Vineyard

Drake Wines, Volume 1

Chelle pimblott

Published by Chelle pimblott, 2021.

VINEYARD

First edition. May 5, 2021.

Written by Chelle pimblott.

DEDICATION

To my book bitches without you I wouldn't be writing xx

To my editor in chief, thank you for all that you do and it goes way beyond editing and being a sounding board. Love ya guts!

To my family, thank you for allowing me to write and forgetting to cook for you sometimes. Love you always xx

****

***Please note ***

VINEYARD

was written by an Australian Author, in Australian English.

As such you may assume there are some spelling errors within, however it's just how we spell things downunder.

****

Chapter One
MAKENNA

"I wish Mum and Dad were here to see this."

"Me too Kenna but I'm sure they're watching you today from wherever they are."

My big brother Logan always seems to know exactly what to say to make things feel at least a little better. I don't know how he got to be so smart, or so in touch with everyone else's feelings around him but I know he had to grow up pretty fast after our parents were killed in a car accident a few years ago. He took on the running of the family business and the family. I'm hoping that my marriage will allow him to relax a little bit and take back his life. He spends too much time worrying about my brother and I, as well as the business. He needs to concentrate on his own love life.

"Are you excited sis?" My little brother, Caleb asks me.

He knows the answer already and I can feel the smile spreading across my face as I answer him.

"I can't freaking wait!" Suddenly, I'm engulfed in both of my brothers arms.

"We love you sis and we're glad you're bringing Brady officially into the family." Logan says, resting his chin on top of my head.

"Even if he has been around for forever already and is just another brother to me. I'm glad you're making it official too." Caleb says, kissing my cheek.

I have to take a few deep breaths to control my emotions. Thinking about my wedding day brought me all kinds of different emotions but trying to decide between which one of my brothers would walk me down the aisle today almost tore me apart. In the end, we came up with a plan that everyone was happy with. Both of them would walk me down the aisle, one on each arm and then they would stand next to my groom.

"I swear to the heavens if you two are making that girl cry, I will cut you both to pieces and throw you in the dam." Rochelle, my cousin and bridesmaid warns my brothers as she walks in the dressing room door, closely followed by Beth, Brady's sister and my maid of honour.

"Roch, it's OK we were just taking a minute to remember our parents." I tell her, knowing that she'll feel slightly guilty about breaking us apart, or threatening her cousins.

"I know that and that's why I threatened them. You're getting married to that gorgeous man who is bouncing on the balls of his feet out there waiting for you. If I didn't know better, I'd say the man was high out of his skin and searching for his next hit. I guess in a way he is, he's waiting for you after all."

Beth walks over to me and embraces me. "You make him *so* happy Makenna and that makes me happy." She says quietly in my ear.

I squeeze her a bit tighter and whisper back, "He makes me all kinds of happy too, Beth."

"Alright, enough with the lovefest, you can do that later." Rochelle announces. "We've got a wedding to get started here."

Logan holds up my veil, the last piece of attire that I need to add before I meet my future husband in a few minutes. "Can I help you put this on, or do you have other plans Roch?" I can't help but laugh. Rochelle is a force to be reckoned with and we all love her for it, but sometimes, Logan can't help winding her up a little. I have a simple silver crown, with the veil flowing down the back of my dress.

My dress. Oh my dress is amazing. I'm not really a frou frou, frilly kind of girl. Don't get me wrong, I love getting all dressed up whenever the occasion calls for it but walking in the vineyard means going for comfort first. When Brady takes me out though, I love getting into beautiful dresses and heels, but this dress. This dress is something else. I didn't ever see myself in something so, well poufy when I got married but it's the dress that called my name when I started trying them on and it's the one I kept coming back too.

With its sweetheart neckline, wide cap straps, lace bodice and then full, ballgown skirt made of tulle, with the lace from the bodice cascading down the top half of the skirt, all in a beautiful champagne, it's my dream come true that I didn't even know I had.

The best part? Yeah, it gets even better. The damn thing has pockets! Pockets in a wedding dress! The most amazing thing ever created on this planet I can tell you that. I wasn't sure at the time exactly what I would *need* to put in them, but I *loved* knowing they were there. Today, I know that I have a few things in them. Lipstick, my something old and my Mum's hanky from her wedding day, is my something borrowed. My something new is my dress and let's not forget the amazing shoes as well. Something blue, well you'll just have to wait until the reception to find out that one.

"So, are you ready to get this show on the road Kenna, or do you need a few minutes to run?" I know what she's doing. She's trying to make the room feel a little less, I don't want to say maudlin, but I guess we're all thinking the same thing. So I drag myself out of my daydreaming and smile the biggest smile of my life. I've never been more ready to do anything in my life.

"I'm not going anywhere, except out to that garden and marrying the love of my damned life." I loop my arms through my brothers, who are standing on either side of me, take a deep, shaky breath and say. "Let's get married!"

"I'm not marrying Brady. I mean I love him like a brother but this isn't my deal you know, a love triangle or whatever this would be." Caleb squeaks out.

We step out into the hallway, and I stop to look at my little brother in confusion. "You mean this isn't going to be a marriage with the four of us in it?" I can feel Logan shaking with laughter beside me.

"W-what do you mean? No. No way Makenna. He's becoming a part of the family and we're close but never ever *that* close. Nope. No fucking way." His voice is getting higher and higher pitched. I have to stop him now because the guests will be able to hear him soon and think something has gone wrong.

"I'm marrying Brady. Just me Caleb, relax." Logan loses the plot next to me and laughs. Loudly. Too loudly.

"Oh my god man, you should have seen your face. I've never seen a more horrified look on anyone's face ever in my life and I've seen some disturbing shit."

"Shut up." Caleb yells at Logan. Guess I didn't think that one through properly huh? "I can't believe you did that to me Makenna."

"I'm sorry Cal, but you should have seen your face. Like I would let either of you anywhere near my relationship with Brady." I look over at my big brother, who looks like he's struggling to stand upright and is still wiping the tears from his eyes. "Look, if you two can't get your shit together right now, I'm walking down that aisle to marry the man I love by myself. I'm sorry I teased you Cal but you left yourself wide open and Logan, just cut it out."

My threat to walk towards my groom alone brings them both out of their moods and back into the game. How on earth did my mother ever wrangle these two when we were kids, I will never know.

"You're not walking down there alone, so come on Cal, let's get our sister married."

I look up to see Rochelle just staring at us like she has no idea how the hell we're related to her. To be honest, if I were her I'd be wondering the same thing but she's her own special brand of lunatic as well, so she can't talk.

Sweet Beth is standing there smiling at the three of us and having a laugh herself. This is why I love my soon to be sister in law, she gets my humour and doesn't think I'm crazy. Well not too crazy to marry her brother anyway. I smile at her, she smiles back and she nods at me, her smile almost as wide as mine, as we reach the door that will lead us out to the garden and the beautiful archway where my soon to be husband is waiting for me.

The music starts and Rochelle gives me a kiss on the cheek and starts the walk down the aisle. When she reaches the halfway mark, Beth starts her walk down too, right after she gives me a kiss on the cheek and tells me she loves me.

Then the music changes to the Bridal Chorus, signalling our turn to walk down the aisle. Brady and I chose the traditional Bridal Chorus for me to walk in because we knew it's what our parents wanted, but the music we walk back up the aisle to after we become husband and wife? Yeah, that's slightly less traditional and I can't wait, but first we have to become hitched to one another.

"Let's go boys. Let the wedding begin."

As we walk down the aisle, I hear gasps and exclamations of how pretty my dress is and how gorgeous I look today. How proud our parents would be if they were here with us but I barely register any of it. All I see is the man I've loved since we were fifteen years old, standing at the makeshift altar that he built with my brothers, under the arbour that my parents erected, covered in flowers my parents planted. It makes me feel like they're here with us, even if it is just in spirit.

When we reach the arbour, the music stops and the celebrant asks who gives me away to be married and my brothers say together, "We do." Then I'm facing Brady and now that I'm up close to him, I can see the tears in his eyes. My brothers move to stand beside Brady and then I hear the murmurs go through the guests again but I don't care what any of them have to say, because Brady takes the opportunity to mouth, "I love you" and just when I think my smile and my heart can't get any bigger, he mouths, 'You look beautiful'.

The celebrant, Julie, coughs to clear her throat and the ceremony begins. Honestly, it's a blur of words and I don't think I'll remember what I said later. Then there are the vows where we promise to love, cherish, and not sleep around with others, no obeying for either of us, in sickness and in health and then suddenly Julie is pronouncing us husband and wife, then the groom is kissing his bride. I can't believe I'm married to Brady Harris. I'm now Mrs Makenna Harris.

I'm in a daze as we get photos taken around the vineyard and the old family buildings. I don't let go of Brady's hand the whole time we move around the property. I can hear our guests having a few drinks in the restaurant we have on the property that today is closed for a private function. In fact the whole property has been closed to public access for the past few days so that we could get things set up.

"Are you ok sweetheart?" Brady leans down and murmurs in my ear. To anyone else, it must look like he's whispering something sweet in my ear and I guess he is, checking on me is what he does, and I love him for it.

"Of course I am. I'm Mrs Harris now, life can't get any better." I hope my smile tells him just how happy he's made me today, it feels like it might split my face in half it's so damned big. My heart is so full today, even with my parents absence weighing on me.

"When we start making babies, that's when life can get better sweetheart, but that can wait. I want to enjoy having you as my wife before we add any little people to the mix." He leans down and kisses the tip of my nose. "But I'm going to enjoy practising making babies with you for as long as I can."

"Dude really? That's my sister you're talking about making babies with!" Caleb says, the horror obvious on his face, *and* in his voice.

"I know." My new husband smirks back at my little brother. "Don't you want nieces and nephews?"

"Yeah of course, but I don't need to know how the fuck they got here!" Caleb groans.

Logan claps a hand on Caleb's shoulder, "Dude, if you needed Brady to explain it to you, it explains a lot of things."

"What do you mean by that?" Caleb asks.

"Well, brother, it explains why you're still single if you can't work out the where's and how's of pleasing a woman!" Logan says with a straight face. How he keeps from laughing I have no idea, because I can't help the loud laugh that escapes my mouth.

With a hard shove, Caleb pushes Logan who trips over his own feet but mainly because he's suddenly laughing so hard he can't stand. Logan is built and Caleb, well, he has muscles but he's nowhere near as built as Logan is. "Shut up arsehole." Our little brother mutters.

"Awwww it's OK we still love you little bro." Logan says, engulfing him in a hug.

"Fuck off." Is his muffled response from Logan's armpit.

"Language please boys. You promised me your best behaviour today." Brady's mum says as she walks up to give both her son and myself another hug, sending both of my brother's the 'mum look'.

"Yes Mrs Harris." My brother's say together, both of them looking down at the ground watching the shoe that they're scuffing through the dirt. They look and sound like little boys again. Mrs Harris has been a godsend since our parents accident. I'm not sure what we would do without her and her husband, luckily, we haven't had to find out. "Hi Pauline, where's Jeremy disappeared off to? We need to get a few photos with the two of you, then you can get back over to the party." I ask her.

"Oh, he'll be back in a minute sweet girl. Don't you worry about us, we've got everything sorted, you two don't need to worry about a thing." She answers me, with a sneaky look on her face.

Before I can ask Brady what his folks are up to, Jeremy is back, smiling like a Cheshire cat and corralling everyone for another set of photos. When they're all done, he asks everyone to head over to the reception so that they can have a few minutes with us alone. They lead us over to a couple of bench seats near the garden and ask us to take a seat.

"I know you're probably wondering what the hell is going on, but we just wanted a few minutes alone with the pair of you before everyone wants their few minutes with the new couple." Jeremy says. I look at Brady and he looks about as worried as I feel.

"Is everything OK Pops?" Brady asks his Dad. "You haven't had another scare have you?" I can hear the barely controlled panic in my new husband's voice. His Dad had a heart attack a year ago and although things have been really good since, I know he worries a lot about his Dad, and how his Mum would cope if anything happened to her husband.

"No son. I'm fit as a fiddle, I promise." Jeremy says, laughing, and I feel Brady relax beside me.

"Then what's going on? You two look like a pair of cats that got the cream."

"We kind of feel like we did." Pauline says, linking her arm through her husband's and smiling up at him. "Go on, tell them I can't wait any longer."

"Well, stop talking and I will honey."

"Can you both just tell us what's going on, please?" Brady begs them. I must admit, I'm feeling a little tense now myself.

"Well, you know how we were waiting for that pay out?" We both nod yes, because we know what they're talking about, and just want them to explain. "We got it last week."

"Why didn't you tell us last week?" Brady demands quietly.

"If you stop asking me questions, I'll explain." Brady holds up the hand that isn't holding mine and his Dad continues. "We didn't tell you because we wanted to surprise you today and give you a gift."

"But you don't need to give us anything else Jeremy. You're help with everything for today, financially, physically, and emotionally is more than enough." I say, reaching my free hand out to take his.

"Oh, we know you pair don't want anything from us honey, but that's what makes this so much fun." Pauline says, excitedly.

"Now we know you can't take too much time away from the vineyard Makenna, but we also know that you two organised a week away up the coast." Brady and I look at each other, then back at his parents and once again just nod yes. "But we think you deserve more of a break than that."

"Makenna, honey, you've been through so much over the last couple of years and you are like a daughter to us. Brady, you know you'll always be our baby and we wanted to do something special for you both." Pauline says, her left leg jiggling up and down.

"Go on, you tell them, I know you want to." Jeremy tells his wife.

"We've booked you a four night, five day stay in one of those over the water bungalows in Bora Bora. Now before you say no you don't want us to spend the money on you pair, and that it isn't necessary, you can just stop before you speak. We didn't do it because we knew you were expecting it, we did it because you could *both* do with the break *and* because we wanted to." Pauline says.

We both try to speak but Jeremy speaks before we can. "We couldn't get the money back from the holiday on the coast that you booked, so Beth and Rochelle have decided to divide the week there between them. Rochelle decided they both deserved some time away after the wedding."

"Of course she did." I mutter and Brady laughs. "Hang on, so those two knew about this and didn't say anything? Normally Roch can't keep her mouth shut. The whole family knows never to tell her anything unless you want the entire family to know shortly after." I say, shocked.

Pauline laughs. "In fairness, Rochelle only found out about an hour ago. She's been slightly busy since and had quite a few other things on her mind, and those things didn't give her the chance to spill the beans to anyone."

"You know we can't take this, right? It's too much." Brady says, and I understand what he means. As much as I would love to spend a week lazing in one of those beautiful bungalows, I don't feel comfortable taking the money to do so from Brady's parents.

"It isn't too much, and you *are* going." Jeremy says the tone of his voice is stern and not to be argued with. "You two kids are so damned independent and need to do everything yourselves, it's frustrating. You barely let us help out with the wedding. We can't help setting you up in a new home, because you're already living in it and have been paying it off for a couple of years now. So please, let us do this for you?"

"Please let us do this for you both." Pauline adds. It's almost like she's begging us to take this damned holiday. The pleading in her eyes is hard to take, and I feel myself crumbling, but this is Brady's parents, and if he feels like he can't accept their exceptionally generous offer, then I have to stand by his decision.

I watch as Brady closes his eyes, making the decision on whether to accept his parents very generous gift or not. I'm happy either way, but hey, a trip to Bora Bora would be amazing!

"We know that neither of you can take too much time off work right now, but you'll only be gone one extra day. Please say you'll go." Pauline asks, breaking the silence.

Brady opens his eyes, looks at me and then smiles. Turning to his folks he says, "Thank you Mum. Dad it's a very generous gift, and we didn't expect it at all but yes, we'd love to go spend five days in a bungalow over the ocean in Bora Bora."

Pauline jumps off the seat and engulfs us both in her warm embrace, crying happy tears all over us both. "Mum, you're going to get Kenna's dress all wet if you keep on with the waterworks." Brady jokes with his Mum.

"Oh my gosh, I'm so sorry Makenna, I haven't done any damage, have I?" She asks me in a panic.

"No, of course you haven't, your son is just being a jerk." I answer, while slapping Brady on the shoulder.

Brady and his Dad stand up and shake hands sealing the deal man style. "I'm so glad you said yes son. Your new wife deserves this trip, and so do you." Then he pulls his son in for a manly hug, including the traditional hard slap or two on the back.

"Thank you Dad." I hear Brady whisper to Jeremy and it almost breaks me. It almost brings me to tears and I've survived most of the day without any.

Pauline reaches over and loops our arms together, directing me towards the reception and party. "Thank you for accepting our gift Makenna."

"That wasn't my decision to make Pauline, but I *am* very appreciative of your gift. It's very generous."

"You're welcome darling." She pauses as we step onto the path before we walk into the room and pulls me close. "Thank you for making our son blissfully happy, and thank you for making Jeremy and I very happy. We're very proud to be able to officially call you our daughter. We love you, and your brothers, as if you were our own children." Her eyes well with tears and I don't know if I can hold mine back after that, but before I can tell her I love her too, Caleb yells out wanting to know how long they have to wait for us to grace the guests with our presence.

I guess he didn't realise we were right outside the door, because he kind of squeals a little when Brady opens the door and says in his loud booming voice, "You don't have to wait brother, you can leave any time you like." Making the rest of the crowd laugh.

From somewhere further back in the room, Logan's voice comes out the speakers, "Ladies and gentlemen, and the rest of you riff raff, please join me in welcoming the new Mr and Mrs Harris to the party."

We enter the room, holding hands to loud cheers and whistles. I'm not a huge fan of being the centre of attention, but for today, I'm going to pull on my big girl undies and just let it happen. With Brady by my side, I know I can do anything.

Chapter Two
BRADY

Today is my wedding day. The day I marry the love of my life and make her mine forever.

Makenna Drake was always going to be mine forever. Since the day I laid eyes on her when we were fifteen years old, I knew I wanted to marry her. You can call me crazy, and many have, but I've never felt differently, even when her brothers tried to scare me off, I kept my eye on my girl. Always.

Today, I watched as her brothers walked her down the aisle towards me, knowing that while it's a day of so much happiness for Kenna, there is also some sadness behind her beautiful smile. The Drake siblings lost both of their parents a few years ago in a car accident, and I know that Kenna didn't want to choose between her brothers walking her down the aisle.

When Logan and Caleb kissed their sister to hand her over to me, they stepped up to stand by me. They're there for their sister, but they're also standing up with me. I have to be honest, the rest of the ceremony went by in a blur. All I truly cared about were the promises we made each other and the fact that Makenna became my wife. When the celebrant told to me kiss the bride, I have never felt happier.

We make our way out to the gardens of the vineyard to take some photos while our guests have a few drinks. Caleb yells out wanting to know how long they have to wait before we grace them with our presence. I can't help laughing when he kind of squeals a little when I open the door and say, "You don't have to wait brother, you can leave any time you like." The guests laugh at our banter.

My parents giving us a trip to Bora Bora for our honeymoon, telling us it's from *both* sets of parents, I know I can't refuse their generosity. I know

11

that I can't deny my wife that gift. My Mum and Kenna are both happy, even as the tears flow.

Before Caleb can respond, Logan's voice comes booming out the speakers, "Ladies and gentlemen, and the rest of you riff raff, please join me in welcoming the new Mr and Mrs Harris to the party."

We enter the room, holding hands to loud cheers and whistles. I know Kenna isn't a huge fan of having a room full of people looking at her, so I wrap my arm around her waist and pull her in close to me, leaning over to whisper in her ear, "I can't wait to get you alone tonight. I need to taste my wife all over and make her come on my tongue." Her quick intake of breath, and biting her lower lip are the only reactions I get and no-one else in the room would ever know why. Kenna has a smile a mile wide, spread across her face and she doesn't even look my way until we reach the table at the front of the room that is set up for the bridal party. Before we turn to face our guests, she leans over and whispers in my ear, "And I can't wait get my new husband alone so that I can taste his cock in my mouth and ride him until he's screaming my name." Then she turns to face the crowd, the smile never leaving her face. I know I have to give myself a few seconds before I turn around because otherwise Aunt Myrtle on my mothers' side is going to get a photo of the bride and groom with the groom sporting a very obvious tent in his pants. I knew I should have gone with the looser pants but no, I wanted to show off the butt I'd worked so hard for so that my *wife* could appreciate it.

I'm an idiot.

"Brady. Dude, are you going to turn around soon, because everyone is waiting to take a few photos of their own." Caleb asks me, and I give him a quick smirk, think of Grandma, and turn myself around. Kenna is struggling to keep her laughter in check, and everyone thinks she's adorable and just so happy to be married, when in fact she's just pleased with herself because she can torture her husband.

I lean over to kiss her on the cheek, in a show of affection for all the cameras pointed our way, and whisper against her cheek, "I'm going to pay you back for that one, wifey." I feel shivers work their way over her body and I know, without a doubt, she can't wait for me to get my revenge.

The excitement finally dies down and we sit down to our meal. As we're finishing our meals, music softly playing in the background and the murmuring of voices chatting away, Logan stands up and clears his throat. He taps the side of his glass and the room quietens down and I start to feel nervous.

"Family and friends, I would like to make a toast to the bride and groom, Mr and Mrs Harris." There is some more glass tapping and cheers, until Logan clears his throat again and silence descends. "I just want to say a few words before we get on with the rest of the night. I promise, I won't take up too much of your time." There's some light laughter around the room, but we all understand why he's doing this speech and the room is filled with emotion. "As you all know, our parents can't be here tonight, but I know, without a doubt in my mind that they would be very proud of everything that Kenna has achieved and how beautiful she looks today. My sister is one amazing woman, and I know that our parents have watched over her today and made her day a special one." He smiles and looks at Kenna, his emotions clear on his face. " I know that they loved Brady like a son and were proud to welcome him into the family. Now, Caleb and I weren't always so welcoming." Light laughter fills the room again. "As her big brother, I felt the need to give Brady here a very hard time when they first started dating, and being the dutiful little brother that he is, Caleb joined my cause." Logan takes a deep breath and looks over at me, his face full of affection. "But the truth is, we couldn't have chosen a better partner for our sister. He's helped her through some pretty tough times, in fact he helped all three of us through losing our parents and I couldn't be happier to call him my brother. So, let's toast the happy couple." He holds up his glass, and the rest of the room join him and then as one the room says, "Cheers!"

I don't know how he does it, but my father follows Logan's speech and his is just as heartfelt, loving, and emotional as Logan's. Welcoming not just Makenna but Logan and Caleb into the family officially he said, even though they've been a part of the Harris clan for years now. There is barely a dry eye in the house once he finished, between his speech and Logan's, everyone is kind of wiped out. He offers my mother the chance to speak but she declines, and I can tell she's just too emotional to speak.

Instead, my sister Beth stands up and welcomes Makenna into the family. "Even though I've long considered Makenna my sister, today she is officially my little sister and I couldn't be happier for my brother. I've watched their love grow and bloom over the years, and I can't think of a happier couple than my brother and new sister." Beth takes a deep breath and continues. "And yes, before you want to make the distinction that she's my sister-in-*law*, she's not. She's my sister, in every sense of the word and I can't wait to see their love blossom even more now that they're married." Leaning over, Beth lands a kiss on Kenna's now damp cheek and raises her glass, "To the bride and groom." And everyone follows suit.

Rochelle, Kenna's other bridesmaid and cousin declines to make a speech and I'm surprised, because that girl could talk under water, but when I look over to see if she's OK, I can see her tears rolling down her cheeks, and I know the emotions of the day have gotten to her. Just like they have Kenna.

Just when we thought the speeches were over, someone gave Caleb a microphone and his voice booms through the room. "Take care of my sister bro, or I'll have to kill you, and I don't want to do that because I actually like you. Be warned though, you hurt her, and I *will* have to hurt you." Then with a clang and the squeal of feedback from the microphone getting too close the speaker, the entire crowd erupts in laughter. That is Caleb wrapped up in one speech for you. Always the class clown he gets a laugh and lightens the mood in a room. I know he's feeling the loss of his parents today as well, but he's trying to make Kenna happy today and not dwell on it.

Kenna and I move around the room, thanking our guests for coming out today and catching up with people we haven't seen for a while. By the time we make it back to our table, I can see that the day is starting to take its toll on her, but we barely get to sit down for a few minutes before we're back up again and cutting the cake. I know this event is signalling the end of the time we're expected to be here, and I can't wait to get out of here.

"How are you doing baby?" I lean over and whisper loudly in her ear. She looks up at me and I see the tears sitting the edge of her lashes. I can't stand that she's sad on our wedding day. On *her* wedding day. "I love you

Makenna Harris. Forever and always." Then I kiss her, leaving no room for thinking.

When we come up for air, she's smiling at me and the tears in her eyes have faded away. "I love you too Brady Harris. Always." Then she kisses me lightly on the lips. "And forever." She whispers as she nuzzles into my neck, and we sway to the music the DJ is playing. I don't think either one of us could tell you what he was playing, but we don't care either.

"Let's give the new Mr and Mrs Harris one last toast and send them off to their honeymoon." Logan is at the microphone again and I can't thank him enough for taking the reins today. Normally I'd be giving him shit about not being able to relax, and being too controlling over everything that's happening, but I can't help appreciating him today. He's taken the load off his sister and myself.

"Where are you headed?" Someone in the crowd yells, but before either of us can answer Caleb does it for us.

"If you think they're telling you lot, you're kidding yourselves. They're not giving you the chance to crash their god damn honeymoon. You'll find out where they went when they get back." Caleb yells.

I can't help laughing. I doubt anyone can take an impulsive trip to Bora Bora, but I guess you never know, and why they'd want to join us on our honeymoon, well that just baffles me honestly. Logan moves up beside me and says, "Get out of here while you can guys, I'll block them at the path."

"Thanks man, you're a legend." I say to Logan, giving him a quick hug and slap on the back.

"Thanks boss. I love you." Kenna says, as she holds her brother in a tight hug and gives him a smacking kiss on his cheek.

"Go on, get out of here." He says, pushing us out the door.

"Your chariot awaits to whisk you off to Bora Bora." Caleb says, as he swings open the car door and ushers us inside. I swear I hear him mutter, 'you lucky bastards,' as he closes the car door and hits the roof of the taxi, signalling the driver to take off.

"I packed for a week up on the coast here Brady, not a week in Bora Bo-ra!" Kenna says panic in her voice and all over her beautiful face.

"It's OK baby, we'll work out something. We're not heading straight to the airport now." I say, trying to calm her down. Then her phone chimes with a message from somewhere amongst her dress folds, and she pulls it from a pocket I didn't even know was there.

"Oh my god!" She sighs, then starts laughing.

"What's going on?"

"It's a message from Rochelle."

don't panic I repacked your clothes and Beth did your husbands. Everything you need is in you suitcases AND you both have a carry-on bag that has everything you need to board the plane AND be comfortable. She says.

Kenna starts to type out a message to send back, but before she can, another message comes through.

and before you start worrying some more, everything is taken care of. Go! Enjoy your time away with your husband. There's a change of clothes in your bag and the driver will bring your dress back home

"I guess they had it all organised then, hey?" Kenna looks at me and asks, I can see the confusion and worry still written all over her face. "They thought of everything."

"I guess they did baby. Let's just go with it and relax. You've worked so hard the past few months. You've organised our wedding and worked hard at the Vineyard as well. It's time for just us." Kenna looks like she might fight me and then all of a sudden I see all the fight escape her.

"You're right." She leans over and kisses me. "That's why I love you."

"I love you too baby. Now relax. If they missed anything, we can buy a replacement." I smile at my wife and pull her into my side. I make sure her head is resting in the crook of my arm and rest my cheek on the top of her head.

The ride to the airport goes smoothly and quickly. Once we get there, Kenna heads into the ladies to get changed. When she comes out, all I see is my beautiful wife. She hands her wedding dress which is now packed away in a garment bag back to the driver, who nods and leaves us to our own devices.

"Why are you smiling like a lunatic for Brady?" Kenna asks me.

Pulling her body close to mine, I kiss her. I kiss her like it might be the last time I get the chance, hard and passionately. I vaguely hear someone yell, 'get a room' and a wolf whistle. That's when I realise I got a little carried away and my hands are squeezing her butt cheeks. When I break the kiss,

Kenna's cheeks have a beautiful blush to them. "Sorry baby, I think I got a little carried away." I say with a smirk.

"Well, you didn't go there alone. It takes two to tango babe." She says, laughing. We link our hands together and walk over to the check in desk. That's where we discover my parents booked us business class flights the whole way.

"My parents really went all the way with this trip, didn't they?" I ask, shaking my head.

"Well, not *all* the way." Kenna says and when I look at her curiously she laughs and says, "Well, it's business class, not first class."

"I wish I'd known what a princess you were *before* I made you my wife." I say, and she laughs, linking her hand back in mine and pulling me along to the gate for our flight.

We pass through security without a hassle, then grab a coffee each, before we sit down to wait for our flight to be called. Thankfully, we don't wait for long before our flight is called and we board the plane, find our seats, and settle in. Our pods, while right next to each other, have privacy screens between them, so I can't see my new wife and I'm kind of annoyed that I won't get to see her for the entire flight. As much as I appreciate what my parents have done for us, I think I'd rather be back in economy so that I could at least sit *next* to my wife.

"The screens in between your seats can be removed if you want, you just have to push this button here." The flight attendant says, pointing at a button to my right, just to the side of the privacy screen, almost as if she read my mind.

"Thank you." I reply, smiling at her. She smiles back at me and walks away to tend to another passenger. I push the button and my wife's beautiful smiling face appears in front of me. "Hey there beautiful, any chance you want to join the mile high club with me today?" I ask, winking.

"You never know your luck handsome, but we'll have to be careful, I wouldn't want my husband to catch us." Kenna replies, winking right back at me. This is one of the many reasons I absolutely adore my wife. She loves joking around and teasing me.

I lean in closer, and say in a loudish whisper, "I guess we'll have to be really sneaky then. I wouldn't want to anger your husband, there's nowhere to run to on an aeroplane."

"I guess you can always jump out, but you better make sure you know where the parachutes are first." I can't control the burst of laughter that escapes me. This woman of mine kills me with her sense of humour and undeniable wit.

The flight attendant comes back around asking us if we want a drink. Kenna asks for a Chardonnay, while I ask for a water. I had a few drinks with the boys back at the reception and I'd rather keep a clear head for the flight. By the time our drinks arrive, the plane has taken off smoothly and Kenna has her reading app open on her phone and she's sitting back in her chair, relaxing. I let my head fall back on the soft cushioning of the head rest and close my eyes, letting the day play out in my mind. I feel a smile spread across my face as I replay seeing my now wife for the first as she started to walk down the aisle towards me on both of her brothers arms. It's then that I realise that I never told her how beautiful she looked or how amazing her dress was. I open my eyes and turn my head to tell her just how amazing she is, and I can't help but chuckle. My wife is sitting snuggled up in her reclined chair, a blanket wrapped around her, a small pillow behind her head and her phone resting on her chest, her mouth slightly open and her eyes closed. It took her just a few minutes to fall asleep and while most of the time I envy how quickly she can fall asleep, today I understand exactly why she's so exhausted. It's been a long and emotional day, and while I'm going to let her sleep, I can't resist pulling out my own phone and taking a photo so that we can remember just how my adorable wife spent the first few minutes, quite possibly hours, of our honeymoon. Guess we won't be joining the mile high club on this trip. Guess I'm out of luck!

I relax back into my chair, turn on the TV in my amazing pod, and look through the movies on offer. I choose one, put on my headphones and pull my blanket up over me, and promptly fall asleep. It's been a busy few days and apparently I'm tired.

"Do you want to join the mile high club?" I feel Kenna's hot breath in my ear as she climbs into lap.

"Well, that's one way to wake up, but you better hope my wife doesn't see us." I haven't opened my eyes, yet I still brace myself for the inevitable punch in the arm and I am not left disappointed. "Ouch!"

"You deserved that Brady!" Kenna grumbles.

I reach up, my eyes still closed and pull her down to me. "I love you Mrs Harris."

She lets out a small huff, but says, "I love you too, Mr Harris." Then we're kissing. I pull the blanket over Kenna, covering both of us from our waists down and I've got the hem of her dress up around her waist in seconds. "What are you doing Brady?" Kenna asks, her lips resting lightly on mine, not wanting to be apart for too long.

"What do you think I'm doing baby?" I ask her, as my hand travels down her stomach to rest on the silk between her legs. She hisses a breath in between her teeth. "Shhhh baby. You have to be quiet. If you promise to be quiet, I'll make you come." We're in the back corner of the business class section, and I'm hoping it will lend us a little bit of privacy. "Can you come quietly Kenna?"

"Yes." She takes a deep breath as I run my finger along her pussy lips. I can feel the heat building between her legs, and how damp the silk is getting. I know my wife is turned the fuck on right now. "Yes, I promise I can be quiet Brady, just please make me come."

"Your wish is my command my beautiful wife." I murmur as I graze the shell of her ear with my tongue, sending shivers through her body.

Without giving her the chance to take a breath, my finger dips in underneath the silk of her underwear and I push a finger into her pussy. Kenna gasps as I slowly start to pump my finger in and out of her body.

"Remember your promise baby, you have be quiet. No sounds." I remind her, quietly.

"Yes." She says on a gasping breath. "Please Brady."

I can feel her pussy squeezing around my fingers, looking for release. I add a second finger and start to pump in and out of her body a little faster and a little harder. Her breathing becomes harsher, faster and when I push my thumb onto her clit and put just the right amount of pressure on it, I can feel her orgasm building fast. A few seconds later, Kenna bites down hard on the base of my neck, right where it meets my shoulder and I hiss in a breath. I don't stop moving my fingers though, the sharp bite of her teeth driving me on. "That's it baby, come all over my hand." And that's exactly what my gorgeous wife does as her orgasm hits her hard. We sit like that for a minute, forgetting where we are, before I bring my fingers to my mouth to clean her orgasm off them. Kenna groans as she watches me, then I do her pants back up and we relax, just lying there quietly together until there's a quiet cough right beside us.

"I don't mean to interrupt your … cuddling, but you need to go back to your own seat Mrs Harris. The seatbelt sign is about to go on and we'll be descending not long after that into Tahiti."

Kenna buries her beautifully blushing face into the crook of my neck. "Thank you. She'll be in her own seat in a second." I say with a smile. The flight attendant could have busted us, but she didn't. She spoke quietly, so no-one else heard her. "Welcome to the Mile High Club Mrs Harris." I feel her body shake, as she laughs quietly into my neck.

"Do you think she heard me Brady?" she asks, pulling back to look me in the eyes.

"No, I don't, but even if she did, who cares? She doesn't know us, and we'll likely never see her again." I push Kenna's hair behind her shoulders and off her face. "I'm pretty sure she's seen worse displays than what we just did, so let's wear our sexual prime like a badge baby." I say with a smile.

"You're right. We don't know her, so who cares." Kenna nods in agreement, but I think it's more about her convincing herself that's the truth than actually agreeing with me.

"Move your cute butt back over into your chair so we can get onto the last leg of our travels." I says, gently smacking her on the arse, making her squeal quietly, which of course, makes me laugh.

As Kenna settles into her own seat, the seatbelt light turns on and we do as we're told and buckle up, ready for the descent and next leg of travel before we finally hit Bora Bora.

Reaching over, Kenna squeezes my hand, "I love you Brady Harris."

"I love you more, Makenna Harris." I say, lifting our hands so that I can kiss the back of hers with a sloppy kiss. We don't let go until the plane lands and we need to carry our bags to get off the plane.

Chapter Three
MAKENNA

I haven't forgotten what my husband did to me on the plane earlier. He will be repaid handsomely as soon as we land and have some privacy in our secluded bungalow. I'm not sure if the flight attendant knows what we did, but I can't find it in me to care too much. Brady's right, we don't know her, and we'll probably never see her again anyway.

After the plane lands, we're driven in golf buggy's to the main office. When we get out of the buggy and Brady tries to grab our luggage, but our buggy driver isn't having it and says , "No!", as he smacks Brady's hand away. "It's time for you to relax." He says with a smile and leads us towards the front desk.

Checking us in is the simplest thing I've ever done. "Brady and Makenna Harris."

"Good afternoon Mr and Mrs Harris, I'm Samantha and this here is Tomas. We will be available to help you with anything you need during your stay here with us." Samantha smiles and nods at Tomas, the golf buggy driver and luggage carrier. I smile at him, because he just has that smiling aura about him and I'm sleepy happy. "Your parent's booked you into the Honeymoon suite, with a full butler service. Which means, you don't have to leave your bungalow again, unless you want to, until you leave us to go back home again in five days."

"Wow!" Brady says quietly to me. "I didn't know they'd booked all that Kenna, did you?"

"No, I found out about it all when you did Brady." How on god's green earth could I have possibly known what his parent's had booked for us when I found out at the exact same time as he did that we were coming? "But they've surprised us at every turn so far, so I guess we should have

21

known, honey." He looks at me suspiciously but doesn't say anything as we're lead to our bungalow over the beautiful ocean that will be our home for the next week. A home I intend on not leaving for the entire time we're here, I'm going to make the most of the time I have alone with my *husband*.

Talking of being alone with my husband. While I've been dreaming of our alone time, Tomas has dropped our bags in the bedroom, given us a quick tour of the bungalow, and explained how the butler service works. I barely notice when the door clicks shut behind, I'm too busy thinking about how much Brady is going to enjoy his pay back sex. I *did* think of doing something a little more, shall we say public, to get his pulse racing, but decided against it. I'm not an exhibitionist and I sure as hell am not a sharer. I'm not sharing my husband with *anyone*.

"Come here wifey." Brady growls, reaching for my hand and pulling my body tightly into his. This man does the most amazing things to me, I guess that's why I married him. I don't get the chance to say anything to him before his lips have taken mine in a kiss that would shame any porn star. His hands roam up and down my body, then make their way under my loose cotton dress, and squeeze my butt cheeks. My hands have automatically reached up and planted themselves in his hair, pulling his lips closer to mine. My hips move with a mind of their own too, and I grind my pelvis into his. Our bodies know each other so well, they're just drawn to fit together so neatly. For a second I've forgotten what I had planned for my new husband.

I struggle, but I pull back from his lips, cradling his face in my hands. "Hold on to that thought honey." I take two steps backing away from his body and his hands grip tighter onto my butt.

"Where do you think you're going?" He asks, holding on a little tighter. "I've finally got my wife to myself and you're not getting away from me easily baby."

I place a finger on his lips, and he sticks out his tongue to lick it. I suck in a breath, then he sucks my finger into his mouth and rolls his tongue around it, sucking on it like it's a lollipop. I groan, he knows my pussy is now wet and making a mess in my underwear, so he sucks even harder. My eyes roll into the back of my head and I close them, drinking in all the sensations of him touching my body. My pussy clenches, and I know I'm starting to lose sight of my plans, again!

I step back, out of his embrace too far and so quickly, that he has no choice but to let go of my body, otherwise we're both going down onto the ground and causing who knows what damage.

"Where are you going, baby?" He asks, rubbing his hand over the bulge in his pants, making sure I see his hard and ready cock waiting for me. I almost give in. *Almost*, instead I take a few more steps away from him before speaking.

"Keep those thoughts, right there," I say in a squeak and gesturing with my hands up and down his body, then stopping to point at the bulge. I clear my throat and continue, "Keep those dirty thoughts going and I will be back in a minute. I promise, you're going to love what I have in store for you Mr Harris." Without waiting for a response, I turn and book it out of the room into what I hope is our bedroom. I know if I stay anywhere close to him, I'll give in and just fuck his brains out, but I can wait. He can wait for a minute so I can make it even better.

"I'll be waiting Mrs Harris, because I can't wait to fuck my wife." He says, his voice thick with need and desire. I pick up my pace, grab the hand luggage that I've been carrying with me everywhere, and duck into the bathroom. My excitement ratchets up as I open the zipper to find exactly what I'm looking for.

Quickly I strip out of my dress and underwear, swapping it all for the outfit I just pulled out of my bag. Conveniently, there's an almost full length mirror in the bathroom and I give myself a quick once over, my smile gets even bigger when I see the white lingerie that I picked out for our wedding night finally on my body.

"What's taking so long baby?"

"I'm coming, Brady." A low growl comes from the other side of the closed door.

"You better not be, that's my job and I'm going to make you come more than once today, wifey."

"Oh god I hope so." I mumble to myself. Out loud I say, "Didn't I tell you not to move?"

"No, you just said wait. So, I'm waiting, and I decided to wait for you in comfort."

I open the bathroom door and lean against its frame, hoping like hell I look sexy. By the look on Brady's face, I'm doing the job right. His eyes have gone dark chocolate in colour, filled with desire and making my knees weak, but he doesn't move a muscle, he's sitting completely still on the edge of the bed.

I slowly walk towards him, swinging my hips in an exaggerated swagger bringing a little bit of humour to the tension filled moment, but he still doesn't move a muscle, and his eyes follow the movement of my hips. My mouth goes dry just watching him, watch me and seeing the absolute desire on his face. I stop in front of him, and drop my mouth down to meet his, while my hands dive into his hair and I scrape my nails on his scalp.

I let my mind go blank, allowing my body to take over. I know what I want to do , now I just have to do it. I straddle his legs, and he moves back a little on the bed to give us more stability, his hands holding onto to my hips making sure that I don't fall. Moaning as I start grinding my hips into his hips and pushing my hot pussy on his hard cock that is pressing against the zip of his pants, begging to be released. When he reaches down to play with my pussy, expecting to find a barrier of lace and satin in his way, I smile against his lips not breaking our kiss. He just discovered that I'm wearing crotchless underwear, giving him easy access to my pussy that he wasn't expecting.

Before I know what he's doing, he stands up turning us around and putting me down on the bed, easily changing our positions. Now instead of straddling him, I'm underneath his body looking up at him, and I watch as he drops down to his knees, placing his hands on my thighs ready to spread them wide so that he can access my pussy with his tongue. My brain jolts back into action and I lean up on one elbow so that I can reach out the other one to push on his chest. He stops, but he's not too happy about it.

"No!" I say in a breathy but stern voice that doesn't sound like me. "This was supposed to be about you, not me."

"What do you mean?" He asks me confused. "This *is* for me." He tells me without reservation and starts moving his face back between my legs.

"No! Brady, I already came today, and I want you to come for me, I need to make you come." I almost feel like I'm begging my husband to let himself come, how ridiculous is that?

"Oh, I will baby. Right after I get a taste of your pussy and make you come all over my tongue." A shudder runs down my spine, and he knows he's got me. "Once I'm done licking your pussy, you can continue on with whatever you had planned for me. Deal?" He asks, with a knowing smirk. I nod, not knowing if I have enough breath to voice my agreement and fall back onto the bed. I know what he can do with that tongue, especially when he combines it with his fingers.

His low laugh vibrates through my thighs, working its way through the rest of my body until I can feel it everywhere, but I don't get any time to process those feelings, because his lips latch onto my clit and gently suck on it. "Oh my god!"

I feel him smile against my pussy, "Yes, can I help you?" I don't get the chance to answer because his mouth is back on me, and it's dancing between licking at my clit and sucking it, to fucking my pussy. My mind blanks and all I can do is feel. When two of his fingers join in and his mouth concentrates on my clit, my hands scrape along his scalp and twist in his hair, pulling on the dark caramel strands making him groan. His groan rumbles through my pussy and when he crooks his fingers into a 'come hither' motion touching *that* spot, as well as sucking on my clit and then licking it, I see stars. I swear I forget how to breathe as my orgasm hits me, making me black out for a few seconds. He slowly drags his fingers in and out of me while I come back down to earth. When I open my eyes, he's lying beside me on the bed, his head resting on one hand, his other hand resting just under my breasts.

"Holy shit Brady!" I say, my voice still hoarse from the heavy breathing and chanting of 'more' and 'yes, yes, yes!' I just did. "If I'd known married sex was going to be *that* hot, I would have married you years ago honey."

"Sex with me has *always* been *that* hot baby and you know it." I crack one eye open to look at his gorgeous face, he's got a cocky smirk on his face because he knows he's right. We might have been each other's firsts *and* only sexual partners, but we didn't lack anything in that department. We've always been adventurous and happy to learn new things about the other person's body. Never stop learning. He nuzzles my neck, leaving light kisses on my skin and I can feel the dampness on his stubble, my orgasm still on his face. Then I feel like I'm floating, until I realise Brady's picked me up and moved me under the covers of the most comfortable bed on earth.

"You're right, sex with *me* is *always* amazing!" I reply without opening my eyes and smiling. "We really need one of these beds at home Brady, it's so damned comfy." He doesn't answer me, just gets in beside me and pulls me into his arms. I curl my body over and around his and feel myself sliding into sleep, until I jolt and try to sit up. Try because he's got his arm so tightly around me, that it's hard to move.

"Stay there and get some sleep baby." He murmurs, sleepily into my hair.

"But I had plans for you Mr Harris." I mumble into the hair on his chest as I do what he asked and relax into the warmth of his body.

"That can wait, we've got the rest of our lives baby. Sleep now, more sex later. I promise." He sighs and holds me even closer. "I love you Mrs Harris." He declares quietly as he drifts off to sleep.

"I love you, Mr Harris." I say, allowing his quiet breathing to lull me into sleep as well. I can have my way with him, just as soon as I recover from my blinding orgasm and we both get some sleep.

Chapter Four
BRADY

I know Kenna had some wild plans for me when we got here earlier but seeing her standing in the open doorway to the bathroom with nothing but a few scraps of lace and satin on her delectable body was honestly, too much to resist. When I discovered that I didn't need to take those scraps of material *off* her body to gain access to it, she had no chance of getting to me before I could make her come on my tongue and my hand.

Despite my new wife's plans, I knew I could make her come hard enough that we would *both* be able to sleep afterwards without her needing to go through with any of plans her for me. Kenna gets sleepy after she orgasms and knowing that I didn't get much sleep on the flight over here, I knew I would be asleep not long after as well. We have almost a week here, but we have the rest of lives for anything else.

When I wake up, I don't know how much later, the sky is dark, and I can smell food. My stomach rumbles and I start to laugh, reaching over to find Kenna, but she's not next to me.

"Hi there handsome." Kenna says as I feel the bed dip at my feet, but when I try to move them I realise she's actually crawling up my legs, her hands and knees straddling my body. It almost feels like we're back to where we started when we got here.

"Hi there yourself beautiful." I say reaching down to draw her up my body. I want skin on skin, but that little white bodysuit thingy that's she got on is fucking hot. "What is it baby?" I ask, wondering if we should skip bed and eat for some energy.

"It's time." She says, lightly kissing my expecting lips. "For you.", She kisses along my jaw and I suck in a harsh breath between my teeth. "To lie back." She kisses my neck, sucking on it lightly just before finishing with.

"And enjoy your." Her tongue travels down my chest and circles a nipple, before she sucks it into her mouth and uses her teeth to nibble on it, not too gently either. "Wedding present." She says, as her tongue travels across my chest and starts to play with my other nipple.

My hands reach down, trying to grab hold of any part of her body, just to feel her, touch her, but she ducks away from my touch and I growl. I go to sit up, to chase her body, to feel her against me, but she plants a hand right in the middle of my chest and pushes me back down.

"Down boy. Just relax Brady, I swear I'll make you feel good. Great even." She says with a playful smile. I know she can and will make me feel good. Fucking fantastic as a matter of fact, but I hate being a passive participant in sex with her. She *knows* I love to touch her and kiss her gorgeous body. I'd let her do anything to me, as long as I could feel her with my own two hands or lips. Still, I do as she asks and lie, not so gently, back down on the bed, watching her watch me. A pleased smile spread across her face, one that I would do anything to see, including letting her take the reins sexually every now and then. "Good boy." She says with a sexy glint in her eyes.

I'll give her good *boy*. "Baby, I'm all man and – " I don't get to finish my thought because she sucks my cock into her mouth, swallowing it to the back of her throat, causing all the breath to leave my body and taking away my ability to speak.

With a pop, she releases my cock from the warm dampness of her mouth, licks her lips and smiles innocently up my body. "And what? Cat got your tongue?" I roll my head back and forth across the pillow in what is supposed to be a shake of my head, no. "I know you're all man honey, I've got your *manhood* in my mouth." Before I can even think of trying to answer her, she's got her mouth wrapped around me again and she's sucking, licking, and moving her mouth up and down my hard cock again with no break in sight. My hands, which have been buried in the sheets at my side, fly down and grasp as much of her hair as they can. I'm not trying to hurt her, or even control her movements, I just *need* to be touching her anyway I can be. My hips jump off the bed, or try to anyway, when she reaches down and starts playing with my balls.

"Fuck Kenna! I don't know how much longer I'm gonna last baby." I hiss through clenched teeth. "I want to be inside you when I come baby. Please." I'm not above begging to be inside my wife.

She releases me from her mouth, her hand is still rolling my balls around making my eyes cross when a finger slips and touches my asshole, my body jumps in surprise. "You like that, don't you?" She asks, as her hand continues to roll my balls and her finger follows that movement rubbing further down. I can't answer, I don't have the capacity. "You want to fuck me, Brady?"

"Yes!" I grind out as I reach down and hook my hands under her arms, then drag her up my body before she even knows what's happening. She squeaks a little in surprise and then smiles, while rubbing her wet, hot pussy over my hard, pulsing cock. I sit up, bring her with me and her eyes widen in shock as the movement allows my cock to enter her in one swift movement.

"Oh fuck!" She leans back, pushing her boobs into my face and I want to lick, suck, and bite them but I can't get to them. I push and pull the material around until I've freed her boobs and they're now sitting, plump and gorgeous in my hands. I run my thumbs over her nipples, and she groans. "I thought I was in charge here, Mr Harris?" She asks, grinding her pelvis into mine, wrapping her hands around my neck, her fingers tugging on the ends of my hair.

"You are baby, but I *need* to touch you like I need to fucking breathe right now. You can set the pace of the fucking, but I have to touch you while you do it." I explain, just before my head dives down and my mouth draws in a nipple to suck and bite. Her fingers dig deeper into my hair and she pulls on it harder, trying to pull me away, then pushing me into her breast, asking for more without using words. I swap breasts and give it the same attention as I gave the other one. I've got one hand resting in the middle of Kenna's back, holding her steady and pushing her to me when she begins to pull away. The other reaches up and starts tweaking, pulling, and pinching the nipple I sucked to a hard point.

"Oh fuck me Brady." She says, he breathing coming in ragged pants. "I need to fuck you. I need to move, to feel you moving in me, now."

"Yes Kenna, I need you to move." I say, letting her nipple fall out of my mouth, but not too far away and she shivers when my hot breath wafts ever so lightly across her wet nipple. Without a second thought, she starts moving up and down on my cock. My hips roll up and down to meet her movements, making me go deeper and deeper into her body with every thrust.

Her hands release my hair and fall down onto my chest. I think she's trying to push me back, but I'm not lying down on the job. Not today. So, instead her hands find my nipples and she starts to pull, twist and massage them with her fingers. I'm in sensory overload and my self-control isn't going to last for too much longer.

"I need you to come baby." Taking her face in my hands, I look deep into her eyes. "Come for me baby." Her movements become erratic, she's out of control and I love it.

She's rising and falling, and my hips are moving up and down to meet her in the middle. There's only the sound of slapping bodies, grunts, and moans of pleasure.

"BRADY!!" She screams so loudly I can't help but wonder if the people in the nearby bungalows can hear her, but I don't care if they can, because I can feel her pussy pulsing around my cock and that's enough to finish off my self-control.

"Holy shit, Makenna. I'm gonna." I don't get to finish because I come in my wife as she collapses on my chest, and we collapse back onto the bed, my arms wrapped around her, bringing her with me.

"That was." Kenna begins, but then shudders wrack her body and I feel her entire body move. "You can't be ready again already Brady!" She half laughs, half groans.

I laugh, and shrug my shoulders under her, "What can I say? I'm attracted to my gorgeous, beautiful, sexy wife and I plan on having her as many times as I can on our honeymoon." She moans in what I take as agreement and I can feel her breathing getting deeper, if I don't move now we'll both fall asleep again, but I need food before I do anything else. "Come on baby, I'm pretty sure I can smell some food and I think we could both do with eating something. When was the last time you ate?" I ask her.

She snuggles deeper into my chest, so I smack her on the backside to get her moving, and it works because she jumps up, sitting on my thighs.

"That was uncalled for Brady, honestly." She says, looking for all intents and purposes, angry with me, but I can see the smile playing at the corner of her mouth. So I grab her around the waist and run my fingers up and down her sides, knowing that I'm tickling her and she's about to either kick me in the balls, or get off the bed to get away from me. Luckily for me, this time she chooses the latter. "I'm going to have a quick shower. I'm all sweaty and sticky."

"I like it when you get sticky and sweaty, especially when I'm the cause, baby." I wink at her, knowing she's about to roll her eyes, and there it is.

"I need to get out of this bodysuit too. It's a damned mess." She growls some more.

"I love it when you're naked. I'll see you with food when you get out of your *quick* shower." I throw a smirk and a wink her way, and she huffs as she closes the bathroom door. We both know that woman doesn't know *how* to take a *quick* shower, which is why we had to get an endless hot water service installed at the house. Otherwise, no one else on the property would be able to access any hot water for hours.

I'm tempted to join her in the shower, but I need food and so does she, so instead I discover there's an outdoor shower, so I quickly jump under that and rinse off under the cold water. Then I wander back into the bedroom to take off my wet boxer briefs and put on a pair of workout shorts. Once I'm changed, I go out to the dining area to check out what food was brought in for us earlier while we were sleeping. It's kind of creepy knowing someone was in here while we were asleep, but they were very quiet and respectful, so I guess it's all just part of the service,

I was thinking about serving us up some plates in bed, but I think it might be better if we sit out at the dining table to eat. I'm not saying that I wouldn't take my wife on the table, kitchen bench or any other hard or soft surface in this amazing bungalow, but I think we'll at least think twice before we do anything out here and give us a chance to fuel up.

I lift the silver domed lids and look under them to see what we have. The piles of fruit, crusty bread with olive oil, cheese and crackers are on two of the plates. I pull the last lid off and there are two very delicious looking chocolate lava cakes, complete with a note on the side letting us know there is some cream in the fridge. There's a bottle of champagne in an ice bucket with two glasses as well. They've thought of everything! Normally I'm a beer kind of guy, not a wine guy, but I'm especially not a champagne guy, and yes I do see the irony of marrying into a wine making family. For tonight though, I'm happy to make an exception. Celebrating marrying the love of my life deserves bubbles and whatever else my beautiful wife wants.

Deciding to wait for Kenna before I pop open the champagne, I pour myself a glass of water and add some ice. It's cold and refreshing. Leaving all the food covered, I take my drink and sit out on the small wooden deck out the back of the bungalow, overlooking the beautiful clear blue ocean. It's so peaceful and I can feel my body relaxing.

Chapter Five
MAKENNA

I must admit, I was expecting Brady to join me in the shower and when he didn't, I was a little disappointed. Even after all these years together, and never knowing anyone else, sex with Brady was amazing. Did what we do together in the bedroom, well not always confined to the bedroom, always work out for one or both of us? No, it didn't, but wasn't that the fun part? Working out our limits, what we like, what we don't like and what does or doesn't work for us?

I felt a comfort with Brady that I felt with very few people in my life. I could laugh with Brady when things went wrong. Like falling off the bed in the middle of sex, or bumping into a wall, stubbing a toe or even just being able to say no, not tonight honey, I just don't feel like it. Sure, we were serious when life called for it, but together we could be as goofy and silly as we wanted to be, but there was still that tingle in my body whenever he touched me. He could still set my heart and pussy pounding with need.

Turning off the water, I step out of the shower and grab a towel to dry myself off. I walk into the bedroom and I'm again surprised to find my husband not in there. I thought he would pick out some food that Tomas delivered earlier and bring it into the bedroom to eat while we sat naked on the bed.

I opened a suitcase and reached in and pulled out the first thing I touched. Luckily, it was one of my favourite sundresses. Rochelle really did think of everything when she packed for this trip. At least I hope she did, I guess I'll find out tomorrow when I actually go looking for clothes or bathers. I shrug my shoulders, tonight I got lucky and I'll worry about tomorrow, tomorrow.

I drop the white, almost see through sundress over my head, sans underwear because, I'm on my honeymoon and it's just my husband and I in this bungalow.

As I step from the bedroom into the living room, I start to speak, but as I look up, I see my husband, glass in hand and relaxing out on the deck watching the moon light play over the sea, I don't want to disturb him. It's been a crazy few months with the wedding plans, but in all honestly, it's been a hectic couple of years and this beautiful man has stood by me and my brother's, through it all. The visit from the police to deliver the bad news of our parent's accident and their deaths as a result. Dead on impact they said. They wouldn't have felt any pain, they said. I know they say it as a means to comfort the grieving families, but does anyone *ever* truly take any comfort from that? Yes, it's a blessing in disguise that they didn't survive for minutes or hours in pain, but they're still dead.

We mourned and buried our parent's, but we couldn't bury the pain with them, we then had to go through the court case where the other driver who caused the accident was charged with driving under the influence among other things that I don't even want to remember. We had to give victim impact statements. How does a child explain the loss of their parent's, both of them, in an accident that could have been prevented? I'm not really sure, I just know that we helped each other write them, and then handed them over to the court to be read out. We didn't have to be there for it, and I chose not to. The guy who did this, he's suffering as well, and I didn't want to watch that or his family suffering either.

We got through all of that and then we had to deal with lawyers and the legal system for the ownership of the property. I had already been running the vineyard and Logan was running the winery, while Caleb was finishing up his business studies at University. We all agreed on what we were doing in regards to the business and our parent's, bless their souls, had thought ahead, and set it all up legally with their lawyer in case something happened to either or both of them. Yet, there were still legal loopholes, and hoops we had to jump through to set it all up so that the three of us got equal shares in the business.

Through it all, Brady Harris was my rock. He was my sanity, my shoulder to cry on, he repaired my broken heart and shared his parent's with not just me, but my brother's as well. I knew I loved him as a boy at fifteen, but as I stand here, staring at the profile of the man he has become, I feel an overwhelming sense of pride and love. *So* much love.

I know he hasn't heard me enter the small space, even though the bungalow isn't that big. I know he wasn't expecting me to be finished my shower this quickly, it's pretty rare at home, but when he didn't join me, I didn't want to stay in there for too long by myself.

So I sneak quietly across the short distance and lightly touch him on the shoulder making him jump a little.

"Hey handsome, fancy seeing you in a place like this." I say and then I laugh, because catching him by surprise is a very rare delight.

"Startling me is amusing to you is it, Mrs Harris?" He asks, as he pulls me sideways to sit on his lap, causing my laughter to get lighter even as I squeal at the abrupt movement. "Are you hungry baby?" He asks, and I make him laugh by answering that I could eat a horse. We both know that I can eat a *lot* of food, but even *I'm* doubtful I could manage an entire horse. At any time, but I surely wouldn't today.

"Well, I don't think I can offer you a horse my love, but we do have a few other delectable things on offer here." He says with a laugh.

"I already sucked on the most delectable thing in the bungalow." I say, batting my eyelashes and flirting with my husband. Making him still with surprise and excitement will never get old. At least I hope it doesn't. I jump off his lap, because his grip on me loosened the minute I mentioned sucking his cock, all the blood rushed to his groin, and he's going to need a few minutes to calm down. How do I know? I felt him grow and get hard under my right butt cheek. I walk towards the plates with covers on them, putting an extra little sway to my hips and throwing him a flirty smile over my shoulder.

"Damn it all to hell Makenna Drake, I mean Harris. Are you trying to kill me on our first day of marriage? You know there were easier ways to get to my billions of dollars. You could have just asked me for them."

He walks up behind me, and wraps his arms around my waist, resting his chin on my shoulder. "And would you have just given it all to me if I had just asked Mr Harris?" I ask, playing along with his teasing game.

"Every last cent Makenna." He murmurs into my neck, leaving kisses as he goes. "I will give you everything you ever ask me for, as long as it is within my power to do so baby. Never doubt that, not even for a second."

"Everything?" I ask, already knowing the answer. Knowing he's already given me one of the most precious things another human being could. Unconditional love.

"If I can yes. If it's even remotely possible I will find a way baby." He suddenly pulls away from me, leaving my hands that were holding tightly on to his that were resting on my belly, to drop to my sides. "Right now, I can give you food, sustenance and that's what you need." I'm almost disappointed in where this conversation leads, that is until he looks at me with hunger in his eyes and that sexy smirk on his face. "You're going to need your strength while we're here my sweet wifey, so my need to feed you is purely selfish."

"Oh yes, and why is that may I ask, hubby of mine?" I ask putting every ounce of sass I have in the question.

He leans over and growls in my ear, all deep and husky like, "Because I'm going to fuck you until you look like you've been riding a horse bareback for a month." My breath catches in my throat at his dirty promise. Then he rubs his chin, like he's thinking about another plan, and when he speaks again, his voice is even rougher than it was a minute ago. "Or maybe I'll fuck you until you can't walk at all, and you need a wheelchair to get from our bungalow to the lobby." My breathing is so ragged I don't know how I'm not hyperventilating.

"Holy shit." I gasp.

"Holy shit is *exactly* right baby. So here," He says, passing me a plate full of delicious food and helping me to sit down in a chair at the table, because I'm still too stunned to speak or move by myself. "Sit down and eat some food and drink some water, Kenna." He passes me a glass of water and I down almost half of it immediately trying to douse the flames that he's stoked to life. "Eat Kenna."

I look across the table at my husband and see his adorable smiling face. He's always been a bit of a dirty talker, and I love it, but that just went above and beyond anything I've heard him say before. Ever. And it was as hot as hell!

"You want me to eat after that?" I ask him, not quite believing his request.

"Yes baby I do. So don't be flashing those beautiful green eyes at me and fluttering your lashes either. We *both* need some sustenance before either of us can go another round."

"Alright then."

"Champagne?" He asks, and I nod my head, because I can't speak after filling my mouth with food, causing him to laugh loudly.

"What?" I ask, after swallowing the mouthful of delicious crusty bread drenched in the best olive oil I've ever tasted. "You know my weakness is great bread dipped in perfect olive oil." I scrunch my face up, thinking. "Did you order this?" I ask and I know I sound suspicious.

"No, I didn't. I didn't even know it was here until I walked out to see if I could order us something to eat at this hour." He takes a breath, and I can see him thinking about it. "I bet my parents did it when they booked the resort."

"Of course they did!" I realise as soon as Brady says that his parents are behind the feast in front of us that he's right. Pauline Harris would definitely be thinking about her son and daughter in law getting some decent food once they were off the plane. "Your Mum wouldn't let her boy go hungry for too long, even when she's a million miles away from you."

"Yes, because I'm the only one she's thinking of in this scenario Mrs Harris." He walks around to my side of the table, lifts me up then sits back down in my chair with me in his lap. "My parents love you like you're their daughter, you know that. You're not their *daughter in law*, you're their *daughter*."

"I know." I whisper. Brady's parents have loved me unconditionally since I've known them, but when my parents were killed, they really stepped up for me, and my brother's.

"Sometimes I think they'd take your side over mine." He jokes, trying to lighten the mood. "In fact, I'm positive you and Beth can do no wrong and the rest of us just have to behave and do what you tell us."

I reach up and smack him on the chest, and I feel his laughter vibrate through him, because I'm resting my head on his chest. I won't let sadness here in our little bungalow over the sea in paradise. As he pulls me closer to him, I feel his whole body stiffen. "What's wrong Brady?" I can't look up, I feel like if I do he's going to tell me there's some freaky creature in the bungalow.

"Are you sans underwear Mrs Harris?" He asks in a husky voice, as his hands travel down my back to cup my buttocks in his hands.

"We're in a tropical paradise honey, and I decided it was too hot and I didn't need any underwear in our very private, very secluded bungalow." I answer him and then wiggle a little in his lap to loosen his grip so that I can stand up. He's too stunned to notice what I've done for a few seconds.

"So, what's on the third plate that's still covered Mr Harris?" I ask, looking up into his eyes, as I reach for the silver cover.

"Hmmmm? Why don't you lift the lid and have a look. I think you might like it." He says with a grin, recovering himself after a few seconds. He looks like the cat who got the cream and he's *very* happy with himself, even though it's his Mum that ordered the food.

"OH MY GOD!" I squeal. "You're Mum is a freaking angel!" Brady throws his head back to laugh loudly.

"I knew you'd be happy baby." He gets up and walks over to the small kitchen and opens the fridge. "There's even some cream for you to have with your dessert."

"This isn't just a dessert Brady, this is *the* dessert. This is my favourite. There is *nothing* better in this world than eating a decadent chocolate lava cake, and cream makes it even better."

"So, you don't want the ice cream I found in here too?"

"Nope. Keep it for yourself." I reach for the bowl of whipped cream, and scoop out a huge spoonful, putting it in the middle of the small bowl. "This is my favourite dessert ever! I love your Mum!"

"She loves you too, and let's just notice that it's *your* favourite dessert she ordered, and not mine shall we?" He laughs, but I stop bringing my first spoonful of deliciousness to my mouth and I find myself asking him a question.

"Do you mind?" He cocks his head in question. "That she ordered my favourite and not yours?"

That makes him laugh even louder than before. "No baby not for a second. Anything that makes you this happy, makes *me* happy. That being said, I've got ice cream to eat *and* chocolate lava cake. I'm very happy right now."

"Let's eat these out on the back deck and listen to the waves." I suggest and when we get out there, Brady wraps an arm around my waist and pulls me down onto his lap as he sits down.

He leans down and kisses the side of my head, "I love you baby."

"I love you too Brady." We sit there, quietly eating our lava cakes, listening to the waves break on the small beach not far from the bungalow. I can't see any other bungalows that are close to ours, only a few in the distance. "I wonder if anyone can see us over here?"

"I'm sure they can make out the shapes, but I doubt they can actually *see* us Kenna." I put our bowls on the table beside the chair and cuddle into Brady's chest. We sit like that, relaxing for I don't know how long.

Brady's got his arm wrapped around my waist, holding me close to his body, and his other hand is caressing my thigh, and getting closer and closer to where I'm not wearing underwear. I let my legs fall open so that he has a small amount of access to tease both of us.

"Do you think people can see us from that pool right there in front of the bungalow?" He mutters into my hair, his voice husky with need.

"The lagoon in front of your bungalow is private Mr Harris, no-one can see you from outside." I jump out of Brady's lap, a frightened scream escaping me. "Holy shit Tomas!"

"Sorry Mrs Harris, just let me clean up your dishes and I will be out of here until tomorrow morning when I come by to drop off your breakfast." He comes out and takes the small bowls back inside and they join all the other dishes in a trolley he bought in with him. He walks towards the front door of the bungalow, then turns back to us. "If you don't want to be disturbed in the morning, or at any other time, either call the front desk, or there's a sign for the outside of this door. If that's on the door, I'll just leave your food at the door in the trolley. It will keep warm or cold, for a little while."

"Thank you Tomas." Brady says, with amusement in his tone. "Do we have to order food by a specific time?"

With the door already open and the trolley outside, Tomas says, "No Mr Harris. It's all part of the service that was booked. Although, there are a few dinners that you need to think about coming out of the bungalow for, unless you notify me that you want to stay in, but I'll go through all of that tomorrow." He says with a knowing smile and quietly leaves.

"Oh my god! I didn't even hear him come in!" I say surprised.

"I know, but in fairness you were a little distracted. So was I." Brady replies with a wicked grin. "Now, where were we?" He asks, stalking towards me. "Oh I remember. I had my hand in your underwear, sorry not underwear, almost on your pussy, and that's exactly where I want to be now too." He growls, putting his hands on my butt again, and pulling my dress up over my head in one swift move.

"Brady." I say, my voice husky and I can't decide if I'm warning him or begging him to keep going.

"Hold that thought baby." He quickly moves to the front door and puts the do not disturb sign out and then locks the door. Walking back towards me he drops his shorts, and they join my dress on the floor at our feet. He swoops me up off my feet, I automatically wrap my legs around his hips and my arms around his neck. When he starts walking, my pussy rubs up and down his already hard cock and even though I knew where he was taking us, when the water hits my hot body I draw in a shocked breath. "You OK baby?"

"Couldn't be better my love." I'm even better when we're both submerged in the cool water and his lips are on mine in a hot and sensuous kiss. This is where I want to be for the rest of my life.

Chapter Six
BRADY

Taking Kenna's dress off once we were alone again, felt like unwrapping the best present of my life. No matter how many times I do it, or she strips herself of her clothes for me, seeing her naked still takes my breath away. Getting her naked and into that private pool is the only thing on my mind. I don't care if anyone can see or hear us, I just want my wife, naked and in the water with me. Now!

I hold out my hand to help her get into the pool, and she drops down to straddle my hips and we kiss. It's a deep, passionate kiss. I grab her hip with one hand, grinding my hard cock into the softness of her pussy. My other hand tangles into her hair at the base of her head, allowing me to pull her lips in closer to mine. I can't get enough of her, even after all these years together. It will never be enough. "Kenna." Her name comes out as more of a moan, and I feel a shiver run through her body. I pull back slightly, "Are you cold out here baby?"

"No honey, I'm not cold." She answers with a small shake of her head, barely breaking our kiss. "I'm hot, horny and I need you inside me." She finishes with breathy voice and barely open eyes. My wife could not look or sound any sexier if she fucking tried right now.

"If my beautiful wife commands it, then who am I to tell her no?" I ask, while fisting my cock and positioning it at the entrance to her pussy.

"Don't tease me Brady." Kenna groans, trying to press herself down and get what she really wants. The only problem with that is, I've got a tight grip on her hips holding her up so that her pussy lips are spread around the head of my cock. "*Brady*!" My name comes out like a growl.

I know it shouldn't, but that sound makes my cock grow even harder, hearing just how desperate she is to have me inside her, and my restraint, that's been holding on by a string, finally breaks. Without warning, I push my hips up as I push her down and I'm inside her body before she knows what's happening.

"Yes!" I'm a happy man right now. "Don't move." I can hear the begging in her voice and I'm worried that I hurt her.

"Did I hurt you baby?" I ask, through gritted teeth. I don't know how long I can hold back and not move.

"No." she shakes her head slightly, rolling her forehead across mine as she does. "No Brady. I just." She takes a deep, stuttering breath before speaking again. "It's just so *much*."

"It shouldn't be a surprise baby, this isn't our first time *here*, never lone first time *ever*." I can't help but chuckle at her as she whacks my chest with her splayed hand.

"Not. What. I meant. And. You. Know. It." She says between breaths. "It's just *so much*, Brady. So much love and feelings. I don't know what to do with them."

My hands leave her hips, giving her complete control of the movements where our bodies are connected. I reach up to hold her face in my hands instead, pulling her gaze to meet mine. I need her to see that what I'm about to say is the truth. "I know baby. I get it. I love you with everything in me and I will never knowingly hurt you in any way. You know that don't you?" Slowly she nods her head but that's not good enough for me right now, I need to hear her say that she understands me. "I need you to answer me baby. I *need* to know you understand what I'm saying and that you believe me. I love you more than anything else in my life Makenna Harris. You. Are. My. Life." I need her to believe me.

"I love you too Brady Harris. More than I can ever explain or show you." She closes her eyes and drops her lips to mine, leaving a soft kiss on my lips and moving slightly back from me again. The moment is so tender, and loving it almost breaks my heart. Only because I completely understand what she means, and I hate that she doesn't know that I feel the exact same way about her.

"I know baby, I feel it too." I say quietly in her ear. I bring her lips back to mine and kiss her slowly, hoping that I can show her just how I feel. When she starts slowly moving her hips, her mouth opens as she gasps, I run my tongue along her bottom lip, and she flicks her tongue out to touch mine. She uses the bench I'm sitting on to leverage her body up and down, riding my cock in a perfect rhythm. One that we've perfected over the years, and I can't hold back. I pull her head down even closer to mine and groan into her mouth. She moans back into mine and I feel the vibration of it through my whole body. Pulling my lips from hers, I run them along her jaw, over her collarbone and up her neck, nibbling her skin as I go, until I reach her ear and I nibble on it. I whisper in her ear, "I love you with every fibre of my being Makenna Rose Harris, and I always will."

"Brady." Her head has fallen back to give me the perfect access to all her most sensitive parts. Well, above her stomach anyway, and I enjoy tasting every single one of them. Her hair is floating on top of the water, and the moonlight is playing off her skin. She looks like the most beautiful, sensual mermaid a man could ever hope to find and I want to commit how she looks to my memory, so that when I'm an old man I can bring myself back to tonight and fall in love with my wife all over again. "Brady. I need to. I need more Brady." She begs.

"What do you need baby? Tell me and I'll give it you." I promise.

"More. I need more Brady. More you. Harder, faster. I need to come Brady. I need you." She almost sounds panicked, but I know my wife and I know that she's right on the edge of being able to orgasm and she needs a little bit of help to get there. Thank god because I'm not going to be able to hold myself back for much longer.

"More of me? More of this baby?" I ask, already giving her exactly what I know she needs. I reach down between us and rest my hand over her pussy and rub my middle finger over her clit, making her moan, deep and long. My other hand holds on tight to her hip, holding her down so that I can push my own hips up, helping her ride up and down my cock.

"Yes!" she cries out hoarsely, and I know she's close. So close she can feel it and I can feel her clenching around me, making my balls tighten but I'm done for, for sure when she runs her hands through my wet hair, running her nails along my scalp. "Brady! I'm gonna."

"I know baby, I know. Let go!" I am truly done when her hands leave my hair, and she scrapes her nails down the back of my neck and then they're scratching and digging into my shoulders. "Makenna. Baby you really need to." I don't get to finish my sentence, as she screams my name out loudly to whoever is listening. In the distance I hear a bird cry out and then, I follow her over the edge as she drops her head onto my shoulder and leaves light kisses up and down my neck. A few seconds of completely uncoordinated hip movements and I'm done too. I rest my head on her shoulder and attempt to bring my breathing back to normal.

When my breathing is finally normal again, and I've come back down to Earth, I wrap my arms around the most beautiful woman on the planet and pull her in close. "I will love you forever Kenna." I know that no matter what happens in our future, this is the truth. She sighs in my arms and then a shiver runs through her whole body again, only this time I'm pretty sure the cold breeze that has arrived is the cause. "Come on baby, let's go inside." I say, lifting her off my lap and setting her down on the seat, then I pull myself out of the pool and hold my hands out to help Kenna out as well. Luckily, I used my brain before we got in there and grabbed a couple of extra towels from the room. I pick one up off the chair and wrap it around Kenna, then I wrap one around my waist. I finish securing it around my hips as Kenna takes a step away from me. "Where do you think you're going?"

"Ummm inside. Like you said." She answers me, confusion all over her face as she looks between me and the doorway. Before she can take another step, I sweep her off her feet, literally, by bending down and putting one arm behind her knees and the other behind her back, pulling up into my arms. She lets out a high pitched squeal and then laughs loudly. "Geezus Brady you just scared the living daylights out of me!"

I laugh, and carry her inside, pushing the door closed with my foot and then throw her down onto the bed, causing her to squeal again.

"Brady I'm all wet, I can't lie all over the bed!" She yells at me and moves to get off the bed, but I lean over her, almost pinning her to the bed. She can move and get away if she *really* wanted to.

"You're wet are you? I wonder what we could do about that?" I ask, a smirk spreading across my face and I raise my eyebrow at her in question. It takes a few seconds, and I think I might have actually failed in my humour for a second there, but then she starts laughing. Hysterically. "It wasn't *that* funny." I say, sitting back, resting my butt on my heels, effectively releasing Kenna from the bed.

Sitting up, she reaches over and pats me on the cheek. "Oh honey, you are *so* adorable and *such* a dork. It's one of the thousands of reasons I love you so much, but I'm glad you never had to try to use a pick-up line on me, we might never have gotten together in the first place." She laughs, getting off the bed and walking towards the bathroom.

"Are you saying you don't think I could have picked you up if we were in our twenties instead of our teens when we met?" I ask, absolutely shocked by her admission.

"No, I just think you would have to work a little harder if we had been in our twenties baby. If you'd used a line like that on me, I would have laughed in your face and walked away." She says over her shoulder from the bathroom doorway.

"But you just said you loved my dorkiness. Are you saying that wouldn't have been enough if we had been older when we met?"

"Oh I would have still been attracted to you physically, make no mistake about that honey, and I do love your humour and dorkiness, but I don't know. Lines like that are a passion killer honey." She says as she drops her towel to the floor and smirks at me. She can't get out of this conversation with her sexy body.

"I could have picked you up if we were older." I say, not quite as confidently as I was hoping to sound. I hear the shower turn on and I wonder why she needs to have another shower. I'm still sitting on the bed where she left me, staring off into space thinking when I hear the shower turn off. That was quick, especially for Makenna. I look up to see her strolling out of the bathroom with a towel wrapped around her hair and a fluffy white robe wrapped around her body.

"Aren't you cold? That towel must be wet and cold by now." She asks, like she didn't just tell me that I don't have any game.

"What else do you love about me that you might never have found out if we'd met later in life? Hmmmm?" I ask, curiosity winning over self-preservation.

"Your big cock." She says, a bigger smirk spreading across her face. If she thinks the way to win me over is by complimenting my cock, well she'd be almost right, except that I'm feeling a little fragile right now and being reduced to just my cock and his size is kind of insulting.

"You know, it's the not the size that matters, it's how you use it." Geezus, how did I keep a straight face while spewing that one out?

"And you use it *very* well Brady Harris."

"You better believe I do Makenna Harris." I say with a smirk. She thinks she's smart, but she's walked over by the bed and she's so close that I can reach out to pull her in by the belt around her waist. So, that's exactly what I do, and she doesn't look quite as smug as she did a second ago. "Still think your husband has no game and couldn't pick you up if we didn't get together as teenagers?"

"You know I didn't mean it Brady." She says quietly, leaving a light kiss on my lips. "I was just teasing you, but you have to admit, that was a shocking pick up line honey."

"I don't need pick-up lines, I've already got you baby. You're my wife now." I say pulling her in close to me so that I can leave kisses along her neck and shoulder.

"That doesn't mean either of us should stop making the effort to make the other person still feel special, does it?" She asks, unsure of what? My answer or that she should be asking the question.

"You're absolutely right. Let me prove to you right here and now that you are the most important person to me."

As I lie my wife back onto the bed, among the pillows and white sheets, I plan to make her feel *very special* right now.

My last thought before losing myself in her pleasure is, always make sure Kenna knows how special she is and how much you love her.

Chapter Seven
MAKENNA

Falling asleep in Brady's arms is a feeling I never want to take for granted. Waking up in my husband's arms is an even bigger treat because he makes me feel safe, loved, and treasured.

"I don't want to go home baby. Can we just stay here and enjoy each other for the rest of our lives? Please?" Brady mumbles into the crook of my neck, causing me to laugh. "Don't laugh at me woman!"

"You know we can't stay here Brady. We *both* have responsibilities waiting for us at home and let's face it, neither of our families would stay away so there wouldn't be a lot of peace here either." I laugh even harder and he growls against my skin and pulls my body even closer to his, trying to hibernate in the bed.

"We only have a few days in paradise Brady, and we've already spent half of it in our little bungalow of debauchery." I tell him trying to disentangle myself from his ever tightening embrace. "We need to get out and see some sights and other people honey."

"Why?" He grumbles into my neck again.

"Because your parents for one are going to expect to see some photos of our trip and I doubt they want to see just the bungalow, the bedroom and your arse." I say, only to get *another* grunt. "And for two, we need to get *some* sun or everyone, meaning my brothers, will give us grief about never getting *out* to see the sun. I for one do not want to have that conversation with either of them." I say, putting a bit more effort into trying extract myself from his crushing embrace. I don't succeed.

"We're on our *honeymoon* baby, no-one, not my parents or your brother's expect us to have a tan when we get home." He pulls me impossibly tighter to his body and groans. "Can't we just enjoy the fact that we can be alone, doing whatever we want, wherever we want, however we want in privacy? Without one of your brother's walking into the house like they still live there?" He sighs. "I know, I know. It's the family home and I knew what I agreed to when I moved in there, but can't I just enjoy some privacy with my *wife* while I can?" How can I argue with that?

"OK husband we can stay in bed this morning, but we *will* get out and see some sights before our time here is over. Do you understand me?" I can feel his lips on my neck as they spread into a smile. He knows he's won this round, but he won't win forever. "Now, let me get up so that I can pee."

"You'll come back though, right? Because I'll be waiting here for your return." He says sleepily as he releases his stranglehold on me.

"Yes Mr Darcy, I shall return post haste." I laugh back at him and stretch out my body when my feet hit the floor. There are kinks in muscles I didn't even know I had and I'm relishing every one of them.

"You keep stretching like that in front of me Kenna and you won't be getting to that bathroom anytime soon." Brady's sleepy, sexy voice says behind me, making me jump into action. "Thought that might make you move."

I can hear Brady's deep, throaty laugh follow me the whole way to the bathroom. I shake my head as I close the door. My new husband can be such a wise arse sometimes, but he's *my* wise arse and love of my life. I couldn't imagine life without him.

Opening the bathroom to go back to bed, I look up and stop in my tracks. I watch as Brady rolls over onto his back, his right hand resting behind his head and the sheet moving to settle low on his hips, showing off his impressive chest. The sheet starts moving and I realise that his left hand is stroking his cock.

"Are you going to just stand there and watch me, or are you going to come here and help me out?" Brady's deep, husky voice makes me jump, again. I didn't realise he was watching me or really aware of my presence. My eyes travel up his body to meet his eyes, only they're closed. "I know you're there Kenna, come here baby and help a guy out. Or I guess you can just watch me, I won't object."

I can't move, my feet are rooted to the spot. It's not like this is the first time I've ever watched Brady jerk himself off, it's not. We've been together for so long and learned everything we know about sex together, but as the sheet falls off his thighs and I get to actually watch what I assumed was happening, my mouth dries up and I can't speak. Or move.

"So, you're going with voyeurism this morning then baby?" He asks, his eyes never leaving mine.

"Uhuh." Is all I manage to whisper, as I swallow deeply, breaking our eye contact to look back over his impressive chest and watch the muscles work in his arm as he works his cock. Geezus, he's a gorgeous man and I'm lucky to call him my husband. I might have given him some grief last night about lame pick-up lines, but I know deep within my soul that I would have agreed to our first date no matter how old we were when we met. Or whatever lame lines he used.

"If you keep looking at me like that Mrs Harris I won't last very long." He grounds out between clenched teeth. I know he's close, because his hips start to jerk up and down in time with his hand, and he lets out a loud groan. Then his right hand drops to cup his balls and he finally breaks our eye contact as he closes his eyes. Standing there watching him jerk himself off, my hands move of their own accord to my breasts, kneading them and my fingers pull at my nipples. Watching Brady pleasure himself makes me hot all over and I need some relief. "Yes Kenna, baby I'm gonna. Argghhh-hh." I watch as streams of his cum land on his washboard stomach and it's my turn to groan loudly. "Guess it's time for a shower now, huh?" He says and my eyes that I didn't realise I'd closed fly open to see him stalking, yes he's stalking towards me. His release glistening on his stomach.

"What?" I ask dumbfounded. He's going to have a shower?

"I'm going to have a shower and clean off baby." He says quietly in my ear when he gets close to me. "Unless there's something else I should be doing right now?" Is it a question? I can't tell. I look at his gorgeous face and one side of his mouth is lifted up in a lopsided grin. Gawd he's sexy! He continues walking past me and I shake my head.

What did he ask me? I can't think. My hand drops from my breast and slides its way down my stomach to my pussy. He's got me so worked up that I can't stop myself from wanting my own relief from this tension he's built up in my body. I'm so distracted that I don't notice that Brady's back by my side.

"Oh no you don't, that's *my* pleasure baby." He knocks my hand out of the way and then places my hand on his shoulder. "Hold on tight baby." Then without hesitation he pushes two fingers inside me, and I feel my knees buckle slightly at the feeling. "Hold on to me baby, I won't let you fall."

I wrap my hand tighter around his bicep and hold on. His other hand reaches up to grip the back of my head and neck to steady me. All the while, his fingers never stop. They never stop dragging in and out of my body. Then he adds a third finger, and his thumb presses hard onto my clit and starts rubbing it. My head tries to drop back but Brady's got a tight grip on it. He leans in and drags his lips across my shoulder and up my throat, nibbling on my ear when he reaches it, then he whispers, "Come for me baby." His fingers move faster, and his thumb pushes harder on my clit, rolling it around with just the right amount of pressure and then it hits me.

"Brady!" I sigh on a loud sigh. He steps away from me, leaving me panting and standing in the middle of the room, wanting his touch back.

"Still think I don't know what I'm doing, Makenna *Harris*?" He asks, emphasising my new last name, with that smirk on his face. "Still believe you would want to miss out on my skills?"

"We learnt them together Brady." I say, barely able to speak still.

"Exactly. I can play your body like a musical instrument baby, just like you can play mine." He reaches out, grabbing my face and giving me a searing kiss. When he breaks the kiss, I feel the loss of his touch immediately. "Look at you, you got all messy. Guess you'll need a shower as well." Then he saunters, yes fucking saunters off to the bathroom leaving me stunned in the middle of the room.

What the hell just happened? I went to the loo and then I was admiring how handsome my husband is and now. Now I'm befuddled. I hear the shower turn on and that gives me the jump start that I needed. I turn around and walk back into the bathroom that I just left.

"Move that cute butt of yours, I need to clean up. Some dirty bastard got me all messed up." I say, pushing my way passed him into the open shower and standing under the steaming water. He chuckles behind me and then wraps his arms around my waist.

Brady's lips press against my neck, sucking gently on my skin. "I love you Makenna Harris. More than I could ever hope to explain to you. I will love you forever." His words are mumbled against my skin and I feel them through every pore of my being.

"I love you too, Brady Harris. More than you could ever understand. I will love you forever and always." I pull his hand to my lips and kiss the palm of his hand. "I've loved you since I was fifteen years old and just so you know, I would have gone out with you even if you *had* used the corniest of corny pick-up lines."

"I knew it!" He yells, pulling his hand from mine and smacking me on the butt, making me squeal. "I knew I was irresistible!"

I turn around in his embrace, cup his face in my hands and say, "Only to me honey. Only to me." Then I kiss him until we're both breathless. Again.

"Only you baby." He whispers against my lips and then he takes my mouth in a kiss that could steam up the mirror. Reaching behind me, I fumble around until I find the soap and I rub it all over Brady's chest. Not once does he break our kiss.

We're both hot and breathing heavy when we've finished washing each other and I know where his mind is, it's the same place mine is, but we *have* to get out of this bungalow at least a few times while we're here. I feel like it would almost be a waste of a trip if we didn't, and as much as I understand his joy at being alone with me, because I feel it too believe me, I also know I'll regret not getting out and seeing some of the sights on the island.

I pull away from Brady and step out of the shower to dry myself, but he reaches out grabbing my hand to stop me.

"Where do you think you're going Mrs Harris?" I look over my shoulder back at him. He looks so damned sexy with his hooded eyes, his mouth slightly open, almost searching for my lips and I can feel my body being drawn back to his. This magnetic pull that has always existed between the two of us, even when we were teenagers and didn't understand what it meant. Knowing I have to fight it, I gently pull away from Brady and I can see the hurt flash across his face.

"I'm going to get dried and put on some clothes, so that we can leave this bungalow and see other people and some of the island." I stop to wrap the towel around my hair so that it stops dripping down my already dry body. "I love you Brady, but we can't stay in here having sex all day every day." I look at him when I reach the bathroom door and see the disappointment on his face and can't help laughing. "I'm not saying no more sex for the trip darling husband of mine, I'm saying we need to leave the cave and experience some things other than each other. So, I've booked us some things to do on the island."

"If you say so beautiful, but just for the record, I would be more than happy to stay here in the so called cave with you for the rest of our stay, never to see another soul until we pack to leave." He says, rinsing the final remnants of soap off his gloriously naked body, tempting me to step back into that shower and letting him have his way with me. Of course, this was his intention, which helps me have the strength to pull my eyes away from him. Seeing the smug grin on his face as my eyes meet his, gives me the last push to walk out of the room. He knew what he was doing rubbing his hands all over his body while I stood there watching. Jerk! "Are you sure I can't change your mind baby?"

"Jerkface!" I say and poke my tongue out at him as I walk out of the bathroom and back into the bedroom, his bellowing laughter following me as I do.

Opening my suitcase properly for the first time since we got here, I can't help laughing. My cousin knows me so well it's almost scary. I'll have to remember to thank Rochelle when we get home, because she most certainly packed for a sexy time *and* even managed to buy me some new things to come away with that would have made my in laws blush! I hear the telltale noises of Brady rustling around in the bathroom and know that he'll be back out here soon enough and if I'm not dressed, we won't be going anywhere for a while.

As appealing as it sounds to be locked up in here with him, I need to get outside. Grinning to myself I see just what I need to wear. Not only will I be clothed but Brady is going to wish we weren't in public. Which will just make coming back into the bungalow delightfully hot and I couldn't wait for it.

I just finished pulling a dress over my body and as the hem settles at my ankles Brady speaks from the doorway, making me jump.

"What the hell was that?" He growls out in a strained voice.

Turning around, I smile my sweetest smile at him and say, "That was my underwear Brady. You know the things we wear *under* our clothes when we leave the confines of our homes so as not to scare the natives?" I can't help the sarcasm that comes out of my mouth. I think I might just enjoy this day a little more than I had anticipated earlier. "Hurry up and get dressed babe so we can get out of here."

"You think I'm letting you out of here knowing what you've got under that flimsy sundress?" He chokes out. "Not on your damned life, *baby*."

"You're not *letting* me leave? Are you for real right now Brady Harris?" I ask him, hands on hips with a scowl on my face. Does he really want to fight with me here, on our honeymoon? The man wanted to get laid 24/7 while we're here and he's picking a fucking fight?

"I won't be able to concentrate or enjoy whatever we do today knowing what's underneath that dress and I don't want anyone else *seeing* what is underneath that dress!" So, *that's* his issue.

"No-one but you and I are going to know what's underneath my dress, so get your arse moving so we can go do the things." I tell him, not leaving him any room for argument. At least I didn't think so.

"No. Not with you dressed like that." He counters, crossing his arms across his chest. I try not to watch his forearms, biceps, and pecs flex, but they look so damned tasty that I can't pull my gaze away fast enough that he doesn't catch me. One side of his mouth curls up in a lopsided grin that makes me instantly wet, but I can't give in.

"Fine." I tell him, and turn away, starting towards the door. "Don't join me, I'm sure I can find someone to talk to on the island." Before I make it more than four steps, Brady is behind me and wrapping an arm around my waist.

"Fine, let me get dressed and I'll leave the bungalow with you, but you're going to pay for it when we get back here later." He snarls roughly in my ear.

"Is that a threat Mr Harris?" I ask snarkily.

"That's a promise Mrs Harris." He barks out as his arm drops from my waist and his body pulls away from mine. "That's a god damned fucking promise Makenna." He says again, sending a shiver of anticipation down my spine as he walks away from me to get dressed.

I hope his sister got as creative with the clothes she packed for her brother, as Rochelle did with mine. Just the thought brings a smile to my face and then he walks in front of me, reaching for my hand, ready to leave. I can't hold back my laugh. Yup Beth definitely had a little fun at her brother's expense.

"Shut up Kenna. You wanted to leave, so let's go." He grumbles.

"Sorry. Let's go." I say, drawing my lips into my mouth to stop me from smiling. "I think you look adorable." I'm rewarded with a look that could kill the most innocent of innocents and laugh again. He drags me by the hand, out the door, locking it behind us and getting us on the path to the main building without saying a word, at a quick pace.

Beth is definitely getting an extra tight hug off me when we return. She deserves it.

Chapter Eight
BRADY

I am going to *kill* my sister when we get home. *How* the hell did she have the time to go out and find these clothes, honestly? I swear mum and dad said they didn't tell her until a day or two before the wedding.

"I think you look adorable." Kenna says to me, but I can hear the laughter in her voice. It isn't bad enough that I know what's under that dress and I have to control myself for the rest of the day. I also have to make sure she doesn't flash to anyone else, not that she'd do that on purpose, but I'm also self-conscious about the way I'm dressed. I can hear my sister saying, 'but it's how they dress on the island Brady, you look great', I *still* want to kill her.

Where the hell did she even *find* Hawaiian shirts and shorts in the shops near home? Thank god she put in plain coloured shirts and shorts as well, otherwise I'd look like a man-child in kids pyjamas! Considering I'm already in a mood because I want to enjoy my wife, alone, while we can but she insists we leave the damned bungalow.

Walking over to the main building, takes us less than ten minutes and I know I'm grumpy the entire time but I'm annoyed. When we get inside, I'm hot and a little sweaty but Kenna is still holding my hand and smiling wide. She's *so* happy to be here, getting out to see the sights, with *me*. Screw Beth and her skewed sense of humour. We're on an island where no-one knows us and I'll never see these people again, except for my new wife and she doesn't care about what I'm wearing.

I'm still going to kill Beth when we get home and I'm already plotting my revenge. Believe me, it will be *exceptionally* sweet too.

"Nice shirt Mr Harris." Tomas says with a huge grin. "You look like a local." He continues, spreading his arms to show off his own brightly coloured Hawaiian shirt.

"Thanks, I'll let my sister know you approve."

"I think I like your sister, Mr Harris." He says with a chuckle.

"I think she'd like you too." I grimace just thinking about them meeting. "Come on, Tomas I've already told you to call me Brady, I'm on vacation, Mr Harris got left behind at the office." I beg him this time.

"No worries Brady." He replies, his grin spreading even wider than I thought possible. "You look beautiful as always Makenna." He says, turning his attention to my wife, and causing her to grin as widely as him.

"Thank you Tomas. You're charming as always." She says and blushes. She fucking blushes! She married me a couple of days ago and I've rocked her world since before we even hit the island, and she's *blushing* because Tomas the Adventure Specialist compliments her? "So, what have you planned for us today Tomas?" She asks so innocently I almost can't believe she's the same woman who just whispered dirty plans for my cock in my ear, except I know my wife.

"I organised a dolphin and whale watching boat trip for you today. I thought that might ease you into activities outside of your room." Tomas says, causing Kenna blush even deeper and I don't know whether to chuckle or punch his lights out.

"Tomas!" Kenna squeals, hitting the man on the arm.

"Don't be shy now Makenna! You guys aren't our first or only honeymooners and hopefully you won't be our last, but I *am* glad you're getting out to see the island, it's a beautiful place."

Like an idiot, I'm just standing there with an arm wrapped around Kenna's waist, having pulled her in tightly against my body. My attention ping pongs between the two of them trying to keep up with the conversation and what the hell they're up to. I break out of my thoughts when I see Tomas gesture wildly with his arms swinging around.

"Thanks Tomas, I appreciate all your effort to sort these things out for me." She breaks out of my hold and kisses him on the cheek . My hands itch to pull her back to me, but before I can, she's back by my side and wrapping her arm around my back, tucking her hand into the back pocket of my shorts. I've never been a jealous or possessive guy and I know, without a doubt, that Kenna doesn't have feelings beyond friendship with Tomas, but for some reason I can't help myself today. As if Kenna can sense my inner turmoil, the hand in my pocket squeezes my butt cheeks and I can't help my reaction, my butt clenches, causing Kenna to squeeze it again and makes her smile to get even broader when I jump a little.

"You're welcome Makenna, that's what we're here for after all. You kids go off and have fun. We'll be here when you get back and I've already made a reservation for the two of you for dinner tonight as well."

"Thanks again Tomas." Kenna says, and leads me out the door before I can thank him as well. Or ask what the hell he means by dinner reservations, although I guess that's not too hard to work out if I think about it.

We walk in comfortable silence to the jetty, until we're a few steps off the wooden walkway and then Kenna stops, forcing me to stop with her because our arms are wrapped around each other.

"Everything OK there Kenna?" I ask, wondering why she stopped us so suddenly and before we could get on the boat. I mean she went to all the trouble to organise the trip with Tomas after all.

"I just wanted to tell you I love you. I'm so happy that we're married finally and I wouldn't want to do this trip with anyone else." Then she drapes her arm over my shoulders, holds the back of my neck and head in her hands and pulls my lips to meet hers. This woman has my heart and has done since almost the moment we met.

"I love you too baby, always." I tell her when I break our kiss to rest my forehead on hers, giving us time to catch our breath before we keep moving towards the jetty. I don't know what brought on that sudden need to reassure me, but I'm glad she did it.

When we get to the boat, Kenna introduces herself to the captain but when he smiles at her, I can feel my body tense and go all caveman, possessive prick, again. I just don't understand it. Then I hold Kenna's hand as she gets on the boat and I realise what has got me so tense, I know what she *doesn't* have on under all that material and its driving me insane that some other dude might get an eye full.

I step onto the boat right behind Kenna, hiding her body from the guy still standing on the jetty, plastering her back to my front.

"What are you doing Brady? I need to be able to walk across the boat and I can't do that with you attached to me honey." She laughs as she tries to pull away, but she doesn't get very far.

"No you don't. Where you go, I go baby." I tell her, leaving a few light kisses on her neck, knowing what they'll do to her and that I can distract her from what I'm really doing.

"Brady." Her voice is low, raspy and I can feel my body react to it. "We can't." She says it like she means it, but at the same time her hips sway, grinding into mine.

"If you keep doing that baby, you better hope this boat has a bedroom or two onboard." I whisper low and raspy in her ear. I hear her groan quietly, and I push my hips into her, letting her know that's she's not the only one feeling aroused and she pushes back into me again. "Screw it, I don't need a bedroom, just a private place so that I can have my wicked way with you."

"Brady. We can't." She says half-heartedly, while she moves her hips against me again, until someone coughs behind us bringing us both out of our trance.

"Sorry to interrupt, but we're about to get moving and I need you guys to take a seat." The captain says. I turn around to look at him, only to find a knowing looking on his face. He leans in and quietly says, "Once we get moving, we'll be out on the water for a while before we reach our destination. There's two berths under the deck, use the one with the number five on the door." He says, pushing what I can only assume is a key into my hand, because I don't look. He takes a couple of steps back and I notice that Kenna has half turned to face him as well, a blush creeping up her neck and into her cheeks. "There's only myself and another staff onboard, and one other couple. If you can wait ten minutes until we get out to sea, you can spend some time below deck." He says with a wink and a nod, then he turns and walks away.

"Oh my gawd, that wasn't embarrassing at all!" Kenna whisper yells at me, mortification all over her face.

"You know, he knows we're on our honeymoon and I'm sure he's seen worse displays of affection on this boat than what we just did. At least we're still fully clothed baby."

"But he knows. He knows what we *want* to do and what we *plan* on doing *on* his boat!" She turns herself in my arms, burying her face in my chest to hide her embarrassment.

"I've never known you to be ashamed of our sex life Kenna, what's going on?"

"I'm *not* ashamed Brady, but we don't announce what we're doing to the world either."

"We may not announce it Kenna, but we get walked in on all the damned time and I'm more embarrassed that your brothers find us in compromising positions, than strangers I'll never see again in my life." I say, gripping her face in my hands and making her meet my eyes. "That I have to face your brothers after they've seen my naked arse, or worse, like oh I don't know, *fucking* their sister like it's the last time I'll ever get to do it. Or knowing that they've had more than one opportunity to see certain parts of my anatomy in various states of arousal and *still* sitting at the dinner table with them and sharing a meal like nothing happened. You and I both know they've seen more of my body, and yours for that matter, than any of us should be comfortable with. A random guy captaining a boat and being aware that I want to have sex with my amazingly sexy and hot as fuck wife? Yeah baby, that doesn't bother me at all. Not even a little bit. I'm even happier knowing that he's also very aware that my wife wants to fuck *my* brains out as well, because it means that he has no hope in hell of having you himself and believe me, he was thinking about it."

"He wasn't Brady. Not every guy does."

"Oh trust me, every guy *does* Makenna. Most guys would never even entertain the idea of making a move, especially when you're with another guy, but some guys. Some guys they don't care. I could be standing next you in your wedding dress with my suit on, and some knuckle dragging moron would try his luck." I say, running my fingers through her hair and she wraps her arms around my waist. "Some guys will look at us together and wish they had what we have. Some will pity us but none of them matter to me, not really, because I know I have you."

"But you've been all growly and possessive today, and that's not your normal behaviour Brady." She's right it's not. "So, why today? I married you. We're on our honeymoon honey and while I'm not saying that stupid shit like that doesn't happen to people on their honeymoon, it's not happening to *us*. I only have eyes for *you* and I only *want* you."

"I know that Makenna, I don't doubt you, your love or your loyalty. Not for even a second but I *know* what you have on under that flimsy dress of yours and I *know* that if you happen to flash some guy, he won't hesitate to look, and I might have to punch him and then I'll ruin our honeymoon."

"I put underwear on Brady." I can't help the shock that I know must be written all over my face. "Did you really think that I would come out of that room and step foot in public like this, without a bra and knickers?"

"You tricked me?" I ask.

"No, I teased you, but I can't not wear a bra on a boat honey. I'd end up with black eyes." She laughs at me and I look around to see if anyone else is close enough to hear our conversation. "And there is no way on this earth that I would come out on a boat, when I have no doubt it's going to be as windy as hell, with a dress on without knickers!" She laughs, loudly, attracting the attention of the others on the boat.

"Keep your voice down will you!" I say, laughing along with her. "I don't want anyone else thinking about your underwear or lack of it."

"Now who's embarrassed?" She says, kissing me hard and quick.

"Not embarrassed baby, I just don't want anyone else thinking about what's underneath your dress. That's for my eyes only, it's no-one else's business." I say, returning the hard kiss and dragging my tongue across the seam of her lips, seeking permission to enter. She lets out a moan and I take full advantage to slip my tongue and deepen our kiss.

She pulls back after a minute, her hands resting on my chest and her eyes closed, as we catch our breath once again. "Brady." I know that tone in her voice and I can feel myself harden even more if that's at all possible. "Let's take this below deck."

"I thought you'd never ask Mrs Harris, follow me." I turn around while taking her hand in mine and weaving our fingers together, I lead the way below deck without looking to see if anyone else on the boat is watching us.

I don't care if they know where we're going or what we're planning. All I want is some alone time with Makenna and I'm going to have it.

Chapter Nine
MAKENNA

I don't have any more time to think about the what if's or how to's, because Brady turns me around to face him and pushes me up against the wall, where he proceeds to kiss me until I can't remember who is who. When he suddenly pulls away, I realise he was unlocking the door to the cabin the entire time he kissed me. I have no damned clue how he does that, but for those people who say men can't multi-task, they sure can when there's a promise of sex because he always opens doors while he gets me hot and ready to go.

I love the way Brady Harris kisses me. I'd kissed other boys before him and maybe we were just too young back then, but nothing before has ever felt like when he kisses me. It's like he can't get enough of me and it makes me want him even more. We're made for each other, we fit together perfectly, and I can't get enough of him.

His lips leave mine, leaving me breathless all over again and travel down my throat, dropping wet kisses on my skin. He breaths in deeply, the hot and cold air sends a chill across my skin where he was just kissing and creating goosebumps. I groan and my hands dig into his scalp, pulling him back to my skin, begging for him. I feel his smile against my throat, the bastard knows exactly what to do to get me going, as he should after all the years we've been together. Not to mention, everything we know about sex, we learned together, on one another's bodies as well as our own.

"Stop thinking baby. Relax, you know I'll take care of you, I always do." He promises, as he runs his tongue up my neck and sucks my earlobe into his mouth, nibbling on it. A shudder runs through my body and my hands drop to his shirt, desperately attempting to undo the buttons to get to his skin. I need to feel his warmth against me.

While I fumble with his buttons, Brady's hands drop to my thighs and work their way up under the skirt of my dress. When they land on my butt cheeks, he squeezes them and pulls me in tight to his body, squashing my hands between us, effectively stopping me from getting his damned shirt off him.

"Brady." I say with a growly moan.

"What's the matter Makenna?" He asks, his voice deep and raspy with desire, as he smiles against my skin again!

"You know what the matter is Brady." I whine. "You're driving me crazy."

"That's the plan baby." He says way too cheerfully. I try to push away from him, assuming I'll do it easily because my hands are splayed palm down on his chest, but I underestimated his grip on my butt and his determination to keep me close. "Where you going baby?"

"I'm losing my patience Brady." I sigh in frustration. "Don't tease me right now."

"You don't want to be teased today?" He says, looking up from where he was kissing the tops of my boobs, his eyes sparkling with desire and mischief.

"Not today Brady. Not here." I say, my frustration growing.

"No?"

"No! I need you." I growl, ready to explode! Pulling my hand out from between us with great difficulty, I grab a hold of his face and tell him exactly what I need. "I need you inside me Brady. I need you inside me now!"

He growls in response and before I know it, he's stripped his shirt and shorts off, leaving him in just his boxer briefs and my dress is whipped up over my head. I'm standing there in white lace and nothing else.

"God damn Makenna you *are* beautiful and I want to taste every single inch of you." His normally milk chocolate eyes turn a deep dark brown and the look on his face tells me he's going to devour me in about five seconds. And guess what? I'm going to let him!

"You've tasted every millimetre of me a million times before Brady, what's so different today?" I can't help the giggle that escapes me. Nothing makes me that girl who is bubbly happy, except for the way Brady is looking at me right now. I'm not the quiet, coy shy girl, never have been honestly, but when this man looks at me like this, that's where I go.

"Doesn't matter. Yesterday doesn't count. This morning doesn't count." He says, taking a deep, shuddering breath. "You. Are. My. Everything. And I will never get enough of you. Ever Makenna. I promise you that."

The words this man says, how can I not love him with all of my heart?

"I love you Brady." I say, breathless and not moving.

"I know." He says with a cocky smirk and drops his boxers to the floor, then he takes the two steps required to reach me. Before I even know what he's done I'm standing naked before him, then he picks me up by the waist like I weigh nothing and tosses me onto the bed.

"What the hell Brady?" I squeal in shock, but before I can react any further, his warm body is covering mine, stopping me from bouncing again.

"I'm so glad you agreed to be my wife Makenna. I love you so much baby, I can't imagine my life without you." I don't get the chance to answer him as his lips crush mine in a bruising kiss that takes my breath away. There's no more words, only actions.

My hands slide up and down his back, occasionally I scrape my nails along his skin, and I feel him shiver and goose bumps rise in their wake, urging him on. His lips leave mine and my head moves to follow him looking for more, until he kisses me along my jaw, flowing down my neck to my collarbone. I give up searching for his lips and throw my head back to give him easier access to my body.

"Kenna." He mumbles quietly against me as he pokes out his tongue, tasting my skin.

"Brady." I whisper into the air between us. "I need you honey."

"You've got me. Always." He replies so quietly I would have missed it if the room itself wasn't dead quiet.

I don't get the chance to respond because he stretches his body out above me and the feeling of his skin on mine takes my breath away. His hips settle between my legs, spreading them wide. My hands reach up, my fingers digging into his hair and pulling his lips to mine, as he enters me making us both groan. I know how corny it sounds and I'm not quoting a certain movie at all, but he completes me. I feel whole when Brady is around and even more so when we're connected in this more carnal, baser way.

He draws his cock out and then pushes back inside of me and I groan. Nothing could ever feel as good as having sex with the man I love unconditionally without any barriers. "Brady. I'm going to." Again, I don't get to finish as he takes his lips from mine and sucks a nipple into his mouth and lightly bites it and then quickly moves onto the other one, doing the exact same thing to it. He knows exactly how to push my buttons to make me explode.

"Come for me baby, I need you to come with me." He leans over and growls in my ear. That's enough to send me off the edge and I'm flying. Somewhere in the distance I hear him roar out his own release but I'm so far out of reality it sounds muffled and not even close to me, even though I know that's not possible right now. "I love you Makenna." Brady says, his voice barely above a whisper, but I feel his lips move against the skin on my collarbone. He kisses me softly, pulling out of me as he rolls to the side, pulling me in tight to his side.

"No, wait! I need to go to the bathroom." That's when I remember where we are and ask, "Shit, does this room have an attached bathroom?" We were a bit too busy for the tour when we arrived.

Putting his arm over his eyes, he chuckles and says, "Yeah, just to your left baby."

"How did you know that? Forget it, I don't want to know." I say, pulling out of his arms and crossing the very short distance to the door he just pointed to. Slowly I open it and peek through the crack, checking to make sure he's not sending me out into the corridor instead of the bathroom.

"What? You don't trust me?" His voice rumbles from the bed behind me. "That hurts Kenna. You know for a fact I would never send you out naked in public. I don't share what is *mine* with anyone."

I roll my eyes at my Neanderthal and open the door wide so that I can do what I need to do. Peeing after sex should be written into every sex manual for women everywhere. After cleaning myself up and washing my hands, I open the door to go into the bedroom but stop when I see Brady spread out on the bed like delicious smorgasbord just for me. His arm is still flung over his eyes and his other arm is resting on his stomach, so I figure I'll take my time drinking my gorgeous husband in while he's not looking because then his ego can't get any larger.

"Are you just going to stand there and perve on me like a creeper, or are you going to come back to bed and wrap that gorgeous body back around me like before you rushed off?" His satisfied, sleepy deep rumbling voice asks, scaring the crap out of me.

His lips curl up in a lazy smile when I squeak out my surprised. "Arsehole."

"But you love me anyway." He says, still smiling. "Now get over here and give me what I want woman, before we have to go back up on deck and show our faces."

I huff out a disgruntled sigh, but we both know I'm going to do what he's asked. I love snuggling up with Brady at any time, but after we've had sex and he's still all relaxed is the best cuddle ever. I climb onto the bed as he stretches the arm he had resting on his stomach out in invitation and I wrap an arm over his stomach and throw my leg over his, wrapping myself around him, sighing in satisfaction.

"See, that wasn't so hard now was it?" His smirk growing as he tightens his arm around my waist, guessing I'm going to pull away from him for his smarmy attitude, but I have no desire to leave the position I'm in, so he doesn't need to hold on so tightly. I'm not going anywhere.

"I love you Brady." I whisper against his chest.

"I know." Is his reply and I lightly smack him on the stomach where my hand is resting and he pretends it hurt him, but we both know it didn't. "I love you too Kenna." He whispers.

Then we just lie there, enjoying each other and the quiet of the boat, because even though we can hear the rumble of the engines, they're quite muffled, we're also being rocked by the movement of the boat on the waves. It's relaxing and before I know it, I've dropped off to sleep.

"Kenna. Baby, you have to wake up!"

"Mmmm." I don't know why Brady is insisting I wake up. I'm comfortable, warm, and wrapped up in his arms, why would I want to leave. I hear an engine rev and then shudder off, reminding me where we are.

"Come on Kenna, up you get." Brady says, with a chuckle as he starts pulling away from my body.

"No!" I say, my voice husky with sleep, and I make a grab for his quickly retreating arm. "Give me another minute, maybe two, please Brady?"

"One more minute Kenna, but then we're getting up, getting dressed and going back up on deck."

"Fine!" I grumble, as I wiggle my butt back into his groin and enjoy listening to him groan. "Seems like someone's already up."

"Stop it Kenna." He warns, lightly smacking my butt cheek, making me wiggle even more. "That's it!" He pulls abruptly away from my body and stands up next to the bed, looking for his clothes.

"Come back to bed Brady. Just another minute. Please?" I look over my shoulder at him, catching him just as he pulls his boxer briefs up over his erection. I flutter my eyelids and smile, hopefully seductively, at him.

"No! Stop it Kenna. You wanted to leave the bungalow and explore, now you'll get your gorgeous self up and dressed without any more of your tomfoolery."

I sigh. He's right, I wanted to get out and explore, not spend our days and nights cocooned in each other and the bungalow. I wanted to come whale and dolphin watching, so I force myself to sit up on the edge of the bed. I stretch and start looking for my clothes to put back on. I don't have to look too far, because Brady's picked them up and laid them on the bed ready for me. "Thanks honey." I start as I look over at him, but he's just frozen to the spot. "Is everything OK Brady?" His glazed over eyes come back into focus and he shakes his head.

"Hmmm? Yes, yes everything is perfect. Now get dressed so we can get out of here and back up on deck." He sounds kind of stressed, so I do as he asks and put my clothes back on so we can go see some whales and dolphins.

"I'm ready." I announce unnecessarily as I put on my shoes but with Brady hovering waiting for me, I feel like I'm totally justified.

"OK, let's get out of here."

He steps towards the door and I step in front of him, placing my hand on his chest. There isn't a lot of room to move but I manage to manoeuvre around to stand in front of his. "What's wrong Brady?" I ask quietly.

"Nothing's *wrong* Kenna." He closes his eyes for a second and sighs. "If you want to get out of here and look for dolphins and whales, then we better leave now, otherwise we'll have swapped the bungalow for the bedroom on a cruise, because I won't be able to leave. Not when you stretch your body out like you just did and I get to see everything I *could* be touching if we were alone and not on a boat with other people. So move your gorgeous arse above deck *before* I change my mind and strip us both naked before you can say my name and have you again, and again and again." His eyes turn a shade of dark brown I've never seen before and they're begging me. I don't know whether they're begging me to leave or stay, but I do know I need to make a choice and as much as I want to let my husband give me another orgasm, I *really* want to see the dolphins. So, I drop a light kiss on his cheek and turn towards the door.

"Damn it!" I hear him mutter behind me and I smile knowing I made the opposite choice to what he wanted, but a girl needs a rest every now and then, no matter how much she wants her man.

I reach behind me and take Brady's hand in mine, leading him back the way we came from earlier. At least I think I can and well, he's following me, so I assume I'm going the right way.

The sunshine blinds me as we come out on deck. "Do you want a drink?"

"Yes please."

"Stay here and I'll go get us one." Brady says, kissing me and then walking away. I watch him and he catches up with the Captain, a huge smile on both of their faces, as Brady hands him back the cabin key. They laugh at something and then the captain points in the direction of a bench with a couple of coolers on them and I assume that's where the drinks are.

Turning away from them, I lean on the railing and look out to sea, enjoying the peace and quiet of it all. I love the ocean and the beach, I always feel like I'm refreshed after I've had my feet in sand and salt water.

"Mrs Harris, here's some water for you." Brady says and I laugh as he hands me a bottle over my shoulder.

"Thank you Mr Harris. It's warmer out here than I thought it was. That sun has quite a kick to it and I wish I'd thought about bringing a hat."

"Not to worry gorgeous, I've got you covered." Brady promises as he places a big, floppy straw hat on my head, making me laugh. I turn around to thank him and laugh even harder. He's got what I guess you'd describe as a straw cowboy hat on his head.

"Thank you honey." I say, pressing my hand lightly to his cheek.

"You're welcome baby, I'll always protect you." I look from his eyes to his hat and laugh lightly again. "What? They didn't have a huge choice in there, but I thought I'd get into the spirit. I mean, what happens on the honeymoon, stays on the honeymoon." He says, with a shrug and pulls me in to him, tucking my head under his, he kisses my temple and whispers, "Unless it's a baby."

I shiver. From his lips, to the honeymoon gods and goddesses. I can't think of anything I want more than to start a family with Brady.

Chapter Ten
BRADY

This hat, teamed with this shirt, makes me feel ridiculous and uncomfortable. Forgetting how stupid I feel evaporates when I see the smile beaming across Makenna's face when she looks at me. I'd look ridiculous every day if it made her this damned happy. Well, not for work but at home, for sure. Placing the floppy hat I got for her on her head, I lean in and kiss her. I can't help myself, I need to have contact with her.

Turning her around so that she can keep looking out to the ocean, I stand behind her, putting my arms around her and bracing myself against the handrails, holding Kenna steady with my body. She gently leans back, resting her back to my front and that's how we stay for the next fifteen minutes or so until she says so quietly that I almost miss it.

"Oh. My. God Brady! Look!" We both managed to remember our sunglasses but I'm still struggling to spot what she can see against the glare off the water, until she bumps her shoulder into my chest, grabs my hand and points where she wants me to look and there they are.

A pod of dolphins appear in the distance and Makenna barely contains her excitement, I can feel her shaking. Then, a whale breaches the surface of the water a few feet in front of us and just as she's starting to calm down from that, a couple of dolphins rise up and leap over the bow and her enthusiastic squeal cannot be contained. She bounces up and down on the balls of her feet, turning in my arms.

"Did you *see that Brady?*" She squeals in my face, holding my face in her hands and squishing my cheeks, making it a little hard to speak.

"Yeah baby, I saw." I say quietly, kissing her softly.

"Oh my god Brady, I'm so glad we came out here today!" She sounds like she's about to explode, she's so happy.

"Me too baby, me too." I say, smiling at her and then turning her around so that she's facing the water again. I don't want her to miss anything, she looks at me any day she wants to, but this is a once in a lifetime experience for her. I feel like an arsehole for trying to get her to stay in the bungalow now. It was selfish, I knew it then and it's glaringly obvious in this moment.

I resolve there and then, as I watch Makenna's face light up with joy. She's so animated, pointing at every splash, hoping that another whale or dolphin is showing themselves to us. She's so beautiful in this moment, so amazing, that my heart feels ready to explode with love. I've loved this woman since we were teenagers, and there has never been anyone else that has even come close to Makenna Drake for me. Ever. Even when she tried to push me away, telling me I needed to 'explore my options', I didn't leave her. I've never been with anyone else, Makenna has always been enough for me, and I don't see that changing any time soon.

Watching her light up, enjoying this amazing experience and I make myself and her, a promise. I will make sure she enjoys every second of this trip. She was right, of course, that we shouldn't spend all our time here holed up in the hotel and not out here, experiencing everything we can. It wasn't that she didn't want to spend that time with me, it was that she wanted us, *both of us*, to have more.

"You're meant to be watching the ocean and the beauty of these creatures." Makenna tells me when she turns to look at me.

"I am watching the most beautiful thing out here." I tell her, watching her blush.

"You don't have to be so charming Brady, you're going to get sex when we get back to the hotel anyway."

"Am I?" I ask, a serious look firmly in place on my face. "That is nice to know." I say, pursing my lips and nodding my head gently. "I thought we were going out for dinner?"

Makenna leans over, one hand resting on my chest, the other holding onto the railing to balance her, puts her lips right up to my ear and says, "We have to get cleaned up before we go to dinner, Brady and that shower is divine." Then, she nips on my earlobe and spins back around to watch for more dolphins, leaving me trying to regain my balance.

She takes my hand in hers as we walk up the jetty to the sandy path that leads us back to the hotel in silence. When we get around a bend where the jetty, sand and boat are no longer in sight, I stop and pull my gorgeous, amazing, beautiful wife back into my body. Holding the one hand in mine between us, and wrapping my other arm around her waist, pulling her in tight to me. Looking in her eyes, I see the questions and amusement there. "You are fucking amazing Makenna Harris. I love you more than you will ever know." She doesn't get the chance to answer me, confirming or denying what I said, because I slam my mouth onto hers and devour her. After a second, I feel her body relax into mine, and she kisses me back. Passionately, and relentlessly. It turns into something more heated really damned quickly and I pull her hips against mine so she can feel exactly what she's doing to me. The pressure makes her moan into my mouth, urging me on even more.

"Get a room!" Someone yells from a distance, causing us to pull our lips apart.

"We've got one, but thanks for the reminder!" Makenna yells back to no-one in particular, resting her forehead against mine, laughing quietly. We hear them laugh loudly as they walk away.

"One day baby, you're going to get us into trouble." I say, shaking my head while still leaning against hers.

"Nah, I know when to keep quiet." She says with a wink and pulls away from me, starting to walk backwards towards the hotel, one hand still in mine, pulling me along with her. she doesn't need to drag me anywhere. All she has to do is ask, and I'd follow her anywhere. Any time.

She turns to watch where she's walking, but doesn't drop my hand and I follow behind her as we walk towards the entrance of the hotel, she veers to the right and walks right through the side entrance for staff. This woman never ceases to amaze me.

"It's a shortcut to our bungalow." She says quietly, holding her finger to her lips.

I *feel* her laughter rather than hearing it because of our closeness. "Yeah but that's one of the things you love most about me honey. You never know what you're getting yourself into when we're together. Never a dull moment with me around honey." She says while leaning back against my chest. The next thing I know, she's walking backwards and she's sending a lopsided, cheeky smirk my way. God I love this woman! "You coming Brady?" She yells, while she turns and makes her way back to the bungalow.

"Not yet!" I yell back, but I don't move yet. I figure I can give her a fighting chance to beat me to the door and get inside. I think she sometimes forgets how long we've known each other, because she's never been a runner and watching her try, especially in those sandal things she's wearing, is amusing as fuck, and I can't help chuckling to myself. Makenna Harris is a *lot* of things. Beautiful, caring, loving, adorable and smart as a whip, but anything to do with being athletic, except dancing, she fails miserably at.

When she's about ten steps away from the door, I take off after her. She thinks she's won and she's concentrating on reaching for the door handle, not listening to my approach. Just as her fingertips touch the handle, I wrap one arm around her waist and lift her up off her feet. Her squeal of surprise almost deafens me as I place my other arm under her knees and sweep her up into my arms.

"Where's the key Kenna?" I whisper in her ear and feel her entire body shiver. I love that I still have that effect on her after all these years.

"In your back pocket." She whispers back, her voice all husky and sexy.

"Guess you better grab it then, I appear to have my hands full." My own husky voice matching hers. The hand she had wrapped around the back of my neck, slides slowly down my back, tracing along my spine, until she reaches the waist band of my shorts and she hesitates. "Whatcha doing Kenna?"

"Trying to decide whether to grope your butt while I'm here, or just get the key so we can go inside and get naked faster."

"Ladies choice, as always, but I can tell you what I'd prefer."

"And what's that Mr Harris?"

"I think you already know the answer to that Mrs Harris, seeing as though you've forgone the grope and gone straight to the key. So, get that door open woman!" I demand and move closer to the door so that she can reach it. She has to wiggle around in my arms a little to be able to reach it comfortably and my body's reaction is unmistakable, and she'll be able to feel my hard cock pressing against her thigh. "Hurry up Kenna."

"Am I getting too heavy?" She asks, innocence mixed with sass.

"No, but if you don't want another audience, you better move faster." I say as she pushes the door open, laughing.

"Fast enough for you Brady?"

"Not really, no." I kick the door closed and don't bother locking it. I walk us into the bathroom, drop Kenna's legs and she slides her body down mine. It feels amazing, but it's going to feel even better when we're both naked. Neither of us say a word, we just work on getting the other one naked. The only sound in the room is our clothes hitting the floor and the key landing somewhere on the vanity.

Taking Kenna by the waist I walk myself backwards into the shower, she reaches over and turns on the water. I push my head under, wetting my hair and rinsing the sea water off, then I turn us around so that Kenna's under the water. That's when I notice her shoulders are a little red from the sun today and I hope that she's not too sunburnt. I'm distracted when she runs her hands over my chest, tweaking my nipples, before dropping a hand to my already hard cock.

"Fuck!" I moan and close my eyes briefly, enjoying the sensation of her holding me in her hand.

"We don't have much time Brady." She says softly against my chest, while leaving gentle kisses on my skin, driving me fucking wild.

"I won't need much if you keep doing that baby." My hands are kneading her hips, trying to pull her in close to me, but she gets us just apart enough that she can keep running her hand up and down the shaft of my cock.

"You mean this?" She asks, as she runs her thumb though the slit in the tip of the head of my cock, causing me to growl in pleasure.

"Yeah, that." I growl. I open my eyes and look in her eyes. In them I see love and amusement. She knows how to make me lose control and she's damned good at it, but I know how to make her lose control too. Running a hand from her hip to her pussy, I push gently past her lips and slowly push into her.

"Fuck Brady!" Now it's my turn to smile, because she's distracted for a second from my cock, but only for a second. "That feels so damned good."

Her head drops to my shoulder and she leaves light kisses along my neck and shoulder. We're both gently rubbing each other just the way we both like it and I can feel myself getting close to the edge. I lean down leaving my own gentle kisses along her shoulder and up her neck until I reach her ear. I nibble on her earlobe for a second and then I whisper in her ear, "Come for me baby."

"Together." Is all she says, as she wraps her free hand around my neck and holds on.

"Yes." I say, wrapping my arm around her waist to hold us both up as we come in each other's hands.

Chapter Eleven
MAKENNA

Leaning against Brady in the shower as we both wait for our heartbeats to slow back down, I take a few deep breaths to steady myself before I can even *think* about starting to wash my body. I take one more deep breath and start to pull away from Brady, but he pulls me close.

"Let me." He murmurs into the top of my head, and before I can respond, he's soaping up his hands and running them over my body.

"We don't have time for another round you know Brady." I mumble into his chest. "We have to get to dinner."

"I know baby. Just let me take care of you." I nod against his chest and let him wash the day away from my skin. The truth is, I'm feeling tired after being out on the water today and then he gave me an orgasm to top it off. I always feel sleepy after a Brady induced orgasm, he gives them so damned well.

"No, don't go." I say, as Brady untangles my arms from around his neck and drops to his knees.

"Hold onto my shoulders baby, I'm not going anywhere." I do as he says, and he washes my feet, legs and between my thighs. His big hands grip my waist, and he rests his head on my stomach. "I love you Makenna Harris. I will always look after you the best that I can."

"I know." I say, reaching up for the shampoo and washing his hair. "I love you too Brady Harris. I always will." Rinsing his hair, I take his face in my hands and gently draw him to his feet. "My turn." I say softly and he nods, his hands still resting on my hips as I wash his shoulders, arms, and chest. He stops me when I trail my hands down his happy trail towards his cock.

"We don't have enough time for you to get me hard again." We smile at each other, because he's already half hard as it is.

"If you're sure?" I tease him.

"I'm positive, baby." He laughs tenderly. "I can't bounce back as quickly as I could when we were seventeen Kenna, I need some time and it'll take me a while before I can come again. Now, I'm not saying that I wouldn't enjoy you jacking me off, but sometimes a guy needs a chance to recover."

"Maybe later then."

"I'll hold you to that, baby." He says, turning off the water and stepping out to get a towel.

"It's a promise." I reply, as I step out behind him and watch as he wraps a white fluffy towel around his waist. I'm enjoying the show, so I don't notice that he's got another towel in his hand until he's wrapping it around my shoulders, and he starts rubbing up and down my back and arms to dry me.

"Come on, let's get dried and dressed again. I want to take my wife out for dinner and show her off." he says with a lopsided smile.

"What if I booked this dinner so that I could show off my gorgeous husband?" I ask, smacking him on the butt as I walk by him, into the bedroom.

"You really should stop doing that Makenna." He says, gruffly. To anyone else he might look like he's pissed off, but I know he's not.

"You love it! You'll hate it if I ever stop smacking you on the arse as I walk by." I say, without looking back at him.

"You know, if I did that to you as often as you smack me in public, someone would call the cops and accuse me of abusing you. The double standards are atrocious woman!" He continues to grumble.

"Except we're not out 'in public' and you're not *really* complaining." I say, as I bend over to find some undies to wear. A loud crack vibrates through the room as Brady's hand lands on my butt cheek. "Holy fuck Brady!" I screech, straightening up in half a second in shock.

"Well, you wanna bend over like that in front of me, you're inviting me to smack your arse and being that we're in private, it's ok." He says, standing behind me, but not touching me. I can feel his warm breath on my neck, so I know how close he is.

"That's going to leave a mark!" I say, my voice just above a whisper.

"Exactly! You'll know it's there while we have dinner, and so will I, but no-one around us will. What happens in private stays there." He steps away from me and starts to look for his own clothes to wear out to dinner. "Are you going to stop smacking me?" He asks, without looking up.

I don't answer him right away, I pull my undies up and pull on my bra. He doesn't normally go all alpha on me like this and I think I could enjoy it.

"Makenna."

"Yes."

"Yes, you're going to stop?"

"No."

"No?" He asks as he turns to look at me, while he buttons up his shirt. I shake my head, no. "Just remember, what's good for you, is good for me as well baby." Is all he says, then he walks back into the bathroom to do whatever he's doing in there. I imagine he's combing his hair, maybe combing the couple of days growth on his jaw, putting on deodorant and brushing his teeth. Why the hell am I thinking about what he's doing in there?

I'm frozen to the spot in my underwear, my butt cheek still stinging and his promise hanging in the air, while I contemplate what he's *doing in the bathroom*. What the hell? I shake my head to clear it and keep getting dressed.

As I finished doing up my sandal I look up and Brady's standing there, looking sexy as all get out and smug as fuck. Then I realise how I'm sitting on the edge of the bed. Only on one butt cheek. Yeah the other one still stings a little. Arsehole. I get up and walk by him to go into the bathroom myself. His mouth opens, like he's about to speak and we both know it's going to be a smart arse remark about my butt still stinging.

"Don't go there Brady." I warn.

"Or what?" That sexy lopsided smile on lips. "What are you going to do to me Kenna?"

"What am I going to do to you? Guess you'll just have to wait and see." I answer him as I look back at him before I disappear into the bathroom. The look on his face cracks me up and I'm glad he can't see me laughing at him. I half expect him to follow me into the bathroom and ask me what I've got planned. It's what he would normally do, but nothing about this trip has been normal for us.

The constant sex for one thing. Brady and I have been together since we were fifteen and sixteen, I'm a couple of months younger than him, and back when we were teenagers and supposed to horny and having sex at every opportunity we could, we really didn't. Did we touch each other all the time? Hell yes. Were we by each other's side every second that we could be? Another hell yes. Did we get physical earlier than any of our parents would have approved? That one is a definite hell yes, and yet, as attracted as we have always been to one another, as much as we need and want to be close to one another, I wouldn't have said we were sex maniacs. Now, I'm sure Brady would blame my brother's for that, but that's a recent development. They never have and never *would* walk into my bedroom or the cabin that Brady and I were sharing before we moved into the main house, without knocking.

This trip, our honeymoon, Brady just seems to be insatiable and I can't say I don't feel the same way. He's the same gorgeous, attractive, beautiful, caring soul he's always been. I don't think I could have survived my parent's death without him by my side, but being here, in the tropics has just done something to both of us.

"What time do we have to be at dinner Kenna?" Brady says, and when I turn around I see him leaning against the doorframe of the bathroom, looking so freaking handsome I can't speak for a minute.

"Soon."

"How can you possibly know that when you haven't even looked at a clock yet?" He asks, his smirk spreading further across his face.

"I don't need to." I look at his reflection in the mirror as I run the brush through my hair a few times and his lifts an eyebrow in question at me. "Tomas told me we could 'freshen up' after our outing and they would have dinner ready for us just as soon as we get there."

"Ahhh of course, Tomas. I should have known." He says, the smile dropping from his face.

"Are you jealous? Of Tomas?" I ask, I'm surprised that he could feel that way towards anyone, but especially Tomas. The man works here, it's his *job* to make sure the guests are happy.

"No, I'm not jealous, just stating a fact it's all fine because you organised everything with Tomas." He says, pushing off the doorway and turning to walk back into the other room. I've never seen Brady any shade of jealous before, I'm not even sure that's what this is honestly, but I put the brush down on the bench and move over to rest my hand on Brady's arm, stopping him from turning away from me completely.

"Brady, honey, it's his job to help guests organise trips, outings and make reservations for them for dinner. Any meal in fact. Every meal that has been delivered here, to our bungalow, has been organised by Tomas." I grasp a handful of his shirt in my hand and gently tug on it to get him to turn around and face me fully. "I love *you* Brady Harris. I will *always* love you. There is no other man on this planet that I can see me living my life with or having a family with. Tomas, whose last name I don't even know, and I have no interest in actually finding out, is doing his job. Me, I'm doing *you*!" I smile, trying to lighten the mood a little.

"Let's go to dinner."

"Stop being grumpy, and we will." I say,

"I'm not grumpy." He says, and I swear, I can hear the stamp of his foot! I tilt my head to the side, and raise an eyebrow at him.

"Really? You're not grumpy?" I ask, reaching out to take his stubbled cheek in my hands, and rubbing it gently. "Cause you seem grumpy, and I don't want a grumpy husband on my *honeymoon*. I love you Brady. You."

"You're right, and I'm sorry. I don't even know why I'm grumpy." Brady shakes his head, and then leans his cheek into my hand, his eyes closing for a second. "Let's go see what Tomas has set up for us tonight." He says when he opens his eyes. That sexy lopsided smirk is back on his lips, and there's a spark of mischief back in eyes.

"Lead on Mr Harris." I say with a sweep of my hands in front of us both. "I'm right behind you."

Brady takes my hand in his, looping our fingers together, and leads us out the door towards the restaurant. When we get there, Tomas seats us, and introduces us to our server for the night, Olivia. Scanning the menu, we both order, then sit back, and relax. Enjoying each other's company, and the magnificent view.

It doesn't take very long for our food to arrive.

"This looks, and smells amazing, thank you Olivia." I say with a smile, and she gives us a small smile, and then leaves us alone. Brady and I don't talk for a few minutes as we simply enjoy our meals.

"That was delicious." He says with a low moan that sends a shudder through my body. "Do you want to get dessert?" He asks, as Olivia clears the table. Do I want dessert? Look, the fact is, I *always* want dessert and Brady knows it. What he's really asking is, do I want to eat dessert here or back in the bungalow, in private.

A smile spreads across my face, my decision made. "Back at the bungalow."

"Was that a question or a request Kenna?" Brady asks me, his face serious, including the blazing heat in his eyes.

"A request, Brady, definitely a request." I respond with a smile.

"Done." Is all he says and when Olivia comes back to ask us if we want dessert, Brady answers for us and orders exactly what I wanted off the menu. That's what happens when you've known each other for as long as we have.

"That will be delivered to your bungalow in around twenty minutes." Olivia tells us. "Is there anything else I can do for you?"

"No, thank you." Brady says, walking around to help me out of my chair and leading me out of the restaurant.

We take our time strolling back to the bungalow hand in hand, enjoying the evening breeze and all the stars in the sky. I feel happy, content, and relaxed. Brady takes the key out of his back pocket and opens the door, gesturing for me to head inside first. I head straight for the bedroom and kick off my shoes.

"Where did the Aloe Vera gel come from Brady?" I ask, because I didn't see him go and buy it while we were having dinner and he sure didn't go before dinner, we were a little preoccupied.

"I asked Tomas to get some sent to the room. He was more than happy to oblige, being that you're his favourite guest right now." He replies, a twinkle in his eyes.

"How did you know I'd need it?"

"I saw your skin starting to pink in the shower earlier, but then at dinner you started getting a little uncomfortable and thought I'd rather have some than not,." He says with a shrug like it's nothing, but it's not nothing, it's something. He notices these things and then takes care of me. It makes me feel loved, cherished and I adore him for it.

"Oh Brady. Thank you." I take a step closer to him, so I reach my hand up to caress his cheek and he rubs his stubble into my hand. I feel my body warming up and I'm pretty sure it's not from the sunburn. I step in even closer to him, pushing my body into his, but he pushes me gently away, even though I can feel how hard he is already.

"No." He says, shaking his head. "No sex tonight Kenna." Before I can protest he continues, "Let me look after you baby. I'm going to put you in a warm shower and then I'm going to gently rub this aloe vera into your shoulders. Then we're having that dessert that we got sent back here and you, my love, are going to get some sleep."

"How can I argue with that?"

"That's the point, you can't my love. Now, get yourself naked and move that sexy butt into the shower. Let the warm water take some of the sting out of your shoulders and I'll take care of the rest." He says, with a gentle push towards the bathroom. "Go on, go." He says pointing the way.

"I love you Brady."

"I know, Kenna. Now move it before I carry you there myself."

For some reason since we've been here, he's taken a real liking to picking me up and carrying me around. I walk into the bathroom and without closing the door behind me, I strip out of my clothes and step in the shower. Turning on the shower, I step under the water and start to relax some more. I'm half expecting Brady to come in and join me, but he doesn't. True to his word, he waits for dessert to be delivered.

"Dessert is here baby. It's your choice whether you have it before or after I rub this gel into your shoulders or not." He says from the doorway, not venturing any further into the bathroom, possibly to avoid temptation. So, I'll take temptation to him!

I turn the water off and step out of the shower, as I walk towards him I can see the heat ignite in his eyes, but he doesn't move. He's standing still until he realises he's standing next to the towels and reaches out, unfolding it with a flick of his wrist and a flourish, making me laugh, and handing it to me.

"Come here and let me wrap up your glorious body." I go to speak but he interrupts me. "I told you already, no sex tonight Makenna. I'm taking care of you in a totally different way tonight." He wraps the towel around my chest, tucking the end into my cleavage like he's seen me do probably a million times, takes my hand in his and leads me out of the bathroom, towards the bed.

"Lie down on your stomach and get comfortable." Brady insists, and I do as I'm told, wiggling around until I get comfortable. "Are you good?" he asks, his voice deep and gravelly.

"Yup." One simple word is my answer. Then he reaches underneath me and yanks the towel out from under me, throwing it on the floor. I'm about to protest but then his hands are on my shoulders and the cool gel is so nice I forget what I was going to say, instead I let out a moan of pleasure.

"Fuck." Brady mutters under his breath and I know he's struggling to control himself. I'm about to say something, but he adds a bit more of the cooling gel and I relax into the relief. Then he starts massaging my back and my legs and before I know it, I'm drifting off to sleep. The last thing I remember is Brady lightly kissing my temple and telling me he loves me. I think I mumble back that I love him too, but I'm relaxed and sleepy, so I'm not sure if I manage to get the words out or not.

Chapter Twelve
BRADY

As much as I'm tempted to get in the shower with Makenna, I knew that I wouldn't be able to resist touching her. One, if not both of us, would have ended up coming. Again. I need her to know that I heard what she said earlier, and as much as I don't want to agree, we *do* need to experience more than just each other while we're here, even if it *is* our honeymoon. I want her to experience everything that she can here on the island because, it's a once in a lifetime opportunity.

So yes, I *was* enjoying the privacy this bungalow was offering us, but on the boat today, I saw the joy on her face and the way she relaxed in my arms while we sailed across the ocean. She was still, quiet, just enjoying us, and I knew she was right. I want her to keep that feeling, so, no sex tonight. My resolve was even stronger when we got back to the bungalow and I saw that her shoulders were already going pink.

After I know Makenna is fast asleep, I quietly leave the bedroom, closing the door behind me. I pick my phone up off the bench and look at my messages. When I see one from my Mum I decide that instead of messaging her, I'll give her call.

"Brady! Why are you calling me? Is everything OK? Is Makenna OK? Are you OK?" She rattles off in one breath.

"Hey Mum, slow down. Everything's fine. Perfect in fact. I'm fine and Makenna is asleep in bed so I thought I would call you rather than message you back. I didn't interrupt anything did I? You guys aren't having dinner, are you?" I ask, suddenly realising the time difference between here and home.

"No, no, we're not doing anything. Your Dad and I are fine, we were just watching TV. Is Makenna OK? It's a bit early to be sleeping isn't it?"

"We had a big day today and she's pretty tired. We haven't really stopped since we got here." I say, hoping that my Mum doesn't ask any questions about what it is exactly that we haven't stopped doing. I should have known better though.

"Yeah, I bet you haven't stopped. I remember our honeymoon, and I know we barely saw outside our hotel." She says with a chuckle and I hear my Dad laugh and mumble something in the background that I'm pretty sure I don't want to hear. "Oh stop it Jeremy, Brady doesn't need, nor want to hear about our antics." I can hear my Dad laugh loudly this time and my Mum giggles like a schoolgirl.

"I could tell you some stories son!" My dad yells out.

"Tell Dad thanks, but I think I'll pass." I say, laughing to myself. I'm so glad my parents are still so happy with each other. It gives me faith that Kenna and I can make it as long as they have. Kenna parents were still very much in love as well, I guess that shows in the fact that they died together? I'm not sure one could have survived without other one around, so the accident may have been a blessing in disguise, not that I would ever say that to the Drake siblings. Ever.

"So, what did you do today that wore your gorgeous bride out then if it wasn't the obvious thing you'd be doing on your honeymoon?" My mum asks, and I can still hear amusement in her voice.

"We went on a dolphin and whale watching boat tour. It was really amazing, Kenna loved it." I say, and I can feel the smile stretching across my face. Seeing her happy is my greatest joy.

"That sounds like something I imagine Makenna would absolutely love! You're a good man for taking her out on that trip." Mum says excitedly. I could take the credit for it, but I know they'll talk about our trip in detail when we get home so there's no point stretching the truth.

"I can't take the credit for the trip actually. Kenna booked it and the other activities for the rest of the week. She didn't agree with my plans for the week, so she booked us a few activities for the rest of the week."

"So, what you're saying is, Makenna wanted to see more than just the bungalow." My dad laughs as he asks. Mum must have put me on speaker.

"Well, you know it *is* our honeymoon, but Kenna wanted to have some photos to show our family and friends of our trip that didn't include the inside of the bungalow, yes." I laugh quietly, not wanting to wake up my sleeping wife. Not yet anyway.

"Of course she did Brady!" Mum exclaims and even though I can hear the admonishment in her voice, I can also hear the humour there too. My folks have become very protective of Makenna since her parents' deaths. They're protective of the boys too, but sometimes I wonder who they would choose if Makenna and I ever split up. Not that, that is ever happening if I have anything do with it, but still, I can't help but wonder. "You're both having fun though, right? You both needed the break away from everything, but Makenna needed it more." See what I mean?

"Sure Ma, it's not like your only son didn't deserve a holiday as well." I only half joke.

"You know I didn't mean it like that Brady, but Makenna has worked too hard to make the business succeed since April and Jack passed away. Both Makenna and Logan have worked too hard, and Jack wouldn't want them to work so hard that they didn't stop to enjoy life, you know that."

"I know Ma, and I try to make both of them take time out, but it's not easy you know? Both of them are so damned driven to make the business a success. They were both like that *before* their parents died, but since that terrible accident, well let's just say they've both been more determined." There's a minute of silence between us, until I break it by saying, "I'm trying Mum." Really quietly, I'm not even sure she can hear me.

"I know you are sweetheart, we know you are. It's one of the reasons we wanted to give you *both* this time away from Drake Wines. You both needed the break, you work hard there too Brady, not to mention you've got a job that doesn't include Drake Wines as well." My mum says, and it means the world to me.

"We're proud of the adults you've all become Brady, and that includes your gorgeous wife and her brothers. I know that the Drakes would be proud too son, but they also wouldn't want their kids to lose themselves in work. Jack never wanted that." My Dad says.

"I know Dad, but it's just so hard for them. They want to continue on Jack's hard work, but I know they're pushing a little hard some days."

"I know it's hard, but you can work it out and we're always here son, for all four of you."

"Thanks Dad. You guys are the best."

"Well, we have great kids, that always helps." My Mum laughs, trying to make things light again.

"Yeah, we are all pretty awesome, aren't we?" The three of us laugh, breaking the tension that had built up.

"Brady, honey? Who are you talking to?" I hear Makenna's voice from behind me and I turn around to see my bedraggled, sleep tousled wife stumble out of the bedroom, grateful that she thought about throwing her dress on before walking out to see what I was doing. So much for thinking she was out for the night.

"I called my parents."

"Hi Mum and Dad." I hear my Mum gasp on the other end of the phone and there's a little bit of rustling, and I imagine my Dad is now hugging my Mum.

"OK, we're all on speaker, so everyone behave yourselves, OK?" I laugh, trying to keep the mood light.

"Of course. How are you Makenna sweetheart? Brady said you two had a pretty busy and amazing day." My Dad asks, giving Mum the chance to pull herself together.

"Oh yes it was incredible. Have you ever seen dolphins and whales in the ocean Mum? It's absolutely amazing, and they're *so* much bigger than I was expecting."

"No. No I haven't seen them in the ocean Makenna, darling. I'm glad that Brady isn't keeping you in the bungalow and is letting you get out to experience these amazing things."

"Yeah your son is the most amazing man I've ever met. You guys did an amazing job with him, truly. I can only hope we do as well with our kids." Kenna kind of mumbles as she snuggles into my side, dropping her head on my shoulder, but I don't miss my mum's second gasp in minutes.

"You mean..."

"No, Mum we're not pregnant, you guys will definitely be one of the first people to know if we are, I promise." I cut her off before she can get any ideas on what Kenna might have meant, because there isn't anything that excites my mother more than thinking about having grandchildren to love and spoil.

"Oh." My Dad chuckles. "Leave them be Pauline, it will happen when they're good and ready."

"Alrighty, on that note I'm going to hang up because my wife needs to go back to bed and get some sleep. She's already almost asleep nestled into my side."

"Of course." My Mum sniffles. "I forget about the time difference. It must be getting late there. You two take care and enjoy the rest of your trip. We look forward to seeing all your photos when you get home." I can't help laughing at her very subtle dig at me, because Kenna is way too sleepy to catch on.

"Oh, I can't wait to show you Mum, it's been amazing." Kenna says sleepily.

"Oh." I hear my Mum's sniffling getting steadily worse and my Dad says, "Alright kids, we're going to let you go. Enjoy the rest of your trip and we'll see you when you get back."

"Thanks Dad." I say.

"Love you guys." Kenna says, and I hear my poor Mum openly sob.

"We love you both, very much." She says and then we hang up. I'm not sure my mum could take too much more of my sleepy, loving wife tonight.

"Your Mum is so sweet." Kenna mumbles into my neck.

"Yeah she is, but what are you doing up? I thought you were out cold after my massage." I ask, running my hand up and down her back.

"Oh that massage was amazing, and I was out cold, but I missed you, and then I heard you talking. I needed a drink, so I thought I'd come out to see who you were talking to and I could cuddle you."

"Well, that's sweet baby, but you're almost asleep out here so how about, I take you back to bed and then I'll bring you a glass of water. How does that sound?" I ask, kissing her lightly on the head.

"Sounds perfect honey, but I can get myself to bed."

"I know you can baby, but I'll take you anyway."

"Are you going to stay with me this time?" She asks, as I stand up, scooping her up in my arms causing her to squeal quietly and carry her back to bed.

"Yeah baby, I'll stay with you. Always."

"Always?"

"Yeah, you're stuck with me forever baby."

"Good, because I want to be stuck with you forever." She says as she snuggles back under the sheet that I pull over her. "I think we'll make adorable babies, Brady Harris."

"I think so too, Makenna Harris." This brings an enormous, sleepy smile to her face, her eyes already closed again. I pull away from the bed to go get a glass of water when her hand reaches out to grab mine.

"Don't go anywhere Brady, come to bed."

"I'll only be gone for a couple of minutes baby. I'm just going to get you that drink of water and then I'll be back, I promise." Her hand drops to the bed, but she doesn't utter another word.

I walk out to the small kitchen and grab two bottles of water from the fridge. When I get back into the bedroom, I can't help but chuckle. I don't think Makenna is going to be needing that water, but at least it will be there for her when she wakes up in the morning and I guess that means that dessert is now breakfast as well.

I strip out of my clothes, take a quick shower, and after I've dried off, I join my wife in bed. Pulling her close, her back to my front, she wiggles her butt into my groin, and I groan. There's no way anything is happening right now, but my cock doesn't know that and he's standing at attention.

"I love you Makenna Harris." I mumble between her shoulder blades. She mumbles something back that I choose to interpret as she loves me more than I know, and I close my eyes. Happy to be with my Kenna in paradise. Alone.

Chapter Thirteen
MAKENNA

I slowly become conscious and I'm wrapped up in the warm cocoon of my gorgeous husband's arms. His body wrapped around mine, arms holding me to him and his head resting on my shoulder. I have no idea how the hell he managed to sleep like that, it can't be very comfortable, but there he is. He is always there, protecting me, comforting me, holding me, backing me, and letting me be me. This is why I married him, because even when we were teenagers and trying to navigate the world and work out how we fit in it, he always let me be me, while having my back at every turn as well. I've always been able to rely on Brady Harris to be by my side, because he knows I can fight my own battles, but he likes to show that he's my back up. That's if my brothers weren't there to kick arse as well. I'm lucky to have the three of them in my life.

I snuggle in to Brady's embrace, trying not to wake him up, because he needs some more sleep, but I can't get comfortable, and I know why, but I don't want to move just yet.

Brady's hand moves off my stomach to my butt cheeks and he smacks it lightly. "Go have a pee and then come back. I won't move and we can snuggle for as long as you want then, because you won't be needing to go." He says this sleepy, sexy husky voice that I love.

"Oh my god, Brady! I didn't realise you were even awake."

"Well, I wasn't until you started to grind that sweet butt of yours into my groin, and while I don't mind at all baby, I know you need to go to the bathroom. So, go get done what you need to, and come back to me, then we can get back to canoodling the morning away again."

"You promise?" I ask, already knowing his answer.

"Abso-freaking-lutely, baby. I won't move a damned muscle until you get back here." With another smack to my butt, he pushes me gently out of the bed. What can I say, the man knows me pretty well after all these years I guess.

Making my way to the bathroom pretty quickly, because he's more than right, I *really* need to pee! I do what I need to and then fill one of the glasses on the vanity with water and take a few large gulps. I remember getting up last night and snuggling up to Brady on the couch while we spoke to his parents. That's when I giggle a little, because he went and got me a water that I never even took a sip out of.

"Don't stand there being a creeper baby. Come back to bed and let me hold you." How can I resist the man when he speaks to me like that, his voice still husky with sleep and his eyes barely open? He's freaking adorable! I love ruffled, barely awake Brady because he's usually so well put together and so in charge and confident, this is him in his ultimate relaxed state. The fact that he can relax and leave himself open to me like that is a *huge* turn on. I guess it comes with knowing each other forever.

"I was just admiring the view. My husband is a very sexy man you know, and I like taking in the perfection that is Mr Brady Harris." I say with a grin, as I lower myself back down onto the mattress, and in a split second he's pulling me back in close.

Nuzzling his nose into my neck as he pulls me in tight against his body, he sighs. "Are you good there honey?"

"I am absolutely perfect right here, in this second baby." He sighs again, not in annoyance or frustration, but contentment. "And do you know why I'm so perfect in this moment Makenna?"

"No, I truly do not, Brady." I answer him honestly.

"You sure you don't know baby?" He mumbles into the fleshy part of my neck where it meets my shoulder, his breath hot on my neck as he breathes out and chilled when he breathes in again. Over and over, and he leaves goosebumps up my neck and down to my fingertips.

"I'm sure I don't know honey." I whisper, not trusting my voice if I speak any louder.

"I think you do, but I'll pretend you don't and explain it to you anyway." He says, his voice still husky from sleep, as his hand lazily sweeps up and down my thigh, over my hip and up to caress the side of my boob, only to start it's trip back down the path and then back up again. It's kind of hypnotising. "This right here is perfect, because it's just us. No-one else can get in here, they don't have the key that lets them, and we're not going to get interrupted no matter what we're doing."

"You know Tomas has a key right? And so does Samantha, I mean, they could get in here any time they like." I say, struggling to hold back my laughter when his body stiffens, but just as soon as there's tension, he's relaxed again.

"That's what you think baby." I can feel his smile across my skin, and I try to turn around to look at him, but he's holding me so tightly, I can't.

"What the hell is that supposed to mean?"

"It means, baby, that I made a little deal with your friend, and he won't be visiting unless we call him in here *or* he knows we're *not* in here." I reach behind both of us and swat him on the butt cheek that I can reach, and when I feel him clench it under my hand, and he lets out a growly moan against my skin, I know I hit just the right spot. "I already had that deal with Samantha, but she couldn't get Tomas to agree, until yesterday. Now we're best buddies, just like the two of you are."

"Tomas and I aren't 'best buddies', as you put it. He helped me out with booking some activities for us to do, that's all. The man did his *job,* so stop harassing him." I say, exasperated with the man. The man has the balls to chuckle behind me, and I realise too late that he's holding both of my wrists in his hands, meaning I couldn't hit him even if I tried. While it might look and sound like, for all intents and purposes, that I'm stuck here like this, I know that if I made a serious move to get out of his hold, he would let me go in a heartbeat. Especially if he thought he was hurting me in any way, so I relax. "He was helping me, us out, just like he's supposed to Brady."

"I know, which is why he's now just doing his job and helping *us* out by keeping everyone out of the bungalow unless we ask them in here, or we're out on one of the adventures he helped you to book for us." He says, slowly releasing my wrists from his grip. "Wanna have a shower with me? I promise to wash you until you're all squeaky clean. I'll even let you do the same for me baby."

"You're a very generous man, Brady Harris." I say with a smile.

"What can I say, I like to give back to my wife." He says, shrugging his shoulder as he moves off the bed, holding his hand out for me to join him. I hesitate, not because I don't want to join him in the shower, but because I want to see the look of frustration on his face. Instead, he surprises me by grabbing onto my hand, pulling me to my feet, and then lifting me off my feet, to swing me over his shoulder.

"What the hell Brady?" I squeal, while holding onto his naked butt cheeks with both hands, feeling them flex with every step that he takes. I'm not complaining, obviously, but it's not every day my husband throws me over his shoulder and carries me to the shower. In fact I don't think he's ever done it before now. "Put me down!" I demand, but we both know I don't mean it.

"OK." He says while pulling me back over his shoulder, letting my body slide through his hands and down the length of his body. "What the? Damn it Brady." I say, smacking him on the pec, my hand resting there and feeling him up. I mean it's hard to resist, it's an amazing freaking pec!

"You just wanted to keep your hands on my arse baby, and we both know it." He says knowingly, easily reaching out to flick on the shower, and leading me in to stand under the warm water. "Now stand still and let me take care of you." Before I can protest, not that I'm sure I actually *would,* he soaps up his hands and drops to his knees in front of me.

"What are you doing Brady?" I ask, but he doesn't answer me. I guess that *is* my answer, if I don't know what he's doing perhaps I shouldn't have married him. "Argghhhh." I say, not getting to finish my inner dialogue be-cause, "Oh my lord Brady! What the?" My hands grip his hair all on their own and my right leg lifts up off the ground to give him better access to my pussy. That tongue of his should be registered as a weapon of mass orgasms, because damn, the man knows how to use it! His hand grips my thigh, and helps to lift it to rest over his shoulder. If that wasn't the smoothest, sexiest move I've ever seen him do, I don't know what is. I'm sure nothing could beat it, but obviously I'm not really thinking too well right at this moment.

"Move back baby." Brady mumbles against my thigh and I start to hop on one foot, but I'm scared I'll lose my balance. "It's OK baby, I've got you. I won't let you fall, and if you do, you'll land on top of me." I can feel his grip on my thigh. Just as I'm about to ask him what the hell his plan is, my back hits the cold wall and I let out a small squeak, but Brady doesn't skip a beat. His body fits back to where he was before I moved the daring couple of centimetres back on the slippery floor of the shower.

My breath hitches as his tongue goes back to work fucking my pussy and flicking my clit until I don't know where he begins, and I end. My hands grip his hair tightly in my hands and my left leg starts to shake a little and then, oh my god, he pushes two fingers into my pussy and curls them just right to hit the spot, as he sucks my clit into his mouth, biting it lightly. You know, the one that makes women blackout and scream out her man's name, not to mention squirt everywhere.

"That's it baby, come on my tongue and I'll lick you clean." As the aftershocks rip through my body, Brady slips my leg carefully off his shoulder, making sure my foot is steady on the floor, before he rises to his feet, but not before he kisses as much of me as he can on his way up. How he can concentrate on anything other than breathing is beyond my comprehension. "Are you all clean now baby?" He asks, his voice a low rumble in my ear, causing another tremor to surge through my body.

"Not even close honey." I reply with a quiet, spent laugh. What he doesn't realise is I have plans of my own to make him wobbly in the knees as well. He should know better than to think I wouldn't return the favour, I mean what kind of wife would I be if I didn't drop to my knees and take his cock into my mouth and suck him until he comes?

Chapter Fourteen
BRADY

"You don't have to do that." I start to say but hell, maybe she really does need to do that. "Fuck Kenna." I ground out between clenched teeth. I know we've learned everything about sex together, but fuck she's good at giving me head. No, not good she's fucking amazing! "Ohhh Kenna, baby." I'm right on the fucking edge of coming, I'm not sure how long I can hold back. I can still taste her on my tongue and the memory of her falling apart on my face is making it harder to keep a hold on my own orgasm.

She drags her mouth up the length of my cock, flicking her tongue across the slit in the tip and tonguing it for a few seconds, causing a buzzing feeling in the base of my spine, and I know I won't be able to hold back for too much longer.

"Kenna, baby." I groan, my hands twist in her hair, without taking control of her movements, I just need to touch her, to feel connected to her by more than just her mouth and my cock.

"Mmmmhmmmm." She hums on the tip of my cock before swallowing me to the back of her throat.

"Baby, I'm gonna come." I tell her even though I know I don't need to. My eyes are squeezed shut and I'm all sensations. Her hands are rubbing up and down the backs of my thighs, squeezing my butt cheeks every now and then as well, it's too much and not enough all at the same time. She drags her mouth off my cock with a last swirl of her tongue around the ridge of the head and holy fuck!

"Isn't that the aim Brady, for you to come?" She asks, as I open my eyes and look down, meeting her green eyes that are glittering with understanding. She knows that's the aim, we both do obviously, but the warning is just something I've always done. I never wanted her to feel pressured to swallow, especially when we were first together, and we were still learning the basics together. My hips move on their own as she strokes me from root to tip, jerking off has never felt so damned good. "Come Brady." She says, her voice quietly demanding.

"Kenna." I growl. My hands draw her face up to look me in the eyes as my orgasm hits, and I explode all over her boobs.

"Good thing we're in the shower, that makes clean up much easier." She says with a laugh that I'd love to join her in, but I'm still trying to catch my breath. She gets to her feet, slowly dragging her boobs up my torso spreading my cum over the both of us. "Now we both need to clean up. It's only fair and my Mum always taught me to share." She says, wrapping her arms around my waist, pulling me in close and spreading the mess around even more.

"If I had more energy I'd smack your arse, but as it stands, you're right why not share the love around so that we can clean each other. Again." I say with a raspy laugh.

"I knew you'd see it my way honey." Kenna says, balancing on her toes to kiss me gently on my chin. I dip my head and catch her lips with mine before she can escape, not that she can get too far but I want my kiss.

"I love you Kenna." I say against her lips.

"I love you too Brady." I feel her smile against my lips, before she lands back on her feet after stretching up on her toes, taking her lips with her.

"Come back here and let me kiss you." I demand, my hands that were wrapped up in her hair a minute ago, are now holding firmly onto the back of her head, encouraging her to move closer, but not really expecting her give me what I want when I ask like that. She does come back though, and I kiss the life out of her, letting her know exactly what I think about her giving me what I asked for and more, every day.

"Let me clean you up honey. I mean it seems only fair seeing as I *did* get you messy to begin with." She says with a chuckle that shouldn't sound as sexy as it does.

"Well, I could argue that it was me who got us both dirty considering it was my mess to begin with, but I'm not going to split hairs with you. If you want to rub your hands all over my body under the pretence of cleaning me, feel free baby, but know that I reserve the right to reciprocate the pleasure at my leisure." Yeah, I'm impressed with my rhyming as well, especially when it makes Kenna crack up and laugh loudly as she reaches for the soap.

"It only seems fair I suppose." She says with a smile as she soaps up her hands, places the soap back on the shelf and starts running her hands all over my chest. When she reaches my hips, I grab her wrists and stop her from moving any further down, why? I'm not really sure considering I'm already hard again. "What's wrong?" She asks, her face scrunching up in confusion.

"Nothing baby." I tell her. "It's just that if you keep touching me we're going for round two this morning and I know you already have plans for us today. I don't want to be late."

"We won't be late, I promise." She says with a grin that promises so many dirty things, but when I drop her hands to rest my hands on her shoulders and she flinches, I know we need to get some more aloe vera into them.

"Come on, let's clean up so that we can have last night's dessert for breakfast, and I can rub some more aloe vera into your shoulders."

"Oh my god! I forgot about dessert last night, how on earth did I do *that?*" She asks and I can't say I disagree with the bewilderment I see on her face or hear in her voice. In all the years I've known her, I can't say I've ever seen Makenna Drake, sorry Harris, ever not have dessert, especially when she's ordered it.

"Well, you were pretty tired, and I did give you a good massage last night you know. You were asleep before I could even finish." I answer her, my tone and face very serious. "Although, it is highly unusual for you to give up anything sweet, which is obviously why you married me." I nod my head with an intense sincerity that can't be beaten. At least not until Makenna cracks up laughing so hard she can barely stand up. "Hey, that's uncalled for, I'm sweet and you know it!" I say defensively, hands on my hips, soap running down my chest and abs, and water spraying in my face.

Straightening up, Kenna wipes her eyes of tears, which seems useless considering she's actually standing *under* the water, but I'm not going to mention that. "Oh honey, you really are the sweetest, most handsome, loving, and sexy man I've ever had the pleasure of knowing." She takes a deep breath to settle her breathing down and continues. "But you're right about dessert, I can't believe I forgot about it. Even when I got up and we were talking to your parents, I was so tired still that I forgot about my sugar rush."

"You weren't awake then baby." I take a deep breath, trying to decide whether or not to broach a certain subject, but decide to just go for it. I'd rather have the conversation before we talk to my folks again, because I'm pretty sure my Mum will bring it up, and I'd rather Kenna have a heads up in case she doesn't remember what she said. Reaching behind her, I turn the water off because we've cleaned ourselves in the process of talking, it wasn't a conscious thing, we just did it. "So, I have to ask you something."

"OK, sure." When I don't speak again right away, I just let her step out of the shower and get a towel first, Kenna looks up at me. "Is everything OK Brady? You look kind of worried."

"Do you remember what you said to my folks last night?" I ask, using the excuse of grabbing a towel myself for not looking my wife in the eye. We don't keep secrets from one another, well not big ones anyway, I'm sure we have things the other doesn't know about, I mean every one's allowed a certain amount of privacy.

"We told them about our trip out on the boat. I asked your Mum if she'd ever seen a whale or dolphin in the ocean herself."

I nod, agreeing with her. "Do you recall what you called her?"

"Your Mum?" She asks, and by the confusion on her face I think I already know the answer.

"Yeah."

"Pauline?" She asks, unsure. I shake my head, no.

"Oh my god Brady tell me right now! What did I call your Mum? It wasn't anything mean was it? Shit! I couldn't live with myself if I upset Pauline." Kenna walks from the bathroom into the bedroom and paces the room, the towel she wrapped around her body firmly in place. To this day, I don't know how she manages that, my towel falls off my hips every damned time.

"No, I don't think she was insulted, but she was emotional." I say, and before I can react she's standing front of me, slamming her hands on my chest and demanding to know what she said.

"What do you mean I made her emotional? What did I call her?" OK, well now she sounds panicked, so I need to tell her.

"You called her Mum." I say quietly, looking down at my hands holding hers, that haven't moved from where she hit me on the chest.

"Oh." Is all she says.

"Yeah, oh."

"Do you think she was upset that I called her that?" She asks quietly, resting her forehead on the front of my shoulder, just above our joined hands.

"What? No! She wasn't upset about it Kenna, she was emotional because she knows how much you miss your Mum and trust me when I say, I think you made her day complete."

"As long as she's not upset."

"I'm more worried about how you're feeling about it Kenna."

"If you're not upset and your Mum isn't upset then I'm OK with it." She starts to pull away from my embrace, but I don't let her.

"This isn't as simple as you calling your new mother in law, Mum, Kenna. I want to know how you feel about it. If it was a slip of the tongue we can all deal with it." I promise her. "I can talk to Mum before we get home and explain the situation, it's not like she wouldn't understand."

"No, I might not remember saying it Brady, but I wouldn't want to take it back. She *is* my Mum now and I know she would never want to take the place of mine and she never could, so that's OK."

"Are you sure?"

"Yes, definitely. If Mum was still alive, I would have chosen to call Pauline, Mum as well and no-one would have had a second thought about it, so why should things be any different just because she's not here? It doesn't change a thing. Your parents have been like a second set of parents to us all these years, anyway, marrying you just makes it official."

"If you're sure baby." She nods her head and I lift my hand to tilt her face up to look at me, then I kiss her. "Just know that no feelings will be hurt if you change your mind and you can't bring yourself to do it again."

"I know, but I won't change my mind." She swats me on the backside and my towel falls to the floor. How the hell does that happen? I swear I can tug at the towel she wrapped around her body and struggle to get the damned thing off, but mine, yeah it just drops to the ground like that was its whole purpose of existing. "I love you for your concern Mr Harris and I do appreciate the reminder of what I said last night, but I need my sweet breakfast and that is not you sir." Without another word, she's dropped her towel, put on her underwear, and slipped a dress over her head. Meanwhile, I'm still standing naked in the middle of the room with my towel in a puddle at my feet.

"How the hell do you do that Makenna?" I ask, bewildered, and amazed at her skills.

"Do what exactly?" She asks me innocently.

"Get dressed so quickly after getting yourself untangled from the fortress of your towel?" I ask, not joking in anyway, but she laughs at me anyway.

"It's not magic Brady, just plenty of practice in changerooms where no-one wants anyone else to see what's under the towel I guess." She says with a shrug like it makes perfect sense, and maybe to her it does. No such lesson is learned in the male changerooms, that I can assure you.

"You don't get that kind of privacy in the male changerooms at any age baby, so I still think it's magic."

"You mean guys just walk around naked?" She says her eyes widening in shock.

"Sure, the more you cover up the more likely you are to get called out for it, so you're better off just not giving two shits about who sees what in the change rooms. I've certainly never had to learn any magic tricks to get from undressed to dressed like that. How have I never seen this before?" I ask, a little bewildered myself.

"Join me at the table to eat dessert and I'll tell you everything you ever wanted to know about the female change rooms." Then, she sweeps out of the bedroom, swaying her hips from side to side in a way that makes me wish we could stay in the bungalow for the day again, but I know we're going out somewhere to do something. It takes me a couple of minutes to pull myself out of the day dream, before I pull on my boxer briefs, shorts, and a t-shirt. I laugh when I realise which one I've put on and remember I have to get my sister back when she least expects it.

Kenna almost chokes on her mouthful of coffee when I walk out to join her at the small dining table. "Cute t-shirt honey." She says, barely stifling her laughter.

"Yup, my sister is a comic genius who's not going to know what hit her when we get home." I'm serious, but I can't help laughing along with Kenna. It's nice to see her relaxed and having a laugh, even if it *is* at my expense thanks to my not so funny sister.

"She's just having some fun at her little brothers expense and I think it's adorable." She says, covering her smirk with her coffee mug.

"Well, she'll pay one way or another when she least expects it, believe me."

"Are you going to wear that out today?' Her eyes wide with amusement and maybe a little bit of mortification, and I can't help laughing.

"Maybe." I reply sitting down opposite her and bringing the coffee she poured for me to my mouth and taking a gulp. Damn I needed that coffee. "So are you going to tell me the secret business of the female change rooms, or shall they forever remain a mystery?"

"I think I'll break some girl code if I tell you them all. I can't believe you've waited all these years to ask how I manage to get dressed without dropping my towel. It's definitely an artform that takes plenty of practice." She says with a laugh.

"I can't believe you didn't know guys walk around pretty much buck naked in change rooms from a young age. You have to own what you've got baby, otherwise the wolves descend, and you never hear the end of it. I felt sorry for the kids that always hid away to get changed. The teasing never relented even as we got older." I shake my head at the memory. "Anyway, if you're not telling me anymore secrets about changing room rules, then you can tell me what Tomas managed to organise for us today." I say smiling, because I truly mean no harm towards Tomas. Anymore.

"Well, after our breakfast of champions, we can take you to get a new t-shirt if you want and then we're going on a four wheel driving tour of the island." She says, taking a large bite of chocolate cake, filled with chocolate buttercream, and smothered in shiny chocolate. The moan she lets out after that first mouthful is damned sinful.

"You don't want to be seen with me in my sexy t-shirt? I thought it was 'cute' and Beth was just having fun?"

"Well, you don't seem comfortable wearing it so I thought you might like a different one. I'm sure she's packed others in your suitcase." She answers, her eyes wide in an effort to keep a straight face.

"Yeah, let me finish this breakfast of champions and then I'll have another look in my case to see what other surprises Beth packed for me, and then I'll decide about wearing this particular gem."

"But Pinkie Pie is a very popular character in My Little Pony. I'm sure you would be very popular with the under ten set." She says barely managing to keep a straight face. "At least the t-shirt itself is a nice dark grey." Then, she can't hold it in any longer and the tears of her laughter roll down her cheeks.

"The colour is it's only saving grace Makenna." I say with a little more irritation than I mean to. It's not Kenna's fault that my sister has a twisted sense of humour. "Finish your cake and I'll go look for another top to wear today." Even as I stand up, I know that when I get back there's no way my piece of cake will still be waiting for me, but that's ok, I can't really stomach cake for breakfast, so I'll grab some fruit before we leave.

Opening the suitcase my darling sister packed for me, I rifle through the few clean tops left in there to realise that I have one nice shirt to wear to dinner tonight and then a whole bunch of very inappropriate t-shirts to wear outside of the bungalow. My mother will be horrified when she realises my older sister and her only daughter, hasn't managed to mature yet, and quite possibly ruined Makenna's holiday. She won't mind too much that I've been embarrassed, but to ruin Kenna's holiday, well that will bring down some anger on my sister.

I guess I'm buying something to wear on our four wheel driving trip around the island, just so I don't embarrass my bride.

"Are you ready to go?" Kenna calls out as she walks to the doorway of the bedroom.

"Yeah sure, mind stopping off at the gift shop on our way out?"

"She didn't fill your suitcase with stuff like that, did she?" She asks, and even though I can tell she's upset that Beth did this, I can also see the glimmer of amusement in her eyes as well.

"Yes, she really did. The only saving grace is that she did pack something that I can wear for our last dinner on the island tonight, so I don't have to kill her, just torture her for a while." Kenna snorts a laugh and holds her hand out to me.

"Come on bruiser, let's go get you a normal top and then head out on our trip."

So, to the gift shop is where we head. I'd rather wear a touristy top around the island, than this silly My Little Pony one I'm currently wearing, and if I remember, I'll grab myself something quick to eat as well. I'm starving!

Chapter Fifteen
MAKENNA

I don't know whether I want to hug Beth or message her and tell her that she's ruined her brother's holiday. Either way, I think the funny clothes are just that, damned funny. I mean, a my little pony t-shirt on a guy in his twenties is kind of cute, but only if he has the little girl to go with it. I can't help the giggle that escapes my lips at the thought and Brady gives me the side eye.

Just as he reaches to open the door to the gift shop, Tomas's voice booms out from behind us.

"Good morning Harris', how are my favourite newlyweds this morning?" Brady hesitates to turn around to face Tomas, and I know why.

"Good morning Tomas, we're great, how are you today?" I ask, trying to distract him with a huge smile and a hug, but I can tell the minute Brady has turned our way and Tomas's spotted what he's wearing. Tomas's body stiffens for a second and then he releases me from our embrace, taking a step away from me, before bending at the waist and resting his hands on his knees, his laughter ringing loud and clear through the peace of the island.

"Oh my god! What is that? Why on earth do you have a little pony thing on your shirt." He asks, between gasping breaths.

"I'm wearing it because my sister has a terrible sense of humour and I'm going to kill her when we get home." This sets Tomas off into another fit of laughter.

"Our trip here was a surprise wedding gift from our parents." I explain once Tomas calms down again. "We were packed for a trip up the coast near our house, and instead we came to a tropical paradise. Brady's sister volunteered to repack his suitcase when their parents told her their plans, and well, like he said, Beth has quite the sense of mischief, especially when it comes to causing any kind of havoc in her brother's life. This is why Brady has had some, shall we say, questionable clothing chooses since we've been here."

"I wouldn't call what she has a sense of humour Kenna." Brady grumbles behind me and I can't help laughing, he looks so damned cute when he's annoyed. "I think she actually volunteered just so she could mess up my holiday." I want to disagree with him and defend Beth, but I don't think I can with a straight face.

"In all fairness, I don't think her intention was to ruin your holiday, Brady, I think it was just to have a laugh." So, I *did* try to defend her after all, but I can't keep a straight face.

"To have a laugh *at* me. She didn't even think about how this might affect you either and I think that's what annoys me the most." He really is annoyed about the clothing situation.

"I'm going to let you guys get your shopping done, because if you don't get a move on, you're going to miss meeting up with the guys taking you out on your trip today. You're going to love it. I've done the trip a few times, with the guys and by myself. I love getting out into the smaller communities and helping them out on my days off. It's where I came from you know? So I like to give back whenever I can." He says while guiding us into the gift shop. "You two get whatever you need, and Suzie here will sort you out."

"Thank you Tomas." I say with a smile, leading Brady over to the men's tops.

"Any time Makenna." He says with a smile. "Oh and Brady?"

"Yeah Tomas?"

"At least the shirt wasn't pink to go with the picture, you have to grateful for small mercies my man." He says with a smile, turning to speak to Suzie.

"You're not wrong there Tomas, not wrong at *all*." He grumbles behind me and I can't help laughing again. "It's alright for you, Roch never feels the need to give you a hard time and look at you, she looked after you for sure. All these gorgeous flowy dresses you've been wearing."

"I think Rochelle and Beth had different agendas Brady." I laugh as I show him a t-shirt with a whale breaching the water on it, and he shakes head no, so I hang it back up. "Beth was thinking about annoying and embarrassing her baby brother, trying very hard not to think about him being on his honeymoon and all that might entail. Roch was thinking about her best friend being on her honeymoon on a tropical island with her sexy as hell husband, and all the sex they were no doubt going to have." I blush a little as I watch Brady's eyes darken with lust.

"She's done an amazing job thinking about our sex life, which is pretty creepy when I put it like that, but it's not like she had to work too hard Kenna. I mean, you're sexy no matter what you're wearing and even better if you're not wearing anything but me." He grabs me around the waist, pulling me into him. "I always want you."

"Well, you can't have me in here, because we'll get arrested and unless you want the guys running the tour to see you wearing that t-shirt, you need to choose another one, and soon." I say checking out the clock above the register.

"OK, fine let's get this one." He says, pulling a dark grey top off the rack.

"You sure you don't want to check what's on the front of that before you buy it?" I ask, thinking maybe he'd learn from his sister packing his clothes. "I think you should grab two, you know, just in case, for tomor-row."

"You're right." he says, holding two different tops to his chest. "What do you think, do they bring out the colour of my eyes." He asks, batting his eyelashes and tilting his head to the side, his brown eyes resembling dark chocolate I want to devour.

"You're an idiot." I laugh.

"Yes I am, but you love me and want to ..." He leans in, his hot breath in my ear, "Fuck my brains out." His words send a shiver down my spine, because at this moment, he is most definitely right and could be convinced to forget all about the trip Tomas booked for us. That thought alone brings me crashing back down out of my lust filled thoughts.

"You're right, on both accounts, but Tomas went out of his way to help me book this today and include lunch for all involved, so we really should get moving." Then, as much as it pains me to do it, I pull my body away from my gorgeous husband's, and walk towards the register, because I know if I don't, we're just going end up back at the bungalow for some wild monkey sex and I'm the one who told him we couldn't spend every minute there. I want to explore the island and have photos and stories to tell our family and friends when we get back.

"Do you want a drink or something to eat Kenna?" Brady asks me from the snacks close to the front of the shop.

"No thanks, I had breakfast, remember."

"That wasn't breakfast Makenna, that was dessert the next morning because you forgot to eat it last night." He laughs. "I'll grab a few things so that we can have some on this trip." With that he grabs a handful of nut bars, two drinks and looks around to find a backpack to carry them all in, and plonks them all down on the counter, smiling at the lady behind the desk.

"Is that all Brady, or is there something you else we need for this fully catered for trip?" I ask, smiling broadly at him.

"Nope, I think we're good." He looks around the store looking, for all intents and purposes like he's just looking at nothing, but I know this man and ask the lady at the counter wait just a minute. Then in five, four, three, two and he doesn't let me down.

"Oh, and this." He says, passing a pen over. "Thank you Stacey, that's all we'll be needing today. I know how much you like pens baby, especially from the places we visit." He says with a grin that melts ladies underwear clear off them. Lucky I'm not a jealous woman, because otherwise I might be ready to jump the counter and attack Stacey, seeing as how she looks like she's melting into a puddle right before my eyes.

I cough a little, pretending to clear my throat, bringing Stacey back to the here and now so that she can do her job, but I notice she isn't actually entering anything into the register. "Aren't you supposed to, you know, enter everything into the register there?" I ask as politely as I can.

Stacey smiles and says, as she hands over the back pack full of goodies, "Tomas said it was on him."

"No, we can't let Tomas pay for our stuff." Brady protests.

"Oh no, sorry I didn't mean it that way. Tomas asked me to add your purchases to the company account, not his personal account." She smiles at us. "Before you argue any further, Tomas insists and I'm not going to argue with him or you. Enjoy." Her smile broadens as she pushes the bag into Brady's hands.

"Well, thank you, that's very kind." I say, smiling at Stacey, and gently pushing Brady out the door.

"You're more than welcome, Mrs Harris." I smile at her again, as we walk out the door, not even bothering to ask her to call me Makenna, it's too time consuming and I don't want Brady to argue about a few complimentary things.

"Stop pushing me Kenna, we're out of the damned shop now." Brady digs his heels into the soft ground, and I don't have the strength to keep pushing him. The truth is, he was going willingly before as well, I don't have that kind of muscle power. "What was that Kenna? I'm surprised *you* didn't argue harder than that about someone giving you stuff for free."

"Normally I would argue Brady, but places like this, just like we do at Drakes Wines as well, they have accounts for giving customers complimentary things. Whether it be purchases, meals, bottles of wine or free tours. So, while I get your annoyance at Tomas giving us something for free, it really isn't. The business will use it as a tax write off and it will all balance out in the end." I sigh. "I thought you'd gotten over this thing about Tomas, Brady."

"I *am,* Kenna, I swear. I just don't like people giving us handouts, especially when we don't need them."

"So, you're saying you would have reacted the same way if it had of been Samantha that we ran into and she decided to give us some complimentary gifts?" I ask, hands on hips daring him to deny the fact that he *still* hates that Tomas helped me out.

"I think I would have reacted the same way." He says, his arms crossed over his chest. "Samantha is doing her job, not coming on to me every chance she gets."

"So, she's never batted her eyes at you, or blushed when you've thanked her for doing something for you?" I demand.

"I have no fucking clue Kenna. I don't notice these things and you damn well know it!" He turns away from me and starts to walk away, the backpack bouncing up and down slightly on his back with each step. I can't even remember him putting the thing *on* his back, but it reminds me of when he used to storm away from me when we were at school. The thing is, it's adorable and I can't help smiling at his retreating back.

"Hey." I say as I try to catch up with him, but it's a losing battle, his legs are longer than mine. So I yell instead. "Hey Harris, I know you weren't flirting, but don't you think it's insulting that you think your *wife* did to get free stuff?" That stops him in his tracks, mid step. He puts his foot down on the ground, spins, and stomps back to where I'm standing.

"I never accused you of *flirting* with Tomas." He growls.

"Yeah, you kinda did Harris. You seem to think I 'charmed' him into helping me book these outings and just now, into giving us free stuff, but did you ever think, even for just one fucking second, that he's running a business? Or that perhaps your wife, who also runs a family fucking business, promised him a case or two of Drake Wines to try out in the restaurant here? Do you consider that perhaps I was offering him just as much as he was offering me, in *business* terms? No, no you fucking didn't!" I ask him, and yes I do actually stamp my foot.

"So, even on our *honeymoon* you're still working? Still thinking about Drake Wines and what you can do for the *business* huh?" We're standing toe to toe now and I'm about to stamp on his foot, then storm away when I see both Tomas and Samantha out of the corner of my eye.

"It's not like I did it on purpose Brady. Tomas and I were talking about wines and I mentioned Drake Wines, he'd vaguely heard the name. I wasn't networking, it wasn't intentional. I was, in fact, planning our last dinner on the island, and I asked what wines they had available. I asked for one of your favourites from our selection and he didn't have it. He also mentioned that he didn't have any contact details for Drake Wineries, and he had heard about us. Imagine his surprise that Mrs *Harris* was his contact in. I also told him I would contact him when we got *home* from our *honeymoon* to talk business with him." My rant now over, I can unclench my teeth and loosening the grip I didn't realise I had on his shirt.

"God damn it you're so fucking hot when you get all worked up like that." Brady says and then I lift my foot and kick him in the shin, before storming off towards the ocean.

Chapter Sixteen
BRADY

How the hell did I manage to fuck that one up so badly? We rarely fight, so when we do, it really hits me. Don't get me wrong, we disagree all the time, we just rarely fight about anything. So, watching my wife, the woman I married just a few days ago, storm away from me so angry is a real shock.

"Makenna." I yell after her, but she keeps storming towards the water, and I know I'm going to have to move to catch up to her, she's not going to stop and wait for me, or come back. Well, she might, but it will only be to cause me some physical damage! "Makenna, wait! God damn it slow down!" She got a pretty good head start on me, but she's shorter than me and I'm not used to having to chase her.

"Go away Brady. I don't want to talk to you right now." She yells over her shoulder without looking back at me, still stomping her way to the edge of the water.

"God damn it woman!"

"Don't you 'god damn it woman' me, Brady Harris!" I smile, because I knew it would get her to turn around to look at me, even though I can see her rage, I'm glad she's looking at me now.

"Well then, don't walk away from me! We don't *do* that, remember?" She scowls at me, because I've reminded her of a promise we made each other so many years ago I'm pretty sure she's surprised that I remember it.

"You remember?" She asks quietly, looking at the ground, not meeting my eyes.

"Makenna, of course I remember. We made a promise to each other when we knew we would get married someday. I have no intention of breaking that promise. I will never let you walk away from me angry and not settle things between us. Ever."

"I promise to never let you walk away from me angry either. We'll always settle things Brady, because." She chokes back tears, and I reach out to pull her into my arms as her sobs break free.

"Because you never know if you'll make it home to see each other again." I kiss the top of her head. "I know Kenna. I didn't mean to upset you. I'm sorry."

"I'm sorry too Brady." She gasps out between the sobs that have quietened down.

"It wasn't about jealousy or Tomas, Kenna, it was honestly about paying my way. You know I hate it when people try to give me things for free. People accuse me all the time of getting to where I am because I've had it easy. That I have Drake Wines to fall back on if I need a job, that I have you. That my parents have plenty, so therefore I've had it easy, but I've earned everything I have, including my gorgeous wife."

"You run one of the area's most well-known and respected bars and restaurants Brady. You earned that and you *made* that happen. That place wasn't anything special until you took over managing it. You've earned the right to be proud of your accomplishments, but you also know, that businesses give guests complimentary things all the time. That's all this was, Tomas giving some guests gifts."

"Can you forgive me for being an idiot?" I ask, batting my eyes at her as she looks up me, hoping that by doing so I can make her laugh. She usually does when I behave like this. I just don't usually behave so badly beforehand.

"You're an idiot." She grumbles, breaking eye contact to bury her face into my chest again. I'm taking it as a win that she hasn't pulled away from me yet.

"I know and I'm sorry." I say quietly, kissing the top of her head again. "It wasn't about the Tomas thing, honestly. You networking while here isn't the issue either. I just, I want you to relax while we're here Kenna. You work too hard. You think about Drake Wines too much. You want to start a family, but we can't do that if you can't learn to slow down baby."

"Are you saying it's my fault we're not pregnant yet?" Her entire body stiffens against mine, and I pull her closer to me, because I can feel her desire to run again, or rage against me.

"No, I'm not saying that at all. I know why you're working so hard Kenna. I do, but you need to slow down a bit Kenna, and not just because we want a family. You're going to burn out baby, and I don't want to watch you fall. Not when I can stop it from happening to start with."

"But I'm working just as hard as Logan is and you're not telling him to cut back."

"Well, you're not wrong there, you're both working yourselves too hard, but you are wrong in your assumption that I haven't had the same discussion with him. Caleb is back from school and more than willing to take on more responsibilities around the business, the problem is you and Logan still see him as your little brother. Don't get me wrong, he's always going to be the youngest Kenna, obviously, but he's a man now. He's done business school and he has ideas. He deserves to be more than a glorified handyman at Drake Wines, that's all I'm saying."

"You've spoken to Logan about this as well?"

"I have, yes."

"What did he say?" She asks me, lifting her face off my chest to look at my face.

"That is a conversation for when we get home, and you pull back a bit. For now though, we're going to go on this amazing four wheel driving tour that you organised with the help of the amazing Tomas." I say with a smile, and kiss her forehead.

"Ohhhh now he's amazing huh?" She laughs, kissing me on the cheek.

"Well, he is standing with Samantha just over there, and they're watching us, so yeah, he's pretty amazing at the moment. Mainly because he looks like he might want to hurt me right now. So, you know, if you could throw a genuine smile and a wave in his direction I sure would appreciate it ma'am." My behaviour has the desired affect and Kenna laughs, loudly.

We walk towards them, hand in hand, because we have no other option if we're going to meet these guys with the four wheel drives.

"Everything OK Makenna?" Tomas asks, as he gives *me* a death glare.

"It was a simple misunderstanding." I start to explain but Tomas isn't having it.

"I wasn't asking you, Mr Harris, I was asking Makenna here if everything was OK."

No doubts for where Tomas's loyalties lie, not that I actually had any. While I'm happy for Kenna to have as many people in her corner as possible, I am her husband and this guy, well this guy's customer service leaves something to be desired.

"Look, Tomas, thank you for the concern, but my *wife* and I are just fine, thank you." Tomas makes to take another step closer to me and I take a half step towards him as well. I won't back down from this guy, he's known us all of a couple of days and thinks he knows what's going on inside my marriage? I'm sure some people, men, and women, need this kind of protection but Makenna isn't one of them.

"Tomas, don't." Samantha says quietly, taking his arm in hers.

"Brady, honey don't, please?" Kenna asks me, her arm wrapping around my waist, assuring that I won't leave her side. "Everything is fine, more than fine, Tomas. We had a fight, I'm sure it happens a lot."

"Yeah, it doesn't happen as often as you'd think, but it certainly gets dealt with pretty swiftly, if you know what I mean?" He says to Kenna, but doesn't break eye contact with me.

"We understand plenty, Tomas." I reply, trying so hard not to growl at him. Makenna is not his concern, at all. "Thanks for your concern though."

"Tomas, honestly, you don't need to worry about us, or more specifically *me*. Believe me. I've got two brothers who would kill him if he did anything remotely like you're thinking. So, you have nothing to worry about, honestly." Stepping away from me, she touches *him* lightly on the arm. "I do appreciate that you're looking out, not just for me, but other women as well. Brady would see it the same way, if you two weren't in some weird male competition about who's the better man. I do believe you're both amazing men."

"Once things calm down, I'm sure Tomas will see it the same way, Makenna. Thank *you* for understanding." Samantha says, struggling to get Tomas to move back into the building. "Why don't you guys head out with Max and Lee. You're the only couple going today, so you have their full attention." Samantha says, pointing towards two guys leaning up against a cream coloured Land Rover that looks like it belongs out on an African Safari, not in the tropics.

"Thank you Samantha." I say, taking Kenna's hand in mine, and leading her towards the four wheel drive.

"Look after her Max." Tomas yells out and I can't help the way my body stiffens at his words.

"Relax Brady, he doesn't know us, and he's looking out for me." I open my mouth to speak, but she holds her hand up to stop me, then rests that hand on my chest and continues. "We both know that there are women, and men, who need someone like Tomas to have their backs. I think you should look at it this way, at least he's protecting me."

"From *me*. He's protecting you from *me* Kenna. Me!" I say in amazement. "Me! I wouldn't hurt you or anyone else, unless a guy was lifting a hand to you." Yeah, I know I just won her argument for her, but come on! "We've known each other for over half our lives. We *just* got married for fucks sake."

"You and I both know that being married doesn't make anyone safe from violence, Brady." I know she's right, I *know* she is, but I can't help feeling insulted by a guy who barely knows me, thinking I would ever hurt Kenna.

"Don't mind Tomas, he gets a little over protective of all females. Let's just say that he understands more than most that not every guy is as nice as he appears to be, and leave it at that." The guy who spoke reaches out, offering his hand for me to shake, and I do. "I'm Max and this is Lee." He nods his head towards the other guy standing next to him.

"I'm Brady and this is my wife, Makenna." I say, and we all shake hands for the next few seconds.

"I'm just waiting for..." Max doesn't finish his sentence, he gets cut off by Samantha's voice, loud and clear behind us.

"Oh my lord Tomas, move your butt inside, now!"

"Really Samantha? You're going to full name me now?" Guess it's Tomas's turn to growl.

"Yes, if you're going to behave like an idiot in front of our guests. Especially guests who have given you no reason whatsoever to go all caveman on them, then yes I'm going to full name you. Be happy I haven't used your middle name yet, you idiot. Now move your butt and let Makenna and Brady go on their day trip, without you."

"What do you mean, without me?" His head whips around to meet Samantha's eyes. "I was going on the trip today. Max and Lee asked me if I wanted to go, because they haven't got any other guests going."

"I know, and now you can stay here and help me." She smiles at him sweetly, but it's a look that means business and I wouldn't argue with her.

Max chuckles and says, "OK, I guess we're not actually waiting for Tomas now, so let's get this show on the road." Lee nods to Max and opens the rear door for Kenna and I to get in. "Normally we'd have to take a more safari looking truck, but seeing it's just you guys we're going for a bit more comfort today."

"There's a truck that's *more* safari than this one?" Kenna asks, her voice filled with shock and I laugh.

"Ahhh yeah. The other one we use if we have a group only has two seats up front. One for the driver and one for a passenger, then two bench seats along the walls that face each other. That way, we can get more bums on seats at a time, but with it only being the three of you, well two of you now." He chuckles again. "We decided we'd go for a little more comfort." Lee nods in agreement as they both buckle their seatbelts and ask us to do the same.

"Comfort." Kenna mutters as we bounce along the road, and I can't help laughing. I know she booked this trip for me, and I truly appreciate it, but I'm pretty sure she was thinking this was going to be something else. I rest my hand on her knee, and her hand grips onto mine tightly, as we bounce along the unpaved roads.

I know the minute we reach the first village, Kenna will be in her element but right now, bumping along on the dusty roads in what you could only describe as a pretty basic truck, she doesn't look like she's having too much fun.

"First time four wheel driving?" Max asks in the rearview mirror, a large smile on his face. He must see some pretty interesting things on these trips.

"Not really, but the most rustic, yeah." I say, returning his smile and he nods in understanding. Kenna isn't a princess by any means, but she does like some creature comforts, and this truck isn't it!

Chapter Seventeen
MAKENNA

Look, I'm not a princess and I can rough it with the next person, but this is *not* my idea of a good time. When I booked this tour, Tomas promised me that I would enjoy it, I think he was thinking about Brady's enjoyment for this one, not mine, and won't that be a kick in the balls for my husband? Huh! Isn't that just ironic after the little testosterone show they put on back at the resort?

"Ouch!" I yell a little louder than I'd intended.

"Sorry about that Makenna." Max says. "I'm trying to miss the worst of the holes, but this track can get pretty rough at this time of year." Holy crap! That's Max trying to avoid the worst of it?

"Come here." Brady says, stretching out his arm and waving me over with his hand. I hesitate because I don't really want to unbuckle the seatbelt, but he takes it as me still being mad. I'm not mad, not really. It's kind of hot the way he went toe to toe with Tomas. I mean I don't usually get excited by that kind of caveman behaviour, but I have to admit, sometimes a girl likes it when a guy has her back. Even though she doesn't need him to.

Without thinking for another second, or checking to see if we'll hit another bump before I make the small distance between us, I jump over into his arms. He'd already started lowering his arm, accepting that I wasn't going to move, but that's OK, because it means I'm pulled into his side faster. I pull the middle seatbelt over my shoulder and Brady takes it the rest of the way and just as I hear it click in, we hit another rough patch.

"Well, that was perfect timing." I mumble, louder than I thought apparently because all three guys chuckle.

"I'm sorry it's so rough Makenna, but I swear this will be the worst of it." Unfortunately for Max, I see the look him and Lee exchange and know that he's lying.

"Do you like kids?" Lee asks, almost too quietly to be heard over the rumble of the engine and the tyres.

"Yes." I say simply. There's no point expanding on the truth.

Lee nods and says, "Good, you'll love this first village we're stopping in today then. There are a lot of kids running around and they love visitors, so be ready." He says with a smile, I think it's the first one he's granted us today.

"Thanks for the heads up. I look forward to it." I say, returning his smile. A smile that fades as soon as I answer him, and he turns away from me.

"Just be warned, these kids can get a bit handsy, if you know what I mean? Especially with pretty ladies like yourself." Max grins, until he glances up at Brady who is glaring at him. "I didn't mean anything Brady, simply what I've learned in my years of doing these trips, that's all."

Brady gives Max a sharp nod and pulls me in a little closer and I bite back a laugh. I don't remember Brady being so possessive, ever, and I'm struggling to understand why it's happening now, of all times. We just got married, you'd think that would make him *more* secure, right?

Or perhaps the fact that I've never given him any reason to believe that I would cheat on him in our years together, should be enough? I take a deep breath, and start to pull out of his arms, but he pulls me in tighter. I look up, meeting his eyes, taking in his handsome face that I feel like I've known forever. I feel like I've know this *man* forever, but I'm starting to wonder if I ever did.

His hand comes up, gently taking a hold of my chin, not allowing me to move back or look away from him. "I love you Makenna Harris." He murmurs quietly.

"I love you too Brady, but come on, you're being." I don't get to finish, his lips meet mine and while his kiss is short, it's delicious.

"I'm sorry Kenna, I don't know what's happened to me since we got here." He says quietly, resting his forehead on mine.

"I'm not going anywhere Brady, not without you anyway." I reply just as quietly. I don't want the guys to hear what we're saying to each other.

"I know." He sighs. "I know baby. I'm sorry. Can you forgive me?" He pleads. "I'm not jealous, and I don't think you're going to cheat on me or anything like that, I just don't like the way these guys have been looking at you." He explains.

"Well, I can't stop them from doing whatever they're doing, but I know all I'm doing is being friendly." I reach my hand up to cup his cheek, and his eyes close. "No matter what they think, I'm in love with *you* and they can't ever change that. Let's forget about all of it, nothing matters except having a good time on this trip."

"This trip you booked for me because you knew I'd enjoy it, but you wouldn't, you mean?" He asks with a smirk.

"Well, that's not entirely true. I knew you would enjoy the driving aspect, and I knew I'd enjoy the villages. I thought it would be a win, win kind of situation." I admit with a wry smile.

"If it's any consolation, I think you're going to love the villages and so am I." He says, kissing me lightly again. I can't stay mad at him, I've never been able to. Before we can say anything else Max speaks.

"Makenna, Brady?" We pull just far enough apart that we can both look towards him. "We're at the first village, be prepared for." Max doesn't get to finish, because there are suddenly dozens of kids of all ages surrounding us, yelling and some are banging on the side of the car.

"Hey!" Lee yells out the open window and lets out an exceptionally loud wolf whistle, that has all the kids pulling back from the car. They're watching Lee, but they're still over excited about people visiting.

"Come on kids, out of the way, you know the deal. You have to let me park the car before you can see the people. Move it!" Max says with a laugh and the kids all suddenly disappear.

"Where did they go?" I ask, amazed.

"They didn't go far, trust me." Max says with amusement, but Lee just grunts.

Max coughs behind us, "Well, let's get moving now, before the kids get too restless and starting jumping us?" I laugh again, but by the look on both men's faces, I get the feeling they're not joking and that stops my laughter in my throat. "I told you, they like visitors, especially pretty tourists. I'd hold on tight to your bag and possessions. I'm not saying they'll steal from you,

I'm just warning you to be careful. They're great people, but the only visitors they get, we bring to them."

Then without another word he leads us into the village, with Lee walking behind us like they're our security detail, and I'm starting to wonder what the hell I got us into with this adventure. Tomas assured me it would be a great time and I could buy some local gifts for my friends and family back home, but now I'm wondering if that was just some twisted game he likes to play unsuspecting tourists. It seems like it would be bad for business honestly, but right this second, I can't think of another reason for him to recommend this trip for us. Except for the fact that his mates run it and perhaps he wanted to get back at Brady, but what about me? I thought he *liked* me.

"That's enough!" Lee roars and the kids all jump. "What have I told you about the way we treat visitors to the village?" He asks, his voice gruff, leaving no room for argument and it works. The kids form one line in front of us, and I barely hold back a smile when I look at Brady, I can tell he is too.

"This is Makenna and Brady." Lee's voice booms out, making me jump, and the kids giggle. "There will be no pocket picking." He growls and the kids roll their eyes like they've heard this speech a thousand times before. "You will use your manners and you will *not* ask them a million questions all at once. Do we have an understanding?"

"Yes Lee!" All of the kids yell, but the older ones roll their eyes, then laugh, obviously not capable of holding back anymore.

"If you can't tell, Lee gives this same lecture every time, in every village." Max says quietly beside me making me jump a little. "Sorry I didn't mean to startle you." He smiles at me and then Brady, not seeming too effected by Brady frowning at him and pulling me in closer to his side.

"I just didn't realise you were standing there." I tell him, shrugging like it's no big deal, and I guess it really isn't. "Were you a ninja in a former life or something?" I ask as a joke, because I didn't see or hear him move to stand beside me. The last place I saw him, he was standing beside Lee near the kids.

"Exactly." His face turns to stone for another split second and this time, Brady doesn't need to pull me closer, because I'm almost climbing him to get close to him. These two guys are scary as hell and I'm not sure what the hell Tomas was thinking when he suggested this damned trip to me.

"You OK there Kenna?" Brady asks quietly in my ear. "We can head back to the resort any time you like baby."

"What are you talking about?" I ask, looking at him confused, and he nods towards Max. "Oh! No I want to stay, it's all good Brady. As long as you're with me, I know you won't let anything happen to me and I don't plan on leaving your side. We're here, in this and life together." I kiss him on the cheek and look back towards Lee just in time to see the kids rush towards us.

"Slow. Down." He growls at them and I watch in amazement as they do as they're told.

"How on earth does he do that?" I ask no-one in particular. "We have to learn his tricks before the day is over Brady, we might need them one day for our own kids." I feel like this might be useful knowledge sometime in the near future. Hopefully, but I'm not thinking about any of that while we're here. I promised Brady that we would just relax while we're here and let what happens, happen, but I would love to get home and find out I'm pregnant. It would be perfect.

Chapter Eighteen
BRADY

Watching Kenna with those kids today was incredible, and hearing her reference *our* own kids today as well, was something else. It pulled at my heart in a way I haven't felt in a long time. Not since I got the balls to ask Makenna Drake out all the way back in high school. The thought of giving her the gift of children does something to my insides. I want us to be parents. I know how much Kenna wants to be a mum, and I want to be a dad too. I want to give them everything our parents gave us, and more.

As Kenna snuggles closer into my side, her head resting on the front of my shoulder, her nose buried in my neck and her arm across my waist, I wrap an arm around her waist to hold her steady. I can't remember feeling more content. After a rough start, Kenna enjoyed every second of the day out. The kids in every village were adorable and friendly, I'm guessing that's mostly thanks to Lee.

We had to buy another bag from one of the villages because Kenna managed to find gifts for everyone back home, and the backpack I bought just wasn't going to cut it when it came to bringing everything back to the resort.

We hit a big bump, I brace myself with my hand against the roof of the car, and I'm amazed that Kenna managed to sleep through it.

"Wow, she's really asleep isn't she?" Max asks, his body turned as far as he can to look at us in the back. Apparently, it's Lee's turn to drive us home.

I look down at Kenna, tucked into my side and her feet resting up on the seat. She's relaxed and comfortable, and if you don't tell anyone else, she's snoring quietly too, and that's how I know she's absolutely out of it. "Yeah, it was a big day I guess."

"Sure was." Max smiles at me and I smile back, he's grown on me since this morning and I find myself thinking he's not a bad guy at all. "Lee is a more sedate and gentle driver, so hopefully she can get all the rest she needs for later." And I think he's a douchebag again. "I meant for your dinner this evening Brady, nothing else, I swear."

I guess my feelings were written all over my face, that or Max can just read people damned well. "Right." Is all I say.

"When do you leave for home?" Max asks still turned to face me in the backseat.

"We leave tomorrow afternoon."

"One more day in paradise hey? Well, I hope you guys enjoy it. You've been one of our favourite couples we've had on the tour since we started. Isn't that right Lee?" He asks his mate with a punch on the shoulder that Lee doesn't even acknowledge, he just nods his head in agreement. "You can see why I like taking people on tours can't you? Imagine spending all day with this guy? I mean, I get a headache every day from all the noise." He lets out a loud roar of laughter at his own witty joke and I can't help laughing along with him.

"Brady." Kenna sighs out my name next to me and wiggles around in my arms.

"Shhhh I'm right here baby, go back to sleep." I whisper in her ear and she relaxes back into my hold.

"I want that one day." Max says, almost sadly and turns back to look out the windscreen.

"I'm sure you'll find it man." I say, because what the hell else am I supposed to say?

We don't say another word the rest of the twenty minute trip back to the resort. The mood in the car is almost sombre, and when I see the resort in the distance I'm glad we're almost back.

"Brady?" Kenna stirs next to me and I'm kind of glad I won't have to wake her up when Lee pulls up at the entrance to the office. She's not the easiest or nicest person when she gets woken up, unless I'm between her legs anyway, and that sure as hell isn't happening in this backseat!

"Hey baby, you're going to need to wake up." I say quietly, letting her rest against me still.

"Are we back?" She asks, her voice and sleepy.

"Yeah, we are but you've got a few minutes before you have to wake up properly."

"You take your time to wake up Makenna, we're in no hurry." Max says the smile back on his face as he turns to speak to us. It's like the previous conversation never happened.

"Thanks Max." Kenna sighs without moving and I chuckle quietly. "What's so funny Brady?"

"Nothing baby. Absolutely nothing." I tell her, kissing the top of her head and waiting for Lee to pull the car into the drop off parking at the front door.

When the car stops, Kenna starts to sit up, until Lee speaks. "Don't move until you're properly awake Makenna. Max and I aren't in any hurry to get back to camp, so you stay there for a while. We can take your bags in if you like?" I just stare at the guy, I don't think I've heard him speak that many words in the entire day!

"We're good, we only have the two bags, but thanks Lee." I say after shaking some sense into my brain.

"I'm good." Kenna sits up, her eyes barely open, reaching for the bag she bought today, and even manages to sling it over her head to cross her body.

"Wow, I'm impressed." Max says. "I've never seen someone move that smoothly while also being mostly asleep. She's going to make an amazing mother one day." Without another word he disappears inside the building with Lee, leaving us sitting in their car, keys in the ignition. We can't take it off the island without them finding us, but still, that's a lot of faith in their fellow human beings.

"We could steal their car and go on a joyride if you want Brady. You know, one last hurrah before we settle down into married life. One last act of delinquency before we have to behave because we have children to impress."

"We could, but we won't." I say, getting out of the car, then helping Kenna out.

"You're a spoilsport since you got married you know that? A real fuddy duddy these days!" She grumbles as she steps out of the car and into my waiting arms.

"You don't want to have sex in someone else's car Kenna, especially when you know how dirty it gets, and not in the good way." I can *feel* her smile spreading across her face as she rests her head on my chest. "Come on Mrs Harris, let's get you back to the bungalow so you can wake up properly."

"Mmmmhmmmm." She hums, causing a vibration to ripple through my body, starting at my pec and making it a little difficult to walk. She's close enough to understand exactly what she just did to me too. I hear a low chuckle and then, "Come now Mr Harris, you don't want to do anything inappropriate, do you?"

I guide her towards reception, and see Lee and Max talking to Tomas and Samantha. I hope I can get us moving quickly and quietly enough that they don't notice that we've walked by. I realise I'm completely out of luck when I hear my name and then Kenna's before we can get out the door that will lead us to our bungalow and freedom.

Kenna stops and I try to fight her. I try to make her keep walking, pretending as though I didn't hear a damned sound, but she plants her feet and starts to turn to see who is calling us. Which obviously means I have to stop too, seeing as how she's still tucked into my side, with her arm wrapped tightly around my waist.

Sighing deeply I turn with her, because have no choice. I'm relieved to see that it's Samantha and not Tomas, standing in front of us waiting to talk to us.

"Hi." She says, and kind of waves awkwardly. I don't think I've seen Samantha uncomfortable since we got here. "Look, I ummm, I just wanted to apologise."

"For what?" Kenna asks, her sleepy face crinkled in confusion.

"For earlier. Tomas?" She starts again, holding her hands in front of her looking really damned nervous.

"That's not yours to apologise for Samantha, not even close, but that being said, I guess I can understand where he was coming from." I say.

"You can?" Kenna and Samantha both ask me. Kenna takes a step back from me and turns her cute confusion my way and Samantha's eyebrows are almost in her hair and I nod.

"I'm sure he has his reasons, and a guy being protective of women he barely knows is a pretty redeeming quality, honestly. I'm glad that *if* anything was wrong and Kenna needed help, or a safe place, then Tomas would have been there for her, and offered it." I look between the women who are still looking a little shocked. "He *doesn't* need to worry about Makenna, but that being said, I think I understand where he's coming from."

"He does have his reasons." Samantha says quietly. "Reasons that aren't mine to share, but I will say, your assessment is spot on. Thank you for being so understanding Mr Harris, I appreciate it." She says with her customer service smile.

"When did I become *Mr Harris* again?" Samantha blushes and Kenna just stands there looking at me, but doesn't say a word. "We're Makenna and Brady, Samantha, not Mr and Mrs Harris, please. We don't have much time left here and I'd much rather be able to laugh and have fun like before, than have all this awkwardness between us."

"That's very kind of you Mr, I mean, *Brady*." Samantha says and I can see the relief on her face.

"Brady's right Samantha. We only have a few more hours here and I don't want to spend it being wary of you or Tomas. So please, don't worry about it." She smiles and reaches out to take Samantha's hand in hers. "He's a good man, and I know his heart was in the right place."

"It definitely was." Samantha says, gripping Kenna's and smiling. "Thank you for being so understanding." Kenna hugs Samantha and then wraps her arm back around my waist. "Both of you." Samantha says, looking at me pointedly.

"It's all good Samantha." I say with a smile and a shrug of my shoulders. The fact is there's no skin off my nose. Kenna *is* safe and having someone working here looking out for women isn't a bad thing. Not to mention, we're only here for just over twenty four more hours, and I'm not going to ruin Kenna's time here.

I reach out and pull Samantha into a one-armed hug. "Thank you Brady."

"No worries." I say pulling out of the group hug I instigated. "We'll see you later at dinner, OK? We're going to freshen up and look at the loot

Kenna managed to find today." I say, a grin spreading across my face as Kenna tries to stomp on my foot. She's wide awake now!

"Yes, off you guys go, we'll see you later. We've got something special planned for you guys tonight."

"No, Samantha, please. You don't have to make a big deal out of it, especially after this morning. It's our last night and we just want to enjoy the quietness of paradise."

"Oh, don't you worry about a thing Makenna. It isn't a way of making up for this morning, it was already planned before you know who lost it this morning." She says waving us towards the door that leads out to the bungalows. "Now get out of here and relax for a while." She says while pretty much shoving us out the door.

I'm laughing as we hear the door close behind us and I pull Kenna back into my side, but she resists, stopping me in my tracks. "What's the matter Kenna?"

"What was that?"

"What was, *what*?" I ask, confused. I really hope we're not going to get into anything again, it's been a long day and I want to enjoy our last few hours here.

"You *hugged* Samantha!" She say, crossing her arms.

"*We* hugged Samantha, not *me*." I rub a hand over my face in frustration. "Come on, haven't we done this enough already? I'm sorry about my attitude about Tomas. I know without a doubt you wouldn't do anything to hurt me like that. Ever. And I know you know that I wouldn't do that to you either. I don't know what's come over me while we've been here."

"Did you mean what you said to Samantha?"

"Which part?"

"That you understand where Tomas was coming from this morning?"

"Yes I do." I say taking her hand in mine, linking our fingers, as I start to walk towards our bungalow again. "I honestly do."

"What made you change your mind?"

"I had all day and a quiet car ride back here, to think about it." We begin to slowly walk, hand in hand. "He was wrong about us, I think we can *both* agree to that, *but* I can't imagine what is in his past that triggered that reaction, nor can I understand the things he's probably seen here at the resort to cause him to react like that. I can't fault him for wanting to look after you, Makenna. I guess it makes him a decent man and human being."

"I love you Brady Harris." Kenna says with a broad smile across her face. She picks up the pace and when we reach our bungalow, she reaches into the front pocket of my shorts and pulls out the key before I can even think about it.

"Are you in a hurry Kenna?" I ask, laughter bubbling up in my chest.

"I'm getting my husband inside and then I'm going to strip him naked, then I plan on wrapping my lips around his cock and." I don't let her finish. I take over the task of opening the door, letting us both inside, before locking the door behind us, dumping her bag and mine on the couch. When I turn around to look at her, she's slowly taking her shoes off. I pick her up and swing her over my shoulder, causing her to squeal in surprise. "What the hell Brady?"

"You can't say something like that and not expect a guy to behave like this Kenna." I growl, which makes her laugh, that is until she's sailing through the air for a few seconds and then her back lands on the soft bed. She doesn't bounce more than once though, because my body is covering hers. "Now what are your plans?" I ask.

"I already told you my plans Brady." She says, pushing on my chest as she sits up, reversing our positions. "T-shirt off, now."

God damn it, I love it when she gets bossy! I rip off my t-shirt just like I was told, and I lie back on the bed. Kenna leans down slowly and kisses me, slow and languidly, I feel it in every part of me. I pull back until our lips are just touching. "I love you Makenna Harris. I whisper against her kissed plump lips.

"I know, now let me show you how much." She says her voice a sexy, husky sound that sends goosebumps all over my skin.

"Bring it on baby." I say with a smile, feeling cocky, yes, pun intended, until she draws one of my nipples into her mouth and bites gently before kissing it. "Holy fuck Kenna." She knows just how to drive me crazy and I love it. I love *her.*

Chapter Nineteen
MAKENNA

Brady does that move that it seems like all guys just inherently know how to do, and grabs his t-shirt from behind his neck with one hand and just rips it up over his head. I watch in amazement, not only because he can do it, but I also enjoy watching his muscles ripple and his body stretch out as he does it. So exceptionally tantalising and enjoyable.

Leaning down I kiss one of his nipples and then gently nibble on it.

"Holy fuck Kenna." His eyes are shut, and his mouth is hanging open with a silent gasp, and I know I've got him right where I want him now. I turn my attention to his other nipple, before kissing and licking down his body until I get to the waistband of his shorts.

"Lift." I demand, as I tap on his hip. He lifts his hips without hesitation, and I pull his shorts down his legs. Holy shit! "You were commando all day?" How did I not know this? I mean I know we were around kids and other adults all day, plus we did argue this morning, so it wasn't the best time to say, *'hey babe, guess what? I decided to go commando today,'* but still!

He doesn't answer my question, he just smirks, and lifts his feet slightly off the bed so that I can pull his pants completely off his body. As I'm dropping them to the floor, we don't break eye contact.

"Your turn." He says, his voice husky with desire. "Get naked baby."

I don't answer him, and I don't take off my clothes either. Keeping eye contact I drop my body down and open my mouth slightly.

"Kenna. What are you doing?" Again, I don't answer him, because he's going to know exactly what I'm doing in a second if he doesn't already, which I *know* he does, and now it's my turn to smirk. "I want you naked too Kenna."

He doesn't really finish my name, because my mouth is so close to the head of his cock that he feels my breath blowing over him, and when I stick my tongue out to take a swipe at the slit in the top of his cock, his breath hitches, and his body tenses in anticipation. I roll my tongue around the head and the sensitive ridge, before wrapping my lips around just the head. I don't go any further, I'm still flicking my tongue along the slit and all over the head.

"Holy fuck, Kenna!" Brady hisses out and I know, *I know,* he wants more. His hands start to reach for my head, and I freeze, then a second later I pull my mouth off his cock and he groans in frustration.

"Keep your hands to yourself Brady, or I'll stop." I warn him.

"Don't stop. *Please,* for the love of all things. Don't. Fucking. Stop." He begs, and I love it when I have him like this. At my mercy, begging for more. More is exactly what he'll get if he can behave himself.

"If you can keep your hands to yourself, I'll make you come so hard you'll be seeing stars." He lets out another low growl of frustration, and I can't help laughing. Here is this strong guy, laid out for me to feast on at my leisure and he knows he'll get what he's waiting for, he just doesn't like being the one who is waiting, needing, and begging. His eyes are shut, his mouth is still open, and his hands are gripping the covers like he needs something to ground him. "I promise to make you feel good Brady."

"Oh I know." He growls, low and husky, like he's excited for what he *knows* is coming. His eyes flutter like he's about to open them to drill home the next words out of his mouth, but he doesn't get to be in charge of anything right now.

"Don't Brady, or I'll stop." He growls and his head drops back onto the pillow, but his eyes are still shut. "I will use something as a blindfold if you try that again." His whole body stops moving, I swear he's not even breathing for a few seconds.

"Promises, promises Makenna." He smirks, but doesn't open his eyes, and I wipe that smirk right off his kissable lips when I wrap my lips around his hard cock, all the way down to the base and back up again. "Arghh fuck!" He says but it's merely garbled words that I think I understood. That's OK, I'm not here to listen to him talk, I rather like that he can't string more than a few sounds together right now, it means I'm doing it right.

I can't talk, obviously, I have a dick in my mouth, so I moan my agreement to his sentiment and that causes his hips to jump up off the bed.

"God damn it Kenna, you need to stop." He all but begs me, and I grunt a no, which causes more vibrations to rolls over his cock. "Holy fuck!"

I drag my mouth up the length of his cock and lick the tip, before asking him, "What's the matter honey?" My voice is dripping in sweetness and innocence.

"You know what. I'm going to come, and I don't want to." He growls.

"You *don't* want to come? Are you sure about that honey?" I ask, while I reach between his legs and play with his balls, rolling them around in the palm of my hand and running my other hand up and down his *very* hard cock. Just as he's about to speak, I run my tongue over the head.

"Of *course* I want to come Makenna, it's just that." He doesn't finish, because I wrap my lips around his cock and my lips match my hand, stroke for stroke. "Fuck!"

"Mmmm Hmmmm." I hum and his head, is rocking from side to side as he tries to control himself, to stop himself from exploding but I don't want him to hold back.

"No, no, no, no, no Makenna!" He growls, my mouth busy swallowing his cock deep into my throat. "Fuck! Stop Makenna. No more, I'm going to come if you keep doing that baby." He reaches his hand down to pull my mouth off him.

"Isn't that the point Brady?" I ask, my lips resting on the tip of his cock as I speak, causing a shudder to roll through his body.

"Yes. No! Fuck it Makenna!" He pulls himself up to a half sitting, half reclining position, and grips me under the arms, pulling me up his body.

"What? No Brady! I was enjoying that, and so were you. What are you doing?"

"I know. I know, but I want to be inside of you when I come. I want us to come *together*, baby." Then he pulls my lips to his and kisses me like he's a man starving for my kiss. I can't stop myself from pulling my body the rest of the way up his body and settling in his lap, happily grinding against his hard cock. "Clothes. Off. Now." He demands softly against my lips. My top and bra are off in seconds, landing who knows where on the floor or bed. It's a bit more of a struggle to balance on the bed and his hips while taking off my shorts and underwear without causing any damage to either of us, but somehow we manage. "You are gorgeous Makenna. I love you *so* much baby. I want to give you everything your heart desires."

"Does that mean I can fuck my husband now?" I ask with a grin and nibble on his ear, then I trail kisses down his neck, so that I can bite where his neck meets his shoulder, and he shivers.

"Fuck yes. Ride me baby." He says as he nibbles on my neck and shoulder as well, his hands kneading my boobs, and playing with my nipples.

"Are you sure, because I could really go for a soak in the tub." I say, moving like I'm about to get up off the bed and head towards the bathroom. He doesn't let me get too far though, and I hadn't planned on getting too far either.

"Don't you go anywhere." I laugh at his growl and the frown that's now on his handsome face.

Smoothing it from off his face with my thumbs, I cradle his face in my palms and bring his lips back to mine. "I don't plan on going anywhere, except right here." As I say here, I drop and his cock enters my body in one thrust, causing us both to groan, loudly.

"It turns you on giving me head doesn't it?" He asks, neither of us moving yet.

"Yes." I answer simply, because there's nothing else to say.

"It turns you on to boss me around, doesn't it baby?" He asks, his voice so deep and raspy, I know I'm not the only one turned on and ready to fucking melt from being so hot.

"Yes." I answer again, because there's simply no other answer. Except that I rise until just the tip of his cock is inside me and then I drop back down to sit in his lap again, seating him fully in my pussy.

A few more rounds of rising slowly and dropping quickly back onto his cock, we're both holding on by a thread to our orgasms. We both know that there's only a few strokes left in us before we explode. Brady wraps his arms around my waist and slides his hands up my back to hold on to the back of my shoulders, effectively holding me in place. While I put my arms over his shoulders, wrapping my arms around his neck and twisting my hands in his hair for something to hold on to.

The bed is squeaking quietly with every movement and we're rising and falling together in perfect unison. The only other noise in the room besides the bed, is our heavy breathing and the sound of skin slapping together.

"Kenna." Brady drops his head to rest on my shoulder, leaving gentle sucking kisses there.

"Brady." Is all I can say, as we come together in an almost awed quietness.

I don't know how long we just sit there, my legs wrapped around his waist, my head resting on his shoulder and my hands still twisted in his hair. Brady's legs stretched out behind me, his hands still gripping the back of my shoulders and his lips leaving small kisses on my shoulder and neck.

I don't care how long we sit here. I am with the man of my dreams. My husband and I can't imagine anywhere else I'd rather be right now.

Then my stomach growls and breaks the spell of contentment, letting us both know that it must be almost time for our last dinner on the island. We both laugh quietly, and Brady drops his hands to my waist, and moves to the edge of the bed, making to stand up.

"Guess that means we need to clean up so that we can have dinner?" He says with a laugh, as his feet hit the floor and I'm still wrapped around his body.

"I guess so." I laugh with him, and try to move off him, placing my hands on his delectable pecs.

"Where do you think you're going?" He asks, tightening his grip around my waist, holding me close to his body.

"Umm to the bathroom?" I answer, confused.

"Hang on tight then." He says and then we're moving, together. Me still wrapped around him! My hands quickly move to hang on tightly to his shoulders, so I don't fall backwards.

"What the hell Brady!" Now, you'd think I'd be used to him manhandling me and carrying me around by now, but it's not really something I seem to ever get used to.

Before I know it, we're in the shower, he's turned on the water and is slipping my body down his so that I'm finally standing on my own two feet.

"Now, get yourself clean Kenna, we've got a dinner reservation to get to." He says, with a light smack on my butt to get me moving, and making *me* squeal this time.

"Yes sir!" I say as I salute in his general direction.

"Exactly." Is all he says, but he's got a smile spread across his handsome face. A face I can't imagine living without. Suddenly I'm sad but happy as well. "Are you OK Kenna?"

"I was just thinking that my parents were lucky." I answer quietly.

"Yeah, they were."

"No, I mean, I'm glad they were together when they died. I don't think one would have survived happily if they'd been left behind." Brady pulls me in to a tight embrace as the warm water rains down on us. "I just couldn't imagine living my life without you, if something happened to you, Brady, and I think my Mum would have felt the same way about my Dad. So, they were lucky in the sense that if they *had to go,* they went together, I guess."

"There are no guarantees in life Kenna, you know that better than anyone, but I will do everything within my power to come home to you every damned day. You are my world." He says, still holding me close.

"I know. It's the same for me too Brady, always." We stand under the water in our tight embrace for a minute longer, and then I decide to lighten the mood by smacking his gorgeous butt, making it his turn to jump a little and then we both laugh. "Come on Mr Harris, we've got a dinner to get to, move it along."

Chapter Twenty
BRADY

The love of my life is gorgeous and tempting, even when she's smacking me on the arse to get me moving. I guess it's only fair considering I did it to her not so long ago to get her into the shower.

She turns in my arms to turn off the water, suddenly she bends over to pick up I have no idea what, and her butt cheeks bump into my crotch, and I might I have already come just a few minutes ago, but my dick is waking up again. If only we had for more time, so even though I don't want to, I let her go, and step out of the shower. Grabbing a towel, I make quick work of drying my hair, and wrap the towel around my waist. I grab another towel, and wrap it around Kenna, then I pass her another one for her hair. I know my wife, and she requires two.

"Thanks." She says quietly as she wraps herself up tightly.

"Hey, are you OK? We can stay in and get dinner served here in the bungalow if you want?" I tell her as I pull her into a tight cuddle.

"No way! We are going to have that dinner. My parents wouldn't be happy with me if I let sadness ruin our honeymoon." She says with a small laugh. "Could you imagine the lecture I'd get off my Dad if he was still here?" She shakes her head and steps out of my embrace. "He'd kick my arse for not relaxing and just enjoying myself, and you'd be in trouble too."

"Me? What did I do?" I ask, a hand on my chest, to show her my pretend shock.

"He'd be pissed that you allowed me to wallow." She coughs and when she speaks again, her voice is deeper, trying to copy her Dad's voice. *What the hell are you doing Brady? You're supposed to be looking after her for me and you're letting her get sad because I'm not here anymore. Suck it up princess and take her dancing.*" Oh my god I can hear him saying it Brady." She rests a hand on her stomach and bursts out laughing.

"He might be annoyed at me, but he'd be absolutely appalled at the terrible impression of him you just did. His only daughter disrespecting him like that." I shake my head and tut at her. My words crack her up even more, which is what I was hoping for, and she's doubled over laughing, as the towel on her head unravels and falls with a light thump to the floor in front of her. This has the added bonus of making her snort laugh and I crack up with her. She gasping for breath as she tries to stand up and she looks at me with tears in her eyes and I know what's coming.

"I miss them so much Brady." She gasps and a flood of tears fall down her cheeks. I take a step closer to her and rub my hands up and down her arms. "It's a physical pain some days Brady, it hurts so much."

"I know baby, I know." When a sob wracks her body, I wrap her back up in my embrace and carefully walk us over to the bed, laying us both down without letting her go. "Let it out, don't ever hold it in, not with me OK baby? Promise me Makenna." I need her to promise me, I won't let her keep this bottled up inside her, it's just not healthy. You just have to look at Logan to know that.

"I promise Brady. I swear." She hiccups and then takes a few calming, deep breaths and buries herself into my chest. "I love you Brady."

"I love you too Kenna." We lay there on the bed, wrapped up in towels for I don't know how long, but when I hear her breathing start to slow down and feel her body relax, I know I have to get us moving or we'll miss our dinner reservations. I'm pretty sure that neither Samantha nor Tomas would ever actually let us starve or miss a dinner, but still, after today, I don't want to push my luck with either of them. "Kenna. Baby." I say quietly into her still damp hair. "We have to move sweetheart, we've got dinner to get to."

"Mmmmm." Is all I get as an answer and I know I'm going to have to more forceful even though I don't want to be.

"Makenna." I say a little louder, I'm not going to yell because I don't want to, but I do need to get her moving. "Come on baby." When she still doesn't move, I do the only thing left for me to do and I know I'm about to get into trouble, but I can't help myself. Before I start, I move the right side of my body out from under hers and slide off the bed. Once I'm standing, I lean over, rip the towel from her body and start tickling her. She squeals, squirming all over the bed trying to get away from me and when that doesn't work, she starts swinging.

"Brady, stop it!" She screams at the top of her lungs, as a loud slap cracks through the air and I laugh. She got me on the chest, right across my nipple and it stings like a fucking bitch, but she's awake and up on her knees glaring at me. Naked. Naked and pissed the fuck off. "I hate you." She shouts at me, crossing her arms over her gorgeous chest.

"I know, but you're awake now, and that means you can get dressed so that we can still make it to dinner." She scowls at me, and I'm waiting for her to tell me off some more, but before she can say anything, I get in first, holding my hands up in surrender. "You don't want to disappoint Tomas now do you? On your last night here, really? You know he'll come looking for you if we don't make it to the dining room in time." I see the minute she admits defeat, but I don't relax, and I don't break eye contact.

"You're absolutely right. We wouldn't want to upset Tomas *again* today, would we?" She says with a smile that looks like she's still ready to murder me in my sleep, but I have a plan that I hope gets me out of the trouble I just got myself in. I knew the risks going in, and I'd do it the same way if given another chance, but it's still a dangerous game to play. "I'm going to freshen up and get dressed. I suggest you try to find something decent to wear among the clothes your sister packed for you." She says with a sweet smile, but I know what she's hiding behind that smile. Revenge, and now I'm slightly nervous about dinner. Maybe I should be more worried about when we get back here *after* dinner?

As Kenna's backside disappears back into the bathroom with a sexy sway I don't think she's conscious she's doing, I shake my head to clear it. I don't have time to think about what might or might not happen after dinner, because I have to get ready to go to dinner and put a few things in motion.

I search in the suitcase through the stupid shit my sister packed for me and finally find what I'm looking for. Some nice clothes that were buried at the bottom of the case, hidden in a black suit bag that blends in with the lining of the case. Thank you Mum! I send up a silent thank you to the best

Mum on the world, because she knew what her daughter would do and she knew that I would want to take Kenna out for a nice meal, so she slipped in some dress pants and shirts for me. My sister wasn't a complete dick about it, she did pack me some jeans and nice shirts, but this is what I was hoping was in here somewhere.

I pull the clothes out of the bag to see what I have and realise that Mum thought of everything and I shake my head in amazement, because I have no freaking clue how she managed to slip it by Beth, but I'm very glad that she did. I have a couple of complete outfits to choose from, and she even managed to get some dress shoes in there. I don't know how she did it, but she did and I'm grateful.

I've got a pep in my step after our shower, and I'm dressed in record time even for me, and I'm wearing Makenna's favourite shirt. I'm waiting in the living area of the bungalow for Makenna to come out of the bedroom when my phone dings with a message, I look at the screen, and see it's from my Mum.

I hope you found the nice clothes I packed? I was hoping you two would get the chance for a nice dinner before you come home hehehe

I can't help the smile that spreads across my face as I reply to her message.

I did thank you. We are going out for dinner in a few minutes

It's a whole minute after I hit send when she replies.

I'm glad you're getting out

That causes a deep chuckle to rumble out of me, because my Mum hinting at the fact that we're actually leaving the bungalow for a change is amusing to say the least.

I'm still laughing to myself when I hear movement in the doorway to the bedroom. I look up and the breath leaves my lungs. Makenna looks gorgeous every day, and even though she took my breath away when she walked down the aisle to me at our wedding, the vision standing in front of me tonight is even more stunning.

"Well, what do you think?" Kenna asks, and it's then that I realise I haven't moved a muscle since she walked into the room.

"I think that Rochelle looked after you much better than Beth did me with this whole repacking our suitcase thing, and I won't ever be able to thank her enough." I reply, surprised by the rough sound of my voice.

"I don't know, you're looking pretty handsome over there in my favourite shirt." She says, with a smile as she makes her way over to me, that gentle sway in her hips and the emerald green lace of her dress skimming her knees.

I *definitely* have to buy Rochelle something over the top nice when we get back home.

Makenna stands in front of me, places her hands on my chest and I can feel the heat from her touch through my shirt, and it heats up my body. Maybe we don't need to leave our little oasis tonight after all? I shake my head to clear it of the lust that's taking over, I can't do that to Kenna on our last night here. She deserves to be wined and dined, so I cough to clear my throat before I speak.

"My Mum managed to pack me some nice clothes under all the stuff that Beth put in my suitcase." I tell her with a smile, and she runs her hands over my chest and arms, playing with the button of my shirt. "You know, if you keep doing that, we're not going anywhere tonight, right?" I ask with a smirk.

"You rolled up the sleeves of your shirt." She breathes out like I did something impressive when all I did was roll up the long sleeves of my shirt because it's still fairly warm outside, on the tropical island we're on.

"Ahhh yeah, it's still warm out Kenna."

She laughs and it's a light, happy sound that causes my heart to swell. I love seeing her so relaxed and light-hearted. Especially after the start to the day we had.

"You have no idea how sexy you look right now, do you? When we leave this room, every woman, and some men, are going to be watching you walk by and they're going to wish you were with them."

"It goes both ways baby. Men will wish they were me too, and I'm sure some women too." I wink at her, and she blushes. "Come on, let's go knock some socks off, because if I don't get you out of here and in public, we're getting dinner in, again, and my Mum will kill me." This earns me another laugh, and I want to earn more of them tonight, and every night.

"Let's go Mr Harris, before you ravage me." She says, looping her arm through mine and leading me out the door.

We get to the restaurant much sooner than I was expecting and when Samantha sees us she lets out a low whistle. "Well holy smokes look at you two!"

"Thank you." Kenna says, even as a blush creeps across her cheeks again.

"Follow me, we've got the best table reserved for you two." Samantha leads us to a table, slightly apart from the other diners, on a small deck just outside a set of double doors I've never noticed before.

"Thank you Samantha." I say with a smile as I push Kenna's seat in for her.

"Anything for our favourite couple Brady." She winks at me without Kenna seeing and leaves us to get settled and I smile broadly at her, mainly because she's back to calling me Brady, I have no clue what the wink was for.

"So, what do you feel like eating tonight Kenna?" I ask, as soon as I get myself seated at the table.

"You." She answers, her voice husky. Holy hell what the hell is she trying to do to me? I'm already half-mast because she looks edible in that dress, and now she tells me she wants to eat *me* for dinner?

"Well now, that can be arranged later back in our bungalow, but for now, seeing as though we're in a public place, I think you should keep those plans to yourself, baby."

"Are you sure Brady?" She asks, and there's a mischievous glint in her eyes that suggests she wouldn't say no if I gave her the go ahead, but I'm not sharing her in any fucking way with anyone.

I cough to clear the lust in my voice. "I'm very sure, Makenna. There will be no public display of sexuality tonight or any other night."

"No public displays of affection at all?" She asks with a pout. A fucking pout! I have no idea who this woman is, because my wife doesn't behave like this. I almost jump out of my chair when I feel her foot press against my upper thigh.

"Makenna, stop it!" I hiss at her. She doesn't pull her foot away, but she does throw her head back and let out a loud laugh for a couple of minutes, which garners plenty of attention from the other diners. I grab her foot, and push my thumb into her arch. Her laughter stops, and instead she moans quietly.

"The look on your face was hysterical." She says with her eyes closed as she lets out another quiet moan while I dig a little harder in her foot. "If you don't stop that we're going to have a spectacle of a completely different kind Brady."

"I know." Her eyes snap open and the haze of desire slowly fades to amusement as she tries to pull her foot out of my hands, but I hold on tighter, not letting her get away that easily. We're still stuck in a staring contest when the waiter arrives a minute later for our order.

"I'll have whatever beer is on tap, and my wife will have a margarita please." I say, only breaking eye contact with Kenna when she smiles at me, to look up at the waiter and smile at him.

"Have you had a chance to look at the menu yet?" He asks with a knowing smile. I don't get the chance to answer.

"No, but we'll both have a medium rare of your best steak, with some potatoes and salad, please." She tells the waiter with a huge grin, that he returns like he knows exactly what the deal is at this table, but he has no clue. I'm betting he thinks it's a power play, but in reality, we both just know what the other one will order.

"Dessert?" He asks, looking between us to see who's ordering this time.

"I think we'll pass for now, thank you." I say.

"Your drinks will be over shortly." He informs us and then he's gone, and it's just us again.

"Have you enjoyed your holiday baby?" I ask quietly while still massaging her foot.

"Holiday? It's our honeymoon, not just a holiday Brady."

"I know, but have you enjoyed yourself Kenna?"

"Yes. Every day has been amazing." Her answer is quiet, and I know what she's thinking but I'm not bringing any of that up until we're back home.

"No work talk Kenna. Or anything else." I tell her before she can speak. "Only relaxing things can be spoken about until we land back home tomorrow, OK?"

"OK Brady." She agrees just as our drinks are set down in front of us and I release her foot.

The sun is starting to set ,and I move our chairs so that we can sit closer together, and I drape an arm around the back of her chair and just watch her watching the sky change colours, and we talk quietly about everything and absolutely nothing. Until our meals arrive and then we're laughing and talking, sharing memories of the island and our families. Talking about all the children we met today, all the talented people we met in the villages. What we don't mention is all of her purchases. I know she expected me to stop her from buying so much, but I just couldn't bring myself to do it.

As our table gets cleaned off, the music from inside suddenly drifts outside like they've just now hooked the speakers up out here. Maybe I just wasn't listening before. When I recognise one of Kenna's favourite songs come on. Standing up, I reach my hand out to her, she smiles widely and takes it, letting me help her up from her chair.

We've got room out here to dance together in the way that swaying bodies held close can do. More if I really wanted to get fancy, but I just want an excuse to hold her close. Looking over her head I see Tomas and he smiles and nods. Believe it or not, I managed to talk him into doing a favour for me, and that favour should be coming up next.

I smile as I pull Kenna in closer, with her head resting on my shoulder and my cheek resting gently on the top of her head I wait until I hear Ed Sheeran's voice and I start singing the words to the absolute love of my life.

Chapter Twenty-one
MAKENNA

Tonight has been magical. I couldn't have asked for a better last night of our honeymoon if I'd tried.

First the look on Brady's face when I offered to eat him instead of our meal, I struggled hard not to laugh at him. Then, he had a death grip on my foot, and WOW. Just WOW! I've never done anything like that under the table before, well not with my foot anyway. Mainly because it's your foot, ewwwww.

But my absolute favourite part of our entire trip, and that includes the food, the sex, all of the amazing sex, the time spent together, the trip to the villages and whale spotting?

My favourite part by a long shot is Brady pulling me into his arms, holding me close and slow dancing to Thinking Out Loud by Ed Sheeran. I love listening to Ed, but Brady quietly singing the words into my ear, well let's just say, even Ed can't weave that kind of magic on his own.

As both men finish off the last words in unison I can't wait to get my sexy husband back to our bungalow to celebrate our last night alone in paradise.

"Are you ready to leave?" His husky voice asks still right against my ear, sending a shiver down my spine.

"Fuck yes." I answer him wholeheartedly without pulling out of his embrace, and I feel rather than hear his laughter rumble through his chest.

"Come on then." He pulls away from me just far enough so that he can wrap his arm around my waist, but I don't really have to adjust how I'm holding him at all. "We're heading out now, thanks for everything." He says, as we walk past Samantha and Tomas. The smile on his face could light up any room, it lights up my soul that's for sure.

"You're welcome." I look up to see Samantha grinning from ear to ear. "I'm glad you enjoyed your night and your stay. Despite some people behaving badly." She sends a frown to her left.

"I made up for it tonight, didn't I?" Tomas asks, giving me a genuinely warm smile, and I suddenly feel sad. I'm going to miss these two when we leave here tomorrow. "Oh, now come on Makenna, don't give me that look."

"I'm going to miss you two, you know that? You've made our stay here exceptional." I tell them, proud of myself for not sounding like I'm going to burst into tears, to my ears at least, but I assume not to Brady's because he gives me a squeeze.

"Well, we've certainly made it an interesting stay if nothing else." Tomas says, and Samantha laughs, as he drapes an arm over her shoulders.

"I'm not sure *we* did anything, but *you* sure made your presence known." She admonishes him, but there is an affection in her tone that you can't miss, and Tomas has the good grace to look sheepish.

"In an attempt to make up for my rather unprofessional behaviour, I've left a couple of surprises in your room." He holds up his hand to stop any of us from talking. "Before any of you speak, no, it's nothing offensive Samantha, they'll love it. Yes, Makenna and Brady, I *did* have to, and you can't say no. It's my business, not yours."

"I sure hope you guys like whatever it is that he's done." Samantha says with what can only be describe as a grimace.

"I'm sure everything will be fine." Brady says to Samantha, and to Tomas he says, "You have nothing to make up for Tomas. You're a true gentleman and you were protecting Makenna, I can't fault you for that. Now, if you don't mind, I'm going to take my wife back to our bungalow so we can enjoy our last night in paradise."

"Good night you two." Samantha and Tomas say together.

"Good night." I say, as let Brady lead me back to our room.

We don't speak on the way back. I'm feeling a little nostalgic which is strange considering we haven't even left yet, but I've enjoyed our time here so much. Even with the disagreements and weirdness, it kind of made it feel like home, and that made it all the more fun.

As Brady opens the door my mind wanders to the night ahead and that's how I miss him sweeping me up off my feet.

"Brady!?" I shout out.

"I have to carry you across the threshold." He says with a sexy lopsided smile.

He looks so handsome and I can't wait to strip him out of his charcoal grey dress pants and my favourite deep burgundy shirt. He has no freaking idea what those roll up shirt sleeves do to a woman. Maybe I can convince him keep the shirt on, and I'll just undo the buttons so that I can get to his chest. What the hell is it about strong forearms that drives us crazy?

He places me on the bed, runs his hand from my thigh to my ankle. He rests the heel of my shoe on his chest, and removes it, dropping to the floor. Then, he kisses my ankle and places my foot back on the bed. He does the same thing with my other shoe, but when he places my foot back on the bed, he follows it and kisses up my leg until he reaches my hip, then he works his way down my other leg, back to the ankle.

I sit up as he leans back, one foot on the floor, one knee resting on the bed. I draw the zip on my dress down my side, allowing it to fall open and I hear Brady groan. I get up on my knees and pull the dress up over my head. We're now almost eye to eye.

Brady's hands are frozen on the top button of his shirt and I smack them away. I want to unwrap my husband tonight, and of course, he lets me. One button at a time, I unwrap my favourite gift of all. Brady Harris.

When I undo the last button, I don't remove the shirt, I reach for his belt buckle instead and undo that, moving quickly onto the button and zipper on his pants, letting them fall to the bed. He moves to stand up, and I reach for him. He doesn't move too far away, just enough so that he can let his pants drop to the floor and step out of them.

He stands in front of me in just his boxer briefs, with his shirt hanging open and I can't wait to make love to him any longer.

"Make love to me Brady." I whisper into the quiet room.

"Every day of our lives Makenna." His voice is husky with need. I reach behind me to undo the clasp on my bra, but his hand on my arm stops me, and I tilt my head at him in question. "Leave it on." His eyes flash with heat and desire, and I drop my hand from my back to rest on his arm.

He makes a move to take his shirt off, and it's my turn to protest. "Leave it on." I demand, sending him my own version of his lopsided grin.

"Whatever you want, Makenna." His hands move to the band on his boxers, and he raises an eyebrow at me. "How about these? Do I leave these on too?" His eyes spark with mischief.

"Off." I breathe out. "Take them off Brady, now."

"I love it when you get bossy Makenna." In the time he's spoken, his boxers have disappeared, and his cock is standing proud, ready for action.

"I love you." I tell him. He pulls the cups of my bra down to expose my breasts, then he pulls my underwear off my hips, down my legs and tosses them on the floor, then his body is above mine.

"I love you." He kisses me like it's our first and last chance.

"Show me. Make love to me Brady."

"Every day, Kenna." And that's exactly what he does, with his shirt undone and hanging off his shoulders, because I asked him to.

Lying in his arms afterwards, I sigh in contentment. Brady's got one hand behind his head, the other one is lightly scratching up and down my back, his eyes are closed, and he's relaxed. He looks like he's almost asleep, but I know he's not.

I've got one hand over his heart, resting my cheek on it, and the other one running through the hair on his chest, our legs tangled together. Every now and then his stomach twitches because it tickles, but neither of us move.

"I kind of don't want to go home." I whisper into his chest. I love my brother's, and I love the vineyard, but being here, slowing down and just enjoying some alone time with Brady, without any of the normal day to day pressures, it's been amazing.

He kisses the top of my head, "I know exactly what you mean baby." His voice is just as quiet as mine.

"But I *do* have to go to the bathroom." I feel the vibrations of his soft chuckle and then his hands that's scratching my back, smacks me on the butt.

"Well, off you go then. I'll go and see what Tomas's surprise is." He untangles our bodies and sits on the edge of the bed for a second before getting up and walking out to the living area. I enjoy watching him walk away, his shirt flapping in the gently breeze, his leg and butt muscles flexing as he walks. Damn he's sexy and I am one lucky woman.

I get up and take myself to the bathroom, do what I need to do and as I walk back into the bedroom I hear Brady's chuckle.

"So, what is Tomas's surprise for us?" I ask, a smile on my face.

"You're never going to believe this." He says as he walks back in the bedroom, carrying a tray. "We've got a bowl of chocolate covered strawberries, and a bottle of champagne."

"How very cliché of Tomas." I laugh, even though I appreciate the effort. I adore him even more for it actually.

Brady waits for me to sit on the bed and get comfortable before passing the tray to me. "That's not all that's on there either, check out the envelopes."

I look at the tray and see there are two envelopes, one with each of our names on it. I look up at Brady and he shrugs his shoulder, as he opens the bottle of champagne.

"You didn't look at yours yet?" I ask, because he definitely had time to.

"No, I thought I'd wait for you and we could open them together."

"Scaredy cat." I laugh at him, as he pours our drinks and then sits next to me on the bed, handing me a glass. "He's not going to do anything bad to us Brady."

"Well, not to you maybe." He mumbles into his glass, but I hear him and laugh again. "Come on, let's see what these envelopes have in store for us."

I pick up both envelopes and hand Brady his. We look at each other and take a deep breath, then I start laughing, because the look on Brady's face tells me he's absolutely petrified as to what might be inside the folded up paper.

"Just open it Brady, he won't do anything bad to us, I promise." He gives me a look of, 'you promise but how well do you actually know this guy?'.

"Don't make promises you can't keep baby." He sounds serious, but I can see the smile making his lips twitch as he looks nervously at the white envelop in his hands.

"Just open the damned thing." I tell, bumping my shoulder into his, as I slide my finger along the edge to open it. I pull out what looks like a very nice wedding invitation, but is in fact an appointment card for the onsite spa, and I can't help the little squeal that escapes. Then I look at the time I have to be there and grimace. Damn that's early!

"What did you get?" Brady asks me, and I hold the card close to my chest so he can't see it, before answering him.

"I'm not telling you before you open yours." I'm really going to laugh *hard* if Brady has an appointment at the spa as well. "Well, come on, what did you get?" I ask, smiling. He hesitates for a few more seconds before putting his glass down so that he can open the envelop in his hand. As he pulls out a not so fancy card, I can't wait to see what it is. He looks at the card, looks at me, and then back to the card.

"Wow!"

"Come on Brady, just tell me what it is!" I complain. I'm not above begging him, and I *am* still naked, so I could probably get it out of him easier than I am if I really tried.

"He's got me swimming with the fishes Makenna!" I know it's a quote from 'The Godfather', but I have no clue as to how it relates to Tomas or Brady for that matter.

"What the hell does that *mean* Brady?" I ask, completely baffled.

"It means I'm not sure that Tomas has my best interest at heart with this. I wonder if he plans on coming to this one too?" he asks, mostly himself. "What did you get?"

"An appointment at the spa, very early in the morning, but I guess there wasn't much choice, after all we are leaving tomorrow afternoon." I say, while showing him the card.

"Nicer card and nicer place to visit too." He grumbles.

"I'm sure whatever it is, it's not that bad Brady. Don't be ungrateful. Tomas made an effort to make up for something we told him he didn't need to make up for."

"Well, we'll both be up early in the morning then." He says, popping a strawberry in his mouth, then he places one on my lips and runs it along my lips until I open up and take it into my mouth. Then he kisses me. "Mmm-mm chocolate lips." He hums as he licks his lips.

"So, where are you going so early in the morning then?" I ask.

"On a fishing charter." He finally tells me.

"Oh!" It's all I can say. I've never known Brady to go fishing, ever, so I don't know how he'll go on a charter boat, but I guess he's in for an experience.

Chapter Twenty-two
BRADY

The sparkle in Kenna's eyes is definitely worth Tomas's surprises, even if I am still wondering if he has plans to have me *swim with the fishes.* A fishing charter of all things! I've never been fishing in all my life, but Tomas wasn't to know that, and it's definitely the thought that counts. Without a doubt.

The amusement in Kenna's eyes when I tell her what's in my envelope is about what I was expecting when I saw what it was. She knows me all too well.

"A chartered fucking fishing trip. Does he plan on them pushing me overboard or what?" I ask, only half joking if I'm being honest. "Oh fuck! What if Tomas plans on coming with me? Makenna." I say, dropping the envelope and its contents, and taking her hands in mine. "Baby, if I don't make it back, know that I love you and you're not allowed to move on with someone else. You're mine and only mine, no other man has the right to put his hands, or tongue, on you." I wink to soften the blow, but I mean every damned word.

"Don't be ridiculous Brady, of course you're coming back, even if Tomas *does* join you." She says with a laugh. "How could you even think that. He wouldn't hurt you Brady." She shakes her head at me like she can't believe my thought process, but she forgets I'm a guy and I know how we think.

"I wouldn't be so sure about that." I mumble as I pop a strawberry in my mouth, then offer one to Kenna. She pokes out her tongue, and it kind of curls around the strawberry as I drop it in her mouth, and my cock twitches with interest. Kenna being Kenna, she notices my dick twitch and smiles. Not that it's hard, well it's getting there, I have no pants on!

"You know we both have early mornings now, right?" Kenna asks with a smirk she's trying to hide behind her glass, as she takes a strawberry and pops it in her mouth, the action also covering her smile.

"I do know that all too well." I agree with her, not taking my eyes off her lips. "Tomas is a fucking cock blocker." I mumble. Kenna chokes on her strawberry and I reach over to pat her back. "Sorry about that."

"Oh my lord Brady!" She cries, then takes a gulp of her drink. "I truly doubt Tomas gave us gifts with that in mind. In fact, I hope he didn't think about us having sex, or not having it for that matter. I think he just want- ed to do something nice for us to make up for that mess this morning, and the fact that tomorrow is the last day of our trip, means he was limited as to what and when it could be done."

I think she's right, well, honestly, I know she's right on most of those points, but I'm still not convinced that Tomas didn't do it on purpose. I mean, who plans separate activities for a couple on the last day of their *honeymoon* and thinks *that's* a brilliant idea? Tomas, that's who!

"Promise me you won't say anything to Tomas." Kenna begs me, as she takes another strawberry out of the bowl and holds it to my lips. "Nothing except thank you, that is." She clarifies as I suck the fruit into my mouth, and drawing her fingers into my mouth in the process. Her breath hitches, and she pulls her fingers out of my mouth. Slowly.

"So glad you made that distinction my dear." I say around the fruit in my mouth, and she gives me a dirty look that I know means that I shouldn't mess with her. "I promise Kenna." I say around my mouthful. She shakes her head.

"Swallow Brady." She's smirking again, so I place a strawberry on her lips, and when she opens her mouth to take it, I drag my fingers along the inside edge of her lip, and she gasps. "We should really sleep." She says when she pulls away just far enough that my finger can't touch her.

"You're right, we should." I say, taking her glass from her and putting it on the bedside table along with the bowl of strawberries.

"Hey, I was enjoying those." She says, reaching over me to try to get the drink and fruit back. Luckily for me, it means she's stretched across my body, with her butt up in the air and I can't resist that. I spank her and while she squeals in surprise, I manage to switch our positions so that she's facing my feet and her pussy is in my face. "Brady." She says my name in a breathless plea. I think she means to ask what I'm up to, but she's going to find out in less than a second.

I don't give her time to think. I run my tongue through her pussy, spreading the lips so that I can taste her. She tried to pull away, but I've got her thighs gripped tightly in my hands. I flatten my tongue, and run it up and down her slit.

"Ohh Brady!" She says with a moan. I release one of her thighs from my grip, bringing my hand up to her sweet pussy, I push one finger in her pussy and wrap my other arm around her waist to pull her closer to me, but I didn't need to worry, because she's now pushing herself back into *me*. I push a second finger in with the other, and run my tongue all around them, leaving her clit until I can feel her orgasm building. Then I curl my fingers into her favourite spot, bend my head down so that I can reach her clit, and I suck it into my mouth, flicking it with my tongue.

"Fuck!" She says with a hoarse gasp. "Brady! I'm going to." She doesn't finish her sentence, but she does finish, as she comes all over my fingers and my tongue. I pull my fingers out and lick her clean.

"Come here baby." I say, gathering her up in my arms.

"Already did Brady." She murmurs, and I chuckle as I pull her upright against my chest and then lie us both down.

"Yes, you did Kenna. Yes, you did." I pull the covers over her and move off the bed.

"Where are you going?" She asks, reaching behind her in the empty bed looking for me.

"I'll be back in a second Kenna. I'm just going to take this food out to the kitchen and turn off all the lights."

"Oh, OK." She says quietly, already almost asleep, still spread out looking for me in the bed.

I made quick work of putting the bottle of champagne and the rest of the strawberries in the small fridge. Then I move around turning off the lights and making sure the doors are locked. I swipe my phone off the small table where I left it when we went for dinner and set an alarm for the early start we both have in the morning, and put it on the bedside drawer. Then, I crawl back under the covers with my gorgeous and sated wife, pull her into me so that we're spooning. I feel her sigh and relax into me.

"Oh! We have to set an alarm Brady!" She says in a panic, trying to sit up, but I have a tight hold on her, so she can't.

"Already sorted Kenna. Now, go to sleep." I murmur into the crook of her neck.

"But what about you Brady?" She asks.

"What about me?"

"You didn't get to come." She says, and starts to try to turn in my arms so that she's facing me.

"I don't need to Kenna, I'm fine."

"But that doesn't seem fair."

"It's not always about what you think is fair Kenna. It doesn't always have to be reciprocated baby."

"I know, but." I don't let her finish talking, I turn her head so that I can *just* reach her lips with mine, and I kiss her.

"No buts. Just sleep now. It's not about a scorecard, or keeping things even Kenna. It's about bringing you pleasure and before you say it, I know it brings you pleasure to pleasure *me,* but I don't go down on you, so that you'll give me a blowjob. So, how about we just call it even and go to sleep."

She sighs in my arms and I press a kiss into the crook of her neck again and then another between her shoulder blades.

"I love you Brady." She whispers, so close to being asleep, that I know she'll be there in a few short seconds.

"I love you too Kenna, more than you could ever know." Then she's asleep and I follow her a few seconds later.

I wake with Kenna wrapped up in my arms and the most obnoxious noise I've heard in just on a week. I reach behind me, straining my arm to find my vibrating phone on the bedside table.

"Brady. Turn it *off!*" Kenna begs.

"I'm trying, but it's just out of my reach." I tell her as I stretch a little bit more to try to at least touch my phone. Where the hell did it go? I give up and pull my arm out from under Kenna and untangle our legs as well, before rolling over to my side of the bed. By the time I finally have it in my hand, I'm sitting on the edge of the bed, naked, with my eyes barely open and Kenna grumbling behind me about it being too early to be awake. Not bad from the woman who is normally up before me when we're at home, but I guess you can't fault her when we're supposed to be on a freaking holiday, can you? "It's time to get moving baby." I tell her, knowing she's going to protest.

"No, it's time for *you* to get up *honey*. Personally, I have some time before I *have* to get up." She mumbles, her face buried in her pillow. I rub my hand across my face and try to wake up, because she's right, I'm the one who has to be up at this ridiculous hour.

"You're right, but you have to be up soon too you know."

"I know but we don't *both* have to be up right *now*, Brady."

"Fine, but you asked me to set the alarm Kenna." I grumble at her, before hauling my arse off the bed and stomping to the shower.

Standing under the steaming hot water, I start to wake up and relax all at the same time. Do I want to go on this fishing trip? I'm not really sure to be honest and while I'd like to believe that Tomas did this out of the goodness of his heart, I'm not completely convinced that's true. What I *do* know for certain is that he has a soft spot for my wife, and I think he'd do almost anything she asked him to do.

Do I think they're trying to kill me off? Hell no! Not to mention, I'm pretty sure he's in love with Samantha, and I'm pretty sure she feels the same way about him, I just think he's a little protective, too much some would say.

I've washed everything and I'm just soaking in the warmth of the water and debating with myself whether or not I can get out of this stupid fishing trip. It's not like I can cook or eat anything I catch, we're leaving today. I'm getting grumpy about going on the trip again, and trying to work out a way of telling Kenna that I'm not going on it, when I feel her arms wrap around my waist, settling on my stomach, her cheek resting between my shoulder blades.

"Hey there, I thought you were staying in bed for a while longer?" I ask her, resting my hands over hers.

"I decided spending time with my husband was much more important than getting a few more minutes of sleep." I squeeze her hands, and pull her as tightly as I can get her to me. "Not to mention, you're naked *and* wet, how am I supposed to resist that temptation?" She asks, and I can feel her smile on my back.

I turn in her embrace to face her, and kiss her forehead, because I know if I kiss her properly I won't be able to stop and we just don't have time for that. "Well, you're naked and wet now too, do you expect me to resist the temptation now as well?"

"You can't resist Brady." She smiles up at me, knowing all too well that she's speaking the truth. I close my eyes to try to resist kissing her deeper than a quick peck on her forehead and shake my head. "You know you can't." She laughs and then she disappears from my embrace.

I open my eyes to see where she went, and I feel her grip the backs of my thighs. Looking down, I see Kenna on her knees, looking back up at me with hooded eyes. "Kenna." There's a question, a statement, and a warning, all rolled into one word.

"I told you last night I'd even the score."

"You don't have to." I start, but I don't manage to finish because Kenna wraps her lips around the head of my cock, and I can't think. "Christ Kenna!" I hiss, and put my hands up on the shower wall to steady myself, as Kenna runs her mouth up and down my cock like it's the last time she'll ever get the chance to taste me. I don't know if I have time for this, but I'd rather miss the boat or have to run to get there on time, than to walk away from having her mouth on me. When she starts playing with my balls as she continues to drag her mouth up and down my hard cock, I lose all thoughts about anything except Kenna and her mouth. "Kenna." I say in a voice I don't recognise as my own.

"Hmmmm." She hums, her lips still wrapped around me and the vibrations run down my cock and settle in my balls. My knees buckle and I have to concentrate to keep myself from falling to my knees.

"Kenna." I repeat. It's a warning, one she's not heeding. "I'm going to come." I think I say, I'm not really sure.

"That's the whole idea Brady." She says as one of her hands pumps me long, tight, and fast up and down my hard cock, while the other still rolls my balls around, pulling and squeezing them.

Shit. Fuck. Crap. Fuck! I'm going to explode! It's too much, my nerves are sparking all over.

"Come on my boobs Brady." Kenna demands and that's all I need to hear to break that small amount of control I have left. I hang my head between my outstretched arms and look down to Kenna on her knees, pumping my cock and I'm coming all over her tits just like she told me to.

"Geezus Kenna that was something else." I tell her still trying to catch my breath, as she stands up, and kisses me.

"You're welcome." She mumbles against my lips and I can't help laughing. "But you should get a move on, or you're going to be late." Then she smacks my butt and pushes me out of the water so that she can wash herself. My cocks back at half-mast watching her wash my come off her gorgeous breasts, but she's right, I'll be late if I don't get moving and I'm pretty sure Tomas will come looking for me if I don't turn up.

So, against my better judgement and by sheer will, I turn away from my wife who is soaping herself up in the shower, dry myself off and leave the bathroom without looking back. If I look back, I won't be leaving. It's still a bit chilly this early in the day, so after pulling on shorts and one of the t-shirts from the gift shop yesterday, I pull out a hoodie for the first time since we got here.

I grab my phone off the bedside table, look at the time, and swear. Shit! I'm going to be late if I don't move now.

"Kenna, baby, I have to go." I yell out.

"OK honey, I'll see you when you get back." She yells back, and I start walking towards the door, think better of it, and walk back into the bedroom just as Kenna walks out of the bathroom. I was so distracted getting ready I didn't even realise she'd turned the shower off! "Geezus Brady!" she yells and places a hand over her heart. "I thought you'd already left and then you come bursting back into the bedroom like you're being chased!"

"Sorry, I didn't meant to scare you, but I couldn't leave without saying goodbye." I tell her.

"You *did* say goodbye Brady."

"Not like this I didn't." I say, stepping into her body and taking her face in my hands to pull her lips to mine, kissing her until we're both out of breath.

"Wow!" She says as I pull away. She's not wrong.

"Now I can go." I smile at her, and take two steps away from her, because she's still naked and I'm tempted not to go. "I love you Kenna, enjoy your spa treatments." Then I'm walking back towards the door. "Don't forget to lock up when you leave too, baby." I call out.

"I love you too Brady! Enjoy your fishing trip." She yells back. Enjoy a fishing trip, I think as I close the door behind me and start towards the jetty that we used the other day.

I'm almost there when Tomas joins me, and I can't help sighing. I don't know what it is about this guy that annoys me so much, I'm normally a pretty laid back and easy guy, I need to be in my job as a bar manager, there are plenty of idiots to deal with in a bar, trust me. This guy has just managed to get on every last one of my nerves, and in a very short time.

"Good morning Brady, I was just about to come and get you." Tomas says, in a happy voice that seems to contradict the look in his eyes. They seem to be shooting daggers my way, and I'm still struggling with the why, but it's our last day and then I'll never have to worry about Tomas again.

"Yeah, sorry. I know I'm running a little late." I apologise.

"No, no that's not the reason why I was heading over to your bungalow."

"Why were you coming over then?" I ask, suspicious of his true intentions.

"I thought you might struggle with wanting to leave Makenna behind this morning." He says with a bit of a chuckle. Geez, does he think I wouldn't struggle to leave my new wife on our *honeymoon*?

"Well, it *is* our honeymoon Tomas, so yeah it's tough to leave Kenna for a few hours, but you gave us both such generous gifts, I feel like it would be rude not to take up your offer." That was polite while making my point, wasn't it? It earns another chuckle from Tomas, so I guess I didn't offend him.

"Truth be told, I didn't think you'd show." What the hell? I stop dead in my tracks.

"What the hell does that mean? Did you book this trip or not? Because if you didn't, I'm going back to Kenna and we'll get a couples massage at the spa later." I'd rather that, than a *fishing trip* if I'm being honest. My outburst earns me another chuckle from the guy who seems to be way too involved in my relationship.

"No, I booked it, but I didn't think you'd show. If I'd known you'd be OK with having a massage, I would have just booked you both one." I mean, who *wouldn't* be up for a massage while they're on holiday, or any time really? "The thing is, I'm booked to go on it as well."

There we have it, he really does have every intention of throwing me overboard and leaving me there!

"So, I guess we get to spend the morning together." Tomas says, while slapping me on the back and steering me towards the boat tied up at the jetty. I let him lead me, because I'm in a bit of a daze really and even though I'm not sure I want to go on this trip, I was kind of looking forward to it up until ago minute when Tomas appeared anyway. "Morning fellas."

I look up to see who Tomas's talking to, only to find Lee and Max from our four wheel drive adventure, doing what looks like some last minute checks of the boat and the gear.

"Good morning guys." Max says, a little too cheerily for my liking. "Looks like you two get to spend some time together after all." Even Lee laughs at his joke, which makes me nervous, and for the first time on my honeymoon I wish Logan and Caleb were here as well. "Don't look so nervous Brady. We promise to bring you back safe, and in one piece, alive and well for the beautiful Makenna."

"Uhuh, sure you do." I mumble, and Max lets out a big belly laugh.

"Insurance will skyrocket if we lose anyone else." He tells me with a hard slap to the shoulder. "Oh you should see the look on you face Brady! Absolute classic! We haven't lost anyone yet and I don't plan on starting now. I promise you, you're safe with us. We didn't put you in any danger yesterday, did we?" He asks sincerely.

"No, no you didn't." I reply, thinking hard to find something that means I should stay on dry land, but coming up empty.

"Good. Well come on then, let's get this show on the road. Well, boat on the water shall we say." Max cracks up again, while Lee just shakes his head, but he has a small smile on his face.

"How the hell do you put up with this guy?" I ask Lee as he helps me onto the boat, and pulls in the ropes tying the boat to the pier.

"Some days, I wonder that myself, but while he talks too much, he's a great guy." He says with a shrug. "Not to mention, he's my business partner and we get to work in paradise."

I can't argue with that, and even if I wanted to, he doesn't give me the chance before he walks off to organise some equipment and check them out.

Tomas and Max are standing at the helm talking like old mates, so I take a seat on the back of the boat and relax, as we start to build speed the further we get away from the safety of the beach and the pier.

"I promise you're in good hands." Lee says beside me, causing me to jump out of my fucking skin. "Sorry, I've been accused of sneaking up on people and I'm trying to stop it. In my former career, that skill was necessary, it's hard to just stop doing it."

"No worries." I say, because what else could I possibly say to him?

"Have you ever been fishing before?" he asks, and I consider lying to him, but I decide what the hell, it's going to help either of for me to pretend to know what I'm doing.

"Never." I say, with a smile.

"Trust Tomas, he didn't even ask did he, he just booked it and told you to be here?"

"Something like that."

"I'll run you through the basics now then while those two talk about whatever they're talking about up there." He nods towards the other two men and shows me one end of a fishing rod from the other, as well as a few other basics and before I know it, Max yells out that we're stopping so that we can, 'drop a line in'.

"If you need any help, just let me know." Lee says, and that's how I managed a crash course in the basics of fishing, in a few minutes. Now I guess it's time to put it into action. This should be fun!

Chapter Twenty-three
MAKENNA

Sitting on the couch, I can't help thinking about Brady and hoping, he's enjoying himself. We've known each other for most of our lives, and I've never known him to go fishing, not even once. Thinking about him out on a boat and learning how to fish, makes me laugh.

I've just finished my coffee when there's a knock at the door. For a second I panic thinking something must have happened out on the boat, but I know Brady can look after himself. When I open the door and to see Samantha standing there, I'm happy for a second then panic sets in again.

"Good morning Makenna." She says at the same time as I say, "Is everything OK?"

"Oh goodness, I'm so sorry Makenna, I didn't even think that's what you would think of when I showed up at your door." She says, placing her hand on her heart. "Everything is fine, I haven't heard from the boys except to say that they were all on board and setting out."

"Oh that's good news." I say, taking a deep breath and then slowly letting it out again, releasing tension I didn't even realise I was feeling. "Hang on, what 'guys'?" I spent last night and this morning telling Brady that Tomas wouldn't be going and it wasn't some ploy to get him alone to either kill or get him to leave me. If Tomas went, I can't see Brady being too happy when they return.

"Oh Tomas went today. He goes out all the time with Lee and Max." Samantha informs me without realising all the drama that might cause.

"You mean Lee and Max from our trip to the villages yesterday?"

"Yes, that's them. They're great guys, I'm sure Brady will have a fantastic time. They all know the ocean like the back of their hands, they know where not to go and where it's safe to go as well." Samantha stops talking, and I must have a look on my face that says I don't know that this trip was a good idea for Brady, because she starts trying to reassure me, as she speaks in a jumble of words that are almost too fast for me to understand. "Brady will be perfectly safe Makenna, I swear. They're all good guys, honestly. Tomas means no harm to anyone, well unless of course they deserve it, and of course Brady doesn't deserve it, so he'll be absolutely fine." Her eyes are wide with panic, and I swear that was one word, not a couple of sentences. She takes a deep breath and slowly releases it. "Perfectly fine. He's safe, I promise Makenna."

"OK."

"I mean, both Lee and Max are ex-soldiers, so if anything should happen they'll know what to do." She nods vigorously, and while I know she's trying to placate me, that knowledge doesn't really make me feel much better. To me all that translates to is, 'Lee and Max know where to hide the body.'

"OK." I say, dragging out the two letters for a good few seconds. "Honestly, you didn't really make me feel any better about the situation Samantha, but there's nothing I can do about it right now, so I'm just going to have to trust that Brady can handle himself, because I know that he can, and that Lee and Max don't want to ruin their reputations with a missing client." Samantha laughs, and it's a real, proper amused laughed too.

"Oh, they'll never let anything happen to a client." She smiles what I assume is supposed to be a reassuring smile at me. "Are you ready?"

"For?"

"Your day at the spa." She says a little too cheery.

"Oh, yes. I was just finishing my coffee, and I was going to head over. I didn't realise I needed an escort over there though." I say, hoping I don't sound quite as offended as I feel. I mean, I run a family business and I think I can manage to find my way over to a freaking spa on my own.

"Oh, no you don't, but I thought with Brady gone for the morning, you might enjoy some company."

"Oh, yes that would be lovely. Let me just rinse out my coffee and we can leave." It would be wrong to tell her I was looking forward to the time alone, wouldn't it? It's not that I won't miss Brady, because I will, but I rarely get time alone. At home I'm always either in the office with Margot,

Logan or sometimes, Caleb most recently, or I'm at home with Brady. Nine times out of ten, my brothers join us, with Jules as well. Not that I mind having everyone around, but sometimes it's nice to just relax in the peace and quiet.

"I can leave you in peace if you'd rather, Makenna? I get how hard it is to get some time to yourself, after working all day." Samantha smiles an understanding smile. While I don't think she'd be offended if I said that's what I want, I decide in that instant that I would actually love some company.

"I would love to have your company this morning Samantha." I say and know that I am genuinely happy to share the morning with her.

"If you're sure?"

"Absolutely. We're normally two busy women, so we deserve to have a morning off, and we should enjoy that together. The boys are all out together, so let's do it." I pull the door closed behind us, lock it, and loop our arms together.

"Oh you don't need to lock the door Makenna."

"I know, but it means Brady can't get in unless I'm back from the spa, and that's more fun than you know."

"He can get a key from the front desk."

"I know, but he won't." I say with a smile, and she just nods like I'm a crazy person. Maybe she's right. She might be the one regretting we spend the morning together after all that fuss. "Let's go."

We walk in companiable silence, but we have unlinked our arms. It was so freaking uncomfortable to walk while doing that! Ever the delightful host, Samantha opens the door, and waves me in first.

"Good morning Samantha, and you must be Makenna." The young lady asks as she walks out from behind the front counter, hugs Samantha and then holds her hand out for me to shake, which I do. "I'm Sylvie, I'm the manager, so if you have any problems or issues, don't hesitate to let me know."

"Thank you Sylvie, I'm sure we won't have any issues. I haven't encountered any since we got here, so I'm sure it won't be any different today."

"Well, that's being generous considering Tomas's behaviour, but thank you Makenna."

I can't help the laugh that rings out around the foyer. "Tomas has definitely been, a challenge, shall we say, but his heart is in the right place and as long as he brings my husband home today unharmed, I think we can agree that Tomas's a good guy."

"On that we can agree." She smiles.

"Let me show you ladies back and we can get started. I was thinking we could get you nice and relaxed in the spa, with jets of warm water rushing over you. A few minutes in the steam room to open your pores, then a facial. Which will of course then lead into a manicure and pedicure." Sylvie's plan so far sounded delightful. "We'll finish you off with a nice, relaxing full body massage with some calming oils. How does that sound?" She asks with a knowing smile.

"That sounds like absolute heaven Sylvie, thank you." I tell her honestly. I can't remember the last time I did this. Samantha's standing beside me with a huge grin on her face.

Sylvie leads us into the changing room, and says, "Why don't you ladies get changed? We have some new robes and light slippers there waiting for you and you can put your clothes in a locker just here. No phones or anything disruptive in the treatment rooms, so you're better off leaving them in here, safely locked up. One of the girls will come and get you both in a few minutes.' She smiles and then she's gone.

Samantha and I look at each other, then look around the room. There are a couple of folding screen room dividers at one end of the room with beautiful wooden frames and different coloured canvas privacy curtains on them.

"I guess that's where we change then?" I ask Samantha, she should know, the spa is a part of her business, but I get the feeling this is completely out of her comfort zone, and she's either never been in before, or it's been a while since her last visit.

"Is there a robe hanging up back there?" Samantha asks, so I peek around the edge of one of the screens and smile.

"There sure is. I'll take this one." I smile at her and we both disappear behind our screens. It's quiet except for rustling of clothes being removed, and folded up.

"Knock, knock, are you ladies ready to go? If not I can wait for a few minutes." A quiet voice says from the other side of the screen. I stumbled against my screen, because even though she was quiet and we were told to expect her, she still startles me in the quiet of the room. "I'm sorry, I didn't mean to startle you."

"You didn't." I start as I walk out from the behind the screen, tying the belt of my robe around my waist. "Well, OK, you *did* but we knew you were coming, so it shouldn't have startled me." I say with a nervous laugh.

"Makenna's right, we knew you were coming to get us, but your voice breaking through the quiet was just a little startling." Samantha says, as she appears from behind her screen as well.

"Oh, Ms Holt, I didn't realise you were joining us today." Our beauty therapist says, surprised.

"It's Samantha, please." It's the first time I've ever seen Samantha look uncomfortable in our time here. "I'm not here as Ms Holt, I'm here as a guest, so no special treatment, OK?"

"OK, Samantha." The poor girl kind of trips over the words, and I can't help but wonder if Samantha's a tyrant of a boss underneath all of her genial customer service. "I'm Geri, and you must be Makenna?" Geri smiles when she looks my way, but it's definitely her 'customer service' smile, and not quite as genuine as it was before Samantha joined us. I'm guessing she booked under the name Samantha and, not Miss Holt for this very reason.

"Hi Geri, it's nice to meet you." I say, as I take her outreached hand in mine, and smile as warmly as I can. "So, what's first on our spa morning agenda?" I ask, trying to move this awkward little group along to something new.

"Sylvie said you've got the whole package booked, with a pretty tight time frame. So I thought we could start with the spa for about ten minutes, that will get you nice and relaxed. Followed with a five minute burst in the sauna to open up those pores, before we do the facial."

"Sounds good to me." I reply with a smile and follow her out of the change rooms to the spa. I can hear Samantha behind me, so I look behind me and smile, glad she's still there as Geri leads us through a door into a small room with a spa at one end and what I assume is a sauna at the other end, with some bench seats in between.

"You can hang your robes up on the hooks here." Geri indicates the hooks above the seating. "We've already got the spa going, but if you want to change any of the settings, the control panel is just here. Unless you have any questions, I'll leave you ladies to relax for ten minutes."

"I think we're good, thanks Geri." I smile at her, because Samantha still hasn't spoken and she's wearing a pretty decent frown on her face. Geri returns my smile, and heads back out the door we just came in, like the place is on fire.

"I'm sorry Makenna, maybe I should just leave you to enjoy your peace." Samantha says, her head high, but I can see the indecision on her face.

"Hell no woman! I think you need the break and relaxation more than I do. I'm already on holiday Samantha."

"You're not wrong, but people are behaving like I'm intruding, and I want you to enjoy yourself. You're not my friend, you're a guest, and I invited myself along to your spa day."

"Hey, whoa there. I'm going to stop you right there. I'll admit I was surprised when you came to the bungalow earlier, and said you were joining me this morning, but I don't want you to leave. Truth be told, this is something I would have done with my friends at home, and it would feel really weird doing it alone. So, while it might have been a bit weird at the beginning, no, I don't want you to leave."

"Are you sure?"

"Absolutely! Now drop that robe and join me in the water." I say, as I literally do as I instructed and drop the robe. Although, I do hang it on a hook because I can't not! Then I step into the water, which has the perfect amount of bubbles and is at the right temperature to be comfortable too. "Oh my lord! They know a thing or two about doing things right here Samantha." I say, before groaning in pleasure as I park my butt on the seat and close my eyes. I hear the water splash and smile.

"Thank you Makenna." She says quietly as she settles into her own seat. I let the quiet brew for a few seconds before I speak.

"So, what's with you and Tomas?" I ask, keeping my eyes closed so she doesn't feel like she's under the spotlight. It's a trick that Logan taught me, not to necessarily close your eyes in a meeting, but to look away from them. If people think you're not drilling them for information, they'll relax enough to at least drop a few tidbits.

"Nothing." Her answer is quick, and I try hard not to laugh.

"That's the standard response, but is it the truth?" I push.

"Yes." Her answer is still quick, but not quite as quick as before, and the word is stretch out.

"Are you sure about that?"

"Yes." This time, the word is almost a whisper. "Nothing is going on between Tomas and myself." She says with more conviction.

"Is that because you don't *want* it to, or because you don't think it *should?*" I ask, pushing a little further because while I can sense her hesitation, I also think she wants to talk to someone about it, and she can't talk to anyone here.

"It can't happen. No matter how many times he asks, or how much I want it to." She says, brusquely. I haven't opened my eyes to look at her yet, but I hear her moving around to get more comfortable.

"Why not? If you like him, why can't you date?"

"It wouldn't be right. We tell all staff that while we haven't banned fraternisation, we don't actively encourage it either. What would it look like if two *managers* started dating?"

"But it's not a rule that you can't, right?"

"Technically, no, there's no rules against it."

"And you like him, right?"

"Yes." She finally admits, and I have to fight with myself to not open my eyes and yell hallelujah at her!

"And he likes you, right?"

"Yes." She sighs. "Since the first day he started six months ago, he's asked me out on a regular basis."

I can't keep still any longer. I open my eyes, sit up, and look around the small room that we're in to make sure we're still alone. Our ten minutes in the spa aren't close to being up yet, but I want her to feel comfortable talking to me, and not clam back up again. Confirming we're still alone, I move closer to Samantha and take her hand in mine.

"Is working together the only reason you're saying no, or are you using that as an excuse to keep him at bay?" I ask sincerely, because I get the feeling there's more to her 'no' than she's telling me.

"Of course! Isn't that reason enough?" She asks in that steely voice I didn't know she had.

"If I'm being honest? No, not really Samantha." I say in a voice that I normally reserve for speaking to Caleb because it's soothing. "If you want to go out with him Samantha, then go out with him! I'm here to tell you that life's too short not to do something that has the potential to make you happy, and I might have only met you this week, but I can see that Tomas has that in spades."

"Is it that obvious?" I'm glad she picked up that part and I don't have to explain how I know life is short.

"Maybe not to some." I say with a shrug of my shoulders. "But to me, yes."

"Oh. I just don't want it to go bad and then one of us will have to leave the resort and I don't want to leave. This is my home."

"What makes you think it will go bad?"

"Everything does eventually. I haven't had a relationship that hasn't ended badly. They never want to live here, stay here and work in the resort or on the island." She sighs, and takes her hand out of mine. "Not to mention, my parents aren't exactly great role models. They've both been married four times! That's not a great track record Makenna."

"No, it's not, but you're not them and maybe those guys before didn't work out because they weren't the one. Tomas's already here, on the island and working in the resort, so he's not going anywhere."

"That's what he keeps saying."

"Has he gone out with anyone else while you've been working together, and he's been asking you out?"

"Not that I know of."

"That says a lot too Samantha." I move back over to my side of the spa, because Geri will no doubt be back in shortly, and I don't want to be having this particular conversation when she does. "My parents were very much in love when they were killed in a car accident. That's how I know life and love can be short Samantha, and I don't want your sympathy. What I want is for you to promise me to think about it. Think about how you would feel if Tomas went out with someone else, if he left the resort or something happened to him, knock on wood, and you'd never given the guy a chance."

"I'm sorry to hear about your parent's Makenna, and I promise to think about what you've said."

We sit back and relax into the water and the bubbles in silence until Geri walks back in and announces its time for us to steam those pores open. She hands us a towel each, walks us to the sauna door and waves us in.

"I'll be back in five minutes." She smiles as the door closes behind us, locking us in the dark steamy room.

"He's a good man." Samantha says after we get ourselves settled onto a bench.

"He is the sweetest. Well, apart from Brady, of course." That earns me a laugh and I see the Samantha that I've gotten used to shining through again.

"Brady is definitely a handsome, and kind man, but no offence, he's not my type." She laughs.

"No, he's not your type, but I think I know who is and you need to do something about it woman!" That gets me another laugh, that turns into a coughing fit, because we're in the freaking sauna and she's just sucked down hot steam into her lungs. "Shit sorry Samantha."

"That's OK, despite everything, this is the most fun I've had in a while."

I'm about to respond with something smart about Tomas being fun, when the door opens, and Geri informs us our steam time is over. I know I have a time constraint, but I feel like we're getting pushed around a little too much.

Geri hands us both a clean, dry towel to wrap around us. "If you'd like to put on your robes and slippers, and follow me, we can head over to the facial room now."

"I think I might leave you here Makenna."

"Don't even think it about Samantha. You're coming with me." I don't let her finish what she was saying, and I take her hand in mine, not letting her run away either.

"This way ladies." Geri leads the way once again and leaves us, again, when we get comfortable. Not my business, I remind myself and keep my mouth shut. It's really starting to annoy me that Geri doesn't seem to actually have a job to do, though. Not my business!

There's music playing quietly in the background as the ladies get to work on our facials. We don't talk, and I hope that Samantha is taking advantage of the down time to relax. From there Geri takes us to the ladies who do the manicures and pedicures. When our hands and feet are soaking, we're left alone for a few minutes as the ladies go to get the colours we asked for.

I lean over to Samantha so that I can whisper my question to her, and hopefully I won't be overheard.

"Can I ask you a question?" She nods, so I continue. "What exactly is Geri's job? Does she have qualifications for any of the services you provide?"

"I've been wondering the same thing. I've let Sylvie run the spa without too much interference from me, but I'm wondering if that was a good idea. I accepted that the spa had a higher running cost than other amenities, and I trusted that she was experienced enough to not need me looking over her shoulder. I'm starting to question my decision this morning."

We don't get to continue the conversation, because the ladies are back, and get down to business. Our hands and feet are scraped, buffed, polished, and massaged to the point where I'm not sure I'll be able to walk or hold onto anything for a while.

As we're standing up and thanking them for their wonderful work, Geri comes walking back in.

"Sylvie asked me to give you this note Ms Holt, sorry, Samantha." Samantha opens the card and mutters something under her breath.

"Sorry Makenna, I'm going to have to leave you here. I've got something at the main office to deal with, but enjoy your massage, Joey is the best there is, and I will make sure to catch you before you and Brady leave today. I promise." Her eyes sparkle and I hope that promise includes what we spoke about earlier as well.

"I'm sorry you won't be joining me, but you need to go take care of business." I smile and then give her hug. "Take care and please, think about what I said." I say quietly in her ear.

"I will." She promises back.

I pull out of our embrace and she turns to leave, and Geri walks me to the massage room where I'm about to meet the best there is, Joey.

Geri and I don't speak too much, other than her introducing me to Joey, and then me saying thank you.

When she leaves the room, closing the door behind her, Joey says, "You can either leave your bathers on that you wore in the spa, or you can strip down to nothing. I can work either way, and I won't see anything, because you'll be face down on the bed and a towel will cover your behind." He says kindly. "I'll leave for a few minutes so that you can get comfortable."

I stand there for a second and think about what I would be comfortable with if the roles were reversed and Brady was about to get a massage from a female. I know it's their job, they won't get all touchy, feely, but I shudder at the idea of him being naked with another woman, so I decide to leave the now dry bathers on, and get comfortable on the bed just as I hear the door open and Joey walks back in.

"Are you ready?" He doesn't mention my choice to keep my bathers on, just gets right down to business.

"Yes." I manage to mumble into the hole in the bed that my face is resting in. His hands are warm, and strong as they run up and down my back, and over my shoulders.

"Relax Makenna." He says his voice quiet and relaxing. "If I press too hard just let me know, OK?"

"Mmmhmmm." Is all I manage to get out before I feel myself relax and just enjoy the massage. Samantha was right, Joey is good at his job. I lie there, enjoying the feeling of my muscles slowly relaxing, and I wonder if it would be rude, and put my new friendship in jeopardy if I stole Joey and took him home with me.

"I'm sorry Makenna, I have step out for a second." Joey says and then he's gone. I feel too much like a wet noodle to argue with him and I think I hum out a sound that could mean yes without moving my lips. I'm close to being asleep, I don't know if I'll be on our flight home in time because I can't move.

I hear the door open and close again, but Joey doesn't speak before his warm hands are back on my body. Those same hands slip down to either side of my body, just touch my side boobs, and now I'm feeling a bit more awake, but I pass it off as a slip. His hands return to my back and shoulders for a minute, but then his hands slide a little too close to my butt cheeks for me to be comfortable. I'm about to jump up, when his hands actually *squeeze* my cheeks and I try to leap off the damned bed.

"You don't get to touch me like that, arsehole!" I growl.

"Relax Kenna, it's just me, but I sure am glad to know you won't let just any man touch you like that." He says, chuckling. Brady?

"What the hell Brady?" I demand, but he pushes me back down.

"Let me finish your massage baby."

I'll give him baby. Arse face!

Chapter Twenty-four
BRADY

I am *so* glad that Tomas decided to call it early on the fishing trip. Lee and Max were awesome, and we actually caught a ton of fish. Enough to have some for lunch if I can get Kenna out of the spa quickly.

I love that Tomas pulled some strings, and charmed our way into the spa where Kenna is having her massage, the final treatment for the day, so I'm told. The fact that he even got Sylvie the manager to agree to let me sneak into the room and take over the massage? That was just fucking genius! Joey, the massage therapist, tried to show me how to give her a massage, but hell, she's my wife, this isn't my first massage.

I did what Joey suggested, but I just couldn't resist pushing a little further to see what she'd put up with. Her body goes rigid when I touched the side of her boob, but it's not because she's turned on, no, it's because she's shocked I did it. Her arse was just *so* inviting all wrapped up there with a nice white towel over it, and it was covered up, believe me, because she'd tucked the towel underneath her hips. I let her relax after my boob touch, knowing that she would put it down to an accident, then I moved the towel slightly, like I was going to the base of her spine and her body stiffens a little again, but she didn't move, not until I actually started to rub her cheeks.

Her growl of a warning sent a bolt of arousal straight to my groin. Her *words* of warning bought me to full mast and ready to jump her. Anyone would think I was a horny teenager, not a guy in his mid-twenties who just got married to the love of his life.

"Kenna, relax, it's just me!" I tell her laughing. "I sure am glad to know you won't let just any man touch you like that."

"What the hell Brady?"

"Let me finish your massage baby."

"Fuck you! You just about gave me a heart attack. I was ready to give Joey a real what for!"

"I know. It was really adorable."

She starts to sit up again, and I gently push her back down so that I can continue giving her a massage. I'm enjoying it and I want her to as well. What's not to enjoy? I get to rub my oiled up hands all over my gorgeous wife, and even though I know I can do that almost whenever I like, this feels special.

"What do you mean, *adorable?* I can take care of myself Brady Harris!"

"I know you can Makenna Harris. It's one of the many reasons I love you, but did you happen to notice the size of that guy? I'm not sure even Logan could take him on, and come out without a scratch on him." I can feel the tension leaving her body.

"You're right, but I wouldn't have let him get away with touching me like that. I would have slapped him across the face as hard as I possibly could and then told Sylvie she needed to find a new masseuse."

"Don't be too hard on him Kenna, he's actually a really nice guy. At least I thought so from the few minutes I got to speak to him." A buzzer goes off on a table close to the massage table and I go turn it off. "I think your time is up Mrs Harris."

"I think *your* time is *up*, Mr Harris." She says with a wink, as she sits up on the table, her bikini top falls to her lap, and I think I swallowed my tongue. Even after all our years together, she can still make me as hard as a rock in seconds. I swallow deeply, and most unattractively, still she smiles at me and jumps down off the table, heading my way.

"No!" I say, putting my hands up to stop her from walking any closer, but she keeps coming. "No, Kenna."

"Why not Brady? I'm sure they can do without the room for a few more minutes." Minutes? Well, that's a bit insulting. Probably not untrue right now, but still insulting!

"We don't have time, Makenna." I tell her, both my voice and my will, are wavering. "Stop. Put your robe on. Please Makenna." I beg her and close my eyes. I can't look at her and still tell her to stop. I want her, and she fucking knows it.

"I thought we always had time for fun, Brady?" She's throwing my own damned words back at me, all while trying to imitate my voice. It's cute as hell, but I'm *not* giving in on this.

"No! This is not the time, nor the place Makenna." I step away from her and move towards the door. "Now, please put your robe back on so that we can get out of here." I've made it to the door, and I open it to leave.

Just as I close the door behind me, I hear her mumble, "Well, that was just plain rude." I laugh as I fall back onto the door, hitting my head hard against the wood.

I must be the stupidest man alive to not take his wife up on the opportunity to have sex with her, but I want to leave us enough time to have some lunch, that I caught, with Tomas, Lee, Max, and Samantha before we leave. The door behind me opens and I have to catch myself on the doorframe, so I don't fall.

"I'm sorry, did I surprise you? I thought we were in a hurry?" Kenna asks as she steps around me to head to the change rooms.

"Kenna, baby, don't be like that." I take a couple of large steps to easily catch up to her.

"I'm not being like anything, Brady." She says without turning around. "You rejected my advances, and we're in a hurry to get out of here. So, I'm going to keep walking so I don't waste anymore of your time." Fuck!

"Kenna, I didn't reject you." My voice is full of the annoyance I'm feeling. "Makenna Rose Harris you stop walking right now!" My voice is deep and low, so deadly fucking serious, even an employee walking between rooms stops dead for a split second before scurrying off. It's a rare thing for me to use either that tone or her middle name but right now I need her to stop fucking walking away from me. I will *not* have our honeymoon ruined over a stupid misunderstanding. She doesn't speak, but she hasn't moved a muscle. "Are you going to listen to me, or are you determined to be pissed at me?"

"You middle named me."

"I did."

"You used that growly, sexy voice on me." That makes me smile.

"I did." I pause for a few beats. "Does that mean you're going to listen to me?"

"It does."

"Good." I turn us around so that I'm facing her. "We got back early from the fishing trip and I wanted to surprise you." I reach up and place my hands on her shoulders, dropping them to rub up and down her upper arms. "Tomas and I wanted to hurry you ladies along because we organised to have lunch with the guys before we leave today."

"What guys?"

"Tomas, of course! Samantha, Lee, and Max. If there's anyone else you want to invite, feel free, we caught plenty of fish."

"So, the fishing, it went well then? You enjoyed yourself?" She asks hesitantly, making me realise she was worried that I wouldn't be having fun.

"Kenna, you have no idea how much fun that was! Lee taught me so much, and I caught us lunch. Well, the guys all caught some too, but I caught a *lot* of fish baby. That's why I wanted to surprise you, because it surprised the hell out of me." I laugh.

Kenna flings her arms around my neck and kisses my cheek. "I'm so glad you enjoyed yourself Brady, I was so worried that you would be miserable."

"Well, when Tomas met me on the way to the boat, I thought I'd be swimming with the fishes and not catching them." I laugh when she punches my shoulder. "The truth is though, Tomas's a great guy." I can admit it when I'm wrong.

"Lunch then, huh?"

"Only if you move that cute butt and get dressed. No-one else gets to see you like that today, except me. I'll wait here." I give her a quick but passionate kiss and send her on her way. The sooner she leaves, the sooner she'll be back in my arms.

I watch as the door closes behind her, and lean against the wall to wait for her.

"So, it went well then?" I jump because I didn't notice anyone else in the hallway. I look up to see Joey standing there with his arms crossed, but a smile playing at his lips.

"Eventually, yeah." I smile in response, because a pissed off Kenna, is a Kenna full of passion.

"You're one lucky sonofabitch, that's for sure." He says with a shake of his head and turns to leave.

"Hey Joey."

"Yeah."

"What time do you get a break?" I ask.

"In about ten minutes. Why?" My smile is so wide it just might crack my face open.

"Want some fresh fish for lunch?"

"Sure?" The look on his face is a mixture of confusion and I'm up for food.

"Well, come by the staff quarters in about twenty minutes, and there should be a bit of a feast ready." I tell him and turn back to face the door that Kenna went in. "Just you though, not the rest of the staff here, ok?"

"OK, sure. Thanks Mr Harris."

"Brady." I tell him. "If you're going to share a meal with us, then you should probably call me Brady, don't you think?"

"I'll see you in twenty minutes Brady." He nods to me and I nod back before he disappears around a corner that leads to who knows where.

"Who were you talking to?" Kenna asks as she comes out of the change room, the door closing softly behind her.

"Joey."

"The masseuse?" She asks, surprised.

"The one and only. How many Joey's have you met on the island?" I ask her with a smile.

"Just the one. He's damned good with his hands too." She says with a thoughtful nod. It's almost like she's remembering his hands on her body, and I'm starting to regret inviting him to lunch, but he was such a good sport about letting me take over the massage. Kenna's laughter brings me out of my thoughts. "Oh Brady, if you could see your face right now. That frown is adorable, but if you don't stop, you're going to have permanent wrinkles, right here." She rubs my forehead, right between my eyebrows. Which, of course, causes me to frown even deeper.

"Cut it out.' I say, swiping her hand from my face and hold it in mine.

"You're so damned cute when you get all grumpy like that." She smiles at me.

"I'm not *cute*! I'm handsome, I'm sexy, but I am definitely *not cute*!" I growl at her, and I swing her around so that we're facing one another. We're so close our noses are almost touching. "I'll show you how fucking sexy I am." I announce, before taking her lips with mine and wrapping my arms around her so that I can pull her impossibly closer.

Her mouth opens as she moans her approval, and I take the opportunity to deepen our kiss, just how I know she likes it. One of her hands holds my shoulder in the a tight grip, the other has the same tight hold on my neck, pulling me closer. I turn us around again, and push Kenna against the wall, sliding my leg between hers. Kenna wraps her leg around my hip, and I reach down to hold her there, rocking my cock into the heat of her pussy.

"Are you two joining us for lunch, or are you planning on dry humping each other against the wall of the spa for the rest of the day?"

I pull my lips from Kenna's and rest my forehead on hers, while the two of us catch our breath. "Fuck. Off. Tomas." I spit out, and his laughter rings out loudly, even as it fades as he walks away from us. "I am *so* fucking glad we're leaving him *here* today! The man is a bigger cockblocker than your brothers and baby, that's saying something!"

Kenna's laughter rings out through the courtyard between the spa and the main office. "I'm sure he didn't do it on purpose Brady, and well, to be fair, we probably shouldn't be almost having sex in a public space." She says, still laughing. I'm not sure how she can laugh at a time like this, I can barely think about anything except finishing what we started here. "Guess we better go have lunch, hey?"

"I guess so." Right now my idea of having a group lunch before we leave, doesn't seem like such a genius plan. "Just give me a minute to, shall we say, calm down?"

"Huh? Oh, ohhhh, sure. Take as long as you need." She rests her head on my shoulder and her shoulders shake with barely contained laughter.

"Oh yes, you can laugh Mrs Harris, because as a woman, *your* arousal isn't front and damned centre for the entire world to see!" That causes Kenna's barely contained amusement to burst free, and if your wife laughing hysterically at your erection isn't enough to remedy the situation, I don't know what is, and it's quickly obvious that my cock agrees.

"Oh my lord, I'm so sorry Brady, but that's just funny."

"I'm glad my attraction to you, amuses you so greatly." I say, as I give her a tight hug. "Is there anything else I can do for you before we head over to join them for lunch?"

"Let's go. Before Tomas changes all the stories of this morning to make himself the hero, and me a bumbling idiot."

"I thought you said that Tomas was a great guy? Now just because he caught us behaving like horny teenagers, you're pissed at him again?"

I smile, remembering the fun we had out on the boat. "No, he's a great guy still, but so are your brother's, that doesn't mean they're not all cockblockers of epic proportions, though." Kenna lets out a loud snort of laughter, which at any other time would be adorable, but right now I'm just frustrated as hell.

"Come on then, let's go join the cockblocker and I assume the woman he wishes was his, and maybe Lee and Max?" She asks, trying to work out who is and isn't going to be there.

"You got it baby." I put my arm around her shoulders, and she puts her arm around my waist, as we make our way towards the staff quarters. When we get closer, we can hear loud chatter and laughter.

"This was a brilliant idea Brady, thank you." Leaning over she kisses my cheek, even as we keep walking.

"For the love of all things holy, keep your hands to yourself before you turn us all off our lunch you two." There's the Tomas we know, at his cockblocking best again, but he makes Kenna laugh and that makes me happy, so he can't be all bad.

"You're welcome baby." I lean and whisper in her ear, before moving towards Tomas. I'd do anything to keep this smile. "Alright my man, let's get this fish cooking."

"You know what you're doing?" Tomas asks me, shocked.

"I may not have known how to catch the buggers, but I sure do know how to cook them." I assure him and he looks to Kenna for confirmation, which of course she gives, because she loves my cooking.

"Of course he knows what he's doing, I wouldn't have married him otherwise." Then she freaking winks at him like she's not talking about just my cooking skills, and I can't help laughing. Tomas's loud roar of laughter fills the small space as well, and I'm glad we're doing this. Makenna's not the only one who's going to miss this crazy bunch of people who have become friends.

"Show us these cooking skills you claim to have Mr Harris! I'm hungry!" Tomas roars and lets out a boisterous laugh. Lee and Max join in laughing, and I can't help the smile that stretches across my face too. I didn't end up swimming with the fishes this morning, and I managed to earn myself a new nickname as well. It's not one I'm sharing with anyone back home, but I'm still proud of it while we're here.

"Yeah, come on Brady, get busy. I'm freaking hungry." Max says, and I take that as my cue to do my thing.

I look over to find Makenna standing with Samantha and drinking some fruity cocktail that Lee made for them, and I smile. The smile that she gives me back warms my very soul. I wink at her, and she winks back and then Samantha speaks to her and she turns to speak to her.

I joke and talk with the guys as I cook. I couldn't feel more relaxed if I tried.

Chapter Twenty-five
MAKENNA

This husband of mine is something else. If I needed a reminder of why I love him so much, this lunch is it. I've made some friends here, in fact, I think it's fair to say that we've both made some friends here. Even though I know that we've spent barely a week here, I feel like I've known these people, especially Samantha and Tomas, for a long time, and I'm going to miss them when we leave later today. It might seem ridiculous to some people that I could claim them as friends so quickly, and easily, but it's just the way I am, and that Brady understands that makes my heart melt.

I look over to where he's standing with Tomas, Lee, and Max, laughing, and chatting away. It's something I didn't think he'd be doing at the start of our trip, or even yesterday if I'm being honest. As if he can feel my eyes on him, he looks up, immediately looking into my eyes, and he smiles. It's a broad, sunny, happy smile.

"Hey, dude, are you cooking lunch, or are you making gooey eyes at your wife?" Tomas asks, laughing.

"Cooking *dude*, but can you blame me? My wife's gorgeous and I like looking at her. Your damned lunch, is almost done so I hope you've got everything else ready to go?" Tomas smiles wide and nods.

"Of course I've got everything else sorted and ready to go."

"You mean I got everything else sorted and it's now all ready to go, because you did nothing, as per usual." Samantha says, her voice not really carrying the anger that her face does, which just makes Tomas smile wider. He walks over slowly, and I can feel Samantha stiffen beside me as he leans in close to her ear but not touching her. "You like feeding me, don't you sweetness?" He says just loud enough that I can hear him, but I'm not sure he wanted me to.

179

There's a tension in the air that wasn't there before as he steps back, out of her reach, and just as she opens her mouth to either tell him to go fuck himself or admit that she does in fact love to feed him, another voice joins the fray.

"Whatever you're cooking Mr Harris, I mean Brady, smells damned good."

"You came!" Brady says, walking over to Joey and shaking his hand. "So glad you're here."

"Makenna." He nods my way in acknowledgment and then at Samantha, who blushes furiously. "Samantha. How are you?"

"Good. Thanks." Samantha stutters out. I don't think I've ever seen Samantha stutter about anything in the short few days I've known her. She doesn't even stutter when she talks to Tomas. Joey comes over and starts talking to Samantha. Tomas's standing beside a smirking Brady, looking like he wants to murder Joey, and I'm pretty certain no-one would ever find his body.

I now understand exactly why Brady invited Joey to join us for lunch. He must have seen something that I didn't, and now, he's pushing Tomas's buttons. We both know he likes Samantha.

I walk over to where Brady is almost finished cooking, and lean up to his ear. "You did that on purpose?"

He smiles, but doesn't turn to face me. "Someone has to push him to make a proper move, don't they? Otherwise, they're both going to spend their days working together tortured, and who knows how long it is before one of them decides they can't take it anymore, and leaves? I just want them to be happy, and hell, Tomas's had plenty of fun at my expense this week, I'm just returning the favour. Only, my meddling might actually end with him being extremely happy."

"You're kind of sweet you know?" I tell him, and he shrugs his shoulder.

"He deserves to be happy, and Samantha will make him happy, because she loves him, she just can't admit it yet." I kiss him on the cheek, because if I kiss him properly, Tomas's going to give us grief, then again he may not notice right now. "If the look he's sending those two right now is anything to go by, we might need to employ Joey at Drake Wines soon."

I look at him, shocked, but then I start to think that I might like that idea. Branch out a little at Drake Wines and do weekend getaways with those old unused cottages on the property. I know Caleb is in the middle of looking at them to decide what needs to be repaired so that we can get some overnight stays, perhaps we can get a small spa as well.

"No." Brady turns me to face him, and place his hands on my cheeks, looking deep into my eyes. It would almost be sweet and romantic if I wasn't one hundred percent sure of what he was going to say next. "No. No plotting and scheming for Drake Wines. Give me another twenty four hours before I lose you back to the grapes again, please? Joey's staying here, he already has a job."

"I'm sorry, but you're the one who planted the seed." I tell him, leaving a light kiss on his amazing lips.

"I know and I regret it." He drops his hands from my face and turns to pick up a plate of beautifully cooked fish. He takes my hand in his empty one and walks us over to the table that is laden with fresh salads, and hot, delicious smelling bread. "Let's eat." Brady says loudly and everyone makes their way to the table.

As we all get seated I look up to see Samantha sitting opposite me. I smile, but she doesn't smile back, in fact, she looks mighty uncomfortable, and that's when I realise that she's in a bit of a man sandwich. While Brady and I have seated ourselves on one side of the table, Lee and Max are at either end of the table. That leaves Samantha sitting between Tomas and Joey, and I don't think she's very pleased with this turn of events.

"Are you OK, Samantha?" I ask, concerned for her and Tomas's health.

"Of course I am Makenna. What could possibly be wrong? We're eating some lovely fresh fish caught by your very charming husband, and the rest I know is delicious because I put it all together." Her smile is the kind of smile that I think might mean death to someone, rather than over the top happiness.

"You made all of this?" Joey asks.

"No, she didn't. She organised for the resort chefs to prepare them for us." Tomas snorts, like he knows everything, and Brady just shakes his head beside me. I can't help but wonder how one man could be so freaking stupid? He's digging himself a deep hole if he's insulting her cooking skills.

"Did you just insult Samantha's cooking skills?" Joey asks, and the tension at the tables ratchets up to epic levels. Even Lee and Max have stopped piling food onto their plates. "I can assure you that Samantha here is a very fine cook." He smiles at her like she's the stars and the moon.

"Thank you Joey." Samantha's says quietly.

"And how the hell do you know how well *Samantha* cooks?" Tomas asks. Tomas and Joey are the only two people at the table still actually piling food onto their plates. Samantha hasn't even lifted a finger to start getting herself some food.

"Because I've eaten her food before. Quite often actually." Joey smiles and Samantha drops her head into her hands. Tomas finally stops filling his plate, drops it to the table, making his cutlery clatter, and drops heavily into the seat next to Samantha.

"For business meetings? About the spa and such? I mean she likes to bring food to all the staff and management meetings, that's what you mean, right?" Samantha makes this noise into her hands, it sounds a lot like a wounded animal, I guess she knows what's coming next.

"Well, yes, those too." Joey says with a smile, not realising what he's doing. Or maybe he does, and he simply doesn't care too much about the repercussions.

"You two dated?" Tomas asks.

"No!" Samantha says, her head coming up to look at Tomas so fast, I swear it almost flew off her shoulders. "No, we didn't date."

"No, we had more of a *friends with benefits* arrangement, didn't we Samantha?" Joey chuckles, like he's remembering all the good times they shared.

Lee and Max both make this snort, laugh, choking sound and cover it up by having a drink, and then shoving food in their mouths. I have no idea what to say and Brady, well he tries to break the awkward silence. "Who wants some more fish?"

"What!?" Tomas shouts.

"I said, who wants some more fish? I had such great success on my first charter we called it early and came back here so that we could share a meal with you guys. So that *Makenna* could say goodbye and thank you for your fine hospitality." Tomas gives him a death glare, and Brady returns it, but

I can't take my eyes off Samantha. The woman has more layers to her than I ever gave her credit for, and the fact that she had a *'friends with benefits'* kind of arrangement with Joey is damned impressive. Even more impressive is that until now, they appear to have managed to keep it to themselves too. Well, Tomas didn't know, but I get the feeling the other two guys did. I don't imagine there's much that goes on around here that they don't know about.

"You're right Brady. Let's enjoy our lunch and then we can get you two off on your trip back home, and away from this madhouse." Tomas goes to speak, but Samantha holds her hand up, right in his face because he's looking at her, but she's still looking my way, except down at the table, not at me. "Don't, not here. Makenna and Brady are after all still guests here at Sandy Cove, no matter what else we feel about their friendship. *They're paying guests Tomas.*" Tomas stops talking and starts eating.

Joey, who had been sitting on the other side of Samantha that entire time, quietly eating his lunch, smiles and says, "Thanks for inviting me to join you guys for lunch Brady, I'm having a really good time." Brady receives looks that could kill from both Samantha and Tomas, while the rest of us choke on our food.

"So. How did the fishing trip go?" I ask, trying to get a change of subject happening. It only works because Lee, of all people, starts to entertain us with stories of their trip this morning, with Max and Brady injecting their own versions of the stories as well. While Tomas sits there quietly stewing in the revelation, eating his food, until Lee's story gets completely over the top and it draws Tomas out to tell the truth, as he saw it anyway.

The rest of lunch goes well. Until everyone's finished eating and Joey loudly declares it's time for him to go back to work, and then kisses Samantha on the cheek.

"That was highly inappropriate Joey." She whispers angrily.

"Why? They all know what's going on now." He laughs, as a loud crash of bottles being emptied into a bin as Tomas tosses his on the top.

"There isn't anything going on Joey and you know it. It hasn't been going on for months, close to a year actually, so stop making it out to be more than it is or was." Samantha hisses.

"Wow, that hurts Samantha." Joey says, but he's still smiling. "I'm going back to work now, see you later. Thanks again for asking me to lunch Brady, it was fun. I hope you and Makenna have a safe trip back home." Without another word to anyone else, he's gone, and I take a deep breath.

Samantha starts to clean up, and I make a move to help her. "No, Makenna, you're a guest here. Not to mention you need to go pack so that you can get home."

"I'm so sorry Samantha. If Brady had known, he wouldn't have invited him. If I had known I would have stopped him from inviting him, or I would have made him take the invitation back. I'm so damned sorry." I say quietly, because I don't want any of the guys to hear us.

"It's not your fault Makenna, or Brady's, forget about it." She says, waving her hand at me, but I can see the tears in her eyes.

"He didn't mean to embarrass you. He just thought it would be nice to invite Joey because he allowed Brady to step in the room when he knew he really shouldn't."

"I understand that Makenna, and trust me, I've got no-one to blame for that train wreck except myself."

"Is that why you didn't want to stay for the massage, you knew who was on the schedule to do it?"

"I got called away, but the answer is yes and no. I've suspected for a long time that Geri was suspicious about my relationship with Joey. He was alone when he first arrived, and I felt for him. Yes, it became exactly what he said it did, but that ended almost as soon as it began, and Geri has been trying to prove it happened ever since. Which is why she put Joey up as the masseuse when she realised I was booked in with you."

"Joey is the other reason you don't want to get involved with Tomas. You did it once and now you feel guilty and now Geri is trying to out you and undermine you at every turn." It's not a question.

"Yes. So, now you understand. I can't go there again, no matter how much I might want to." She says the last part so quietly I almost miss it. "Go on, you two get out of here. I'll clean the rest of it up and then we'll come say our goodbyes." She takes the plate out of my hand and pushes me towards the path to our bungalow. "Come on Brady, you've done enough. Take your wife and get organised to head home. Please." She pleads with him, her eyes boring into his. He's looking at her so intently, I know he's trying to apologise without words, and she gives him a small nod.

He takes my hand in his. "Come on baby, Samantha's right, we need to get our stuff organised so that we can head home." He starts to lead me away, before raising his free hand and yelling out, "See you guys before we leave, yeah?"

"Yeah, we'll see you before you go." The three guys chime in together.

"Can I call them the three amigos?" I bump Brady's shoulder as we walk towards our bungalow for the last time, and he chuckles.

"Between the two of us? Absolutely! To them? Hell no! They'll enjoy that a little too much and I don't think I could handle it." He says, dropping my hand and draping his arm around my shoulders, pulling me in close to him as we walk. "I really screwed up today didn't I?"

"With the Joey, Samantha, Tomas thing?"

"Yeah."

"Just a little bit." I tell him honestly, holding up my hand and indicating with my index and thumb, a small space. "I don't think it was anything either of us expected, but I guess it's all out in the open now."

"Do you think Tomas can forgive her?"

"What's to forgive? They weren't together, and they weren't prior to it, nor have they been since. It's none of his business really, and even though I can see why he's upset, I doubt he'd be offering any apologies if the situation was reversed, and nor should he. That being said, Samantha shouldn't have to apologise either. She's a grown woman and she makes her own life choices."

"You're right, completely, but I think I did more to harm any chance they have of getting together now, than I did to help it." Brady sighs, as we reach the bungalow, and he unlocks the door.

"Hey, how did you get in earlier? I locked the door and I know you didn't have a key." I ask, remembering what I joked with Samantha about this morning.

"I was with Tomas, how do you think I got in to shower and change out of the fishy smelling clothes Kenna?" He asks with a laugh.

"Oh, I didn't know you were going to be with Tomas when I locked the door." I say, more to myself than to Brady, but he laughs anyway.

"I figured as much Kenna, but I still got in, *and* I managed to sneak into your massage as well." Damn! He got me on this one for sure, but that doesn't mean I can't get him next time. "Come on baby, let's get packed up, we don't have much time left before the shuttle to the airport arrives to pick us up."

We didn't make much of a mess, we mostly kept ourselves contained to the bedroom and bathroom. After I collect our toiletries I look at the pile of dirty clothes and then the few clean ones we have left and decide to put all the dirty things in one case and the clean and toiletries in the other. We make a sweep of the bungalow and pick up our phone chargers, which I put in my handbag, then we're done. It almost looks like we were never here, and I can't help the sadness that falls over me.

"We'll come back one day Kenna, I promise." I know Brady doesn't make promises he has no intention of keeping, but I think this one might be out of reach.

"Let's get out of here before we miss the shuttle." I say before the emotion drags me down.

"I love you Kenna." Brady says, then he kisses the breath out of me, and before I know it, we've locked the door, and we head towards the main office.

We open the door and hear raised voices, but it's not until we get closer to the office, that we realise whose raised voices we can hear through the closed door.

"It's none of your goddamned business Tomas!"

"I'm making it my business, *Samantha!*"

"Well, you have no god damned right, so shut the hell up and get out of my office. We've got guests to say goodbye to and you've got a golf cart to drive."

"Fine, but we'll finish this conversation when I get back."

"No Tomas, we won't, because there is nothing to discuss. This is my life, my private life, and it has nothing to do with you. You have no say in anything that I do away from the resort, ever."

"This isn't over."

"Yes, it is. Let's go."

The door to the office opens and Tomas storms out, heading straight for the bar, and I'm worried for a few seconds that he's going to down a shot, before getting behind the wheel of our golf cart. I know it sounds ridiculous, but it's still a vehicle of sorts.

I feel guilty when I see him snatch a set of keys out of the bartender's hands, and comes over to our small group. "Are you guys ready to go? You're our only guests leaving today." He says with a smile so forced he almost looks like he's in severe physical pain.

"Just give me a second, please?" I ask him and he nods.

I walk over to the reception counter where Samantha is standing, going behind the counter, I pull her into a tight hug. Then Brady joins us, a few seconds later Max, and Lee join in too. The only one not in the pile is Tomas.

"I'm sorry for ruining everything Samantha." Brady says.

"You didn't Brady. It was going to come out at some point, and now it has. It is what it is."

"You take care of yourself lady." I tell her.

"She's got us to look out for her Makenna, she'll be fine, we promise." Max says and Lee grunts which I take as his agreement.

"Let's go guys, otherwise you're going to miss your flight out of here." Tomas says softly.

The guys grab a bag each, and take them out to the cart.

"Take care of you Samantha." I tell her and give her one last hug.

"You take care of the two of you. Safe travel guys." She waves at us until we can't see her anymore.

Tomas is dead silent the entire trip to the airport, and it just doesn't feel right.

Chapter Twenty-six
BRADY

The silence in the cart on the way to the airport is deafening, and damned uncomfortable. I thought that I'd finally made peace with Tomas this morning on the boat. That we'd become, if not friends, certainly friendlier, but I think I really screwed up this time. I'm rarely that bad at judging people, and their feelings, but didn't come close to seeing that revelation coming out today.

"Tomas."

"Don't." Tomas says, and the anger in his voice is almost a proper growl more than actual words. Even Kenna flinches away from him. "I'm sorry Makenna."

"I'm sorry I invited him to join us, I shouldn't have, but he stepped out so that I could surprise Kenna, and I just thought, well I was wrong anyway."

"You thought you could make me think they liked each other and that I would make my move, but the thing is Brady, I've made my move. So many times, and she says no every time. No matter what I offer her, and now I guess I know why, because if Joey's her type, I'm definitely not. So, I should be thanking you for doing me a favour. I am sorry that you both had to witness the fallout, but it is what it is."

He pulls up at the airport without another word from any of us, jumps out of the cart before either

of us have a chance to move and gets our suitcases for us, walking towards the doors without a backwards glance.

"Tomas, you don't have to do that." I say.

"Yes I do, this is part of my job Mr Harris. You and your wife were guests at Sandy Cove. We're not friends, we're not even business associates at this point, but I am doing my job, because I'm damned good at it. There are reasons why there are rules in place against this kind of thing. Rules that Miss Holt herself put in place, and constantly reminds me of, and I've ignored them until now. She's right in this case, because I liked you and Mrs Harris, I let myself enjoy your company instead of keeping things separate and now, well I'm paying the price. I won't make that mistake again. Which, no doubt, will make Miss Holt very happy."

"And you miserable." Makenna says with hesitation.

"That's not true Mrs Harris. I love my job and I'm great at it. I have friends on the island, and I don't need more. I also need to stop chasing a woman who so obviously isn't interested and move on with my life." He doesn't sound very happy about his decision, despite his words. "It's funny, because I always thought that was part of the reason the owner pushed so hard for me to come here. She thought that Samantha and I would be great a fit, but now I see that she saw it for what it is. We both have our strengths, she wasn't wrong and that's what I'm going to concentrate on from now on."

"Tomas." Makenna says quietly. "She does feel the same way you do, she's just a little gun shy. Joey was over a long time ago."

"It doesn't matter anymore, Makenna." Tomas says with a shake of his head. "I hope you both enjoyed your stay at the Sandy Cove Resort and will recommend us to your friends. I will hand you over to Catherine here, and she'll get you checked into your flight home." He smiles at Catherine, they have a quick polite chat, and then he's walking back outside to the cart.

"Tomas!" Kenna yells out to him as he walks away.

"Have a safe flight home Mr and Mrs Harris, and congratulations on your marriage. I hope you're always happy." He says, without turning back to look at Makenna, and walking out the door, jumping in the cart. I assume he's heading back to the resort, but if I was him I'd be hitting a local bar and getting tanked.

"Mr and Mrs Harris, let's get you checked in, and heading home shall we?"

"Yes, let's do that." Makenna says without looking at me and I know she's blaming me for this, and she wouldn't be wrong.

I'm not going to apologise or defend myself anymore. Do I feel bad that I'm leaving them here to deal with the fallout? Hell yes, but there's not a lot either of us can do about that now. I hand over our passports and paperwork with a smile. When we're done and our baggage is checked in, we make our way to the terminal, and take a seat.

A few minutes later I can't stand it any longer. "Are you not talking to me now?"

"Hmmm? What? Ohhh because of the Samantha. Tomas thing?" I nod. "Am I annoyed? Yes, but not at you honey. You had no idea what you would be unleashing by inviting the masseuse to lunch. The truth is, we don't know these people very well if at all Brady. Tomas was right with what he said as he left here, we were just two guests at the resort that he works at, but that doesn't mean I'm not angry. My anger is with Tomas though honey, not you."

"Are you sure?"

"Absolutely! I guess we did step over the line between guest and friend there the last couple of days, and it's wild to think we spent less than a week here, but he crossed that line with us, and to leave the way he did, even though he's hurt and angry, *that* I'm annoyed at." She reaches up and kisses me. Not a simple peck to keep me happy, but a real, proper deep kiss that probably shouldn't happen in public. "Also, I'm tired. Someone kept me up late last night and then I was up early this morning." She says with a cheeky grin.

"You were up early? I was up earlier than you!"

"You woke me up, remember?'

"Well, if I had to be up early on our honeymoon, especially the last day, then so did you baby." It's my turn to lean over and give her a kiss, mine is a lot more appropriate for an airport, even though she tries her hardest to deepen the kiss.

Over the loudspeaker our flight is called, I rest my forehead on hers and sigh. "I guess this is it. Honeymoon is over baby, back to reality." I grab our carry-on bags, take her hand in mine, and lead her to the gate.

"It's not over yet Brady." She says with a wink. I don't know what she has planned, but I need sleep.

There's a heaviness in both of us as we board the plane and find our seats. We talk while the rest of the passengers are seated and Kenna rummages around in her handbag for something. She pulls out the pen from the gift shop and a notebook I didn't see her get, and puts it on the table in front of her. As soon as the seat belt light is off and we're cruising, I sit back and relax. Kenna's reading a book on her phone.

I settle back in to my chair and I close my eyes for minute, before I start reading my own book that I didn't touch while we were away, and the next thing I know I wake up covered with a blanket, and a pillow behind my head. I don't know whether Kenna did it or the flight attendant, but either way, it's evidence that I was completely passed out. I look over to see what Kenna's up to and I laugh, because now I know that the reality is, my wife didn't make me comfy. How do I know? Kenna is facing me, her eyes closed, and her phone is resting in her hand on her stomach.

"I'm glad to see you awake Mr Harris." The flight attendant smiles as she speaks to me. "Your wife hasn't been asleep for long, and I'm loathe to wake her, but I'm going to need to shortly. I'm giving her as long as I can."

"Is it OK for me to move around the cabin still?"

"Yes you still have about thirty minutes."

"Is it OK then if I wake her up?" I ask, with a smile.

"Of course it is, but no funny business Mr Harris." She informs me with what could only be described as a knowing smile.

"What do you mean?" I ask, my face as innocent as I can make it, and she laughs.

"Just do it quietly and as discreetly as possible. I don't want to have to come back here and reprimand you or separate you two." She gives me another smile that tells me she thinks she knows exactly what I'm planning and then leaves me alone with Kenna.

"Kenna. Baby, it's time to wake up." I say quietly, running my hand up and down her thigh. Above the blanket that she's wrapped up in.

"Not yet Brady. Please?" She mumbles in her sleep. She's so adorable, and if we were anywhere else, at any other time, I would have let her sleep, but I just can't give her more time. "More sleep." She mumbles.

"You can't sleep any more baby, the planes going to land soon, and I can't leave you here." I tell her gently as my hand travels a little further up her leg.

"Mmmm. If your hand keeps moving like that, I might be convinced to wake up!" She tells me with a smile on her face, and her voice a little less sleepy, but her eyes are still closed tight.

"Kenna, we can't do that, we're on a plane." I laugh.

"Didn't stop us last time." She smiles without opening her eyes, and wiggling in her seat. "Remember?" Oh I remember alright! I stand up, and then sit on the end of the 'bed' where she's got her legs curled up so there's a little bit of space. Then I lean my body over hers and she sucks in a breath and her body is wracked with a shudder.

"If you wake up now and don't cause a scene, I will ravish you when we get home." My whispered promise sends goose bumps down her neck.

"You promise?"

"Promise."

"You know my brother's will be there to see us, right? Logan's picking us up, right?"

"Change of plans, Caleb's picking us up."

"What? Since when?" Kenna asks, confused.

"Since Logan messaged to let me know the change of plans."

"Why didn't he message me?" I don't have an answer for her, so I just shrug my shoulders. "Whatever! You know they're still going to be at the house, right?"

"Yes I do, and once the cockblockers are gone, you're all mine baby, and I promise to make the wait worthwhile. You know I keep my promises." I say, then I lean in closer again, run my tongue over the shell of her ear and whisper, "I also deliver on my promises Kenna."

Before she can say or do anything, I move off her seat and smack her leg lightly.

"Ouch!" Her eyes snap open, giving me a look that might kill a lesser man, but it really just turns me on.

"That didn't hurt, and you know it! Now wake up properly, and get all your stuff together. We'll be landing shortly."

"You're mean Brady, and we haven't even been married for a week!" Kenna grumbles at me as she sits up, and the guy sitting in front of her snorts to cover up his laugh. The woman next to him, who I assume is his wife or girlfriend, sends a dirty look his way and he coughs to cover up his laughter.

I can't help laughing as well. "Well, we've been together a long time baby, guess you knew what you were getting in to before you signed the marriage certificate." I tell her as I move back into my seat.

"Maybe I want a refund." She's still grumpy, and a little wrinkled, but a lot adorable as she tried to force herself to wake up a bit more.

"You and I both know that isn't true. You love me too much to give me up baby." I can't help the grin that spreads across my face when I hear her mumbled reply.

"I wouldn't bet on that Mr Harris."

"My beautiful wife. You and I both know I could bet my last dollar on it." My Makenna, she's adorably grumpy when she first wakes up, which is one of the reasons I didn't want the flight attendant to do it. I doubt she'd get aggressive, but you never know.

Another smile spreads across my face as I hear her muttering to herself still, but she's packing up her stuff and folding up her blanket. Which is exactly what I wanted her to do.

I collect my things and put them in my backpack. A light touch on my shoulder makes me jump, knowing it's not Makenna because she's still grumbling to herself in her seat, I turn to find the flight attendant standing there.

"Sorry Mr Harris, I didn't mean to startle you. I just wanted to say thank you for waking your wife up and doing it without any disruptions." There's a sparkle in her eyes as she speaks to me.

"You're welcome. Just don't mention it to my wife, please? She'll be mortified if she thinks you even suspect what we got up to on the trip over."

"It's safe with us Mr Harris. Just be aware that it's generally not the thing to do, but you were pretty discreet about it." She gives me an appreciative once over then walks away.

"What was that about?" Makenna asks, from her seat, startling me again.

"She was just thanking me for waking you up and getting ourselves organised for landing, that's all."

"That look was *not* about thanking you for either of those things Brady Harris. She was quite openly checking you out!"

"So what if she was, Makenna? I didn't do anything about it, and I have no plans to. Let her look. There are two people, and two people only that can touch me in a way that turns me on."

"Oh yeah and who are they?" Like she has to damn well ask!

"Well, myself obviously." I answer and then I pause for effect. She's so damned easy to tease when she's just woken up and worked up! "And this gorgeous woman, who I've known for over half of my life and is the absolute love of my life." I lean over the divide between us and kiss her lips lightly. "Never doubt that for a second Makenna. I will always come home to you baby, and no-one else gets to touch me."

"Promise."

"Absolutely."

"Good."

"Right, so now that's sorted. Are you ready to be back home?"

"If I'm being honest, not really." She says with a laugh that's still a little husky from sleep. "I really enjoyed our time away. It's the first time I've truly relaxed in a couple of years, you know?" The sigh that escapes her lips is huge and full of emotion. "It's been a tough time, you know?" Her voice is so low, I almost don't hear her speak.

Reaching over the divide between us, I take her hand in mine. "I know Kenna, and I can't promise there won't be more hurdles of all kinds, but I will be there for you through every up and every down." I lean over, and bring her hand to my lips. "We'll be there for each other Kenna." I say against her hand.

"Promise?"

"Absolutely baby. Whatever comes along, we'll face it together."

That's a promise I don't plan on ever breaking. Unless I have no choice, but even then, it would take my own death to keep me from protecting her.

Chapter Twenty-seven
MAKENNA

I know, I know! We've been together for ever, and we *just* got married. I *know* I trust Brady, I know it without even thinking about it, but I just woke up and a flight attendant who *knows* he's married basically hits on him while I sit right next to him! Who does that? Talk about unprofessional!

I shouldn't need his reassurances, but they do make me feel better. That doesn't stop me from giving *her* a once over and a glare as we get off the plane. At least she has the good grace to blush slightly as she bids us farewell.

As we move along the walkway behind the other passengers towards the gate, I can feel Brady's body shaking behind me. I wait until we're in the airport walking towards baggage claim before I round on him.

"What's so funny Brady?"

He stops mid-step and looks at me, schooling his features. "Nothing. Absolutely nothing. Let's go find our bags and get out of here." His hand that is already holding mine, tightens its hold and he starts to walk again, but when I stay rooted to the spot he has to stop.

He turns to me, and this time, the frown on his face is genuine. "What's wrong Kenna?"

"What's so funny?"

"Nothing Kenna." He sighs, shaking his head. I just stand there looking at him. We're both tired and looking forward to being at home, in our house and our bed, but I still want him to answer me. So, I raise an eyebrow at him and try to untangle my hand from his, but he just holds on tighter. "Fine." He says sighing again. "If it makes you feel any better, I don't think that flight attendant is going to check out another, obviously married man or woman, again any time soon." Then he chuckles.

"You know, it's not about me being insecure with our relationship Brady. It's more about respect. Some people, men, and women alike, need to have more respect for others. We were obviously together, *and* she knew we were married, not mention returning home from our *honeymoon!* It's about simple respect!"

"I know that Kenna, I do, but there was no chance in hell she was getting anywhere with me, and truthfully, any guy that *does* let her get past simple politeness, to anything beyond a simple touch, then he doesn't deserve his wife or the flight attendant." He's absolutely right, but it still rankles me. "Come on, let's go home, and forget all about her, because I barely gave her a thought at the time, except to think that it was sad that she felt she could get away with it."

He pulls me to him and wraps his arm around my shoulder. "She had no chance" He whispers in my ear.

"I really hope Logan's already here. Now that we're here, I just want to go home."

"Caleb's picking us up, remember?" I screw my face up in distaste. I love my little brother, but he can be a bit flaky sometimes. "He'll be here on time, I promise."

"Don't make a promise you can't keep Brady. You and I both know there's a chance he won't be here yet." I smile at him and say, "You know he would have taken that flight attendant up on her offer with that perusal."

"Let it go Kenna." He admonishes me, but smiles anyway. "I have no doubt, but the difference is, he's not seeing anyone, which means he isn't engaged, or married, so that's his choice."

"He certainly lives his life." We stop at the baggage carousel, keeping an eye out for our suitcases. "Do you know if he's seeing someone?"

"Caleb?" I nod my head. "No, I have no clue. Why?"

"He's just been very quiet lately. You know he's either at work or home. I think he goes into town to have a few drinks with friends every now and then, but I haven't seen or heard him talk about a girl for a while."

"Maybe he's concentrating on the business?" Brady asks, and I can't decide if he knows something that I don't or not.

"Maybe. He does spend a lot of time in Vines. He doesn't have his eye on anyone in there, does he? Brady?" Suddenly, Brady seems very interested in finding our suitcases. "Brady! Does Caleb have his eye on someone who *works* for us? You have to tell me! That's not going to end well, for anyone, you know that right? I can't have him looking for his next lay with our staff Brady!"

He straightens up and looks me dead in the eyes, anger written all over his face. "You have such a low opinion of your little brother Kenna, and it's completely unwarranted. Has he had his fun while he was in school? Yes, but you know what? He had to deal with your parents death, just like you and Logan did, only you two have always stuck together and then treated him like a child. I think you need to re-evaluate your thoughts about him." He leaves me standing there to think about what he said about my little brother to get our suitcases. Before I know it, he's back with our things and directing me out the door. "He's working hard at Drake Wines, Kenna. He's trying to get you and Logan to treat him as an equal. You need to give him more of a chance. He knows what he's doing."

Before I can answer him, our names are called out and I look up to see the man in question smiling broadly. "Makenna. Brady. Over here!"

"I told you he'd be here Kenna. Have a little more faith in the man, because he is a man now, not a child you have to look after anymore." He smiles broadly back at my brother. "Caleb! Brother how are you man? Thanks for coming to pick us up."

"Well, I couldn't let you guys walk home now could I?" he says, slapping Brady on the shoulder. "Here give me Kenna's suitcase, I'm sure it's full and heavy with all of her purchases."

"Hey, I'm not that bad." I protest, as he takes my suitcase from Brady and pretends he can barely carry the damned thing. I sling my arm around his shoulders as we walk out the doors and into the fresh air. "Thanks for coming to get us Caleb. I appreciate it."

"You didn't think I'd be here, did you?" He asks, without a hint of irritation, or judgement. Which makes me feel even worse about what I said to Brady earlier. I look over towards my husband, who's grinning like an idiot. "She thought I'd forget didn't she?" He asks Brady, who shrugs his shoulders and keeps walking with his head down watching where he's walking. Caleb barks out a laugh. "Smart man!"

"I married your sister, I'm a fucking genius." He tells Caleb, as he reaches for me and takes my hand in his, then he pulls me in for a kiss that probably isn't quite appropriate for public.

"Ohhh gross! That's my sister dude!" He thumps Brady on the arm, and I feel Brady's smile on my lips as he pulls away from me. I'm left standing there for a few seconds, stunned, until Brady tugs on my hand to get me moving again. "I was hoping you two would have gotten all of that out of your system on your honeymoon." He says, waving his hand up and down, then in circles at us. "Obviously not though."

"I'll never get your sister out of my system Caleb, and when you find the woman you love, you'll feel exactly the same way." The smile that Brady gives my brother seems to hint at some knowledge that he has that I don't, and I don't like it. The fact that Caleb stumbles a step or two makes me even more suspicious. "Don't worry buddy, your time will come. Everyone falls eventually."

"What do you mean falls?" I ask curiously.

"I mean falls in love baby. Head over heels, arse over tit, helplessly in love." He declares, spinning me around, and then pulling me in for another kiss, just as we get to Caleb's car.

"Cut it out, you're making me feel ill man, and I was going to get dinner on the way." Caleb says, rubbing his stomach like he really does feel unwell.

"Where were you going to stop? Vines perhaps?" Brady asks.

"No!" Caleb says a little too quickly and loudly.

"Are you sleeping with a member of our staff Caleb?" I ask as Brady holds the door open for me. He gives me a look and shakes his head. Caleb, he rolls his eyes at me.

"No Makenna. I am *not* sleeping with one of *your* staff members." He jumps in the car and starts up the engine just as Brady jumps into the back seat with me. "No funny business in the back seat with my sister. Married or not, I don't want that visual or anything else, in my car thank you very much."

"It's *so* nice to be home Caleb." I say as I roll my eyes.

"It's nice to have you home Makenna." Caleb tells me, looking back at me in the rearview mirror.

"So, why didn't Logan come and get us?" I'm curious, sue me.

"He was busy." That's a little vague even for Caleb.

"Busy? Too busy to come and pick us up from the airport like he promised? Actually, he *told* me he would be here, I didn't ask him to."

"He just said he was busy and asked me to come and pick you guys up. I'm not irresponsible Makenna, I can be relied upon to get things done you know?"

"I know you can, I was just curious as to what might be the reason behind Logan going back on a promise. He never does that. Ever."

"We've got a lift home and that's all that matters Kenna." Brady says, resting his hand on my thigh, and shaking his head. "I'm sure that Logan has a valid reason for asking Caleb to come and get us."

"You're right." I agree, because I'll soon find out anyway when we get home, and I can ask him myself.

I rest my head on Brady's shoulder, and listen to the guys catch up for the rest of the drive home. They talk about everything and nothing and every now and then I join in, but my mind can't help wandering to all the things I'm going to have to catch up on when we start back at it tomorrow morning. I'm thinking about Caleb, and the fact that he *does* spend an extraordinary amount of time in Vines, and I wrack my brain trying to think of who he might be visiting in there.

Most of all, I worry about Logan. He may be the oldest, but he carries that weight on his shoulders way too seriously. Before our parents died, I don't think he really planned on working here, but now he spends almost every waking hour here, building it up better than our father ever could have hoped to. I'm grateful he has Jules, but I can see the strains of the workload that Logan takes on, creating cracks there too.

"Don't worry about a thing. Logan and I have busted our balls to keep on top of everything so that you wouldn't have to when you got back." He smiles at me as he pulls into the driveway of the main house and stops at the front door.

Home. I missed it, I truly did. I missed my brothers and Drake Wines as well, but I suddenly feel not ready for my break to be over.

The guys grab all our bags from the car. As I go to unlock the front door, it swings open and there stands my brother. "Logan! What are you doing here?"

"What? I can't be here to greet my sister and new brother home from their honeymoon?" He asks with a giant smile.

"Of course you can!" I answer him with a big smile of my own. "Give me a hug. You too Caleb."

"Oh now I get a hug? Earlier it was just all, 'I can't believe you're here on time to pick us up Cal.'" He whines, but he has a smile on his face and he's already enveloped us both in his arms. I reach over and leave a sloppy kiss on his cheek.

"I love you Caleb. Thank you for picking us up from the airport."

"You're welcome." He says as he steps back from us, wiping his cheek. "But you can keep the slobber for Brady, I just want your hugs, alright?"

"Deal." I say, putting my hand out for him to shake. When he places his hand in mine, I pull him to me and leave another sloppy, smacking kiss on his other cheek.

"Awww Kenna, that wasn't fair. I wasn't prepared."

"You should always be prepared when it comes to your sister." Brady laughs. "Now, help me bring in the bags please. I would like to come into my home and relax for a bit."

"We've got dinner all ready if you're hungry." Logan informs us.

"We?" I ask, knowing full well who I should expect to be cooking in my kitchen.

"Ahhh yeah, Jules is here." He says, rubbing the back of his neck nervously. "I hope you don't mind?"

"Mind? Of course not! Jules is always welcome here. He's family!" I say, as I move towards the kitchen. "Jules, has my brother got you chained to the kitchen sink again?"

"Makenna! Sweetheart, how are you?" Within seconds I'm engulfed in a warm embrace. "Let me look at you lady!" He holds me at arm's length to look me up and down. "Well, I think island life agreed with you Sweetheart! Any honeymoon surprises?" He asks, looking at my stomach.

"Jules! My man how the hell are you?" Brady asks as he enters the kitchen and embraces the man making us a family dinner, just as I whisper,

'One can only hope Jules.' That no one actually hears because the kitchen is suddenly filled with four men all talking over one another.

Brady smiles at me hopefully, over their heads and I feel a sharp pain in my heart, because I want to be able to tell him that we started a family while we were on our honey moon, but one, it's too soon to tell and two, I'm not sure that's in the cards for us. Not naturally anyway.

"Alright, let's get these two fed so that they can go to bed and reset their body clocks."

"Before you say another word Makenna." Logan starts. "You're not coming back to work until Monday, maybe Tuesday, we'll see. Caleb and I have kept on top of things, so there's no need for you to rush back. We can do it without you, not forever mind you, but we can definitely get by without you for a few more days."

"Logan, I want to get back to work."

"Well, you might want to, but I know for a fact that Brady has more time off, and I insist that you spend that time *together* before you have get back to the grindstone. Take some day trips, or even stay somewhere overnight. Enjoy the time off Kenna."

"Thank you Logan." I get up from my seat, and give him a squeezing hug. Then I move to Caleb and give him one too. "Thank you Caleb."

"No problems, just no more of those horrible kisses, OK?" He begs, but he's grinning like an idiot who actually likes those sloppy kisses.

When I get to Jules, and give him another almighty hug, he asks me, "What was that for gorgeous?"

"That was for cooking us dinner tonight, and for looking after my brother, probably both of them, while I was away."

"It wasn't like it was a chore Makenna." He says with a blush, and stealing a look at Logan, who I can guarantee isn't looking our way as he gets the dishes that he prepared with Jules for our meal. I really wish these two would get their shit together and just admit they're in a damned relationship, but Brady's made me promise not to push them, so I won't. For now anyway.

"Well, thank you anyway because I know my brothers can be a handful." His eyes light up with amusement and I realise what I just said and laugh. "You know what I mean."

"Come and eat. Then we can get out of your hair and let you rest." Logan says.

"Yeah, cause rest is what these two are going to do when we leave them alone together. Not!" Caleb says.

"That's enough Caleb." Logan scowls at our younger brother, and I swear if I didn't know that there was a marshmallow under that gruff, grumpy exterior, I would pee my pants when he sends *anyone* near me that look. "What they do in the privacy of their home has nothing to do with us. Not to mention, they're married now, so leave them the fuck alone."

Caleb only falters for a second under that stare, before he tells our brother exactly what he thinks. "Why don't you shut up Logan? I'm just teasing them. Why don't you take that stick out of your arse and learn to relax for once in your damned life."

"I'm so glad I came back home for this. You guys couldn't even wait for twenty four hours before you were bitching at each other." I say disappointed, looking between the two of them.

"Guys cut it out. You haven't behaved like this the entire time they were away, don't fall back into it now, please." Jules tells them gently. "Remember all the things you did for each other this week and how well you worked together." He looks between the two men and they both nod their heads and apologise to him! I haven't seen that since before my mother died, and I have to give Jules credit, that was impressive. "Now, let's enjoy dinner, and then we can leave the newlyweds to do whatever they please. Wherever they please."

There's quiet at the table for a few minutes, and I look over at Jules and mouth, 'thank you' to him. Which earns me a smile that is basically just a twitch of his lips and a curt nod.

Dinner goes smoothly, with easy conversation about our trip and what happened at Drake Wines while we were away.

When Jules dishes up dessert, Brady and I look at each other and smile. Chocolate cake of any kind, with a delicious chocolate sauce, will never be the same again after our stay at Sandy Cove, but will always mean sweet memories.

"Delicious, thank you Jules." Brady says smirking.

"There's a story there, and I don't want to know it." Caleb groans.

"Don't thank me. This delicious pile of yumminess is all thanks to Leila. She's the dessert queen, and I didn't want to insult her by not asking for one of her desserts."

I watch curiously as Caleb stiffens at the mention Leila, but Brady stops me from saying anything.

"Thanks Leila, you've brought back some delicious memories." He salutes the air towards Vines, with his spoon, and Caleb groans his discomfort again, causing me to laugh. I decide to just enjoy the night and the dessert. My questions can wait. As long as he doesn't get himself into any trouble before I can ask him what's going on.

"To Leila." Jules joins in Brady's cheer and we're all laughing, and talking again.

Chapter Twenty-eight
BRADY

Once I get Kenna off the subject of Leila, and the possibility that Caleb has a thing for her favourite employee, dinner goes really well. The guy has it bad for Leila, but I won't let Kenna get in his way. They're still dancing around each other, so I don't think that it's any of Kenna's business.

"Come on guys, let's let the newlyweds get to bed. They look like they're going to fall asleep on each other at the table." Logan announces, and I couldn't be more grateful. It's been a long day and I still have to call my parents. Like they can hear my thoughts, my phone starts ringing and when I look at the screen, my Mum's face is looking back at me.

"Sorry guys, I have to take this." I sent her a message to let her know that we'd landed safely and were home, but I should have called. "Hi Mum."

"Brady, are you and Makenna home safe?"

"Yes, sorry I didn't call sooner. Logan and Jules had dinner ready for us when we walked in the door."

"Well, I won't keep you from dinner. You can call me back later."

"No, they're all leaving now, just give me a second to say goodbye and I'm all yours."

"Here, let me talk to her while you say goodbye." Kenna says and I hand her my phone. "Hi Pauline, sorry we didn't call you sooner." I hear Kenna say as she walks into the kitchen to get away from the noise. My heart sinks a little for my Mum that Kenna's back to calling her Pauline.

"Hey, are you OK?" Logan asks, resting his hand on my shoulder.

"Yeah, of course just tired." I smile at him, knowing that I must look at least as half as exhausted as I feel.

"We'll get out of your hair so you can get some sleep." He says, embracing me tightly. "Welcome to the family Brady."

"He's always been part of the family, Logan, I've known him almost as long as I've known you!" Caleb says pushing Logan out of the way, and giving me a tight embrace of his own. Logan rolls his eyes, because in the real world there's no way Caleb would be able to move Logan out of the way if he didn't want to move.

"I meant it's official now, idiot." Logan growls.

"Stop calling your brother an idiot, he's far from it!" Jules admonishes him, and Logan actually mumbles an apology to Caleb. "Now, step back Caleb, it's my turn for the man hug." Next thing I know, Caleb is replaced with Jules and I feel like I'm everyone's favourite dessert being passed around. "Welcome home Brady."

"Thank you, and thank you for dinner." I tell him as we separate.

"Hey, I helped." Logan protests.

"I think we all know that's a stretch, Logan, but if it makes you feel better, yes you helped with dinner. You supervised." Jules smirks.

"I did more than supervise." Logan murmurs and Jules blushes. I can't help but wonder if those two realise that they're not actually hiding anything from anyone? They're as bad as Caleb at keeping their feelings under wraps. Which means, they're not succeeding.

"Well, thanks again for picking us up Caleb, and thanks for organising dinner for us, Logan and Jules. It was very much appreciated, I can assure you. You are now forgiven for not picking us up like we'd organised." I say looking pointedly at Logan. I think I can work out why he was, 'too busy', and I think Kenna did too. "I'm going to save both my Mum and Kenna from their conversation. I'll send her out here to say goodbye."

I walk into the kitchen just in time to hear Makenna laugh at something my Mum says. "You know Pauline, Mum, I love Brady with all of my heart, but I think I had better warn Beth to keep her distance from her brother for a while." She's silent for a few seconds and then she says, "Don't tell Beth, or Brady for that matter, but those shirts and shorts were close to being the highlight of my honeymoon. He looked so uncomfortable, and yet so handsome in them. The combination made him irresistible." Another laugh rings out and makes me happy. "I know, I know! Beth must never know that she made Brady uncomfortable for even a second, but I sure am going to tell her every chance I get that she made her brother even more attractive to me." Her next laugh turns into a large yawn, and I hear Logan yell at Caleb for something else. That's when I decide that this night needs to come to a close.

"Hey, Kenna?" I say quietly, as I walk up behind her to touch her shoulder. She jumps, but I don't think I scared her too badly.

"I didn't see you there."

"I know." I smile at her. "Your brother's, and Jules want to say goodnight. So hand my Mum back to me and go talk to them."

"Mum? Yeah I'm sorry, I have to go say goodnight to the boys. I'll hand you over to Brady with a promise to come see you guys tomorrow." She's silent for a second, her eyes never leaving mine. "Goodnight, love you too." I reach out to take the phone and kiss Kenna gently on the cheek.

As another yawn shudders through her body, I give her butt a light tap and push her towards the door, as voices raise again. "Go on, get them out of here and make sure you lock the door behind them."

"They have a key." She says smiling and leaving a kiss of her own on my lips, making me want more, but knowing we both need the sleep.

I watch her walk away and as she gets to the doorway, I hear her say, "What's with the loud voices? I was on the phone you know, and now Brady's on the phone with his Mum. Do you want her to think he married into a family of Neanderthals?"

I can hear Caleb's snort from here, but then the door closes behind her and all I can hear are muffled voices and protests.

"Hey Ma, I'm sorry we didn't call you as soon as we got in." I apologise, because I feel terrible, even though I did send her a message to say that we had landed, we were safe, and that I'd call her when we got home. The only snag being, I didn't know that Jules and Logan were cooking us dinner.

"That's more than OK Brady, you let us know you were home safe, and that's all that matters to me. Makenna already explained that when you got home Logan, and Jules had already organised dinner for you. You can't say no to that. Especially when Jules is cooking." Ma sighs like she's actually missed out on good food, and I can't help laughing.

"Are you good there Ma? Should I tell Dad that you've got a little crush on Jules?" I laugh.

"I think we both know that I'm not his type, age aside, Brady." She chuckles. "That being said that man can cook! He's wasting his skills playing with numbers all day!"

I can't help the burst of laughter that escapes me. "You know, I think he's pretty happy 'playing with numbers all day', as you put it. I think he likes cooking for those that he loves. He gets a joy out of feeding his friends and family. I'm just grateful that includes us."

"You're his family Brady." She says quietly, not saying what everyone knows but doesn't say out loud.

"Yeah, I know." I reply sadly, because I just want them to be happy. "Anyway, we're home and Logan told Kenna under no circumstances was she to head into her office before Monday, so we have all weekend to catch up with you." I tell her, knowing it will make her happy and take us away from a subject that is the worst kept secret in the family. "I'll talk to Kenna tomorrow and let you know what's going on. I think we might do dinner for everyone, maybe."

My Mum lets out a loud laugh and says, "You'd better check that with your *wife* kiddo. I'm sure she won't disagree, but you should give her some time to relax too." She's still chuckling like I have a lot to learn about married life, but I don't view our life as any different to before we were married. We were already living together, now we just have rings and a piece of paper to say we're married. "We're happy to just have you guys here for lunch, if you want to keep dinner for your friends Brady."

"Sure but I want you guys to come over. I'll talk to Kenna and see what she says, and then I'll let you and Dad know. Is that OK, or did you have plans?"

"Ohhh there's nothing we can't move around if you want us over Brady. We want to see you kids since you've been away." She says, and I can hear the smile in her voice. "You sound exhausted, so I'm going to let you go and get some sleep. We can talk about details later Brady. Tell Makenna we said goodnight."

"Goodnight Mum. Tell Dad we said hi."

"I will Brady. Goodnight."

"Hey Mum." I catch her before she hangs up.

"Yes darling?"

"I just." I take a deep breath. "I wanted to thank you."

"For what darling?" She asks, sounding confused.

"Well, for everything really. Taking the Drake's in after the accident for sure, but also for being there for all of us."

"You never have to thank us for that Brady."

"I know, but I want you to know that I appreciate it, and I know that Makenna and the boys do too."

"We know they do Brady. It's what April and Jack would have wanted, and they would have done the same for you and your sister, if god forbid, it happened the other way around." She takes a deep breath to steady her voice. "It's never been a hardship. April and Jack did all the hard work, I just wish they could have seen their kids happy and settled before they left us."

"That may be true, but you've helped them all so much since they lost them, and I know we're all grateful." I take another breath and continue with what I really wanted to say. "I really wanted to thank you for the trip. Without you guys and the Drake's, we would have never done that."

"Did you and Makenna enjoy yourselves?"

"We had the best time." I can feel the smile spread across my face. "We met some amazing people, that took us on some amazing trips. I can't thank you enough for that."

"You're more than welcome Brady. It was the least we could do, it was especially wonderful to be able to give Makenna something from her parents." I can hear the emotion in her voice, and I know if I let her get too emotional, I won't be far behind her.

"Well, that's all I wanted to say." I say, coughing to get the emotion out of my voice. I look up to see Kenna walking back into the kitchen and she tilts her head at me, silently asking if I'm OK. I nod my head yes. "I love you Ma, we'll see you soon."

"We love you too Brady."

"Night Ma." Kenna yells out so that she can hear her. "Tell Pops goodnight too."

I hit the speaker button so that they can hear each other, as Mum says, "Goodnight Makenna darling, we love you."

"Love you too Ma." Kenna says as she wraps her arms around my waist, resting her head on my chest. She closes her eyes and sighs.

I hear my Mum suck in a breath at Kenna's use of the word Ma and the affection in her voice. "Goodnight Ma, we'll talk tomorrow. Kenna's asleep on her feet, so I'm going to tuck her up tight in bed and get some sleep."

"We'll talk later then darling. You both get some rest."

"See ya."

"Bye." Kenna mumbles a last goodbye, but I wasn't joking when I told Mum she was almost asleep right here. I hang up and pocket my phone, then sweep Kenna up into my arms.

"Didn't you already carry me over a threshold Brady?" She asks sleepily, a small smile on her face, as she snuggles further into my chest and her arms loop around my neck.

"Into the bungalow yes, but your brothers made sure I didn't get to do it into our home baby, and I want to do this right." I say quietly in her ear.

"It's too cold out there now honey, can't it wait until tomorrow? Or another day?" I love it when she gets all soft and cuddly, because she starts calling me honey instead of Brady.

"It *could* wait, yes, but instead of doing the front door threshold, I plan on doing our bedroom threshold tonight. How does that sound?"

"Perfect. You're perfect Brady Harris." She sighs, and starts leaving light, sweet kisses on my neck.

"You know, if you keep doing that, not only will you *not* be sleeping too soon, *but* you'll be screaming my name for the entire property to hear." I smile against the side of her head.

"I don't think I could even if we tried tonight, I'm sorry honey." She says on a sigh.

"Are you *challenging* me to make you come baby?"

A small giggle escapes her lips, but her eyes remain closed. "Not at all Brady." She yawns, and her eyes tear up. "Maybe we can test that theory in the morning?"

"Which one Kenna?" I ask as I put her on her feet, leaving her arms around my neck to keep her upright, so that I can undress her.

"Everyone on the property can hear me scream your name." She sighs again as I lift her now naked body and lay her down on the bed, pulling the covers over her. "You're coming to bed too, right?"

"I'll be here in a few minutes. I just want to check everything is locked up and turn off all the lights."

"We could have done that." She tells me, her voice quieter than it was just a minute ago.

"We could have, but I wanted to get you into bed." I turn off the lamp that we left on earlier and the room goes dark.

"Of course you did!" She giggles. "I love you Brady."

"I love you too Kenna, now get some sleep. I promise I won't be long." I kiss her on the forehead and walk to the doorway, look back and watch her as she snuggles deeper into the covers and smiles.

Walking quietly through the house, I make sure all the doors and windows are locked. I mean the only people who come here unannounced, always let themselves in with their keys, making my efforts almost unnecessary. I laugh quietly as I turn all the lights off on my way back to our bedroom. I take a second to take in my sleeping wife before I turn off the hallway light. She's adorable, sexy, smart, and she's all fucking mine. I make quick work of stripping out of my clothes, and gently slide under the covers, pulling Kenna into me. She wiggles her butt slightly, making my cock stand to attention as always when I'm near her.

I'm exhausted, but happy. I'm home, in our bed with my *wife*. It doesn't get better than this.

Chapter Twenty-nine
MAKENNA

"Mmmmm Brady." I move to stretch, reaching out to touch him, only to discover I can't move, because there's something between my legs stopping me. I'm not awake enough to work out what it is, and I don't want to open my eyes, I'm too busy trying to keep this very realistic dream alive.

"It's no dream baby." Brady's husky morning voice says from the other end of the bed, his warm breath sending a chill over my wet pussy, making me shiver. I try to move again, but his hands are on the inside of my knees, pushing them down onto the bed, spreading me out for his enjoyment. And mine! "Morning Kenna." He says against my clit, causing vibrations to ripple through my body.

"What." It's not a question, it's just one word. I'm not actually capable of stringing more than that one word together, because Brady runs his tongue through my pussy lips, stopping just short of my clit. He pauses for second and I take a deep breath that gets stuck in my throat, because a split second later he sucks my clit into his mouth, gently biting it as he does. "Fuck!" My hips are trying to buck up off the bed, I'm not sure whether they're searching for more, or to get away from his ministrations. When he pushes two fingers in my pussy, and twitches them in just the right come hither way, in *that spot,* I feel like I'm leaving my body behind as I come so hard, I swear I black out for a few seconds. "Holy fuck Brady!"

I can't say anything else, because his lips are on mine, begging for access to kiss me deeper. I couldn't resist even if I wanted to, as my lips open and I draw his tongue into my mouth and suck on it. I can taste myself on his tongue and his lips, and it's so erotic I can barely breathe.

"Brady, let me breathe." He pulls his lips from mine and starts to kiss down the side of my neck, as he pushes his cock into me, and he stills. We both let out a deep, pleasured sigh and our bodies collide. We're as close as two human beings can be, and I want to relish it, take our time.

"Kenna." My name is barely a breath on his lips. "You feel so fucking good, baby."

Reaching up I take his face in my hands, and pull his lips to mine, kissing him softly a couple of times. "Make love to me Brady."

"Every. Damned. Day." He says each word punctuation with him drawing out and pushing back into my pussy, and I'm already right on the edge of another orgasm.

"Yes." I hiss out between my teeth. "Yes!"

"Kenna. Please tell me you're close, baby." He grunts out between each push back into my pussy. He *must* be able to feel my pussy gripping his cock, surely?

"So close, Brady. So. Fucking. Close."

"Me too." He growls. "So. Fucking. Close. Now!" Then, even though it doesn't happen very often, we come together in a loud mumbling of incomprehensible nonsense.

Brady collapses on top of me, and I wrap my arms and legs around him, not wanting to let him go, ever.

He rolls us over, until I'm top of him, but we're still joined together.

"Ummmm. So guys?" Caleb coughs outside the bedroom door. "Now that you guys are awake, would you like to join the rest of us for lunch?"

Lunch? I look over to Brady's phone on the bedside table and see that it is in fact, after midday! Then it hits me what he said.

"What do you mean, 'the rest of us'?" I scream at him through the door.

"Ahhh well." I can picture him rubbing his hand over his face, even though there's a solid door between us.

"Caleb." I ground out. "Who else is here, or coming here?"

"Well, it would appear that only you two are *coming,* here, and boy aren't I glad I'm the one who discovered that?" He mumbles, but I can still hear him. "I really hate it when I get outvoted on things in this family. Truly fucking hate it!"

"Who else is here, Caleb?' I demand.

"Well, you'll be happy to know that only your brothers and Jules are here at the moment." He pauses for a second and then continues. "Phew, it would seem like your parents *just* arrived Brady, and I'm sure we can all agree, that was a blessing."

"What's taking so long?" I hear Logan's booming voice outside the door, but he's obviously further away. "Why are you standing outside of the door Caleb? You're meant to be making sure they're getting up and moving."

"Ohhh, believe me they were up *and* moving big brother." Caleb tells him with a laugh.

I look down at Brady, because his entire body is shaking with barely held in laughter, but I can't get off him, because his arms are around me so tight, I imagine it's what being held in a vice feels like.

"This isn't funny Brady!"

Before he can say anything, not that I'm sure he could through his laughter, Logan's voice booms out again.

"What the hell are you talking about Caleb? Are they up or not?"

"Well, after all that, I don't think Brady could possibly be *up* anymore, but feel free to ask him."

"I will, because you're not really helping." The door handle moves, and Caleb's laughter gets louder.

"NO!" Brady and I shout together, and the door stops moving.

"I'm telling you bro, I don't think you want to go in there. Not unless you want to see your sister in some kind of position you'll need to bleach your eyes after."

"What are you talking about?" Logan demands, and I can see imagine the face Caleb gives him as Logan starts to stutter out words. "Ohh! You mean? Ohhh! Fuck!"

"Exactly!" Caleb laughs. "We'll see you downstairs when you're ready." He yells as he walks away.

"Ahh Jesus! I didn't need to know that!"

"Imagine walking up here to hear them finish." Caleb says, the amusement in his voice very clear, and we hear a loud slap. "Believe me, you dodged a fucking bullet, and it's the last time I'm going to find them for anything. You got that?" It obviously wasn't Logan hitting Caleb, otherwise he would have screamed and been calling him an arsehole by now.

"Yeah, sure." Logan answers him, as their voices get further and further away.

"Fuck me!" I say as I bury my face in Brady's chest.

"Already did that, but hey, if you want, I think I can manage another round in a couple of minutes." He laughs when I look up to give him a look that could kill, and I punch him in the shoulder. "Ouch!"

"Your parents are here Brady!"

"Yeah, but they didn't hear anything, and I'm sure Ma would just be happy because she wants grandbabies."

"I'm going to have a quick shower."

"I'll join you."

"No, you won't. You can wait until I'm done."

"What? Why?" He looks so genuinely taken aback, and confused, I can't help laughing, despite the circumstances.

"Because, if we get in there together, who knows who Logan might send up here to hurry us up, but they'll get another performance." He lets out another loud, booming laugh, like it's all OK because it was just Caleb. "What if he sends your Dad or your *Mum* up to get us next time?"

That shuts him up pretty quick. "Yeah, OK. You're right. Hurry up and that gorgeous butt clean then."

I clamber off him in a most uncoordinated, and unladylike fashion, causing him to grunt as I press down on his stomach to get some leverage to stand up. "Sorry."

I don't wait to hear his reply, I make my way into the bathroom, turn on the shower to warm up the water, go to the bathroom, and then finally, get under the nice warm stream of water. I stand there for a minute, just soaking it in, and then sigh, because I know I have to get a move on, otherwise I'm going to get a visitor, and I can guarantee, it will end well! I wash my hair, and my body, then step back into the water to rinse off. When I open my eyes, Brady's standing in the doorway, leaning against the doorframe, just watching.

"Umm whatcha doing?" I ask him, as I pour some conditioner into my hand and start to rub it into my hair.

"Just watching." He states simply.

"Just watching? Watching what?" I ask, curious.

"Watching the beauty that is my wife, wash herself." I grunt in reply and shake my head. "You ladies will never get just how fucking sexy you are with water and soap suds streaming down your bodies."

"Uhuh." I reply, but I think we *can* understand, because we watch men in the shower for the same damned reason. At least, that's why I watch Brady shower anyway. Not sure about other women with their men. So, I decide to put on a proper show for him, seeing as how he's already watching, and I soap myself up to the point where you can barely see skin, before stepping back into the water to rinse both my hair, as well as my body.

Brady groans loudly and I try not to laugh. I don't hear him move, the first I know about it is when his hands grip my hips, making me jump in surprise. My eyes snap open and then blink rapidly as I move my head out of the water. The shower is a glass cubicle, there's no door, so there was no change in the air when he joined me.

"Holy crap Brady!" I squeal, slapping both hands on his chest to steady myself.

"It's good to know that I haven't wasted my time on my ninja training sessions." I raise my eyebrow at him. "Not to mention your eyes were closed, and your head was under the water. That might have helped my cause."

"You're an idiot." I say, laughing at his ridiculous story. "I'm clean, so I'm getting out now."

"Stay." He says, but it's really more of a question. "Please?"

The pleading in his voice almost does me in. Until I remember his parents are waiting for us to join them in the kitchen. "Not happening Brady."

"It was worth a shot." He says, with a shrug of his shoulders, as I walk out of the shower, and grab myself a towel.

"You have to try honey, or you'll never know." I agree with him. I manage to get away and out the door fast enough that he doesn't manage to swat me on the butt. "I saw your shadow move."

"Well, fuck it!" He mumbles and I laugh, leaving him to wash his gorgeous body in peace.

I finish dressing, as the shower turns off, and I walk into the bathroom, this time it's my turn to lean against the doorframe to watch as he dries himself off. I may need that towel back to wipe the drool off my face.

He turns around to find me watching him, and a cheeky smirk spreads across his face. "Enjoying the show baby?"

I feel my cheeks blush, but I don't know why they would. I mean sure, I got caught ogling him, but he's my *husband,* not some random dude! "Always." Then I hang up my towel, and start blow drying my hair. I'm not watching him, because he's too damned distracting, so I don't realise he's moving towards me until he's right behind me. His hands grip my hips, as he rains kisses along my neck, and without permission, my head stretches to the side to give him better access. He's warm and a little damp from his shower, and I want so badly to fall back into his warm embrace, but I pull myself away. "We can't Brady."

"I know, but I couldn't resist. You look so sexy."

I snort out a laugh. "I'm just standing here drying my hair Brady. I've done it a thousand, if not a million times."

"Yeah, I know and you're sexy every time." He says seriously, and then he's gone.

I shake my head at his statement, he's crazy! I put all my things away and walk back into the bedroom, to find him pulling on a pair of jeans.

"Please tell me you're going to wear a 'holiday' shirt." I ask him as he picks up a shirt and starts putting it on, a huge smirk across his face.

"Of course baby!"

"Great! I'll meet you in the kitchen, I want to see the looks on everyone's faces when they first see you." I walk out the door, and head towards the kitchen without waiting for his reply. I seriously hope that Beth is joining us for lunch today, because I want to see the shock on her face when she realises her little joke definitely backfired on her, but I love it!

Chapter Thirty
BRADY

I pull on one of the shirts my sister packed for me, as I watch Kenna walk out the door. I really hope that Beth is in the kitchen, because I want to show her that she can't get one up on me. I actually learned to really love those shirts while we were away. I sit down on the edge of the bed to put on my shoes and then walk towards the kitchen. I can hear people talking and I slow my steps to see if I can work out who is actually here.

My smile widens when I hear Jake, my brother in law talking to Kenna, because if Jake's here, Beth's here.

"Son! It's good to see you!" My Dad says, hauling me into a very warm embrace. It's only been a few days since I saw my folks, but I really missed them, which makes me look over at Kenna, because her parents can't be here to welcome us home. There's a sadness in her eyes, but my Mum wraps her up in an embrace as well.

"It's good to see you Dad." I walk over to my wife and Mum, and envelope them both in a hug. "You too Mum."

"Oh my lord, you *actually* wore the shirts?" My sister squeals, as she enters the kitchen, and everyone else breaks out laughing.

"He wore a different one every day." Kenna tells her. "He even wore the shorts out a couple of days." The shocked look on Beth's face is worth the laughter coming from Jules and Kenna's brothers.

"You look like an idiot." Caleb says between gasping breaths of laughter.

"I think he looks handsome, and sexy. A man who is secure in himself is very attractive and sexy. You could learn a thing or two off my husband Caleb. You've got to be secure in your masculinity little bro, the chicks dig that more than anything else you could do or be." She looks towards where

Logan is standing with Jules. "So do the guys." She says, without actually still looking at the two guys, and they remain oblivious somehow.

"You actually wore them? Outside? In *public*?" Beth shrieks! "I didn't mean for you to wear them in *public* Brady! Oh my lord, I am *so* sorry Makenna!" My sister looks horrified, but when I look at Jake standing beside her, I start to think that she's actually playing us with this act.

"Relax Beth, they were fine. If it makes you feel any better, I was pissed when I first opened my suitcase and there were these shirts with matching shorts on top. I thought that was all you'd packed for me, but Kenna made me see it for what it was."

"And what, pray tell, was that?" She asks, the horror still in her voice.

"I look good in them." Everyone but my sister breaks out into raucous laughter. I can't help the smile that spreads across my face, because I just got one up on my sister who thinks she's so damned smart!

"Well, I'm glad you liked them." She says, her voice full of disappointment.

I walk over and wrap her up in a tight hug, *very* tight hug. 'Thanks for packing my suitcase Bethy." I say loud enough for everyone to hear me, and then I whisper in her ear, "You wanted to ruin my honeymoon? Seriously Beth, that's a low fucking blow, even for you." She starts to protest, but I just squeeze her a little tighter. "You're lucky that Kenna liked them."

I pull back, and step away from her. "It was meant to be a joke Brady, I didn't mean anything else."

"Yeah, I know, and now we're all laughing." I walk by her to get to the fridge. "Watch your back Bethy." It's not a threat it's a promise. One we've been giving each other for years, and I feel great satisfaction as I watch her swallow deeply. Standing beside her, Jake just laughs.

"You brought whatever he does next on yourself Beth. You two need to stop doing this shit, seriously. There are going to be kids running around here soon!" He says, shaking his head at our stupid one upmanship in our pranking war. Maybe he's right, but I'm going to let Beth watch over her shoulder for a while before I actually agree with him, and propose a ceasefire.

"Are you two still carrying on with this nonsense?" Mum tuts at us both.

"Nah, we're done now Mum, it's childish and ridiculous." I'm staring right at my sister and I can see she doesn't believe or trust me, and that's just where I want her to be.

"Come on, let's eat!" Jules announces.

"Did you cook something Jules?" Mum asks.

"I did Mrs Harris."

"Pauline, please. I think we've known each other long enough for us to be on a first name basis Jules, don't you?" Jules beams back at her.

"Of course, Pauline." He nods. "Logan helped me yesterday. We were cooking all afternoon so that the newlyweds had the fridge stocked and they'd have something to eat without having to leave the house."

"That's so sweet Jules, and Logan. I'm sure they appreciate the effort and the thought."

"I'm not sure they've noticed yet Pauline." Jules says with a laugh, and Logan grimaces.

"Why not?"

"Because we haven't had any need to check for food yet Ma. The guys had dinner ready for us last night and now, well we got woken up to join everyone for lunch." She nods her agreement, but she looks like she thinks she missed something. "Come on, let's eat." I announce and everyone moves to help Logan and Jules set the table and put out the amazing spread of food.

The conversation flows around the table. Makenna and I regale our family of stories from our trip, excluding all the time we spent together naked, obviously. I know her brothers seem to have a radar for knowing when we're having sex, and they choose those times for visits, but I highly doubt they want to hear about any of the action. I know I don't want to share any of those details while my parents and sister are listening.

When Kenna gets out her phone to show Ma some of the photos from our whale watching trip, I get up and start cleaning the dishes. Beth starts helping me, and no-one moves to stop her.

Beth and I start to fill the dishwasher that, on days like today, I'm glad it's one of the things we included when we remodelled the house.

"You know I only did it for fun, right?" Beth says quietly, so no-one else can hear her.

"Hmmm?" I say, concentrating on the dishes and not looking at her.

"The Hawaiian shirts and shorts." She obviously feels the need to explain, even though I'm positive we both know what she's talking about. "They were for a bit of fun, I never expected you to actually wear them, and I made sure you had plenty of other clothes to wear."

"You bet." I say, smiling at her.

"So, we're good?"

"We're great, Beth."

"I thought you were going to be *so* mad when you got home." She chuckles softly. "To be honest, I was expecting a few angry texts when you first discovered them, and when they didn't come, I figured you'd wait until you got home to yell at me."

"Like I said, my wife found them attractive, and I wasn't the only one wearing them on the island, so it was fine."

"Good, I'm glad."

We finish the rest of the dishes in silence, then as we're walking back into the dining room to join the others, I walk beside my sister, and sling an arm around her shoulders and bring her in close so that I can whisper in her ear.

"I'll get you back when you least expect it, trust me Sis." She stops walking, while I keep heading towards Makenna, and take my seat next to her, pulling her into my side.

"What did you say to Beth?" She asks quietly, looking towards Beth is still standing.

"Nothing, nothing at all. Why do you ask?" I ask with a satisfied smile.

"Why? Because she's still standing where you left her, and she looks a little scared."

"She's fine." I kiss Kenna on the cheek and join in the conversation around the table. After a few minutes, at Jake's insistence, Beth joins us all back at the table, but she never really settles back into comfortable conversation.

Almost an hour later, everyone is starting to say they should be getting back to work and life. Thank the heavens, because I want the house and my wife to myself for a while. Mum gives myself and Kenna another tight hug, and big sloppy kisses on the cheek.

"OK Ma let Kenna go. It's not like you're never going to see us again, we're home now." I laugh, as Dad pushes between his wife and mine to give her a bear hug. He whispers something in her ear, and I see tears well up in her eyes, she holds on tighter to the old man. I can't bring myself to part them, so I drape an arm over my mum's shoulders and start to walk her to the door.

"Subtle son." She laughs as we walk. "Come on Jeremy, I think we've outstayed our welcome. You too boys, let's leave the honeymooners in peace."

"Didn't they just come *back* from their honeymoon?" Caleb mumbles.

"Yes, but they still have a few days off, so you'll leave them in peace Caleb." Logan admonishes his brother. We'll be lucky if they're not *both* back here tonight for dinner, I can promise you that! "For now, we *both* have jobs to do, so let's get back to it."

They both give me a man hug, and then give Kenna a tight squeeze each. Jules has hung back a little, until I pull him in for a man hug of our own, then Kenna gives him a tight hug as well.

"Thank you for thinking about making us a few meals Jules, we really appreciate it. It's definitely more delicious than the takeaway we would have gotten. Especially last night." Kenna says, and kisses his cheek, causing Jules to blush a deep red.

"You're welcome any time." He replies before leaving with Logan, and heading towards Logan's place. Caleb, funnily enough, heads towards Vines. Mum gives us both another hug, before getting in the car with Dad and slowly driving off the property, waving until we can't see her any more.

"Well, that was lunch I guess." I state obviously.

"You think?" Kenna laughs. "That was nice. It was great to see the family, and I swear I might talk to Logan about hiring Jules for Vines at some point." I'm not sure if she's serious or not but I feel obligated to tell her that Jules already has a job, one that he seems to enjoy.

"So." I say, gathering her up in my arms, pulling her back to my front as we stand in the middle of the living room. "We've got a couple of free days ahead of us, what do you want to do?" I know she's burning to get back to work, but I'm with Logan on this one, she deserve the break. I'll still take her up the coast for a few days if I need to.

'Honestly?"

"Of course."

"I'd rather stay home. Mostly anyway." I look at her and raise an eyebrow. "No, not because we're close to work so that I can slip easily into the office. I just want to stay home. We've been away for the better part of a week, and I just want to enjoy being *home*." She turns in my arms, snaking her arms around my waist, and resting her cheek on my chest. "I want to spend some alone time with my husband."

"That I can help you with, baby." I say kissing her on top of the head. "So, what did you want to do this afternoon then?" I could make a few suggestions, but I figure she already knows those!

"We could go back to bed." Maybe she is thinking the same way I am.

"Now, I'm liking that suggestion."

"It wasn't code for sex Brady. I'm tired. Really tired and I feel like having a nap."

"Let's get you to bed then." I say, stepping out of our embrace, taking her hand in mine, and leading her back to the bedroom. "Strip!" I tell her while I waggle my eyebrows at her, making her laugh, and roll her eyes, as she sheds her clothes, leaving on her underwear and a singlet. It looks like she had this planned from the beginning!

"I told you, no funny business. Honestly, I need a nap." She says as a yawn conveniently escapes her.

"Come on then." I say, kicking off my shoes, and leading her to the bed. Both of us lie down, and I pull her into my side. Snuggling in close, she drapes an arm over my waist, and rests her head in the crook of my arm. Before I can ask if she's comfy, she's snoring, and I laugh, she really was tired!

I lie with her for about twenty minutes, and for half of those, I have my eyes closed as well, figuring I might as well try to get some rest as well, but I'm just not tired. So, while I'm lying there trying to work out how to get out from under my sleeping wife without waking her, she does it for me by rolling over to face away from me. Before she can wriggle her butt back into my body, I slide off the bed.

I watch, amused as Kenna wiggles back a bit, and when she doesn't find me there, she sighs and settles into the bed, sleeping soundly. I realise I'm standing here just staring at her sleeping, and it feels kind of creepy.

I head back to where we dumped our bags last night in the living room and drag them into the laundry. I open up both cases, and pull out the dirty clothes, throwing them in the washing machine. Once that's going I take Kenna's bag full of gifts, and set it on the dining table. I guess today's lunch would have been the perfect time for her to give them out, but neither of us thought about it.

With the washing going, the bags kind of tidied up and the kitchen clean after lunch, I decide to lie on the couch and catch up on some of the TV I missed while were away.

That's where Kenna finds me when she wakes up.

Chapter Thirty-one
MAKENNA

Waking up in the bed alone is cold, I miss the warmth of Brady's body next to mine. I strain to hear if the shower is running or if I can hear Brady moving around, but there's only silence. With a final stretch, and a low growl, I head to the bathroom, do what needs to be done, then I get dressed.

The search for my husband finds me standing in the living room watching him snore quietly, lying on his back, book flat on his chest, and his mouth slightly open. He's a sight to behold honestly. I could be offended that he didn't stay in bed with me if he was just going to sleep anyway, but I know him pretty well, and I'm going to assume he tried to sleep, but he couldn't so he came down here so that he didn't disturb me.

I leave him where he is, and head into the kitchen looking for some of the leftovers from the lunch that Jules made for us, and a drink. I close the fridge door and almost have a heart attack, and almost dropping the can of drink in my hand, when there's someone standing there. Logically I know it can *only* be Brady, but it takes a few seconds for my brain to catch up!

"Did you enjoy watching me sleep, you pervy girl?" He asks, that sexy smirk on his lips, and a still half asleep look on his handsome face.

"Holy crap Brady! You scared the shit out of me." I put my drink on the bench beside the fridge, my other hand is on my heart.

"I didn't mean to scare you Kenna. Who else did you think it could be standing here?" He asks on a chuckle.

"Well, considering the last time I saw you, you were snoring quietly on the couch, I didn't expect you to be standing there. The fact is, with the way my brothers walk in here any time they like, it could have been one of them I suppose." He nods in agreement. "Who the hell just stands behind the fridge door anyway? You can't tell me you didn't think you being there *wouldn't* scare the shit out of me Brady!"

The smirk spreads further across his face. "Yeah, I didn't really think that through, but I'm here. Whatcha doing?"

"Getting something to eat, I'm hungry."

After all that food we had at lunch, you're still hungry?"

I shrug my shoulders, "I'm hungry."

"Me too." Brady replies, but from the look on his face, it's not food that he's hungry for.

"Brady!"

"Makenna!" He growls out, prowling towards me as I back up. It doesn't take him long to 'catch' me, it's not like I'm trying to get away from him.

"My brothers could come in any time." I warn him, even though he knows that they could and will.

"Door's locked." He growls.

"You checked?" He nods his head, yes. "Before you came in here, you checked the door?"

"Yes Makenna." He's caught me, pinning me against the benchtop. Then my stomach growls, and so does Brady, only this time he's frustrated. "Come on, let's get you fed and hydrated, you're going to need it." He promises, taking a few steps back from me, to go to the fridge.

"I'm going to need it huh?"

"Yup, I've got plans for you baby, and you're going to need your energy." He doesn't look up from the fridge when he answers me. "So, do we want the leftovers from lunch, or do we want one of the meals Jules has in here?"

"We could finish off the leftovers." I say, thinking about the cheeseboard that Jules put together. As if he can read my mind, Brady pulls out the covered cheeseboard that he's placed a few extras on top of. "Just what I was thinking."

"I know." He says simply, with a huge smile. There's no point asking him how, we've known each other for a long time, I'm just going to appreciate that he pays attention to the details. He quickly moves about the kitchen, gathering crackers and other things and I'm left standing there just watching him. "Come on." He beckons me to the stools at the bench, pulling one out for me to sit on, and one for himself right next to mine. "Let's get some food into you."

We sit there for a few minutes putting together a handful of things we want to snack on in comfortable silence. We have the first few morsels before Brady speaks as he piles a cracker with my favourite cheese, some ham, and then places another cracker on top, so it's a cracker sandwich, just how I like them. He offers it to me, but when I go to take it he pulls back a little, silently asking me to open my mouth. So, I open my mouth and he places the cracker on my stretched out tongue. I lick the tips of his fingers as I curl my tongue around the food to draw it into my mouth, making him growl. I close my eyes and moan around the food.

"Shit Kenna!" I open my eyes, deciding it's my turn to seduce him with food. I drag a cracker through some dip, and put a small slice of ham on top.

"Your turn." He opens his mouth in anticipation, as my hand moves to his mouth. Then I pull back and shove it into my mouth and moan.

Brady gasps, then lets out a loud laugh as he throws his head back. "Cheeky woman!" His laughter dies quickly though as I stick a finger in my mouth to clean off the small amount of dip left on the tip. I hold his eyes in a hot gaze, as I suck on my finger, then slowly pull it out of my mouth, running the tip of my tongue around the tip of my finger.

"Fuck me!" Brady says in a whispered groan.

"That's the plan. I want to do that to your cock." I tell him.

The plate of food gets pushed to the side, as he clears a space, and then he grabs me by the waist and puts me up on the bench. I open my legs and he steps into the space. I pull him in close, and when his lips are a breath away from mine I say, "Kiss me Brady."

Kiss me is exactly what he does. Deeply, openly, and fully, with his hands tangled in my hair pulling me impossibly closer. My hands are everywhere, running up and down his arms, his back, shoulders, neck, and my fingers tangling in his hair. He grinds his hips into my pussy, and even though there's a couple of layers of clothing in between, I can feel the ridge of his hard cock pressing against my pussy.

"Kenna." My name is a whisper on his lips, and that's all I need to start tearing his clothes off. I pull at the hem of his t-shirt, trying to get it up over his head, but I get distracted when my hands hit his warm, hard flesh. So, instead of getting the t-shirt off, I just push it up out of my way, and run my hands over his tight stomach, and hard pecs, relishing in feeling him under my hands. I drop my lips to his nipple and suck lightly on it, I go to move onto the other one, but his t-shirt drops down onto my face. Growling in frustration, I rip it up over his head and throw it to the floor, making him laugh until I draw his nipple into my mouth and suck, hard. "Fuck!"

"Trying to." I mumble against his chest, as my hand dives to the waist of his jeans, and beyond, to wrap my hand around his cock.

"Ohhh, yeah." His head lolls back on his shoulders, his eyes closed, his hands gripping the edge of the benchtop behind me to steady himself. "Fuck Kenna! If you keep doing that I'm going to make a mess in my pants that I haven't made since I was a teenager and jerking off because of the girl I had a crush on."

"Who was the girl?" I ask, smiling at him as he brings his face forward to look me in the eyes.

"My wife." He growls and then my t-shirt is joining his in a mess on the floor, my bra joins them a second later. "I used to whack off in the shower thinking about your gorgeous blonde hair and sparkling green eyes."

"Ohhh really Mr Harris?" I ask, gasping as he pulls a nipple into his mouth and sucks on it.

His lips come off my nipple with a pop, and he's says, "Really *Mrs* Harris." Before he gives my other nipple the same attention.

"Oh yes!" I scream huskily. "Yes Brady." I push my chest into his mouth, and pull his head close to me at the same time.

"Hey guys, you want to have dinner together? I mean, I know. Oh shit, no, not again! Can't you guys stop fucking?" Caleb screams from the kitchen door, as he covers his eyes.

"Hey, what's for dinner? Do you guys mind if I join you, Jules headed home earlier because he had to go into the office." I hear Logan, but I can't see him yet. "What the hell are you doing Caleb? Why are you standing in the middle of the entrance with you hand over your eyes?"

"They're at it again!"

"Who is doing what again? Speak in sentences dude."

"Kenna and Brady, they're having sex on the *kitchen bench*!" Caleb replies, in a voice so squeaky, I haven't heard it since he hit puberty.

"Maybe you should knock before you enter then Caleb?"

"What, like you did, *Logan*?"

"Well, OK, you've got me there, but still, I was yelling out as I entered the house."

I press my lips to Brady's in a light kiss, and struggle to hold in my laughter. What can I say? I'm not amused by them entering our home without knocking, but I am amused by their bickering, always have been. Logan's normally so responsible and Caleb is so chill, but when they disagree with each other, which is quite regularly, it's comical.

"They're like a bickering old couple." Brady says quietly, not wanting the boys to turn their attention his way.

"They really are." I laugh, and kiss him again.

"Are you guys dressed yet? I'm still hungry."

"And still here!" Brady mumbles against my lips.

Chapter Thirty-two
BRADY

"Why are you still here?" I yell out, wishing with everything in me that they've left, but no such luck!

"Because I'm still hungry!" Caleb yells back.

"Then go to Vines, you're there all day anyway, what's the difference getting dinner there?" I yell back, and my question is met with silence for a few seconds, and for a few seconds I think I might have won this round.

"I wanted to see my sister again, but I didn't want to see her half fucking naked!" Caleb yells back.

"I'm hungry too." Logan calls out. "Are you dressed yet, because I'd like to come in there and work out dinner."

"Fucking hell. They're insane. They're both fucking insane." I mumble to Kenna as I rest my forehead on hers and take a deep breath. "I swear to God, I'm changing the fucking locks in this house baby. Every. Damned. One."

Kenna jumps off the kitchen bench, wraps her arms around my waist and laughs. The woman fucking laughs at me.

"You know, we *could* try locking the ones we've already got."

"I thought I *did*! Not that it would matter too much, because your brothers would still get in. They've got keys!" She buries her face in my shoulder, trying to cover her laughter but her whole body is shaking with the effort.

"Dude, can you put your shirt back on? I don't need to see your hairy nipples out for all to see where I eat, and Kenna, please tell me you've got clothes on again?" Caleb begs from the doorway where he's standing with his back to us still. "You guys should really start locking the doors before you get down to business." He advises, and the bastard is deadly serious.

Kenna can't hold her laughter in anymore, and with a loud snort, she throws her back and laughs. Loudly and with her entire body. In fact, she's so amused by the situation she doubles over, resting her hands on her knees, to catch her breath. As she calms down she picks up her bra and shirt, and starts putting them back on. Chuckling every now and then.

Why on earth did I fucking marry into this crazy arsed family? Oh that's right, I love the snorting mess in front of me with every part of my being.

"Maybe *you* should learn to knock before entering the house, *dude*." I say, my sarcasm sliding off him like water off a duck's back. He's such a pain in my arse, I love him like a brother, a very annoying little brother though.

"Nah. If you didn't want people to come in you'd make sure you locked the doors my friend. That's what people do, you know." He says, helping himself to a cold drink from the fridge, as Kenna does up the last button on her shirt.

"Make yourself at home Caleb, I insist." Some days living on the family property really sucked balls. Most days I love it, but at times like this, I would kill Satan himself for some extra distance from Kenna's brothers, and the privacy that would give us.

"Thanks bro, I will." He smiles at me, and I know he understands that I'm annoyed at his cockblocking ways, but he chooses to ignore the fact.

"Caleb, they're newlyweds, they're going to be at it for a while yet." I hear Logan say as I pick my t-shirt up off the floor and pull it on. "You know what? They've always have been at it, so perhaps you should learn a lesson, and knock on the door, wait for an invitation to enter little bro." He suggests helpfully as he helps himself to a cold drink from the fridge as well. Both of them are right at home here! "Just wait until you get yourself a woman that you can't keep your hands off, then you'll know how they feel. Maybe we'll just walk in on you all the time for payback?" Logan smirks at the horrified look on Caleb's face.

"Did you knock on the door and wait for an invitation, Logan?" I ask, not even trying to hide the annoyance in my voice.

"Well, I no, not *this* time, but I could hear your voices from outside, so I knew you two lovebirds weren't alone." His reply is helped out with his swinging hand, that I can only assume is pointing between my wife and myself.

My reply is cut off when Kenna speaks, softly but firmly. "Look guys, you're going to have to start respecting some boundaries." She holds up her hand to stop her brothers from interrupting her. "No! I know we all grew up here, in this house, and I understand that this is still home, for all of us, but Brady and I live here now. This is *our* home, where we want to start a family, and if you guys can't learn to live with some boundaries and rules to give us some privacy, then maybe we have to think about moving out."

"You mean *off* the property all together?" Logan asks her, suddenly very interested in what his sister has to say.

"Yes. *Off* the property all together Logan, that's exactly what I mean." Kenna replies, looking her older brother dead in the eyes so he knows how serious she is. We've talked about maybe moving off the property, but I don't want to, I know how much being here means to Kenna. Even more so in this house.

"Whoa. Just calm down there Kenna, let's not do anything rash. I mean you *can't* move away from us or the property." Caleb says the panic as clear as day in his voice.

"I can Caleb, and I will." Kenna looks at him. "We deserve some respect, *and* privacy guys. I *want* it." She demands.

Hot damn! My wife is so damned hot when she's bossy and demanding like this, defending us and our marriage. She's beyond hot actually, and if her brother's weren't here right now, I'd bend her over the kitchen bench and take her hard and fast. Maybe even with her brothers in the room right now. I won't, but I *could*. My thoughts have wandered so far off the reservation that I startle when Kenna pokes me in the arm and speaks to me.

"You need to remember that this is home for them too. They're not used to needing permission to walk into this house. This was *our* family home before it was yours and mine. I know you know that, but I can't ask them to never come back here without permission. It's all we have left." Her attention is focused on me, and the lust in my body ratchets up another dozen notches. She's all fire and passion, I don't know if I can wait to have her.

"You boys may want to leave and go to your own homes. Right. The. Fuck. Now." I look at them both, one at a time. "Unless of course you'd like to see what I plan on doing to your sister?"

"Brady!"

"Don't Brady me baby. You're hot when you get all riled up and I was all ready to go before we were rudely interrupted and now, well now I'm about ready to throw you on the bench, brothers or no brothers."

"See ya."

"Yeah bye."

The Drake brothers are leaving the house faster than I've seen either of them move, locking the door behind them, and I'm smiling.

"Brady?"

"Yes wife?"

"Are you ever going to stop calling me that?"

"What? Wife? Hell no, not unless you plan on not being my wife sometime in the future?"

"You're stuck with me husband."

I grin and rip my t-shirt back over my head. "Now, where were we before we were interrupted? Ahhh yes. Come here and put those soft hands all over my body."

"You don't need to tell me twice." Kenna murmurs and then her hands are everywhere. "Just maybe not on the kitchen bench?"

"Oh we're doing it on the kitchen bench Kenna, and then I'm going to serve your brothers food from the same bench, and I'm going to love every fucking second of it."

"Let's do it then." She says with a wicked smile, as she starts on undoing my jeans and dropping them to the floor. Her shirt, bra and pants join them.

I run my fingers through her pussy lips to see how wet she is for me, while she pumps my cock in her hand. "You're so fucking wet. Are you ready for me already Kenna?"

"Yes. Yes I need you now Brady. Please."

I grab her hips and lift her up to sit on the bench.

"Shit! That's cold!" She squeals.

"You won't notice in a second, I promise." I don't give her chance to answer, as I line our bodies up so that I can enter her. Then in one swift movement, I push my cock all the way into her pussy, causing both of us to groan loudly. Kenna grips onto my shoulders, so tightly it almost hurts, and I love it. My head falls back, and I take a few seconds just to enjoy being inside my wife again.

Kenna's lips touch my throat, and she kisses her way up to my ear, where she whispers huskily, "I love you Brady Harris." Then she draws my earlobe onto her mouth, nibbles on it slightly, and lets it go. "Fuck me Brady."

I don't need any further invitation. "Hold on tight baby." I say before pulling out of her tight pussy and then pounding back into her again. Over, and over, and over again, until we're both sweaty, and panting.

"Kenna, I'm close." I grind out in a voice I don't even recognise as my own. I can feel her fingernails digging into the flesh of my shoulders, and I tighten the grip I've got on her hips, as I pull her body in tighter to mine, needing more. More of what, I have no fucking clue, I just need it.

"More, Brady."

"I know." I don't know, I have no fucking clue what more means, I only know that we both want it!

I tear my hand from her hips, and bring it between us to play with her clit, because if she doesn't come soon, she's not really going to get the chance. Not on my cock anyway, I'll make sure she finishes one way or another though.

"Brady."

"Kenna."

"Brady."

"Feel. So. Good."

"Yes." Kenna throws her head back and screams out, and I'm glad we don't live in an apartment building, or close to her brothers right now. "Yes, Brady!"

She's gripping on tight to my shoulders so that she doesn't fall back onto the cold bench. "I'm gonna come Kenna." Suddenly, she sits up, tangles her fingers in my hair and pulls my lips to hers, and kisses me like her life depends on it. That's all it takes to make my hips pump into her wildly, and within seconds, I'm coming too.

I wrap her up in my arms, as she pulls me in close to her as well, her arms around my waist. Sex with this woman just keeps getting better and better.

"We should probably clean up." She says, not moving a muscles to pull away from me.

"You can't be comfortable. That benchtop must be cold on your butt." I say, lifting her off and putting her on her feet.

"Not anymore." She laughs. "My butt had a nice warm spot thank you very much." She says, still laughing.

I grab her around the waist, swinging her around. "Then allow me to put you back up there!"

"No! Brady, stop! You're making a mess!" She shrieks.

"I think that ships already sailed Makenna." I tell her, laughing myself, and putting her back on her feet. "Come on then, let's go get you cleaned up."

"Us cleaned up you mean?" She says, swatting my naked arse.

I skip forward half a step. "Ouch!" I send a frown her way, that makes her laugh even harder, as she starts picking up our clothes. "Leave them there baby, we'll clean them up later."

"What if Logan and Caleb come back?" We both pause, looking at each other for a second, and we both know the answer.

"Fine! You go upstairs and clean up, have a shower and I'll drop these in the washing machine so that the evidence is cleared away, just in case." Just in case, I think we both know that they'll be back within half an hour to get some food. They know that Jules left meals here for *us,* but he left enough for *all* of us, because he knows better as well.

"You've got a deal Brady." Then she's gone, and I watch her as she leaves. Who wouldn't? I mean she's naked and walking away from me, we might be married, but I'm not dead!

It takes me a minute after she's disappeared to collect myself, and re-member what I'm supposed to be doing. Picking up our discarded clothes I walk into the laundry and throw them all in the washing machine. Well, I go to, only to realise I haven't emptied the last load I washed. So I do that, and chuck them in the dryer, while the second load washes.

I was tempted to leave our clothes on the floor so that when her brothers return, because they will, they would see them and know what went on in here, but I know that Kenna wouldn't appreciate it, so I clean up. I look at the bench and smirk. I can't wait to serve food to her brothers off this bench, but first, I'm going to wipe it down with disinfectant because Kenna's arse was on it and while I love my wife and will lick her from head to toe without reservation, I don't want to think about my parents eating food off that part of the bench. Ever. Her brothers, yes, because they're cockblockers, but not my parents.

When I'm done, I join Kenna in the shower.

"You took your time, I thought you'd be up here sooner, so I kept waiting for you." She says as I step in behind her, and take her in my arms.

"Wait no longer, I am now here!" I announce.

"So I can see and feel. Now I can get out and you can stay in." She announces, trying to get out of my arms and out of the shower.

"You don't get to leave me alone here twice today gorgeous." I murmur against her neck.

"I've washed myself though Brady."

"Then wash me, baby, it would be my pleasure."

"So, ummm, are you guys going to be dishing up dinner soon? I'm still hungry." Caleb's voice breaks through the quietness of the house. I guess I should just be grateful he's not standing in the bathroom doorway, and from the sounds of how far away his voice is, he isn't even in our room. That doesn't stop me from growling my frustration into Kenna's neck, causing her to laugh once again.

"It's OK Brady." She says, patting my arm in mock comfort. "You weren't going to get lucky again anyway."

"That's not the point." I grumble, as I let her go and start washing myself. Before she gets too far, I grab her hand in my soapy one, stopping her from walking away. "Tomorrow we change the locks, you hear me?"

She smiles, flings the soap suds at my face, and says, "I hear you honey. First thing we'll get up and head out to the hardware store, I promise."

"And you can't give them a spare key." She looks shocked by my demand. "Promise me Makenna. The whole point is so that they can't get in here unannounced."

"But what happens if there's an emergency?" I raise an eyebrow at her and stare her down. "Fine. They don't get a spare key, but I think it's wrong Brady, one day we'll need them, and they won't be able to get in, and you'll regret this decision."

That may be true, but for now I really don't want those two cockblockers to have spare keys. I'll no doubt give in, in way too short a time, but for now, they don't get one.

I finish washing myself, and by the time I walk into the bedroom, Makenna's long gone, and I can hear her talking with her brothers in the kitchen. Their voices are muffled, and I can't work out what they're saying, or who's actually speaking, but they are most definitely here. Again!

Chapter Thirty-three
MAKENNA

After getting dressed, I join my brothers in the kitchen. Yes, both of them returned, and no-one is very shocked about it, not really. I love them, truly I do, and the truth is, they're not here every day or every night for dinner, but they *are* here a *lot,* and they do still treat this place like it's theirs. Things have to change, so I decide to have a chat with them while Brady's in the shower. It's not that he shouldn't be a part of the conversation, it's just that I think that my brothers need to hear this from *me.* Every time Brady says something, the boys think he's joking, but I really think it's starting to get to him now. I don't know why it means more for him that we have some privacy now that we're married, but it does, and I'm going to make sure they understand that.

"Boys, sit." I gesture for them to take a seat at the kitchen bench. The kitchen bench that Brady cleaned up before he joined me in the shower, don't think I didn't notice that.

"Uh oh what did you do, Logan?" Caleb asks, sitting on the stool and looking at our brother suspiciously.

"Nothing Caleb, if anyone's done something to piss Makenna off, it's going to be you. You're the annoying one." Logan answers him and I know I have to put a stop to their bickering before they go off again. Why Logan can't behave like the grown up and oldest child that he is, is beyond me, but you get these two together and they seem to revert to childhood.

"Stop it." I put my hand up to stop them from continuing to bitch at each other. "We need to have a serious talk about your free access to the house."

"But this is our family home Kenna." Caleb whines. It's at times like this that I remember just how young he is and how young he was when our parents died.

"That's true Caleb, but you both agreed to Brady and I living here. You agreed to us making changes, renovating the house so that it was more like what we wanted. If you guys want us to move out of the house, and move into a new one, built here or not, then now is the time to speak up."

"No! That's not what we want!" Logan hollers.

"Don't talk for me arsehole." Caleb hollers at Logan.

"*Do* you want Makenna and Brady to move out of the house? Do you want them living somewhere else. Somewhere that is possibly not Drake Wines? Is that what you want?" He asks our little brother, his voice deep and kind of menacing I have to say.

"No I don't, but you don't get to answer for me Logan, I'm not a little kid. I'm a grown arse man and I'm here and pulling my weight with the family and the business."

"He's right Lo, I asked you *both,* not just you." His head turns sharply, and he's suddenly looking at me with that menacing look. The only difference is, it doesn't bother me at all. "Look, the fact is Brady has every intention of going to the hardware store in the morning to buy all new locks. For every door in the house. He's also made me promise to *not* give either of you a spare key."

"Well, that's unrealistic, what happens if there's an emergency?" The ever practical Logan asks, and although I agree with him, I'm not going to tell him that.

"We'll work that out when it happens."

"That's the point of it being an emergency Makenna, it's not something that's organised to happen. It's an *emergency*!" My brother, ever the logical one of the family! I send him a scowl .

"Logan's not wrong Kenna." Caleb chimes in, nodding vigorously. "I mean what if I need food and you're not home, how will I get in?"

"You won't." I say, scowling at him as well. "Look OK. This is something Brady needs, and I'm going to give it to him. You guys will have to learn to live with it. We need and deserve the respect of having some privacy." I hesitate, because I haven't really spoken to anyone except Brady and my doctor about what I'm about to say.

"What is it Makenna? What's wrong? Are you and Brady OK?" Logan says, his voice steady as always, but his eyes give away his concern.

"Everything's fine, perfect between Brady and I. We're good, better than ever in fact." I tell him, waving my hand at him, because if there's one thing that's come out of all of this, Brady and I are closer than ever.

"Then what is it?" Logan asks, reaching over to take my hand in his, steadying me. I look over at Caleb, who has been strangely quiet, and he doesn't say anything, but he takes my other hand in his and I can feel the tears building. They annoy the crap out of me, but they're my brothers. My family and they always have my back.

"I've been seeing a doctor for the last year."

"A doctor? What kind of doctor and how did we not know about this? Why didn't you tell us before now?" Logan demands.

"If you shut up and give her a chance Logan, maybe we'll find out the answers to all those questions." Caleb gives Logan the filthiest look I've ever seen on his handsome face.

"Both of you shut up and let me speak." I sigh, close my eyes for a few seconds and when I open them, both of my brothers are looking at me expectantly. "We've been seeing a fertility specialist. We've been trying to get pregnant since before Mum and Dad died. We first saw the specialist just before they died and since then, he kept telling us that it's more than likely linked to the stress of losing them and then building up Drake Wines."

"Then you'll take time off. Caleb and I can run things around here." Logan announces.

"Absolutely. You can count on us sis, you can step back, and we'll take care of things." Caleb says, barely letting Logan finish his speech. I can't help the smile that appears, even though I'm on the verge of tears.

"Thanks guys, but that's not necessary." I give my brothers a weak smile.

"It is if we want nieces and nephews to spoil." Caleb counters.

"You'll only get those nieces and nephews to spoil if you stop being cockblocking bastards." Brady says from behind me, as he wraps his arms around me and presses into my body.

"I told them." I say quietly to him.

"Ahhh well, that explains the hands and the faces, but honestly guys, we've got this sorted." Brady rests his hands lightly on my stomach. "We're hoping relaxing on our honeymoon has helped, but we're going back to the specialist next week and if nothing has happened, then we'll talk about the next step with him."

"What would be the next step?" Caleb asks.

"Hormone stimulation drugs." I say with a shrug. Brady gives me a squeeze.

"What does that entail?"

"We're not quite sure, which is why we have an appointment with the specialist next week." Brady answers Logan, who is looking at me like he wants to say something.

"What is it Logan?"

"I just don't understand why you didn't tell us you were struggling sooner."

"There's nothing you can do to help Logan. Literally nothing, and I knew you would try to find a solution where there isn't one. My body needs a little help to make it work, and you can't fix that." I know that makes him angry, because I watch as his nostrils flare, and his eyes darken. "The truth is, there's not a lot any of us can do except wait."

"We have a plan Logan." Brady assures him.

I look at Caleb, who has dropped my hand, and is sitting on his stool, staring at his hands in his lap. "Caleb?" He doesn't look up, doesn't say anything. "Caleb. What's wrong?"

His eye shoot up to look me in the eyes, then they dart to Brady's, before landing back on me. "I'm sorry."

"You have nothing to be sorry about little brother." I start.

"No. I mean I'm sorry that you're struggling to get pregnant. I know how much the both of you want a family." He says, looking at Brady and back at me again. "But I'm mad too. I'm mad that you didn't let us in. I'm not a little kid anymore Makenna. I don't need you or Logan to look after me, to shield the world from me. I want to be included in decisions. I know this is a private discussion between you and Brady, that you two have to make the decisions that best suit you both, and I'm not saying I want a say in what you do, or how you deal with this. I'm just saying it would have been nice to know, that's all."

I step out of Brady's embrace, and walk around to Caleb. "It wasn't about excluding either of you Caleb. It was about us getting our heads around things first." I take his hand in mine and use the other to tip his chin up so that he's looking into my eyes. He *is* a grown man now, but he looks like my baby brother right now. "We were hoping that we wouldn't have to tell anyone anything to be honest. We were hoping against hope that it would sort itself out, but it doesn't look like that's how it's going to be."

From beside me, Logan says, "That's fair Kenna, honestly, but why are you telling us now?"

"Simple." I tell him, holding his hand as well. "We need some privacy to go through all the steps we'll have to do for this treatment."

"I thought we were finding all that out next week?" Brady asks, confused.

"I've looked it up." I say with a shrug. "I wanted to know what we were getting into."

Logan nods his head, and looks up at Brady. "You don't have to go and change the locks, we'll knock from now on before entering, or message or call before we come over. Won't we Caleb?"

"Absolutely. I'm sorry Brady. I honestly thought you were playing the annoyed brother in law, I didn't realise it was really annoying you." He looks from Brady to me. "And you're right. You guys need and deserve privacy and respect. Especially now, but obviously before as well."

"Caleb, I know that this house brings with it many memories and it's where you grew up, it's where you have memories of your parents. I understand all of that, and I don't begrudge you any of it, but that being said, when we had the conversation about living here, and making changes to make it feel like ours, you both agreed. You agreed wholeheartedly that we could make this place ours. We haven't changed everything, and we compromised on a lot of things between ourselves. So, don't misunderstand where I'm coming from, because you guys are always welcome here. Always. We are brothers, not in laws, *brothers,* but even without all this other stuff going on, we deserve some respect. This is now our home. The place we hope to one day bring up kids of our own." I walk back around the side of the bench that Brady's standing and wrap my arms around his waist. "I don't want to and I'm not banning you guys from coming over, I never fucking would, but some consideration would go a long way."

"We've got a pretty long and emotional road ahead of us, we would like a little bit of space. If that's OK?" I ask my brothers, quietly.

Both of them are up out of their seats in a heartbeat, and smothering us both in a hug.

"Of course it's OK! You shouldn't have needed to ask." Logan says

"Of course! I'm sorry you had to ask, and I'm sorry I've taken you guys and the house for granted." Caleb says at the same time as Logan speaks.

"I love you guys." I say, my tears now falling down my cheeks.

"We love you too Kenna, and you should have never had to ask for privacy." Logan says, squeezing us tighter.

"I love you guys too, but can I escape this group hug please?" Brady asks, and I know he's trying to lighten the moment, but it's too late for that.

"Love you too Brady." Both of my brothers say at the same time and squeeze a little tighter.

Caleb let's go first. "So, can we have a last dinner to celebrate or what?" He asks, his signature cheeky smirk that I'm sure gets him in well with the ladies, on his face. "I mean, Jules made a few meals right? I know the man made enough for *all* of us, because he knows that we *used* to annoy you all the time."

"Yes, we certainly made you plenty of food." Logan says, a sadness spreading across his face.

"Are you OK Logan?" I ask, concerned about my big brother. "Where is Jules tonight?"

"He doesn't live out here you know, he has his own place in town." Logan snaps, and even though I know he's a terminally grumpy man, this is grumpy even for him. "He went home. He's got an early start in the morning, and he didn't want to have to get up any earlier than he had to. Leaving from here cuts into his morning."

"If you're sure?" I ask.

"Of course I am! What else could it be Makenna? Like I said, he doesn't live out here, and he's not going to. Let's eat." Just like that the subject is slammed shut once again.

I look at Brady and he shrugs, like there's nothing we can do about it. When I look at Caleb to gauge his reaction, he's doesn't seem to be paying any attention to how much grumpier Logan is. He's only worried about getting some food into his eternally empty stomach. Perhaps that's why he spends his days in Vines? He's got easy access to food!

"OK, so what else did you cook Logan, and what do you feel like?" I ask the room.

With the decision made we move onto lighter, less complicated subjects, but every time I chance a look at Logan, he looks miserable. He barely joins in the conversation, which is unusual. When we've finished eating, he helps Brady clean up and then says goodbye. Caleb says goodnight not long after when he realises there's no dessert tonight.

There is, but he doesn't need to know that, because we're just not sharing it with him!

Chapter Thirty-four
BRADY

Her brothers are long gone, with the promise of giving us more privacy in the future, and we're cuddled up together, toasty, warm, and relaxed in bed.

"So, what made you tell them tonight?" I ask, quietly. Her back tucked into my front, my arms wrapped around her tightly so she can't escape.

She's quiet for a while, before answering me, her voice quiet but steady. "I wanted them to understand your need for privacy. I needed them to know so that they would back off."

"They won't back off Makenna and you know it. They'll give us privacy, without a doubt and they'll let us do what we need to do, but we're talking about your brothers here."

"I know, but now you don't have to go changing all the locks, and they know where they stand." I don't quite agree with her, but I'm not going to say anything to her tonight. Maybe they can give us the space she asked for tonight. "Are you mad that I told them? I know we agreed not to tell anyone, but it seemed like the right time."

"And they're your family." I feel her nod her head. "No, I'm not mad you told them Kenna." I reassure her.

"You haven't told your parents though, have you? Or Beth?"

"No." I answer honestly.

"Why?" I sigh deeply and exhale slowly, taking my time to answer, because I need to choose my words carefully.

"The simple truth is, I don't want my Mum to stress or worry. I love Beth, even with all the pranks we pull on each other, but I can't trust her to *not* say anything to Mum. I don't think she'd do it on purpose, but she *would* slip." I sigh again, because I don't want to say anything that will hurt

Makenna, but I want to explain the truth of why I don't want to tell my parents too. "Also, I don't want my Mum to get too emotional about it with *you*. You know she loves you, and she's become a little overprotective of you since the accident. She'll be devastated for you, for us, and I don't need to deal with that, I have no doubt that's not something you want to deal with either. I don't want you to feel like she's trying to take the place of your Mum."

"I know that's not what she's trying to do Brady. She's always included me in everything, and treated me like a daughter, right from the beginning like she knew we'd end up here one day." I feel her smile against my arm.

"Well, I also thought that the more information we had when we spoke to her, the better off we'd be so I was waiting until we saw the doctor this week." I confess.

"Then you want to tell them?" She asks, and I can hear the nerves in her voice.

"Only if we need to, and you want to." She stiffens in my arms, and I know what she's thinking. "Telling Logan and Caleb was different, I get that Kenna, honestly I do."

"Do you really think your Mum will try to smother me?"

I laugh at her question, how could she believe anything else? "I have no doubt baby, no doubt at all." I hesitate for a second and then ask her something that has only just occurred to me. "Hang on." I turn her in my arms, and she buries her face in my chest, not looking at me. I gently hold her chin in my hand and bring her eyes up to meet mine. "Do you think she would *blame* you? Do you think that *I* blame you?" When she doesn't answer me, I kiss her lightly. "Makenna that couldn't be further from the truth baby. These things happen, and you've always had trouble with your periods, so I guess it kind of makes sense."

"What if I can't give you the kids you want?" She asks quietly, so quietly I would have missed it if I wasn't still holding onto her chin. She closes her eyes, but I can see the tears building in the corners of her eyes.

"The kids *we* want, right?" She doesn't answer, just nods her head. "Because if you don't want kids baby, that's alright with me. If you've decided this is all too much, or that you just don't want kids, I'm good with that."

"OK." Her voice is barely a whisper.

"Kenna, baby, open your eyes and look at me." I wait until she eventually does as I ask, and my heart breaks when I see the unshed tears, and heartache there. "Makenna Rose Harris, I have loved you since we were sixteen. I have wanted you to be my wife almost since the day you agreed to go on that first date with me. If you don't believe me, ask my Mum. I'm pretty sure I told her I'd met the girl I was going to marry when I got home that day. She laughed, and told me I was crazy, and yet, here we are. I don't want anyone else, I never have, and if you don't want kids, I'm more than happy for it to be just us for the rest of our lives. Do I want kids with you? Yes, but it's your body, and it's you that has to go through all the medical crap. I would never demand you put yourself through that to make *me* happy." I kiss her lightly on the tip of her nose, then her forehead, as she closes her eyes again. "But if you want to go through with all of this, then I'm beside you every god damned step of the way. You will *not* have to do any of it alone. I will be at every appointment, and I will help with every aspect, whatever that means. We're a team Makenna, this is *our* life, not mine, not yours, but *ours.*"

"Are you sure, because if you want out now, I won't stop you."

"You want to get rid of me so soon after I made you my wife?" I laugh, trying to lighten the moment. "You're stuck with me baby. I'm not going anywhere. Today, tomorrow, next week, next month or next year. I love you with every beat of my heart."

"I love you too Brady Harris."

"I'm glad to hear it. Now no more talk of anyone going anywhere, other than to sleep. I think we could both do with some rest. It's been a long day."

"I love you Brady."

"I love you too baby." I kiss her forehead again, and pull her into me. I think I need her more than she needs me right now.

WHEN I WAKE THE NEXT morning, I stretch out my arm looking for Kenna to pull her in for a hug, only to find the other side of the bed empty, and cold. Which means she's been gone for a while. I can't hear the shower running, so I guess she's already up and moving.

"Hey sleepyhead." Her cheery, sexy voice rings out from behind me as she walks in the bedroom door. I roll over so I can see her gorgeous face.

"How long have you been up? Why didn't you wake me?"

"Not long, really, and I didn't wake you because you looked so peaceful." I watch her move around the room, she's restless, which means there's something on her mind. "I wanted some time to think." She takes a deep breath like she's steeling herself to tell me something bad. "I want to do this." She says with a firm nod of her head.

"Do what baby?' I ask, sitting up in the bed, watching her pace around the room.

"This baby thing. This hormone stimulation thing." She stops pacing, and looks me in the eyes. "I want to have a baby with you Brady. I want to have *your* baby." She sounds determined, and I hate to break her bubble by bringing up the reality of the situation, but I have to.

"And what if it doesn't work baby, then what?"

"Then we move onto the next step, and the next." She says with a sharp nod of her head, but looking down at her hands twisting together. "We keep trying."

"When do we stop?" I ask gently.

Her head whips up to look at me, and there's uncertainty *and* steely determination in them. "I'm not sure, but I'm thinking when we have the family we've always wanted." Guess we're going into this thing full on then. As long as I know the boundaries, I'm all in.

"I'm all in baby. I will follow wherever you lead." That earns me a smile that makes the sun shine and my heart warm.

I will do anything to help keep that smile on Kenna's face. Anything.

Chapter Thirty-five
MAKENNA

My head and my heart feels lighter having made the decision that this is something I want to do. I felt weighed down when Brady basically told me this was *my* choice, *my* decision. It felt like a lot to put on just my shoulders. We're a team, we do things together. Decisions are made together after discussing options and making choices. That being said, I've never loved him more than when he told me that it was *my* choice, because it was *my* body. It was *me* that would have to deal with things emotionally, physically, and mentally. That being said, it's Brady that's going to have to deal with the hormones involved. I'm betting they're going to be killer!

We spend the weekend relaxing, and I'm glad we decided not to go anywhere else after our honeymoon. I know Brady still thinks that I wanted to be close to Drake Wines just in case, and he thought that I might try to sneak into the office for a while, but he was wrong. The truth is, I just wanted to enjoy being home with my husband.

My husband!

I'm not sure I'll ever get used to calling him that. I mean, it's been our plan since we were teenagers. Even back then. The fact that we made it makes me happier than I could explain. Brady makes me happy, and I don't think I could have gotten through the loss of my parents without him.

On Monday morning, I find myself dragging my feet. I'm not really feeling like I want to head back into the office, and get back to work.

Margot looks up when I enter, but her smile turns into a frown when she looks at me.

"Are you OK boss?"

"Yeah, I guess. How have you been Margot?" I ask, trying to get myself in the mood for catching up on work.

"It's nice to have you back." She smiles hesitantly at me. "You know I love your brothers, but can I tell you, just between you and me, they're hard work." She lets out a small laugh, which makes me laugh a little.

"I understand just what you mean Margot, trust me." I wink at her. "Your secret is safe with me." I say, moving by her to get to the coffee. "I hope they didn't give you too much trouble while I was away?" I ask her, not really expecting a truthful answer, but hoping like hell she hasn't had to do all the work and they've just harassed her.

"They were fine Makenna, honestly." Her smile is reassuring. At least she doesn't look stressed out or overworked. Actually, now that I look at her, I realise she looks quite relaxed. The exact opposite of what I was expecting on my first day back in the office.

"I'm not sure I believe that they were *both* an absolute joy to work with while I was away, but you look to be very happy, and not at all stressed, so I guess I've got no choice but to believe you." I feel like a bitch saying that about my brothers, but they can be a handful when they want to be, and together they can be downright painful. Especially if they're fighting each other over who's right and who's wrong!

"Oh, I didn't say Logan wasn't his usual grumpy self, but I'm used to that." Margot shrugs her shoulder like that's just a normal thing she has to deal with. "Caleb on the other hand, he's something else." She says with a smile, and dare I say, a bit of a twinkle in her eyes.

"What did he do now?" I ask, and I know I sound like a long suffering parental figure who has had to deal with his tomfoolery for decades, instead of his sister who actually does love him to pieces.

"What?" She looks at me confused for a minute, and then laughs. "Ohh Caleb was no trouble at all! In fact, I'd go so far as to say that his visits became highlights of my week." The giggle that comes out of my assistant sends a cold dread right to my core.

"Please no! Don't tell me it's my *assistant* my little brother has his eyes on. I think I might kill him." I curse under my breath, but apparently not quietly enough, because Margot lets out a loud laugh. Too loud for the small space and early hour.

"Ohh no Makenna, I promise it's nothing like that! Damn woman, I'm a little shocked you would think I'd be even close to being on his radar. I mean, it would be tight, but I'm *almost* old enough to be his mother, and if you breathe that to *anyone* outside of this office, I will deny it with everything in me. However, it is the truth." She scowls at me, and then continues. "That being said, your younger brother is quite the charmer and I do enjoy his company." She says, her smile returning.

"You're not old enough to be his mother Margot, stop it!" I admonish her. She's my assistant, and I know I can check her records, but I know she's nowhere old enough to be Caleb's *mother*! That's insane. "You're not wrong, he certainly has a way about him that people are drawn to and like. He's a lot like our Dad in that way." I tell her, my eyes getting a little misty remembering my Dad charming everyone he met, from the handyman to big company executives that tried to buy him out more times than I could count.

I jump at Margot's gentle hand on mine, because I was on another planet thinking about my Dad. "I'm sorry hun, for startling you, and making you think about the loss of your parents."

"It's OK Margot, it's been a couple of years, it's probably time to move on." I brush off her apology, because I don't want anyone to think that I'm being too sensitive, and I'm over the sympathetic looks as well.

"Well, I think we both know that mourning a loss takes its own time, and you just got married. I doubt you dreamed that you'd be marrying Brady without your Dad giving you away, so I get why you would be feeling emotional right now." She pats my hand, and then turns back to her desk. "I worked with your Dad and Logan for a while before the accident, trust me when I say he's missed. Your Mum too."

"I always forget you knew them." I smile softly at her. "It feels like you came on board with me and then took on some work for Logan as well." She laughs loudly.

"Logan has always been much more, shall we say, independent with his work." She looks at me, and I must look like I'm horrified to think she thinks I'm needy, because she laughs again before adding, "What I mean is, he doesn't trust anyone else to do his work, and won't admit when he does need help, because he's a stubborn bugger."

Now it's my turn to laugh, because her assessment of Logan is perfect. "You crack me up Margot, your assessment of both of my brothers is so accurate it's scary." I place my hand on her shoulder gently. "I'm sorry Margot,

I forget that you knew our parents as well, and that you worked for Dad before me. You must miss him as well?"

"Sweetheart, I miss your Mum and Dad every day, but they weren't my parents, and I can tell you, even though you learned at your Dad's side, you've made this place your own. So has Logan, and your Dad would be amazed and proud of what you've both achieved." I can feel the tears building up, and I know if I don't move into my office, they're going to flow uninhibited down my cheeks. "Mark my words, Caleb is going to make his mark around here too, and Drake Wines will be beyond amazing. You all have something special to bring to the business. Most of which Jack could have never dreamed of, and while you've all got your faults as well, I can see the three of you working well together here. Jack and April would be proud Makenna, they *are* proud of you and your brothers."

I can't speak, there are no words to express what I'm feeling. So, instead I give Margot a tight hug, and a kiss on the cheek, then head to my office. Almost ten minutes later she brings me in a coffee, and I realise she must have ordered it from Vines. I thank her and get back to going through what feels like a thousand emails waiting for my attention. I guess the guys didn't go through these, and why would they?

I lift my coffee to my lips to take a sip, as I realise I didn't have a coffee before I left the house this morning, and decide it's just what I need to give myself the push to get my motor running. Only when I smell it as it gets to my lips, I'm repulsed by the smell, and dry heave a little at the thought of drinking it at all. I put the cup down on the furthest spot on my desk, and have a drink of water from the bottle I keep on my desk, and get back to sorting out my emails.

It's not until Margot comes in an hour later to take the empty cup back to Vines, and realises that I didn't drink it, that it really registers with me that I felt ill just smelling coffee.

"Margot, I have to go back to the house for a while. Do I have anything important I have to get to this morning or early afternoon?" I ask, suddenly really needing to get back to the house.

"No, I made sure today was just a day for you to catch up on everything. No calls, or meetings of any kind. You don't even really need to be in the office if you'd rather spend the rest of the day at the house. I can definitely hold down the fort here." I gather my stuff, phone, keys, bag, and start to rush out the door. "Is everything OK Makenna?"

"I hope so, with any luck, everything might just be perfect Margot." I give her a tight hug, before leaving her standing in the office alone and looking slightly bewildered at my abrupt departure.

I rush through the front door, not needing my key because Brady hasn't left for work himself yet. I guess that's both the plus and negative of him running a bar. Things don't happen early in the day for him, but it can mean some late nights.

"Hey Kenna, what are you doing home? I wasn't expecting you back here at all. Did you miss me?" he smiles and he's sexy as hell, but I don't stop to kiss him hello, I just keep moving towards our bedroom, and bathroom. "Hey, are you OK? What's wrong?"

I hear him ask closely behind me, but I don't answer him, I just throw my bag on the bed and rush into the bathroom, searching through the drawers and the cupboard in the vanity. Damn it, I should have bought a smaller one!

"Kenna, baby, you're scaring me. Speak to me, tell me what the hell is going on, please?" He begs, but I can't tell him until I find what I'm looking for. Then I hold it up like I'm presenting him with an Olympic gold medal. "What's that?" His confusion is understandable, it's been a while since I've needed to even *look* at a pregnancy test, so he would barely know what he's looking at.

"A pregnancy test." I tell him, plain and simple. The confusion on the poor man's face develops into a severe frown. I swear, I've never seen such an epic frown on his handsome face, ever.

"A pregnancy test?" He asks, hesitantly. "For who?"

"Me." It's just one word, but it has an incredible weight to it, and I can't help the smile from spreading across my face. "I think I might actually be pregnant Brady."

"But how?" He asks, his confusion complete.

"Well, there's this thing called sex, and when a guy puts his erect penis into a ladies vagina, and pumps really hard, and sometimes gently, they both end up coming, if he's good at it. Then he ejaculates and if the lady is ovulating, the chances are that she might get pregnant." I get the giggles, because I can't believe I just got that far into explaining to Brady *how* a pregnancy occurs.

He blinks rapidly a few times, and then scowls at me. "I know *how* the mechanics of getting pregnant works you smart arse, I just don't understand how *you* got pregnant! We've been trying for ages, and the few times you've thought you were, you've gotten your period soon after."

"I know! I know OK, but my boobs are sore, and I'm feeling exhausted. I really didn't want to go back to the office this morning."

"Baby, we just got back from our honeymoon, and even though it was a holiday, we were still busy. There were still flights, which are always tiring." He pulls me into a tight embrace, rubbing his hands up and down my back. "I just don't want you to get your hopes up, only to get upset."

"I know honey, but I didn't drink my coffee!." He pulls back from our embrace to look me in the eyes, like he's trying to decide if I've finally lost the plot over this baby thing. "I didn't make a coffee here, at the house before I left for the office, and Margot went to Vines and brought me back a caramel latte, and I dry heaved when it got close to my nose. I didn't even *taste* it Brady. I didn't even put the cup to my lips, I put it as far away as I could possibly get it on my desk, and drank my water."

"When was the last time you had your period?" You'd think the man I have sex with would know that, wouldn't you?

"About four weeks before the wedding. I know this because I was terrified I was going to get on or near the day and have to deal with a white dress!"

"You didn't go on the pill to try to control it before the wedding?"

"No! We're *trying* to have a baby Brady!"

He holds his hands up in defence. "I know, I know but it can be done." He pulls me back in to his embrace. "I guess you better pee on a stick then?"

"You have to let me go first, Brady."

"You're right I do." He lets me go, but I can feel the anxiety radiating off him. "I'll go wait in the bedroom while you do your thing. I'm sure you don't need an audience." I smile at him and he walks out of the bathroom, closing the door behind him.

He's right I'd have performance anxiety with him still in the room, and I wouldn't have been able to pee in front of him, so it's best that he leaves me to it.

Opening the box, I read the instructions, and put everything close by the toilet. Then I sit and wait. Apparently my bladder doesn't require an audience to get performance anxiety, and I have to wait until it relaxes to get down to business.

Chapter Thirty-six
BRADY

Waiting for Makenna to pee on that damned stick gives me more anxiety, apprehension, unease, and utter fear, than walking into a haunted house could possibly give me right now.

We've been here a few times before, and they've either just been her period being out of whack, which is apparently her normal, or very early miscarriages. Which is why we have an appointment with a fertility specialist this week.

I don't want to get my hopes up, because I don't want to get Makenna's hopes up. If we're both up, then the fall is just going to be that much worse.

She's had test after test because there just doesn't seem to be a reason for it. She doesn't have Poly Cystic Ovary Syndrome. She doesn't have endometriosis, or adenomyosis. Everything, for all intents and purposes, appear to be in working order. The only hitch is her period is erratic at best, and no-one can tells us *why*. I've learned so much about the female anatomy, and what happens monthly, weekly, and daily, that I want to hug my Mum, and my sister forever, not to mention Makenna.

Don't get me wrong, I went through a barrage of testing too, but none of them seemed to be quite as invasive as what Kenna went through, and there didn't seem to be as many either. Either the swimmers are working, or they're not really. No infections, or deformities, no cause for it, and we discovered that I am, in fact, not infertile.

Which makes me feel better, and Makenna worse, because now *our* issue is hers, and *hers* alone. I tell her that it's not true, but while she agrees with me, I can see it in her eyes, she doesn't believe me. We've had a doctor say, in a very offhanded manner, that it could quite simply be that we're not compatible. You know, conceiving wise, and modern medicine could help with that. Maybe. I've never wanted to deck a professional more in my life than that day. One flip remark sent Makenna into a down spiral for days.

Now, make no mistake at *all*. If my wife walks out of that bathroom and tells me she's pregnant, I will be beyond happy. My problem is, I'm apprehensive. I'm weary about the positive result from a urine test in our bathroom. A urine test at a clinic doesn't make it any more, or less accurate, logically I know this, but it just seems almost surreal doing it here first every time.

I get up from where I'd been sitting on the edge of the bed waiting, to start pacing the room. I can't keep still. The fear, anxiety, and concern for Makenna if that test says negative is overwhelming. The problem is, they're no less overwhelming thinking about the test coming back positive instead though either.

Either way, I'm nervous as hell and she seems to be taking *forever* in the bathroom.

I pause at the bathroom door, and try to hear what's going on in there, but it's a futile exercise and I know it. So, I start pacing again. Back and forth at the foot of the bed. Then I change it up and pace up and down in front of the window. A window that I don't look out of to take in the view of vines that Makenna wanted, and why our bedroom is on this side of the house. I just keep pacing.

Then the bathroom door opens, and I hold my breath. I honestly don't know what I want to come next. Positive or negative. Either one comes with its own set of heartache to be honest. There are tears in her eyes, but I can't tell if they're good or bad tears. I'm rooted to the spot. I want to go to her, to hold her, but I find that I just can't move.

"Makenna?" Her name means so many different things in that one breathy, quiet word.

The tears pour down her face, as a smile curves her lips, and she starts to nod slowly.

"Yes?" My feet are rooted the spot, I can't move because I'm in shock.

"Yes." Her voice is raspy, and full of emotion. "I'm pregnant."

"Wow!"

"That's all you can say?" Her face morphs from teary happiness, to pissed off and ready to kill me in a heartbeat. But the honest truth is, I have no clue what to say. I know what she *wants* me to say, but my heart and my head are at war. "Aren't you happy? I thought this is what you wanted too?" There are fresh tears streaking her cheeks now, and that's what gets my feet moving.

Pulling her into the tightest hug that I dare, I kiss the top of her head as she buries her face into my chest and the sob she lets out breaks my heart!

"Kenna, baby, look at me. Please?" I wait until she pulls her head up and rests her chin on my chest, her beautiful emerald eyes still glistening with tears, but she's stopped crying. "I *do* want this Makenna, never doubt that, please. I'm just worried." I take a deep breath and keep going. "I want to jump for joy, and shout it from the rooftops Kenna, but with our history I'm feeling a little, shall we say, anxious. It's what we both want, make no mistake about it Kenna, having a baby with you would be bring me immeasurable joy, and happiness, but that doesn't stop me from being worried."

"All pregnancies have a certain amount of stress, Brady." She says softly, running her hands gently up and down my arms, trying no doubt to comfort me. "There are no certainties in the world, honey."

"There certainly are. First and foremost is that I love you unconditionally Makenna." I close my eyes, and pull in a deep breath to steady my voice. "But losing this baby or you, I don't know if I can do it baby."

"How about we just do this one step at a time?" She asks me, pleading in her voice and on her face. "I'll call the doctor and ask what she wants us to do. We already have an appointment with her this week, so maybe we can wait until then, and just enjoy it for now?" She sounds so fucking hopeful, and I can't burst her bubble, so I smile and smile.

"Sure baby. Why don't you call the clinic and see what they say, and I'll go make you cup of coffee. Damn I mean tea I guess."

She smiles at me, and it's radiant. "Thank you, that would be amazing!" I watch as she grabs her phone from her bag and starts to scroll through her contacts to find the clinic's number. She smiles at me as she puts the phone to her ear and I smile back, before leaving her to make the call.

I move around the kitchen on autopilot, putting the water on to heat up, getting mugs and the tea bags all sorted. When that's all done, I stare out the kitchen window, not really seeing anything out there. I can't go into work tonight, which is insane because it *should* be my first night back. I call my second in charge and he's more than happy to cover me for one more day, maybe two if need be. He doesn't ask any questions, and tells me to take as much time as I need. Putting my phone back in my pocket as I stare out the window at nothing. I don't notice anything else going around me, and that's how Makenna manages to sneak up on me. I jump when I feel her arms sneak around my waist, and she presses her front to my back.

"Sorry Brady, I didn't mean startle you, but I didn't want to speak, because you looked so peaceful." She laughs quietly. "I guess in retrospect I should have spoken. That may have been a little less scary than someone coming up behind you and touching you. It's a bit creepy, although, I *am* the only other person in the house right now."

"Well, that's never a guarantee, it *could* have been one of your brothers being weird." I say, taking her hands that are resting on my stomach in mine, and placing them back on my stomach.

"They're both at work. At least they should be." She laughs. "But you're right, it's quite possible that one of them would do that, and it would be creepy."

"Hell yes it would! I don't want either of those knuckleheads hugging me from behind. Or at too many other positions either." I say thinking about it. "We're supposed to be at work too, but here we are." I say bringing our hands up to my mouth and kissing hers.

"Shouldn't you be leaving soon?"

"I called Damien, he's going to cover for me. He said they're not busy so it will be fine." I shrug, because it really isn't that big of a deal.

"You should go back today Brady, it's your first day back since before the wedding."

"It's fine." Kenna circles me to come to stand in front of me, our hands still joined. "Brady, go to work. I'm fine, we're fine, everything is fine."

"Then why aren't *you* at work?" I ask, it sounds a little like an accusation of some kind, but I don't mean it to.

"I came home to do the test." She sighs, then kisses my lips lightly. "Could it have waited? Without a doubt, but I had to know there and then. The fact that you were still home was simply luck. If the penny had dropped a few minutes later, you wouldn't have been here honey."

"Would you have called me?" She thinks about it for a minute, then shakes her head.

"No. I would have waited until later when you got home." I open my mouth to speak, only for her to cut me off. "It would hurt, and annoy me to wait, but you would have come home then, and you need to be at work Brady."

"No, I need to be here with you, looking after *you*. The outside world can wait." Before she can protest any more, I lead her over to the couch. "You get comfy, and choose a movie for us to watch while I get our teas brewing, again."

"Brady." She says, as I gently help her sit down and then head back to the kitchen. "I'm not fragile you know. Even if the worst happens, I'm not made of glass. You can't stay home every day to look after me, and I won't be working from home every day either. Life can and will go on honey."

I close my eyes, and hang my head down, because I know she's right. "I know Kenna, just give me today OK? Just one day. Let me look after you as if you might break just for today. Then we can go back to normal in the morning and let whatever happens, happen. Please?"

"One day Brady, that's all."

I carry a tray into the loungeroom, placing it on the coffee table in front of her, place her steaming hot mug closer to her, moving mine to my side, and place the plate of cookies in the middle. The empty tray goes under the coffee table for later.

"What are we watching?"

"Dirty Dancing." She says with a smirk, and I smile at her.

"A little bit of Baby and Johnny hey? Awesome." She cracks up laughing, and it's a beautiful sight. I send up a silent to prayer to whoever might listen to a man that doesn't believe in anything, to give this gorgeous, amazing woman sitting beside him, the one gift that she wants. For this pregnancy to be the one that ends with a baby in her arms, and not counted as another loss to them both.

"Drink and eat up. If you want something else to eat, just let me know." She side eyes me but doesn't say anything. "Behave yourself or I won't hesitate to put you in the corner, baby." I wink at her when she looks at me, and this time, I get a full body laugh.

"You idiot." She says after she's calmed down. "Let's just watch the movie."

"I'm ready for the time of my life." I say with another grin, which earns me another side eye, *and* a groan. I relax back into the couch and watch Makenna watch as Baby and Johnny's relationship develops. After all these years, and the amount times we've watch this movie, as well as the fact she could possibly recite the movie word for word with the actors, she's still completely taken in by it. It's amazing. *She's* amazing. When she finishes her hot drink, I pull her in to snuggle with me, and I'm glad I didn't go to work today.

"Don't you go to sleep there." I tell her as she gets comfy with a blanket as well.

"I won't, I promise." She says, but when the end credits start rolling, I can hear Makenna's low snoring. I don't move, I keep her just as she is and close my eyes as well. A nap never hurt anyone, I think as I feel myself drift off.

Chapter Thirty-seven
MAKENNA

I wake up snuggled into Brady's side, with my head resting on his chest. I can tell he's asleep because the rest of his body is relaxed. I slowly, and as quietly as I can move back so that I can look at him. I just want to take in the man I love and who I know will make the best Dad.

"How long are you going to sit there staring at me like that Kenna? It's a little creepy." He hasn't moved, his eyes are still closed but the corners of his mouth are turned up slightly.

"Thanks for staying home with me." The corners of his mouth move to make a full smile.

"For you, any time." He lightly smacks my butt. "Come on, let's get some lunch and then we can watch another movie."

"Don't you have some work to do?"

"Not really, it can wait until tomorrow. Do you need to get a few things done?"

"Yeah, I do." I admit.

"OK, lunch first, and then you can sit on the couch with me while I watch a movie and you work."

"Brady, I'm pregnant, not fragile." The look he gives me is both hot, and a little scary. Not in the 'he's going to hurt me' scary, more like in the 'my god he's so protective,' kind of way. I pity anyone who even *looks* like they might hurt me or any of our kids. *Our kids! Multiple!* God I hope there's going to be multiple, but first we have to hope this one becomes a reality.

"I know, but that doesn't mean I'm not allowed to look after you." He leans down and presses a gentle kiss to my lips. "So, let me do it, OK?"

"OK, Brady."

"Good girl. Now let's go makes us some lunch."

"I don't think we need to, to be honest. Jules left so much food in the fridge, I think we could almost eat for the next two weeks without leaving the house, and I'm not sure how he managed to get it all *in* the fridge!"

"I don't think you should question Julian's ability to get things organised Makenna. Everything in that fridge is in containers and labelled. We don't *have* that many containers in the *house*, so he got them from somewhere, and I can't imagine that Logan had them all sitting there waiting to be used." We both snort with laughter at just the *thought* of Logan having enough plastic containers to store this amount of food, because it's insane! "Have you seen the freezer? It's worse than the fridge! He couldn't have cooked it all, even *with* Logan's help, and not just because Logan's help in the kitchen is like a contradiction in terms. I mean you know I love your brother, but cooking is *not* one of his many skills." I let out another snort of laughter.

"You're not wrong." I admit. "He's lucky to have Jules, otherwise he might starve." We give each other a look, an understanding that those two need to get their shit together.

We settle ourselves on the couch, eat lunch and then I get to work, while Brady watches a movie.

Dinner is chosen from one of the many containers still in our fridge, and I know we're going to have my brothers, and possibly Brady's parents over for another meal or three to even make a dent in the amount food we have in the house thanks to Jules.

We watch another movie, because why wouldn't we? Brady wants me to rest, and that apparently means sitting on my butt watching movies. Just for tonight, I indulge him, but I also get a promise out of him that he's going to work the next few days, because I can't deal with this kind of attention from him for too long! We have an early night, because I'm apparently tired and need to rest, which means we're both waking up pretty early the next day, and that's how the next few days unfold.

We get up early, Brady gets me breakfast, I head to work, Brady brings me lunch, then he heads to work himself. Dinner is the only time I get to myself, and I'm in bed when Brady gets home, just like always.

"Hey baby, I'm home." He says as he climbs into bed, pulling me into his body. "How are you feeling?"

"Hey honey, I'm fine. How was work?" I say, still half asleep.

"It was work." He laughs when I jab him in the stomach with my elbow, he knows I hate it when he says that. "It was work. It was busy, which is great, but I'm tired."

"Get some sleep." I whisper, because I know he hasn't slept well the last few nights. It also means I don't have to tell him that I've been having a few cramps tonight. I don't want to think about what they might mean, so I decide I'm going to sleep on it, and deal with them in the morning.

The next morning, I wake up feeling sick. I put it down to nerves, because I have my appointment at the clinic today, that is until I roll over and realise the movement really upset my stomach, and I'm on feet and bolting to the toilet to get rid of what I've eaten in the last week. At least, that's what it feels like anyway. When I'm finally done, I wash my face and rinse my mouth out, and decide a shower is what I need.

While I wait for the water to heat up, I go to the toilet. When I notice the blood on the toilet paper, my heart skips a bit. I know it can be normal for some women in the early stages of pregnancy to bleed a little, for me however, it's never been good news.

Steam is filling the bathroom, but I can't seem to move off the toilet. I'm rooted to the spot, not really knowing what to do.

"Are you OK Kenna?" My head snaps up to see Brady standing in front of me. He kneels to look into my eyes.

"I'm bleeding?" I stutter out.

"Where? Did you hurt yourself?" He asks, looking over my naked body, cataloguing every part of me to see if there's blood anywhere.

"No, I'm not injured Brady. I'm *bleeding.*" He stops looking my body up and down. That's when I see that he understands what I mean, and he notices the toilet paper in my hand.

"It can be normal Makenna, we both know that. It's early and your body and hormones can still be trying to sort themselves out." I can see the panic in his eyes though, and I know we both know that this doesn't end well for me. It hasn't the last few times, and I can't convince myself that this one will be any different. "Come on, let's get you cleaned up, then we can call the clinic and see if we can get your appointment moved up."

He's so matter of fact and takes charge so easily that my autopilot kicks in and I let him lead me to the shower, where he washes me, then himself. Then he leads me out, drying us both.

"Kenna, baby." I look up at Brady like it's the first time I've realised he's even here, but he's already dressed. "You get yourself dressed, and I'll call the clinic, OK?"

"Sure." He's already put some clothes on the end of the bed, and when I see a pad sitting with my underwear I realise that's why he didn't dress me himself. I need to do this. I don't think, I just move my body to get dressed like I've done a thousand times before this morning. Just as I finish, Brady walks back in the room, his phone still at his ear.

"Give me a second, and I'll put you on speaker so that you can ask her yourself." I sit down on the bed, and Brady sits next to me. "OK, go ahead."

"Good morning Makenna, how are you doing?" The doctors voice is gentle, and soothing.

"Good morning Doctor Morris. I'm good, how are you?"

"I'm fine Makenna, but are you really good?"

"No."

"So, can you explain to me what's going on this morning?"

"I woke up, and when I moved I felt sick, so I went to the bathroom."

"Were you sick? Did you throw up Makenna?"

"Yes. I think I lost everything I've eaten in the last week." I chuckle weakly.

"OK, can you tell me what happened next?"

"I turned on the shower, and went to pee, but when I wiped myself, there was blood." I close my eyes at the memory.

"That's when I found her Doctor Morris." Brady adds.

"OK. Are you cramping Makenna?"

"Yes, but they're not much worse than any that I get when I get my period."

"OK, how about we get you to come in now, and we'll give you a check up and see where we go from there. How does that sound?" I don't answer her, I can't. I know what's happening, I've been through it before.

"That sounds good, thank you Doctor Morris. We're ready to leave now, if that's OK? It will take us about half an hour to get to you, will that be OK?" I hear Brady talking, and I understand the words he's saying, but I don't think we need to go to the hassle of going to the clinic. I think we all know what's happening here, and there's nothing she can do for me now.

"No. I want to stay home, and just let it takes its course." I mumble.

"I would like you to come in Makenna, just so that I can check you out. There are a lot of women who spot in their first few weeks of pregnancy, and this is what could be happening."

"It's a waste of your time, and my energy." I sigh. "We all know it, so why don't we just not."

I lie down on the bed and curl up. I can hear them both still talking, but their voices are background mumbles in my head. I don't know how long I lie there for before Brady's helping me to my feet, and walking me out to the car. I feel numb.

"There's no point Brady." I tell him as he pulls the seatbelt over me, and buckles it. He doesn't speak, at least I don't think so. He kisses my cheek lightly, moves out of the way and closes the car door. It's a kind of distant thunk in my head. We're driving out of the gates of Drake Wines before I realise, and even though I know there's no point to the trip, I don't have it in me to protest anymore, so I close my eyes. I feel Brady's hand come to rest on top of mine and give it a gentle squeeze, but I don't have the energy to react, and he just leaves his hand there. He thinks I don't brush him off because it's comforting, when in reality I can't be bothered moving my hand away, and his touch is just making me feel worse. I've let him down.

This man who gives me everything, and I can't even give him a baby.

Chapter Thirty-eight
BRADY

I don't know what to do. Nothing seems to be enough. I'm not enough. I mean what's the point of having decent swimmers if they can't stick the fucking landing?

Makenna is so quiet, and withdrawn. I wish she didn't have to go through this again.

Doctor Morris and I tried to be positive, but Makenna knows her body and she's been through this before, more than once unfortunately, so I trust her gut instinct.

Yet, I still have that small amount of hope living inside my chest, that this time, *this time will be different.*

So, even though I'm looking at Makenna, and seeing that haunted withdrawn look on her face, I can't help but have a tiny spark of hope.

I've read up on all the information I could possibly get my hands on, and I read them in my office where no-one else sees me.

Bleeding early on doesn't always mean a miscarriage.

Cramps early on don't always mean a miscarriage.

Vomiting early on can simply be morning sickness or her hormones settling in.

Exhaustion can simply be her body setting itself up to carry this baby to term.

And yet, as I pull up into the carpark at the clinic, I can sense that this one isn't going to be the exception to our rule. To her rule. The worst part is, no-one can tell us why.

My sperm count is great, and they're healthy, strong.

Makenna's eggs are healthy, and they can't see anything wrong anywhere else.

So, why? Why can't we keep a baby full term?

I know Makenna feels like *she's* letting *me* down, but I feel like I'm not doing enough. Being enough for her. I don't know what to do anymore.

I look over at Makenna. She hasn't moved since I parked the car. Neither of us have.

"We're here baby." She flinches, but she doesn't move. It's not until I see that small flinch though, that I realise my word choice probably wasn't the best one. See, I'm an idiot who doesn't even know what to say to his wife when she's so obviously in pain. "I'm sorry Makenna." I say quietly, before getting out of the car and walking around to her door, and opening it for her.

"I'm not ready." Her voice is a whisper, and I crouch down so that I can hear her properly, and look at her beautiful, sad face. "If we go in there, it's real Brady, and I'm not ready."

"OK. We can sit for as long as you need." And that's what we do. I end up sitting on my butt on the asphalt next to her door, holding her hand in mine. When my phone rings I have no idea how long we've been sitting there like that, and I ignore it. Whoever it is can wait.

"Brady." I jump as a hand touches me lightly on the shoulder. "Brady, I understand if you both need some time to deal with this, but we think you'd both be more comfortable inside. We can bring you in the back, and take you right into a room on your own, but you shouldn't be sitting out here."

I look up and see Doctor Morris. "I'm so sorry, this must look terrible to your other patients, but Kenna, she just couldn't come inside yet." I explain.

"I'm not worried about other patients, or how it looks Brady. I'm worried about you two." She nods to her right, and suddenly there's a wheelchair next to me. "I think this might be helpful, so Makenna doesn't have to walk."

"That's OK, we don't need it Doc, I'll carry her."

I reach over Makenna, unbuckle the seat belt that she left on, then scoop her up in my arms. Thankfully, her arms automatically wrap around my neck and she rests her head on my shoulder, like it's too much effort to hold it up.

"I've got you Kenna." I whisper in to her ear, and then we make the walk to the clinic together, the doctor leading the way, and the nurse bringing up the rear with the wheelchair.

"This way." Doctor Morris says, pushing open the door to a room I've never seen before. It's not quite as sterile or clinical as the other treatment rooms here. "You can put her down on the bed just there. You can even get up there with her if you both want. There's more than enough room." She's right, it's not just a hospital bed.

"Thank you." I say, gently placing Makenna on the bed, then walking around the other side to be beside her.

"The nurse is bringing in a portable ultrasound, but we'll leave you two alone for a while. I'll check in on you shortly and see how you're going." She places a hand gently on Makenna's arm, and talking softly like she doesn't want to spook her, she says, "Whenever you're ready Makenna, we have to do an ultrasound and see what's going on. No hurry though, OK?"

Kenna nods, but doesn't speak. The doctor gives me one more sad look and then leaves with the nurse that bought in the ultrasound, the door closing quietly behind them.

I don't know how long we lie there for, but the doctor pops her head in once, nods, and leaves us be again. We haven't moved. I'm holding Kenna, and she's gripping tightly onto my arms, silently begging me not to let her go. It would take someone tearing me away from her to let her go right now.

The door opens quietly, and Doctor Morris walks over to the bed, rests her hand lightly on Makenna's and speaks quietly. "Are you ready now sweetheart?"

I feel, more than hear Kenna's breath hitch, but she nods yes, and moves to lie on her back. I go to move away to give her some space, but she grabs my hand, pulling me close. She doesn't look at me, but she does pull me close, so I go. Not that I was leaving her, I was just making room for her to be comfortable. "I'm right here Kenna." I whisper into her hair.

"OK, are you ready?" Kenna nods again, but still doesn't speak. "You know how this works. The gel should be warm, I'll squirt some on your stomach and then I place the wand on, and I'll move it around to see what we can find."

The doctor does everything and then sits there for what feels like an eternity looking at the screen. Her face doesn't give anything away. Not until she cleans the wand, puts it away and then cleans off Kenna's stomach. The look she gives me shatters my heart into fucking pieces.

"I'm so sorry Makenna. Brady." Makenna lets out a loud sob, and turns to bury her face in my chest. "I'll leave you alone for a while. There's a bathroom just over there. Take all the time you need."

"Thank you." I barely croak out, closing my eyes and holding my sobbing wife close.

Fuck. Fuck. Fuck. Fuck!

I hate that we lost another baby, but I hate listening to Makenna sob her heart out even more when all I can do is hold her.

I'm not sure how much later, Makenna pulls away from me, gets off the bed and heads to the bathroom without speaking. She stopped crying a while ago, but she still hasn't spoken a word.

I startle out of my thoughts when the door quietly opens, and a nurse steps in the room. "Do you need anything Mr Harris? Is Mrs Harris OK?" Her voice is gentle and soothing, but it still grates on every last one of my nerves. Is my wife OK? What kind of question is that? Of course she's not fucking OK! OK is the last thing my wife is. But I don't give voice to any of my thoughts, because she doesn't mean it like that.

"Makenna just went to the bathroom, she'll be out in a few minutes." I tell her, not answering her question.

"Take your time." I suddenly feel like take your time is code for, come on guys we need the room, or we want to go home ourselves, so move it along.

"Thank you." Is all I manage to say to her, and then she leaves as quietly as she entered, and I'm left sitting on the edge of the bed staring at the wall.

Suddenly my head feels too heavy to hold up anymore, so I drop it into my hands, rest my elbows on my knees and close my eyes.

"Brady?"

My head snaps up at the sound of her voice, raspy from the tears she's cried, and exhaustion she feels. "Can we go home now, please?"

"Absolutely. Just let me check in with the doctor and then I'll get you out of here OK?" She nods and lets me lead her to a chair to sit down in.

I walk to the door, open it to look for Doctor Morris, and I see her as she walks out of another room reading a folder in her hands. "Doctor Morris." My voice is rough. From not speaking for a long time, and the emotions of the day.

"Brady." Her pace quickens, and within a minute she's standing right in front of me. "Is Makenna OK?"

"Umm I guess. She wants to go home, but I wanted to check in with you before we leave." We both walk into the room, but Kenna doesn't look up, she continues staring at her hands. "Do we need to do anything before we leave?"

"There's just a few things to go through before you leave, OK Makenna." Kenna nods. "Have you been to the bathroom since you got here?" Kenna nods. "Was there blood still?" Another nod. "Was there a lot? More than a normal period for you?" Kenna shakes her head. "OK, that's good. Your body will take care of everything and we don't need to intervene. That being said, I'd still like to see you again in a week to check up on you, and make sure everything went the way it's supposed to. Are you OK with that Makenna?" Another nod. The Doctor turns to look at me, the sadness in her eyes almost takes me down. "I already got the nurse to make an appointment for next week. If the day or time doesn't suit, call up the office and get them to rearrange it." She hands me a card with the date and time on it.

"Thank you Doctor Morris." I cough, because my voice is rough, and breaks over a couple of words.

"I'll send a nurse in with a wheelchair, and we can get you back out to your car the same way we got you in."

"That's OK, I'll carry her." I say.

"Sure Brady, but I'll send a nurse to give you a hand anyway." She holds a hand up to stop me from talking. "Before you start to protest, you're going to need some help with the doors and unlocking your car."

"Thank you. For everything."

"I just wish it was better news." She rests her hand gently on my arm. "Take care of each other, and I'll see you next week.

A few seconds later a nurse comes in, I hand her my car key without a word, and I pick Makenna up in my arms again, and walk her back out the same way we came in a few hours ago.

Chapter Thirty-nine
MAKENNA

The drive home from the doctor's clinic is quiet, neither one of us talking, because we don't know what to say. The radio playing quietly is the only sound besides our breathing. It isn't quite what I was hoping for, but it is what I was expecting after this morning.

I really thought that perhaps our time away on our honeymoon had worked its magic and we finally had a pregnancy that would stick.

I've been working on the assumption that it's been stress that's prevented me from staying pregnant these past few years, simply because of everything we've been through.

It wasn't much before my parents' accident that we decided to start trying. We both want a family, and neither of us cared if marriage or children came first, we were always going to get married at some point. They were both going to happen eventually, except now it appears that one of them may never happen, and I can't see the light at the end of the tunnel anymore.

Oh, I know we have options, lots of them, and while I don't need help to *get* pregnant, I *do* need help keeping that baby in my body long enough that it can survive. Something that never even occurred to me might happen. As far as I know my parents didn't have any issues on that front, but of course neither of them are here to ask.

Brady pulls into the driveway of our house, my family home, the one I grew up in that always had kids in it, and I didn't even notice that we'd arrived back at Drake Wines. The garage door opens, he parks the car, and the door closes behind us, keeping the rest of the world out. I can't move, I just sit there, wondering where the hell we go now. If I walk in that house

I'm going to be hit with the reminder that we may never fill it with the kids we were hoping for.

The hand that Brady's had resting on my thigh the whole drive home, rises to hold my head, then he wipes a thumb under my eye. I turn to face him, because I don't understand why he did that, and his other hand reaches up to cradle my face. Now both thumbs are wiping under my eyes.

"What are you doing Brady?" I ask him, confused by the tears on his face, until I realise that I'm crying too. I reach my hands out and cradle his face in mine like he's doing to my face, and we just let the tears fall together.

"I'm sorry Kenna." He chokes out. "I'm sorry I can't give this to you." That's what he thinks?

"No Brady, *I'm* sorry. This is something we *both* want, and I can't give it to *you*." I swallow deeply, close my eyes for a few seconds to gather my courage to say what I need to say. When I open them, the pain I see in Brady's eyes almost kills me, but I need to say this. "You're going to make a great father one day Brady, and if you need to leave, if you need to find someone else to give you that, then I want you to. I want you to go find what you need." My hands drop from his face, and I turn away from his frozen body and move to get out of the car. I can't stay here any longer, I need to get out. I need space.

Before I can even open the door, Brady is slamming his door closed and he's on my side of the car, opening the door for me.

"What the fuck was that Makenna Rose Harris? Can you repeat that because I think I must have heard you wrong. I swear you just told me to leave you and find someone else!" He's not touching me, and I'm still sitting in the car, but that doesn't mean I can't feel the anger vibrating off him. I'm angry too, but not with him.

"You heard me correctly. I'm defective and this isn't what you signed up for. So, if you need to leave, I understand." I tell him while trying to get out of the car, and move past him to get into the house.

"You want me to *leave*?" He asks, blocking me from getting out of the car. Do I want him to leave? No, but I do want him to have the life *and family* that I know he absolutely deserves. "I want you to do what you need to do, Brady. I know how much you want a family, and that means kids of your own, and the truth is, I might never be able to give you that. You were there, you heard what the doctor said today."

"Yeah, I was, and while things might be a bit more difficult for us, it doesn't change how I feel about you Makenna *Harris,* and it never will. Kids or no kids, adoption, fostering, IVF or whatever the fuck else, we'll look into it. We have options Makenna." He sighs, closing his eyes and taking a deep breath to calm himself down. Then he wraps me in his arms, in the tightest hug I think I've had since before my father passed away, before pulling away and holding my face in his hands, tightly so that I can't move, forcing me to look into his eyes as he says, "But none of that, and I mean *none of it,* Makenna, changes how I *feel about you.* You are the love of my life and you have been since I was sixteen, nothing will change that. Do I want to be a Dad? You better fucking believe I do, but I want that *with you,* and not some random woman you've created in your head because you think I need to move on." He rests his forehead on mine and takes a shuddering breath. "I love you, Makenna. I'm not leaving you. Whatever happens, happens to *us,* and we do it *together.* You don't have to make one decision, choice, or step without me. I will be with you every step of the way."

"OK." What else can I say after that speech?

"OK?" He steps back from me, and the car, which means I can get out now, and go inside. His head drops to his chest, and he says, "You don't believe me, do you? After everything we've been through, after all these years, do you *really* think *this* is what is going to push me away?"

Without looking back, I say just loud enough for him to hear me, "You deserve better than this Brady. You need and deserve more."

"Fuck that!" He growls behind me and before I know what the fuck's happening, I'm swept up off my feet and being held tight up against the chest that I know so well that I could tell him apart from all other men blindfolded.

"What the hell Brady?!" I scream.

"Don't. Don't you dare fight me. Don't you dare assume that you know what I'm feeling, or thinking right now, because even though we've known each other for almost half our lives, you seem to have forgotten everything I am." He frowns down at me in his arms and I've never seen that look directed at *me* before, but I have seen grown men shit themselves when it's been directed their way. "Open the door for me please Makenna."

I reach out to turn the knob, and push the door open, without saying a word. Brady pushes through the doorway and shoves the door closed with his foot. A second later we're on the move again and he's walking through the house towards our bedroom.

"I can walk Brady, I'm not fucking disabled, just broken." I ground out between my teeth, not feeling as irritated as I no doubt sound, I just feel, broken.

"You are *not* broken Makenna. Do you fucking hear me? This isn't just your issue baby, this is an *us* issue, and I won't let you take this on all by yourself. No guilt. You get tonight only. Tonight to wallow and feel guilty about something that you can't fucking control, but then you're picking yourself up, and we're getting on with business, and I don't care what that looks like." He says as my feet touch the floor, and that's when I realise we're in the bathroom. Before I know it, he's got the bath running and I'm naked.

"What the hell Brady?" I ask, hands on hips, naked hips, but I'm trying here.

He places his hands gently on mine, but doesn't pull me close. "Let me look after you Kenna, please?" He murmurs. I don't answer, because I can't, there's a lump of emotion lodged firmly in my throat, so I nod instead.

That's all the permission he needed, because he lifts me up and gently sets me down in the warm water.

"Now, lie there and relax for a while. Get all that broken business out, and then we'll talk. We can be angry, sad, disappointed together, but we are *not* broken Kenna." He starts to leave and just because I'm a smart arse I have to respond to his demand.

"Yes, sir." I salute, even though he doesn't turn to look at me.

"Good." Is his only response until he gets to the door. "Did you ever think that you're not the only one who's broken Makenna? Maybe I'm broken too." He doesn't give me the chance to say anything, before he's gone, and all I can hear is his retreating footsteps, and my own heart beating rapidly in my chest.

He's right though, it never occurred to me that *he* could be the reason we can't have kids, or the combination of the two of us is what is creating the issue. The thought makes more tears stream down my cheeks, and I turn off the taps that Brady left running. I pull my legs up until I can rest my chin on my knees and just sob. I guess I'm mourning the loss of the children that haven't come and aren't likely to. I want it so much, and I want it with Brady. I've had so many daydreams of mini Brady's running around the house and yard. Smiling, happy, carefree little boys, with brown floppy hair and chocolate brown eyes that you can just melt into, enjoying the sunshine and life in general.

He can say that maybe he's the one that's broken, but he's not the one who miscarried his baby, I am.

Chapter Forty
BRADY

I don't know if I can watch McKenna go through this again. She's heart-broken and so am I.

We're home from the doctors and she's having a warm bath, then I'm putting her to bed with either a sappy movie or her favourite book to read. She needs to rest for a couple of days, and I'll be here to make sure she does. I've already called Damien at the bar to let him know that I'm going to need a couple more days off. I didn't give him any details, I just told him that Makenna had a medical emergency and I needed to stay home and look after her. The truth is, I think I need to take time off to get my own head straight again as well.

Now I'm leaning on the kitchen counter staring at it like it holds all the answers. I'm supposed to be making my wife a honey tea and getting her a couple of her favourite biscuits, but I'm stuck here, staring at my hands that are pressed to the bench.

I'm not sure how long I've been standing here, but that's where her brothers find me when they, of course, let themselves into our house.

"Hey dude, where's Kenna?" Caleb asks in his always fucking happy way.

"Caleb!" Logan says to his brother in his always stern kind of way, he just has different tones really. "What happened Brady?" He asks, placing his hand on my shoulder making me flinch. I didn't know he was close enough to touch me. Caleb sits on a stool on the other side of the bench and it takes me a minute to realise he has no food or drink in his hands. I must look fucked up. "Is Kenna OK? Where is she? Are you OK?"

"Makenna's having a bath and no, you can't go annoy her Caleb, not to-day."

"I wasn't going to man." I know he's telling the truth because he hasn't moved a muscle. "Are you OK?" He asks, the concern on his face is almost frightening, Caleb is rarely anything except exuberantly happy most days.

'Me?" I ask, shocked because it's Kenna I'm worried about, and they should be worried about their sister too, not me. "Yeah dude, I'm fine, why?"

"Well, for one, we found you staring at nothing leaning on the bench in your kitchen." Caleb says.

"And two, Brady, you're crying." Logan says quietly.

I am? Shit, I am! I didn't even realise, but the pool of my tears on the bench is a dead giveaway. Logan grabs a tissue from the box that Caleb has deposited on the bench and hands it to me.

"Are you guys OK?" Caleb asks, and I can hear the concern in his voice. It's kind of nice to know these guys are as worried about me, as much as they are their sister.

"We're fine." I take a deep, shaky breath, and scrunch the now wet tissue in my hand, leaning a hip against the bench. "We will be."

"You guys just got married, you've been together forever. You're not breaking up are you?" Caleb asks and Logan throws him a look so dirty, Caleb should be using a tissue to clean the mud off his face! I can't help laughing, but it's only a couple of chuckles before it turns into a sob.

I pull myself together after two gulping sobs. Logan's hand grips tighter onto my shoulder, so tight that it's almost painful and I'm kind of enjoying the pain. It's matching the non-physical pain in my heart.

"He didn't mean to say that." Logan growls.

"Yeah, I did. I didn't mean to hurt his feelings, 'cause obviously he's already in pain, but yes, I *did* mean to ask that. I want to know." Caleb declares.

"It's ok Logan." I say, patting his hand, and giving him what I hope is a reassuring smile and then I turn it to Caleb. "We're not breaking up. I'm not leaving, it's not happening. No matter what, OK?"

Caleb nods and Logan says, "You don't have to explain *anything* to us Brady, it's *none* of our business." Logan glares at his brother again, and I can't help the rough laugh that escapes me. I love these two idiots as if they were my own brothers, and although we're not linked by DNA, we are definitely brothers.

"No, it's OK." I take a deep breath and hope that Kenna doesn't kill me when I tell her that I told her brothers what's been going on. "Makenna was pregnant."

"What do you mean *was*?" Logan asks, in his quiet, serious, and yet concerned way. You seriously don't want to be on the other end of a yelling Logan, because that means you've really fucked up!

"She miscarried, again, this morning." I tell them, a sob escaping me.

"I'm so sorry Brady." Logan says quietly.

"Didn't you have that appointment with your specialist today? That's why we came by, to see how that went." Caleb sounds so hopeful, it's painful.

"Yeah we did." I sigh, another deep, full body sigh as I explain the events of the past few days, leaving out a few details that I'm sure Makenna can tell her brothers if she wants to. "When we got home, she told me to leave. Your sister told me to leave and find a woman that, 'wasn't broken, because I deserved better than a woman who can't give me the family I want,' can you believe that?"

"She actually *said* that?" Caleb asks, shocked.

"Yeah, she actually said that as she walked away from me. Didn't even look back to tell me to my face."

"She's hurting Brady." Logan says quietly.

"What the fuck do you think I'm doing Logan? You think I'm getting ready to throw a party? Maybe it can be a divorce party, and I'll invite only single women. What do you think, is that a good idea?" I ask, my voice louder than I intended for it to be, and I hope that Makenna is too involved in her own thoughts to have heard me.

"That's not what I meant Brady, and you know it! You guys were made for each other and we've always known you would get married and start a family. You've *always* been, and will always *be* our brother." Logan says, and Caleb nods his head in silent agreement, which is unnerving because the guy is *never* silent. "I'm just saying that she's in pain, and she knows you are too, and she's just trying to make your pain better the only way she thinks she can. By taking away the problem, her. Whether she's right or not, is a completely different issue." He stares me down, and I crumple under his stare. "I just wish you guys had told us sooner, we might have been able to help."

"Well, we didn't think you'd be *that* interested in your sister's sex life to be honest, and other than lending us your womb, I doubt there's anything you *could* do Logan." I say, with a laugh that sounds watered down, even to me, but when Caleb shivers at the thought of his big sister having sex, I actually let out a loud laugh for the first time in a couple of hours. When I hear him mutter an 'ewwwww' under his breath, my laughter becomes uncontrollable and I double over.

"What the hell? Is he broken?" Caleb asks, and I hope his questions are directed towards Logan, because I have no hope of answering him.

"Geezus Caleb, of course he's not *broken*!" Logan tells him. "He's fucking emotional you idiot, and you just proved his point as to *why* they didn't share what was going on with us, because you're an immature idiot."

I take a few gasping breaths to calm myself and tell them the truth. "Well, that's not entirely true. We didn't tell anyone in the beginning because we wanted to surprise our parents. We all know how much they *all* wanted to be grandparents." I say with a shrug and a sad smile, because the Drakes didn't live long enough to become grandparents and my parents might be waiting a while. "Then the accident happened, and the wedding and we figured that the stress was a contributing factor, and the doctors agreed."

"But it's not?" Logan asks.

"No."

"I'm going up to see Kenna." Caleb says, starting to stand up from his chair.

"No, you're not. She's soaking in the bath and she does not want you in there." I tell him, hoping he gets the picture that his sister is *naked,* and the last person she wants to see is her little brother.

"Right." He says and sits his arse back in his chair, just as my phone chimes with a message.

Makenna: Can I have my tea and biscuits in bed, please?

I smile, because how could she think I would say anything other than yes?

Me: That was the plan baby.
Makenna: Oh OK thanks.
Me: Are you out of the bath already?
Makenna: Yeah. Didn't want to sit there
Followed quickly with:
Makenna: Just want to cuddle up in our bed. With you?
Making me both happy and sad at the same time.
Me: I'll be right there baby, just getting everything ready.

"Is she OK?" I don't even bother asking Logan how he knows I'm messaging his sister.

"Yes." I say, as I move about the kitchen getting everything together to take up to her. "I'm going to go take care of my wife. I'll call or text you later when she's up to seeing you." I say as I finish up and start walking towards our bedroom.

"So, she's out of the tub then?" Caleb asks.

"Yes, Caleb. We're going to lie in bed and relax for a while."

"That's not code for, 'have wild monkey sex' is it?" He asks and Logan does me the favour of clipping his brother on the back of the head. I would have done it, but I've got my hands full.

"Makenna just had a miscarriage, do you really think they're going to have sex right now Caleb?"

"What? They're always having sex!" Logan glares at him. "Sorry Brady, I guess I didn't think, it just kind of slipped out."

"They've been trying for years, *years* Caleb, to get pregnant. Today they lost a baby, and you think it's the time to ask if they're going to have, 'wild monkey sex', because it might offend *your* sensibilities?" Logan clips him around the back of the head again.

"That's not what I meant. I just didn't think alright? I mean, I don't want to think about them having sex ever, you either for that matter, so yeah."

"You're so insensitive sometimes Caleb." I leave them in the kitchen arguing. They can let themselves out, they let themselves *in* often enough, I'm sure they can work out the opposite pretty easily. "Trust me, no-one in this house wants to think about *you* having sex either." Logan grounds out at him.

"It's not like we haven't walked in on them having sex often enough. I mean I didn't think it was out of the realms of possibility that they'd be heading that way today as well."

"Maybe not, but the difference today is, we found Brady leaning over the kitchen bench crying. *Crying*, Caleb!"

"Yeah, OK, you're right, but that doesn't mean I'm insensitive Logan. I know they're both hurting."

That's the last thing I hear as I head towards our bedroom and Makenna. I leave them to it, I don't give a shit what they do, as long as they leave us alone tonight to grieve.

"Hey baby." I say just as I reach our bedroom door.

"Can I hear my brothers' voices?" She asks, and just as I'm about confirm her suspicions, Caleb barrels past me and jumps on the bed, bouncing Makenna around and then settling himself on my side of the bed. The man has no boundaries I swear!

"Hey sis."

"Caleb, what are you doing here?" She asks him, but looks at me. I send her an apologetic look that I hope conveys just how sorry I am for what she's about to endure.

"I came to make sure you're OK, it's what we do right? We're family." He asks, as Logan strolls through the door, concern written all over his face as he sits on the edge of the bed, and pulls Kenna into a tight hug. These two have become really close since their parents' accident, and they've taken on the shared responsibilities of the business that their Dad built.

"I'm sorry Kenna." He says quietly into the top of her head, and a fresh wave of tears starts.

"And you call *me* insensitive!" Caleb mumbles.

"Shut up Caleb!" Logan growls, but Kenna pulls her younger brother into her side for a group hug.

"Come on Brady, you know you want to be part of the Drake snuggles." Caleb says, waving his hand in the air to draw me into their group.

"Harris, Drake snuggles now Caleb." Kenna sniffles and looks over her brother's shoulders at me.

"It has always been Drake, Harris snuggles Kenna." Caleb says, making Kenna cry even more, and making me a little emotional myself.

"Move over." I tell them, my voice rough from all the emotions of the day. They all shuffle over to make room for me, and I force my way into Kenna's side. I wrap my arm around her, and pull her in close. As soon as she's comfortable, with her head resting on my chest, her brothers are on us. I'd say smothering us, but it kind of feels good to not be dealing with this on our own anymore, and I know Makenna feels the same when I feel her sigh and relax into the cuddles.

Chapter Forty-one
MAKENNA

I should have known when I heard my brothers' voices that I wouldn't be left in peace, but I can't say that the group hug isn't welcome. We've always been close I guess, as close as siblings get when they're young children, but when our parents died, we all stepped up, and just looked after each other. Although, I'm sure Caleb would tell it a different way, we *do* love him unconditionally.

I'm not sure how long we all lay there, but my tea goes cold, and Caleb eats my cookies, which pisses Brady off, which in turn, causes Logan to clip Caleb over the ear. Again!

"Let's get pizza." Caleb says after I don't know how long of lying there quietly in between some joking, reminiscing and tears. What I do know is it's dark outside.

"Alright Cal, you and I can go get it." Logan says, as he stretches, and makes to get off the bed.

"No way!" Caleb protests.

"Just get it delivered Logan." Brady says, and the decision is made.

"You guys don't have to stay here for dinner, we're good you know?" I say quietly as the guys all start shuffling about.

"Is that your way of kicking us out?" Caleb asks with a pout I haven't seen on his face for years.

"No, but I know you guys have lives of your own." I look between them and they both just shrug. "You've got, I don't know, friends or girls to catch." I look at Caleb and then to Logan I say, "And where's Jules? Aren't you two having dinner together?" The blush that tinges my big brother's cheeks is adorable, and has me wishing that he could admit not just to us, but himself as well, that Julian is more than his *friend*.

"Despite what you *all* believe, I'm not actually a manwhore, and I don't go out chasing ladies every night or weekend. I am more than happy to stay home, get pizza and watch movies." Caleb says in the grumpiest tone I think I've ever heard from him since he was a hormonal teenager. "In fact, I really like staying home."

"I'm sorry Caleb." I say, raising my hands in defence, then I look at Logan as he makes his way towards the door, trying for a quick exit, but I'm not letting him off that easy. "So, where's Jules?" I have a feeling I know where he is, because he's been staying here at Logan's house a lot more recently.

"He's at my place."

"Waiting for you?"

"Well, no, he knows I'm here and why."

"So, either go home or call him to come over and enjoy pizza with us as well."

"Are you sure you're up for visitors Kenna?" Brady asks, concern written all over his handsome face.

"Jules isn't a visitor Brady, he's family." Brady nods his head, we've talked about these two and we agree on the matter. Then I look over at Logan. "Either Jules joins us, or you go home, simple." Logan looks at Brady like he can or would override me, but Brady just shrugs his shoulder.

"Kenna's told you the deal man, take it or leave it. I'm not arguing with her today of all days, but she's also right, Jules *is* family." Brady claps him on the shoulder like I've seen them do a thousand times to each other, it's so familiar, and normal that a lump of emotion forms in my throat.

Brady pushes my brothers out the door, giving them instructions to order dinner, and to go get Jules. Then he closes our bedroom door on them, and locks it.

"Hey!" I hear Caleb say, and then there's pounding on the door. I hear Logan's mumbled voice, then Caleb exclaims, "Well, I wasn't expecting that, and it was kinda rude, you know? We're her *brothers,* it's our *job* took look after her."

"You're right, we are, but Brady is her husband, and we have to respect that. They've had a rough day Caleb, you should just be happy that they want to share a meal with us tonight. Let them have some time together while we organise that meal, OK? They need each other more than they need us right now."

"But I just want to." Caleb starts and Logan interrupts whatever he was going to say, but I can't hear his answer, just the rumble of his voice disappearing down the hallway until there's an awkward silence left in the room.

Things have never been awkward between Brady and me in all our years together. Not even when we were teenagers, and awkward was expected. I'm not sure how to deal with it, because I haven't had to deal with it before now.

"I'm sorry about that, they just kind of, well you know. They're *your* brothers, and they did what they do best." He says with an almost shy smile, and yet another shrug of his shoulders. I guess it's up to me to clear the air, but I just don't have the energy, or mental capacity to do it.

"You don't have to be sorry Brady, I know what they're like, and honestly, I appreciated them being here." It's the truth, but seeing the hurt on my husband's face hurts me too, but I don't know how to fix that either.

"I'll leave you alone for a while then. I'll get one of the boys to come get you when the pizza arrives." He moves towards the door and I feel like a bitch, because I don't want to be alone. I *want* to be *with* Brady. He's *always* been the one I go to, but I still feel like I'm letting him down, and I don't know how to *not* feel that way. He gets to the door, his hand on the knob, and hesitates. "I love you Kenna." He says, his voice husky with emotion, but he doesn't turn to face me.

That's when I realise that I'm pushing him away, he's not leaving me.

"Don't go." My voice comes out in a hoarse whisper, and I can't stop the tears from falling down my face. "Please Brady. Don't leave. I need you. I'm sorry." I close my eyes and bury my face in my hands, because I can't look at him, not if he's going to leave me, and walk out that door.

In less than a heartbeat, the bed dips under Brady's weight and he's pulling me into his body. "I'm not leaving baby. Ever." I try to take a deep breath, but a loud sob comes out of my mouth instead. "Let it all out Kenna. Let it all out baby, I'm right here, and I'm not going anywhere." He places my head on his chest and I wrap my arms around his waist.

"I'm so sorry Brady." I sob.

"You have nothing to be sorry about Makenna, and I'll keep saying it until you believe me. I love you, and that hasn't changed."

After a few minutes, my tears dry up, and the sobbing stops. I take a chance to look up at Brady's face. I need to see if he's telling me the truth, but what I see breaks my heart all over again. The pain on the man's face is devastating, but when I add to that, the not quite dried tears on his cheeks, my heart shatters into tiny pieces. I reach my hand up to cup his face, and he flinches. He didn't see it coming, because his eyes were closed, but he doesn't open them when he feels my touch. He stays perfectly still, like he doesn't want to break the spell. This isn't about just my pain. This is about his pain as well. I love this man more than life itself, and if life is about just the two of us together forever, then I'm going to be grateful for every damned day I have with him.

"Hey, honey, look at me." I wait, I don't know how long, before he opens his bloodshot eyes, and meets mine, which I'm sure look pretty much like his. "I'm sorry." I say again, but when he goes to speak, I place my fingers on his mouth to stop him. "No, I'm sorry you're hurting as well, and I'm sorry it took me this long to notice. I love you Brady. Always." I've been so wrapped up in my own pain, in my own need to protect myself, that I forgot that he needs me as much as I need him.

"Makenna, baby, there is nothing in this world that I want more than to have a baby, a child, with you, but not at the expense of your health. Mental or physical." He takes a deep, shuddering breath, and I bring my hand up to hold his face, to force him to look me in the eyes. "You're my forever Makenna Harris, I will love you always. I don't care if it's just the two of us for the rest of our lives. It will just mean we can have loud sex wherever, and whenever we want. Eventually, Caleb will stop just walking into our home without permission, because of it."

And just like that, this man that I love, my husband, makes me laugh on what could only be described as a really shitty day. This is how he proves to me every damned day that we belong together. He's not making light of the situation, he's just making the most of it.

"I love you Brady." I tell him, then he takes my cheeks in his hands and kisses me. It's a light, sweet kiss that is so full of the love we share it almost brings me to tears again. We're lost in each other, and our kiss, until there's a gentle knock on the door.

Chapter Forty-two
BRADY

A gentle knock on the door interrupts our kiss, and I know before he speaks who is on the other side of the door.

"Hey Logan." I say so that he knows we've heard him.

"Hey guys, pizza is at the front gate, so it will be here soon." Logan says just loud enough so that we can hear him through the door. How did I know it was Logan? If it had been Caleb there would have been a *lot* more noise, and the door handle would have been rattled. He'd also be asking why we locked the damned door. He's used to having easy access not just to the house but to his sister, and most days I don't mind that at all, in fact, it's one of the things I love most about being a part of this family. Not today though.

"Thanks Logan we'll be down in a few minutes, we just need to freshen up. If we're not down when it arrives, don't wait for us."

"But it's your house."

I don't let him finish. "Logan."

"Yeah, OK. No worries Brady." Then his quiet footsteps become silent as he goes back to the kitchen.

"You know, you don't have to go out there Kenna. I can bring some pizza to you."

"I want to go Brady. I *need* to go out there, and enjoy my family." She says with a smile, but it's a sad smile. Reading between the lines, because I know her so well, what she means is the only family we'll ever have. But I have a feeling, and a strong one at that, that she's wrong, but she's not ready to hear that just yet.

"OK, then let's get cleaned up, and head on out there before Caleb eats it all, because you know if we leave him to it there won't be much left." That makes her laugh, and it's the best sound I've heard all day.

"You're not wrong." She sits up so that I can slide off the bed, and when I get to my feet, I hold my hand out to help her up too. When I see what she's wearing, or should I say *not* wearing, it's my turn to laugh loudly.

"Holy shit! Caleb would die if he knew you weren't wearing anything except your underwear under the covers while he was in here snuggled up to you." I say through my laughter.

"I know. I took great pleasure in knowing that I had no pants on under the covers." She smiles, and this time it's full of joy, and her usual sass, and I love it.

"You're incredible Makenna Harris, and I love you."

"I know." She says, and walks with some extra sway in her hips to our bathroom, where we wash our faces, and stare at each other in the mirror. We both look exhausted, anyone looking at us wouldn't think that we got home from a relaxing week in Bora Bora just over a week ago.

"You know you're going to have to put on some pants before we join them for dinner, right? No-one but me gets to see you even half naked. Brothers or not."

"Maybe I'm trying to impress Jules." She says, with a wiggle of her eyebrows.

"I think you and I both know you're going to have to work really hard to get his attention." I smile back at her, and even though she's still smiling, I see the sadness flash in her eyes. To anyone else they'd probably wonder if they saw it at all it was that quick, but I know my wife, and it was there. "They'll work it out baby, I promise."

"I hope so Brady, I really do." I pull her in close for another tight hug, and then we hear my phone vibrate across the bedside table and laugh, because we both know that's Logan telling us to hurry up before Caleb eats all the pizza. We order more than we think we could all possibly eat, and yet there's never leftovers. "You should probably check that, it could be Damien."

"It *could* be, but I think we both know who it really is." I roll my eyes, and she laughs quietly, making me smile as I walk over to pick up my phone.

"So, who is it?"

"You were wrong, it's Logan reminding us that the pizza is here, and if we don't get to the kitchen soon, Caleb will have eaten it all, leaving us none." I turn to smile at her. The truth is, there was more than one message on my phone, but she doesn't need to know about the other one, I'll deal with it later. She also wasn't right in her assumption of who the other message is from though either. "Are you sure you want to join them? You can stay here, and I can bring you some food, if you don't want to be around people. It's been a hell of a day. No-one would blame you if you didn't want the company. You're allowed to take whatever time you need to yourself."

"I'm OK. I want to have dinner with them."

"If you're sure?"

"Stop it Brady. I'm not broken." I can't hide the look on my face, and she sighs. "I know, OK. I know I shut down this morning. I know I shut down at the clinic. I *know* I shut you out, and I'm *sorry*. I am *so* very sorry about that Brady, but I knew. I knew what was going on. I knew what my body was doing, because I've been there before, and I just wanted to protect myself for a red hot minute."

"You told me to leave Makenna." My voice is barely a whisper, but even I can hear the pain in it.

"I know, and I'm sorry Brady. I'm so fucking sorry." She sighs again, but it's weariness more than frustration. "I love you so fucking much Brady, and I just want you to be happy. I know how much you want kids, for so long, our plans have been to get married and have a family. Well, I can't guarantee you the family we had planned, and I wanted to give you an easy out, if that's what you wanted."

"I don't want out Makenna. I love you whether we have kids that have our DNA, or not. If we choose not to have kids in any way, I'm good with that too. As long as it's *our* decision, one that we make together Makenna. You don't get to make the decisions for *us*, and you don't get to make *my* choices for me either, just like I don't get to make yours. It's just the way that relationships work, the way I thought our relationship worked until today anyway."

"I know, and I'm not going to keep apologising for it, so can you forgive me?" She asks, nervously.

"Forgive you?" She nods, tears glistening on her eyelashes. "There's nothing to forgive. You were grieving, you still are. That's why we'd all understand if you want to stay in here and take some time out for yourself. No-one is going to judge you for that, and if they do, I'll kick their arses! I'd even take Logan on if the need arose, that's how serious I am."

"You'd lose." She says with a soft laugh.

"Probably, but it wouldn't stop me from giving it a red hot go. I could get a few good hits in before he realised what the hell was happening." I say seriously, knowing I'd take on anyone that gave her any grief at all about anything.

"Get that scowl off your handsome face. Logan is the last person you need to worry about." She says as her laughter get a little louder.

"Again, that doesn't mean I wouldn't try to take him on if I truly had to." I promise her, as I pull her into a tight hug.

"I know." She says in my chest, as she wraps her arms around my waist and squeezes me tight. "I love you Brady."

"Good." She doesn't get to reply, because there's a knock on the door before Logan speaks.

"Ahhh guys, if you don't come out now, I'm afraid there won't be any pizza left for you." He pauses for a couple of seconds and then says, "Although, there's still plenty of food in the fridge so you wouldn't go hungry. On second thoughts, if you guys want to stay in there and just be together after today, no-one would blame you. At all."

I look at Kenna in my arms, and raise an eyebrow in question at her. "It's your choice baby."

"We'll be out in a minute Logan, thanks for coming to get us."

"Are you sure? Because I can get Caleb out of here in a few hot minutes, trust me."

"I promise, I'm good."

"I'm happy I won't have to kick your brother's arse!" I tell her, and she laughs happily as she opens the door to find Logan still standing there.

"You couldn't kick my arse if you tried Brady." He says, pulling Kenna into a tight hug, and then walking back into the kitchen.

"After you, love of my life." I say, waving my hand for her to follow her beast of a brother, causing another laugh to bubble out of her.

When we get to the kitchen, Jules rises up out of his chair without a word, and wraps his arms around Kenna. When I hear her sob quietly I growl, but Jules just snickers and pulls me into their hug as well. "I'm sorry, and I know you don't want to hear this right now, but I believe this is going to happen for you two. I believe it with all of my heart." He kisses Kenna on the cheek, and then, without warning, he kisses me on the cheek too. My startled expression must be amusing, because everyone laughs.

"I saved you guys some pizza." Caleb announces with a dimpled grin.

"Only because I threatened your dick if you didn't." Logan mumbles and Jules hits him on the arm, and gives him a dirty look.

I struggle to hold in a snort of laughter as I push in Kenna's seat, then sit down myself.

We spend the next hour eating, laughing, and talking about everything and nothing all at the same time. When Kenna yawns for the third time in a matter of minutes, I call an end to the night.

"Alright guys, thank you for your support, we both really appreciate it, not to mention dinner, again, but it's time for you to leave. Makenna's had a long hard day, and she needs to get some rest." I know that Kenna's first instinct is to tell me off for kicking her brothers and Jules out, but then she yawns again, and smiles at me.

"I think Brady might be right. Sorry to kick you guys out. I do appreciate everything you've done for us the past few days, especially today. It would have been easy for me to continue in my silent, dark cave, and blame myself. So, I'm glad you made me want to come out of our bedroom and eat dinner, and just talk about nothing. The laughter has helped repair some of my broken heart."

Jules gets up and gives Kenna another hug. "You go get some rest beautiful, and if you need anything you let me know."

Caleb comes up, and almost squeezes his sister to death. "Easy dude." I tell him.

"Sorry, I love you sis, anything you need, I'm here." He kisses her on the cheek and collects all the empty pizza boxes. "I'll get rid of these on my way home. Night y'all." Then he's gone.

"Makenna, you're not coming in to work tomorrow, and before you even try to protest, I'm not taking no for an answer. I know you're going to say that you need something to do, and you want the distraction, but the truth is, you need to take at least tomorrow to get your mind *and* your body OK." He hugs her tightly, and then it's my turn. "I know I can trust you to make sure she looks after herself, but you need to take care of you too, OK? Promise me?"

"I promise Logan. I've taken the day off work tomorrow too, so I'll be here to make sure she relaxes."

"Good job. Now both of you head up to bed. Jules and I will clean up the little bit of mess here, so you don't have to worry about it tomorrow." Before we can protest, he's pushing us out the door and towards our bedroom. "We'll let ourselves out, and I promise to lock the doors behind us. Off you go."

"Come on then, I guess we've been told." I tell Kenna as I take her hand in mine, and walk back to our room.

We go through our nightly routines with the ease of a couple that have been doing the same dance for years together. When we get comfy in bed, I turn off the light, and pull her close.

"I love you Makenna."

"I love you Brady."

That's the last thing I remember before the exhausting emotion of the day envelopes me and I fall into a heavy, if restless, sleep.

Chapter Forty-three
MAKENNA

The morning after the night before.

That's how I'm thinking about the day after my miscarriage. You'd think, after having a few, that I would be used to them, that they would get easier to endure, but they're really not. I appreciate Logan telling me to take the week off to rest, but I'm not sure that's what I need. Sure, I would have stayed home today, for sure, but having Brady home with me, watching my every move? That's going to drive me crazy.

I'm awake, but I haven't opened my eyes yet, I don't even know what time it is, but I can already hear Brady's phone getting messages.

"Maybe you should go into work today?' I mumble. It's more of a question than a suggestion though, because I know he's dealing with this loss as well.

"It's not work." He answers quietly.

"Tell my brothers to fuck off then." I smile into my pillow.

"It's not your brothers." He says, sounding distracted.

I roll until I can see him. He's leaning up against the headboard, frowning at his phone. "Who is it then?" I ask.

"They're not the only people who call or message me you know Makenna." He snaps, then closes his eyes and takes a deep breath. "Sorry." He says without looking at me.

"So, do I have to guess?" I ask him, and when I don't get a reply, I continue. "Well, it's not me, because I'm right here. I doubt that Rochelle, or any of the girls are messaging you. It could be either your sister or your Mum."

"It's Mum, OK?" He cuts me off sharply.

"OK." I say, as I roll over the rest of the way to face him. Try as I might though, I can't read the look on his face. He almost looks like he wants to vomit, or cry and run from the room all at the same time. "What's wrong Brady?" I ask softly, placing a hand on his arms. I'm worried now that there's something wrong with one of his parents or Beth. Surely his Mum wouldn't send him a text to tell him that though?

"Nothing's wrong Makenna." He snaps.

"OK then." I say, pulling my hand away, and sitting up. "I think I'll go and have a shower then." I push the blankets off me, and sit in the edge of the bed. As I move to stand up, I feel his hand settle lightly on my arm.

"I'm sorry Kenna. Don't worry about it, why don't you go have your shower, and I'll explain." I sit back down and turn to face him, crossing my legs on the bed, but I don't move closer to him, causing him to sigh. The hand on my arm fell to the bed when I moved, now he places it on my knee. "Mum messaged me last night, and I never messaged her back, so she's been blowing up my phone with messages and calls. All of which I haven't answered." He's looking at the screen on his phone, and not me.

"OK, yesterday was a bad day, and you were distracted, I get that, but why haven't you answered her this morning?" I ask, looking at the time on his phone.

"I did. I told her I was sorry, but we were busy yesterday and then slept in this morning."

"OK, so what's the problem then?" Pauline is a reasonable person, and doesn't expect either of her kids, or me for that matter, to drop everything to get back to her if we're busy. "Your Mum doesn't expect an immediate response Brady."

"Generally not, no."

"What's different about this time?" I'm confused now.

"Someone told her they saw us at the clinic yesterday." He can't look at me, his eyes are glued to the screen on his phone.

"OK, well it wasn't a secret Brady." I say, cautiously.

"No, it wasn't, but now she wants to know why we were there." He says quietly.

"Oh." We're both quiet for a minute or two, and he still can't look at me. "Well, tell her the truth."

"I don't want to break her heart." He says so quietly I'm not sure whether he actually spoke, or I imagined it.

"What do you mean?"

"Come on Makenna, you know why." He argues, throwing the covers off, and jumping out of bed. When he starts pacing in front of the window I know he's got a lot on his mind, but I can't help him work it out if he doesn't tell me everything.

"No, I don't Brady, please explain it to me." I ask quietly.

He stops pacing and looks at me with a look of surprise on his face. "How can you *not* know what I mean Makenna?"

"I don't know what to say Brady." It's obvious he thinks I know what he's talking about, and I'm just playing dumb, but I have no clue what's going on.

"We were *at the clinic.*" He emphasises the word clinic like it should means something, and it does but obviously not the same thing.

"*The clinic that she knows we're going to in order* get *pregnant.*" He says the words as one, and in a rush.

"Yes, I know she knows what was going on, Brady. She knew what we were going to the clinic for, but it's also a doctors clinic, not just a fertility specialist." I say, and as soon as the words leave my mouth, it dawns on me what Pauline is hoping. "Oh shit! She thinks we're pregnant?"

"She hasn't said as much, but if I don't answer her in a more direct way within the next few minutes, she's going to be here, asking a lot of questions. I don't want to put you through that Makenna. It was enough last night with the guys, but they're your family."

"So are your Mum and Dad." I say, getting out of bed and walking over to hug him. "They deserve to know what happened as well Brady. We knew we were going to have to speak to them. Why don't you invite them over for lunch, and we can tell them face to face. Together."

"I don't want to put you through that Makenna. They're going to ask questions you don't want to answer."

"I'll answer them, and if they're too much, I'll tell you." I reach up and kiss him. "I promise Brady. I'm OK. You know me better than that, I'm not a fragile flower. I'm not going to break honey."

"Yesterday." He starts, but I kiss him to stop him from talking.

"Yesterday I was a mess, I know."

"Things don't change that quickly Kenna."

"Well, they probably shouldn't, and in any normal person, they probably wouldn't but I'm OK today Brady." I sigh, and snuggle into his chest, pull him tighter to me as he finally hugs me back. "I'm not going to blow wind up your skirt Brady, and tell you that it doesn't hurt. That I'm not still hurting, because I am. You and I both know this isn't the first time we've been through this, and I'm in no way saying it gets easier or any less painful, because it honestly *does* still hurt. A fucking lot, but we can't keep living like that. You were right. There's more than one way to have a family."

"Are you saying you want to stop trying?" He tries to pull away from me, but I tighten my hold on him not wanting to let him go.

"No, that's not what I'm saying, in fact, I'm saying the complete opposite." This time it's me that steps back, but only far enough away so that I can look at his handsome face. "I want to go ahead with our plans as soon as we can."

"You mean, you want to take the hormone stimulator?"

"Yeah. I know I have to go back in a week to check in with the specialist, but I'm hoping she can tell us we can start sooner rather than later."

"Are you sure that's the best idea Kenna? I mean, it was only yesterday that you were telling me to leave you because you think you're broken."

"I know, but I want this. We want this." I rest my hands on his chest, keeping him from moving away. "You still want a family, right?" I know I sound panicked, but I can't help it.

"Yes Kenna, of course!" He rests one hand on both of my that are still on his chest. "It's just that, I don't want to watch you go through what you did yesterday again. I hate watching you in so much pain."

"You were hurting too Brady."

"I was. I am, but it hurts me more when you're hurting."

"I know honey, but I'm OK." I kiss him, and before we can get too carried away, his phone vibrates in his hand, and when he looks at it and sighs deeply, I know it's Pauline again. So, I take his phone, and message her back.

Me/Brady: Come around for lunch in about half an hour

Mum: Why? What's going on?

Me: Pauline, it's Makenna, please come join us for lunch and we'll explain everything

Mum: OK, we'll see you soon

"They'll be here in half an hour, so we should have a quick shower." I say, handing back his phone, and walking back to the bathroom. "Are you going to join me?" I ask, look his way just as I get to the doorway, and throw my top at him, but he doesn't move. So, to get him moving, I shimmy off my pants, throwing them over my shoulder as I put a little extra sway into my hips as I disappear into the bathroom.

When Brady hasn't joined me by the time I step into the steamy shower, I figure I'm on my own, and start washing my hair. My morning shower is my favourite time. Warm to hot water cascading over my body from head to toe, it's almost meditative, and it gives me time to think. That is, if Brady doesn't join me, then it generally gives me a different kind of relaxing time! I smile thinking about all the different times over the years he's joined me, or I've joined him, it truly is a great start to the day.

"What are you smiling about baby?" Brady asks, stepping in behind me, and wrapping his arms around my waist, resting his chin on my shoulder. I jump a little in surprise, because even though there's only us in the house, I had my eyes closed and didn't hear him enter the room. "Sorry, didn't mean to scare you." He says, kissing my neck, and I stretch to the side, giving him better access. I feel his chuckle against my skin, and it sends a shiver down my spine, making me groan.

"Brady." I say his name in raspy voice that I barely recognise as my own.

"We can't Kenna." I know he's right, and I want to stamp my foot like a two year old, but I don't.

"I know." I say, turning in his arms to hug him back. "But that doesn't mean you can't." I say with a smile, dropping to my knees before he can stop me.

"No Kenna." His hands reach out to pull me back into his embrace, but I don't allow myself to be moved, and when I take the head of his cock into my mouth, his head drops back, and he says my name again on a moan. "Just for a minute."

"Mmm Hmmm." I agree, as a take all of him in my mouth, knowing that the vibrations will go all the way down to his balls. His hands run through my wet hair, gripping on without pulling. We don't have much time, but I know what gets this man off quick. I run my hands up the back of his thighs, massaging along the way. When I reach his nice tight buns, I give them a couple of tight squeezes, then run a finger along his butt crack, before playing with his balls.

"Fuck Makenna! If you don't stop in a minute I'm gonna come." I pull my mouth off his cock, and rest my lips against the head.

"Isn't that the point?" I ask, him before running my tongue around the ridge of the head of his cock, and swallowing him again.

"We can't. We shouldn't. You can't." The poor guy, he can't finish a sentence! His eyes are shut tight, his grip on my hair is getting tighter, his nails are scratching at my scalp, and his hips are slowly moving back and forth to his own beat, while trying his best not to choke me. "We. Don't. Have. Time."

But we do, and we both know it. I continue playing with his balls, while rubbing a finger behind them, and massaging him, never letting up from pumping up and down his cock with my mouth. My other hand gripping him tightly at the base to keep us both steady. I feel his legs start to shake, and hear the growl that works its way through is body, before he lets out a loud roar, and releases in my mouth. "Hell Makenna." He murmurs as I stand up, my hand gently caressing him still.

"I won't do it again if it's hell Brady." I say with a smirk.

"Come here." His voice has that sexy after orgasm hoarseness to it that I love, and I go to him without thinking about it. He pulls me in tight to his body, gripping the back of my head, and pulling my lips to his, gracing me with a scorching kiss. His tongue tangling with mine and I know he can taste himself on my tongue, and when he groans, I wish could take it further, but we can't, and now we really don't have the time.

I pull away before I want to, and smile up at him. "Guess I better finish washing myself and brush my teeth, I don't want to kiss your folks with dick breath." I say as I fill my mouth with water to rinse it. There's five seconds of silence, and then Brady throws his head back to let out a loud laugh, one hand over his heart.

"I doubt either one of them would notice, but you're right, I don't want to think about you kissing my parents with my come on your breath." He kisses me, and then goes about washing himself. We dance around each other like seasoned professionals who knows the other persons next move.

When I'm finished, I go to step out of the shower, and Brady leans over without touching me to whisper in my ear, "When you get the all clear next week, I'm paying you back for that one." Then he steps back into the shower like nothing happened, while I'm stuck with one foot in and one out of the shower, a shiver running up my spine, causing goosebumps to pop up all over my body. The promise of things to come is always a turn on. "Beth and Jake are coming over too. I figured we might as well tell everyone, everything together, that way there aren't a million phone calls or questions later."

His voice brings me out of the turned on haze I was in, and I move to grab a towel, to dry myself off.

"Good idea."

"You're not upset are you?" He asks, his voice closer than I was expecting, and when I look up I realise he's out of the shower as well.

"No, of course not, just thinking."

"About what?" He asks, but he knows what he did, because I see the twinkle in his eyes, and the slight smirk on his lips.

"How disappointed your Mum is going to be when we tell her." I say, and even though it wiped that cocky smirk off his face, I feel mean for doing it that way. "Not to mention all the ways you're paying me back for the best blowjob of your life." I say, walking out of the bathroom, and into our bedroom, with his laughter following me.

"I knew it! You had that dazed look on your face, and your eyes were slightly glazed over. It's the same look you get when I lick your pussy from the bottom to your clit." His words send another shiver up my spine, because I love it when his mouth is on my pussy. "Yeah, just like that." I can hear the smile in his voice, but I don't look around to see the smile I *know* he's wearing, because we really have run out of time now.

"We don't have time for your shenanigans Brady." I admonish him with a smile on my face, but before he can say anything in return, the doorbell chimes. Luckily, we're both dressed just in time.

"I'll go let them in." Brady says as he does up his jeans.

"I'm right behind you." I say, as I do mine up too, and follow him to the front door.

Chaos erupts when Brady opens the door, as a chorus of hello's, good morning, no afternoons are said and kisses on cheeks are exchanged.

"Come on, let's go and sit down." I say, and Brady takes my hand in his, and gives it a gentle squeeze. Once we're all seated, Brady and I sharing an armchair, his parents, sister and brother in law sharing the couch, I take a deep breath, and close my eyes. When I open them again, all I can see is the hope, and excitement on Pauline's face, and it almost kills me to tell her what I have to. "Brady said that one of you saw at us at the clinic yesterday?"

"Well, no, my friend Josie did." Pauline says, barely containing her excitement. I'm not even sure how anyone saw us there yesterday. Granted I'm not the best person to ask about any of the details from yesterday, but I *do* know that we didn't go in the front door.

"Well, I'm not sure what *Josie* thinks she saw, but I don't think she understood what was going on." I say coughing in my discomfort. Brady has a tight grip on my hand, and still squeezes it a little more in support.

Even though he leans in and whispers into my hair, "You don't have to do this."

"I'm not pregnant. We're not pregnant." I blurt out, because I just want it said. "I actually had a miscarriage yesterday." The room is suddenly very quiet, except for the quiet gasps from both Pauline and Beth. "We've been trying, without truly trying, to get pregnant since before my parents' accident."

"Unfortunately, this isn't our first miscarriage." Brady says quietly.

"Oh why didn't you tell us?" Pauline asks us, the sadness in her voice feels like a knife to my heart.

"That was my choice." I start.

"No, it wasn't, it was *our* choice." Brady says. "No-one knew that we'd been trying. Not even the boys. After the first time, we just couldn't bring ourselves to tell anyone."

"This time." I swallow. "This time I thought it was different. I *felt* different, but it wasn't meant to be."

"Ohh Makenna, Brady, I'm so sorry. I wish you'd told us sooner, but I'm glad you're telling us now." Pauline gets up and engulfs us both in a hug. "So, what happens now?"

Chapter Forty-four
BRADY

I can't help cringing at my Mum's direct question. I know that she didn't see Makenna yesterday, so therefore has no idea how this last miscarriage affected her, but it's still a pretty painful, and direct question.

"I'm sorry, was that the wrong thing to ask?" Mum asks, while everyone else on the couch is silent.

"No Pauline it's fine." Makenna says at the same time as I say, "Well, kind of Mum, yeah."

"I'm sorry. I should have asked if you were OK Makenna."

"Mum. Let them speak." Beth says, as she pulls her back down to sit beside her.

For the next thirty minutes, I sit and watch Makenna explain the situation, and answer every question known to mankind about our reproductive situation. I interject every now and then, but Makenna takes the floor like the strong woman she is. Although I watch her closely, I can't see the woman that I had to carry in and out of the clinic yesterday, even so, at the thirty minute mark I call it off.

"Right, that's enough. For today at least. We invited you over for lunch and to let you guys know what's been going on, but that doesn't mean we want to talk about it for the rest of the day. These are some very intimate details you're getting into here, and I'm not sure that you need to know *that* much about us."

"Yeah come on Mum, let's give Makenna and Brady a break from all the questions. We came over to join them for lunch, not interrogate them." Beth says, taking Mum's hand in hers and pulling her to her feet. "Not to mention, I'm hungry. Have you still got some food that Jules made?"

I can't help laughing at her behaviour. "Of course we do, he made enough for all of us to eat for a few weeks."

"I'm not sure what we would do without Jules around." Kenna mumbles to no-one in particular, as we follow everyone into the kitchen.

"Why don't you two sit down and let Mum and I organise something for lunch?" Beth tells us, more than asks. "I mean, it's not like we can't work out something delicious, I'm sure Jules has everything labelled."

Makenna laughs, and it's music to my ears. "You have no idea, wait until you see it all. It's labelled with what's in the containers, and what it all goes with and where it's stored." She shakes her head, while still laughing. "He is amazing! If I wasn't married to your brother, I might just have asked for Jules' hand in marriage."

"Well, that's hurtful." I say, my hand on my heart in mock pain.

"How would your brother react to that confession?" Beth asks, laughing.

"Oh I don't think Caleb would be too upset or shocked by it." Kenna says with a straight face, and everyone laughs.

My Dad pulls out a seat for Kenna to sit in, and when she looks up to smile her thanks at him, he smiles almost sadly back at her. When he pulls her into his arms for a tight hug, she slides her arms around his waist, and holds him tightly back. My Dad doesn't always speak the words, but he always shows he loves us. Jake and I sit down at the table and let them have their moment, and when they pull apart, I can see the tears in both of their eyes. I want to ask Kenna what he said to her, because I know without a doubt that he whispered something in her ear, but I'll wait until everyone leaves before asking her about it. My Dad waits until Kenna's seated before he sits down himself, and when he does, he pats her hand one last time, before coughing and asking Jake about work, changing the subject, and getting conversation flowing.

Mum and Beth bring over a huge platter of roast chicken pieces, and a big bowl of salad, that I swear I never saw in our fridge when I looked in there last night, but was obviously in there somewhere. Jake jumps up to go and help Beth bring in plates, cutlery, and glasses, while my Mum brings in a big pitcher of homemade lemonade, that again, I've never seen before. I don't even know anyone who has *made* lemonade before.

When Kenna made a move to help them, my Dad placed his hand on her and quietly said, "Let them look after you Makenna. You too Brady. It helps them both to know that they can do something for you two at the moment." Kenna squeezes his hand and relaxes into her chair.

Once everything is on the table, and everyone is seated, plates gets passed around and the conversation starts off slowly, and quietly, but it becomes animated pretty quickly. It's hard not to join in and have fun when Jake is giving Beth grief over something she said or did, because giving my sister hell is *always* fun.

When talk turns to our honeymoon, I go and get Kenna's tablet so that she can show everyone the pictures she took while we were away. The modern day version of the holiday slideshow I guess. I sit back and watch as Kenna explains every photo she took, where we were, what we were doing, and who we were with. Everyone else at the table is enthralled with the pictures and the stories that go with them, and Kenna has my family eating out of her hand, entertaining them.

More drinks are poured, snacks and dessert is shared, alongside the laughter, the questions and the women cooing over the villages and the children in them. I enjoy every second of watching my gorgeous wife recall, and tell all of our stories. I barely add anything, except to correct her every now and then, or to add something extra, but, basically, I just enjoy her absolute happiness.

When there's no more photos to show, and no more stories to tell, Kenna turns off her tablet, and a silence settles over us again, and I know what's coming, so I try to head Mum off at the pass, but I can't stop her from asking Kenna all kinds of questions. Kenna answers each one without even blinking an eye, but I still worry that it's all too much.

I'm saved from telling Mum that enough is enough, by my Dad, who stands up and declares it's time they headed home. He hasn't said much today, but I know that he feels much the same way as his wife does, and I know that he loves us.

"Come on Pauline, we've taken up enough of the kids day, we've got things to do at home ourselves." Mum starts to protest, but he doesn't let her. "Come love, we need to get going. Kenna and Brady need to relax for a while." That's what does it, and she starts to clean up the few dishes left on the table.

"Leave it Mum, we'll do it after you guys leave. Thank you for everything." Kenna says, hugging Mum tightly.

"We didn't do anything Makenna." She replies, her eyes glistening.

"Yes, you did." Kenna kisses her on the cheek, and steps away. I wrap her up in my arms and smile at Mum.

"Come Pauline, let's get home, and leave these two kids to relax. They've had a big couple of days." Dad says, as he takes her hand in his, and steers her towards the front door.

"We're leaving too Beth, come on." Jake leads her to the door behind our parents, but she breaks free from him, and throws her arms around both of us.

"I'm sorry. Just know I love you, and I believe that one day soon you're going to make the best parents a kid could have."

"Thanks Beth." I say, my voice croaky with emotion. She coughs, then she's gone, and Jake sends a small nod our way before saying goodbye and leaving in front of our parents.

"Bye kids." Mum says as Dad leads her out the door behind my sister. "If you need anything, anything at all, you just call us, OK?"

"We will Ma." I call out, lifting my arm to wave to them all.

"Enjoy the rest of your day." My Dad says, as he closes his door, and starts the car. I can tell he's saying something to Mum, and she's giving him what for as he does, and I can't help laughing.

'What do you think he just said to her?" Kenna asks, laughing herself.

"I'm guessing she wants to come back up here to hug one, if not both of us, and tell us that it will all be OK, and that she loves us. Then, at a guess, he's telling her that we *know* this, and she does not need to come and reassure us. Again. That she should leave us alone to deal with it the way we want to." We both jump a little when we hear my father's voice boom out of the car with a resounding, "NO!" We hear the locks close, and he opens the window and yells out goodbye, before taking off down the driveway, a little faster than he should be considering he's sharing it with people walking as well.

"Well, that was fun." Kenna laughs and pulls out of my arms to walk inside.

"If that's what you want to call that." I grumble, closing the door behind me. "Now, get back here." I demand, stretching out to take her hand in mine, pulling her back into my arms. "What are your plans for the rest of the day?"

"I haven't really thought about it, but I guess cleaning up the kitchen is the first thing that needs to be done."

"I'll clean." I tell her, without hesitation.

"I'm not fragile Brady." She says quietly.

"I know you're not Kenna, I just want to take care of you, can you let me, please?" I ask, rubbing my hands up and down her back, not quite begging, and not quite telling her this is what's happening today.

"Sure Brady." She sighs deeply.

"Why don't you relax on the couch and watch a movie?" I suggest, and when she doesn't agree right away, I figure that's a no. "Or you could get yourself comfy out on the back deck with a book and enjoy the sunshine out there?" I knew this idea would tempt her. She rarely gets time to sit and read for pure pleasure these day, and when she does, she generally falls asleep.

"Hmmmm. That could work." She looks up at me.

"I'll even bring you a coffee, a snack and a cold drink of your choice." I kiss her smiling lips. "I'll even leave you in peace out there."

"What are you going to do while I sit outside?" I sigh, knowing that she's made up her mind.

"I can log in and get a few things done for work." I'm barely finished speaking before she's trying to step out of my embrace.

"See, I *told* you to go to work today Brady! I knew you shouldn't have the time off." She says angrily, trying to step out of my embrace, but I pull her closer.

"That's not what I said Kenna. It can wait, it can *all* wait. Everything except you and me can wait baby. What I meant is, that if you want to go relax with a book, then I can busy myself with some work I can do online. I don't really feel like reading, and I don't feel like sitting down to watch anything. I'm feeling a little restless, so I won't be able to concentrate on a book, but work, that I can do. It's nothing that can't wait, honestly, but if you're going to relax, then I can do it." I drop a kiss to the top of her head. "If you want, I can sit out on the deck with you?"

"I would like that." Kenna says quietly.

"Done deal then. Go get your book, and get comfy. I'll organise everything else and meet you out there." I turn her around, pointing her in the direction of the back doors, and smack her butt to get her moving.

"Brady!" She squeals, but I know she doesn't hate it, even if she does protest.

"Well, get moving then baby." I smile at her before walking in the opposite direction. I have to walk away, because my cock is starting to pay attention, and we can't take it any further today, or for the next week. She might have taken it in hand in the shower earlier, but I won't let her do it again until we can enjoy each other.

I check to make sure that Kenna did as she's told, and then I get busy making her a coffee, pouring out another cold drink, and put up a plate of crackers, cheese, and the smoked ham that she loves. I take it all outside, and place it on the table beside her lounger, then I bend down, and leave a kiss on her cheek.

"Thanks Brady." She mumbles, she's totally engrossed in the book on her e-reader, and I chuckle quietly as I walk back inside to get my laptop so that I can get some work done. I lied to Kenna before, I *do* have work that needs to be done, it's not anything that can't wait, but it will help when I get back to work if I can get some stuff done today.

When I get back outside and set my laptop down on the table, I pull out the chair to sit down and look over Kenna because she's awfully quiet, I cover my mouth and laugh. She's asleep with her e-reader resting on her face. I get up, and place it on the table. I take the plate and cold drink back inside and put them in the fridge, then I sit down and get to work.

Chapter Forty-five
MAKENNA

I come to because I can hear Caleb talking. Loudly!

"Shut the fuck up Caleb!" Brady shout whispers. "Kenna's asleep, and I'd like her to stay that way."

"Why?"

"Why are you here Caleb?" Brady asks, the frustration in his voice makes me laugh. Luckily, I'm facing away from them, meaning they can't see the smile on my face.

"I came to see my sister."

"You saw her yesterday Caleb, and I know you've messaged her a few times today as well."

"Well, she had a shitty day yesterday, and I wanted to check in on her."

"And the multiple messages today weren't enough?"

"Well, no. I wanted to check on her face to face, because she can hide her feelings in a text or phone call." Caleb whisper yells back at Brady. "I know you're married to her, but I've known her my whole life, and trust me when I say, she doesn't always tell the truth when it comes to her feelings. I need to see her face when I ask her something, otherwise I can't always tell if she means it or not."

"Well, fine, but sit your arse down and be quiet, she's sleeping."

"Fine!" I hear the scraping of a chair on the wooden deck, then Caleb keeps talking. "You know, I'm checking in on you too, you idiot. I love you both, you're just as much my brother as Logan is, Brady."

"I know. I love you too Caleb." A weird silence falls between them for a few minutes, then they start laughing quietly, and my heart swells with love for the two of them.

"She's not asleep you know." I hear Logan before I see him, mainly because my eyes are closed attempting to hold back the tears of joy that are trying to escape. I open my eyes to see him standing in front of me. He must have come in the side gate.

"Crap! Where did you come from?" Caleb says at the same as Brady speaks.

"You don't know that Logan, so keep your damned voice down."

"I damned well do know, she's looking at me right now, with a smile on her face." Logan says in his trademark growly voice, and a frown on his face. He doesn't like being told what to do, by anyone. He sits down at the foot on my lounger, as I turn to look at the other two guys, and he pulls my feet into his lap.

"You know you're brother and sister, not lovers right?" Caleb asks, "Because that right there was creepy shit that only lovers should be able to do. You two shouldn't know each other *that* well!"

"We run a business together Caleb, and we've known each other our entire lives, obviously. We know each other pretty well by now, and can anticipate what the other will do when it comes to business and our personal lives. It's our *job* to understand the other person, and yet I do believe that Brady knows her better than either one of us could, so if he says she's fine, and she needs rest, we should probably believe him, and leave them in peace."

"And yet you still came here to check on her too." Caleb says, narrowing his eyes at our brother.

"You're right, and I came for all the same reasons you did, Caleb, because she says what she thinks we want to hear in messages so that we leave her be. If you talk to her face to face, you can tell if she's trying to hide something. So, yes, I came by to see how she is, and to check in on Brady as well."

I know that Brady's no doubt annoyed that they're here, again, but he can't be annoyed for long after speeches like the two he's received from my brothers tonight, surely?

"So, are we feeding to you idiots again tonight, or what?" Brady asks, as he turns off his laptop, closes it, and starts to stand up.

"No, I'll just head home," Caleb says, standing up.

"No, we're good, I just wanted to check in and see how you were both doing." Logan announces, placing my feet on the ground beside the chair, standing and holding out a hand for me to hold as I stand. I look to Brady, and he gives me a small nod.

"Stay, both of you. Have some dinner with us, again, and then you can go home after you see that we're OK. We're not perfect, but we're doing OK. I promise." I tell my brothers.

"Only if you're sure?" Caleb asks, not me, but Brady.

"Of course we're sure. You're always welcome here Caleb, all I'm asking is for a little respect and consideration." Brady slings an arm around Caleb's shoulders. "I know it's not easy for any of you, and this *is* the family home, *but* just in case you haven't noticed, we're not April and Jack Drake. The truth is, I'm not trying to be Jack, but our door is always open for you, and Logan. I just don't want to share every meal with you guys, or to lock you guys out, so."

"Consideration, respect, and a little bit of distance?" Caleb says, and Brady laughs.

"Yeah, exactly." Brady laughs, and then thumps Caleb on the shoulder. "Just wait until you find the love of your life Caleb. You'll understand what I mean then, and you won't want any of us just barging into your place without knocking, or warning."

"What about Logan?" He asks cheekily.

"What about me?" Logan asks.

"Well, when Logan finds the love of his life, we'll show him the same respect that we'll show you, and expect ourselves." Brady says, not looking back at us.

"You know." I say quietly so that the other two can't hear me. "I was just wondering where Jules is tonight?" Subtle? Yeah not so much, but I don't care too much about subtle where these two are concerned anymore.

"At work." Lo answers me with a shrug of a shoulder. "He said to tell you that he's thinking of you."

"Tell him I said thanks, when you talk to him later tonight." I say with a smile and bumping my shoulder into, well Logan's ribs.

"If I talk to him later, I'll make sure to tell him you say thanks." He hip bumps me back, because our shoulders have no chance in matching.

"Thank him for all the food too. We both know you were more of a hindrance than a help in the kitchen. In fact, I'm surprised he didn't send you to come pick us up from the airport anyway."

"He knew he was leaving town." Logan blushes, but doesn't say any more on the subject. "OK, I'm out of here, if you need anything, you call me, OK? If you want more time off, or you need time off for appointments and treatments, just let me know, and we'll sort it out."

"You mean Margot will sort it out, and tell you what's going on?" I laugh, letting him off the hook from talking about Jules for now.

"Yeah, probably, but either way you know we've got you covered. Caleb and I can keep things afloat whenever you need us to."

"Yeah I know, thanks." He gives me another quick bear hug, says goodbye to Brady, and then he's gone, dragging Caleb yelling out goodnight, with him.

"I know I complain about them, but they're lovable cockblockers."

"You're not annoyed that they came over again tonight?" I ask, around my laughter.

"Not really. They love you Kenna, and they're worried about you. I can't begrudge them for checking in on you, and I never would, you know that, right? It's just that sometimes, a lot of the time, I wish they behaved like normal family members, and called or at the very least, knocked on the door before just making themselves at home and walking in without an invitation to do so." He says, taking my hand, and leading me back inside. "That being said, I get it, and I understand that it all comes from love, and that makes it easier to accept some days."

"They love you too, you know."

"I know they do, and I appreciate that, but like I said, it would be nice to have *some* boundaries."

"I think they understand that now, and you know, once we have kids, they won't want to be here all the time. Too much noise, and they might get asked to change a nappy." I laugh, and try to keep walking but Brady's stopped dead in his tracks and because he has my hand in his I have to stop too. "What's wrong Brady?"

"I think we need to talk." He says, leading me over the couch and pulling me down onto his lap.

"Okayyyyyy." I draw out the word, because I think I know what's coming.

"Don't you think it's too soon to talk about having kids Kenna? No don't say anything, just let me finish. You had a miscarriage yesterday that I thought had broken you completely. I mean you couldn't move, you told me to leave you and cried silent tears that you weren't even aware you were crying baby." He rests his hand on my cheek, the other one holding on tight to mine. "I don't want to rush this. I want to think about it, and make a decision. We don't have to do that now, today or this week."

"I know Brady. I do." I pull my hand out of his so that I can hold his face still so that he's looking me in the eyes when I tell him what I want. I need him to understand what I'm saying, and see that it's the absolute truth. "I'm sorry I said that to you yesterday, and I hate that I worried you so badly that you think I need to be coddled, and I know that it seems too soon, that I've bounced back too quickly, but I know how I feel." I drop my lips to his, giving him a light kiss. "With all of that being said, I also know how I feel Brady. I know I'm ready for this, and I want to fight to have this for us, to have a family with you. I'm not going to lie, yesterday was hard. Really fucking hard, *but* I want to give you this. I want to give *us* this honey, and I'm not going to wait. Well, I'll wait however long the doctor says is healthy, but that's it. Am I still devasted about what happened yesterday? Yes! I'm still devasted from each and every time I got my hopes up and thought I was pregnant, when I wasn't. I'm still devasted from the times prior to yesterday that my body betrayed me. The thing is though Brady, I also know that I'm not giving up. Before you say anything, I know that we can make a family without putting my body and my mental health at risk, but I want to try the hormone stimulant that we'd planned on doing before yesterday happened."

We sit there, me straddling his lap, holding onto his face. His hands resting on my hips, his eyes looking deep into mine to see if this is what I really want and I don't want him to see anything except steely determination, because that's how I'm feeling.

"If you're sure Kenna, but -" I don't let him finish.

"I am more than one hundred percent positive Brady."

"I want this with you, I do Kenna, and I don't care how we get there, but I also want you to be physically and mentally healthy." The pain I see in his eyes almost kills me.

"I know. Can you give me the next six to twelve months of trying this hormone treatment? If it doesn't work after that, then we'll talk about our other options. How about that?" He closes his eyes to think, and takes a deep breath. I know he wants to say no, that enough is enough, but I also know he wants this as much as I do. I know that he wants to give me what I want, I just hope I'm not hurting him in the process as well.

"OK Kenna, you've got a deal."

"Thank you Brady." I squeal, all be it quietly, and drop a hard kiss to his lips, until he pulls away, a scowl on his handsome face.

"But if it becomes too much, for either of us, then we have that discussion sooner, rather than later. We talk about how we're feeling, and how you're dealing with everything. We don't hold anything back. Otherwise, I'm not agreeing to this."

"Deal." I say with a smile, holding my hand out for him to shake it. Instead, he moves us around, and throws me back onto the couch, settling himself between my thighs, and sealing the deal with a scorching kiss that can't really go anywhere, but I still enjoy the hell out of it.

That is until he smacks me on the butt, and sends me to bed while he cleans up the mess we made from dinner. I try to tell him I'm not so fragile that I can't do some dishes, but he just asked me to let him look after me for a while.

Who am I to argue with the man?

Chapter Forty-six
MAKENNA

I'm almost asleep when I feel Brady slide into bed next to me. Either he took his sweet time cleaning up, or I'm freaking exhausted. Maybe a combination of both?

"Sleep well baby." He says, kissing my shoulder as he pulls my body back tight into his front. "I love you."

"I love you too Brady." I whisper, and that's the last thing I remember before waking up the next morning, still wrapped up in Brady's arms. I want to lie here all day, in the safe and warm cocoon of his embrace, but I know that I have to get up. I need to get back to work. I know Logan meant it when he said I could take as much time as I needed off, but the truth of the matter is, I *need* to get back to work. Back to routine, and my normal. I want this week to go fast, so that we can go back to the doctors, get that check-up, then be given the all clear to move forward.

I know my brothers are worried about me. Everyone is, including Brady. He thinks I'm moving on too fast, that I need more time, but the truth is, losing another baby has just given me the drive to make this work. If this treatment doesn't work, then I'll talk to him about our other alternatives, but for now I just want to move forward with the plans we'd already put into place.

Behind me, Brady stirs. I try to move out of his hold, because I want him to stay asleep. He's been worrying about me for the last few days, and he's barely slept. He's going back to work this afternoon as well, so he needs his rest too.

"Where do you think you're going?" He mumbles, his voice deep, and grumbly from sleep.

"To have a shower, and get ready for work." I almost phrase it like a question, but it's not one.

"Are you sure you're ready to go back to work?" He hasn't even opened his eyes yet!

"Yes I am Brady. There's nothing wrong with me honey, I'm fine." I seriously thought we'd hashed all this shit out already.

"If you're sure?"

"More than." I tell him, throwing back the covers, and pulling out of his arms. Now I'm even more determined to get back to work. "Don't you dare make Logan *or* Caleb promise to check in on me either, and if you even *think* of getting Margot to keep an eye out for me, and report back to you, you won't ever be able to have children. Do we understand each other?"

"OK.' He frowns at me, no longer looking sleepy.

"I know you're worried Brady, but you honestly have no need to be. I promise." My voice is softer now, because I know he loves me, and is just concerned I'm moving on too fast.

"If you say so."

"I do."

"OK."

"OK." I agree.

"Well, off you go then." He nods towards the bathroom.

"You're not going to join me?"

"Nope. I'm going to try and get some more sleep. I haven't been sleeping well, and if I'm going back to work this afternoon, I need some sleep."

"Fair enough." He rolls over, snuggling into the covers, and I head towards the bathroom.

I go through my every day routine, and the steam from the shower clears my head even further. Today is the start of the future, I can feel it. When I'm done, I walk back into the bedroom to discover Brady quietly snoring, and it makes him kind of adorable, but I don't want to wake him, so I move quietly about the room getting dressed, and then head into the kitchen for coffee.

"Why are you up so early?" I ask Caleb who is sitting at my kitchen bench, two coffees, and his phone in front of him on the bench.

"I brought you a latté." He tells me, like it's the most normal thing in the world for my little brother to be up and moving *before* me in the mornings, *and* for him to bring me a coffee. From Vines no less.

"How's Leila this morning?" I ask him casually, trying to *not* sound like I'm trying to get information out of him.

"She's busy. Georgie made these for me." he says without looking up from his screen. Again, like it's the most natural thing in the world for him to be here, and getting us both coffee.

"Look, Caleb, I don't need a babysitter OK? I'm fine. Perfectly fine, and more than ready to get back to work." I lean my hip against the end of the bench, bringing the cup of coffee to my lips. There's no way I'm letting decent coffee go to waste. I'm annoyed, I'm not stupid! He finally looks up from his screen, his face wrinkled up in a very adorable frown, and if I told him that, he'd be mad, so I don't.

"You forgot." It's not a question, it's a statement, and now I'm wracking my brain for a meeting that I might have forgotten. "I can't believe Makenna Harris forgot an appointment, a meeting as such." Caleb teases me, crosses his arms across his chest, and resting back on the stool he's sitting on.

"Can you just tell me what's going on? It's been a bit of a busy time Caleb." I know I'm testy, but he's right, I rarely, if ever, forget an appointment or meeting. I regret the tone in my voice the minute I see his face fall.

"I know, I'm sorry. I forgot for a second about, well you know." I don't respond, what could I possibly say? I know he hasn't forgotten because of any malice on his behalf, he's just Caleb. He's always been more relaxed, and easy going. "I decided to come here because I knew you were having a tough week, and I didn't want you to miss the meeting. If you weren't down here soon, I was going to come and wake you up." His smirk is back on his face.

"So, are you going to tell me what I forgot, or are you just going sit there with a goofy smile on your face thinking about interrupting your sister and brother in law having sex? Again."

"Ewwwww I was *not* imagining *that* Makenna, geez. I was thinking about annoying Brady one last time actually, and I mean by letting myself into the house."

"We have a meeting with some contractors about doing some work on those old cottages." Crap!

"I thought that was your project?" He raises an eyebrow at me. "Aren't you working on fixing up one cottage to see if it can be done?" I know we had the conversation, but I can't for the life of me remember what conclusions we came to.

"Yes, we did." He says slowly. "While I *can* do it, I'm not a carpenter, electrician, or a plumber. Neither am I any number of other trades that we may or may not require. I don't have the qualifications for any of that."

"I understand that Caleb." I snap, frustrated by my own lapse in memory, and him stating the freaking obvious.

"Well, Makenna, that may be true, but you also decided that I needed supervision for the project that was classed as 'all mine', because even though you and Logan appointed me nothing more than a glorified handyman in the family business, you still didn't trust me with *this* project, and you needed to hold my hand."

"I'm sorry Caleb, I didn't mean to –" He doesn't let me finish.

"No, you know what Makenna, you told me I couldn't choose a contractor without you being in on the process, and now you can't even remember the meetings we set up. I get that you've got things going on right now, and if you want to put off the project that's fine." He stands up abruptly, collecting his things that I just noticed were sitting on the stool next to him, and gets ready to leave.

"No! OK, you're right, and I'm sorry. I *do* have a lot on my mind, but that's not fair to you. Let's get to these meetings, and you can take the lead. I'm just there to make sure that the contractors aren't dodgy. Even though I'm sure you've already vetted them before getting them here." I rush on, because I know he's about to argue with me about how he's not stupid. "I'm sorry Caleb, truly I am."

Without another word he gathers his things, and starts to leave. "Are you coming with me or what Makenna? The first guy will be at Vines in ten minutes."

"We're meeting them in the bistro?" I ask, surprised. I mean we both have offices.

"No, we're meeting them in the back room at Vines, because it's closer to the cottages."

"Makes sense."

"Are you coming or not? I can do this on my own if you'd rather." He says as he opens the front door and starts to leave.

"No I'm coming, and not because I want to check up on you."

"Sure it's not."

"I want to support you. You wanted this project, and you have some great ideas for the cottages, so I want to see your vision with these guys as well."

"Uhuh." We start walking towards Vines when Caleb stops abruptly to look me up and down. "Are you OK to walk? I mean should we have driven, or maybe I could carry you." He makes a move as if he might just carry me and I take a few steps away from him.

"Don't you even try it Caleb. Ever. I'm not injured, I'm fine, and I am more than capable of walking a short distance." What is it with the men in my life? I'm not fragile glass for fucks sake.

"We know you're not fragile Makenna, we're just trying to take care of you." Can my brother read my mind now? "No, I didn't read your mind, your mumbling, and *that* I can understand. I've got pretty damned good hearing." That smirk is back on his lips, and I'm not sure how a woman somewhere hasn't smacked it right off his face yet.

"Has anyone tried to smack that smirk off your face?" I ask, curiously, because I suddenly need to know.

"Many have tried Sis, but very few have succeeded, and I don't think you want to know how the ones that succeed managed it."

"Ewwww Caleb!" I shriek, and his smirk just gets bigger.

"You're welcome." He says, while he opens the door to the back room of Vines, and waves me inside ahead of him. I thump him on the arm as I walk by, and he laughs.

I take a seat, but before he can there's a knock on the door, and he goes to answer it. He greets the first contractor, and makes the introductions. Then we go over the plans, show the contractor the cottage as we go over the plans once again in there, and he promises to send through an estimate within the next twenty four hours.

That's how we spend the next few hours. Talking to different contractors, going over plans, and showing them the cottage. I have to admit, Caleb has chosen some really reputable contractors, who have done some amazing work in the past. Not that I doubted him, but I am exceptionally impressed.

We're sitting at the table discussing the contractors that we've seen this morning when the door opens, and Brady walks in.

"Mind if I steal my wife to take her to lunch?" He asks Caleb, but it's not really a question, and we're all well aware of it.

"What if I want to take my *sister* to lunch?"

"Husband trumps brother every single time my man. You can have her for the rest of the afternoon, as long as you promise not to wear her out."

"Promise. What's for lunch?"

"We're heading into Vines, because it's right there, and I feel like one of Leila's pies." We both watch as Caleb licks his lips, and looks at Brady, who sighs. "Would you like to join us Caleb?"

"Nah, that's OK, I can get my own table."

"You're not grabbing a second table bro, you're sitting with us." I tell him, as I loop my arm through Brady's and walk into Vines via the connecting door between the two rooms.

"I don't want to intrude."

"Come on Caleb, just sit with us for lunch." Brady says, dragging Caleb through the door behind us.

I love these idiots, more than they'll ever know.

Chapter Forty-seven
BRADY

Having Caleb join us for lunch wasn't part of my plan, but I don't mind, and I hate that everyone is now being all polite about coming to the house. I don't want to give them back the permission to come and go as they please, but now it feels very strained and unusual to *not* have Caleb and Logan around all the damned time. I can't fucking win, no matter what I do.

When we walk into Vines, the three of us seem to notice all at the same time that Logan is already in there. Sitting at a table on his own. We all scan the room to see if Jules is around, but he's nowhere to be found.

"Mind if we join you?" Caleb asks his brother as he slides into a chair next to him. Logan looks up from his phone at Caleb, then sees us there as well, and sighs. It's the kind of deep sigh of a long suffering older brother who is used to having his peace and quiet interrupted.

"How could I possibly say no, Caleb?" He asks, the question is pure sarcasm that Caleb either doesn't get, or chooses to ignore. I'm going with the choice to ignore his big brother, and make himself at home at his table.

"It does make more sense than taking up two or three tables Logan." He sighs and closes his eyes, when he opens them again there's a sadness there that wasn't there the day before.

"I know, Kenna, Brady, please be my guest." He scowls at Caleb again. "At least *they* waited for me to answer them."

"You wouldn't say no, ever, so I just saved us all some trouble. Although, these two took that time I saved, and doubled it." Before they can get into a full blown argument, Kenna drags Caleb up to order, even though normally they come by the tables.

"Is everything OK Logan?"

"Yeah." He sighs deeply, and if it's possible, sadly. "I was just looking forward to having lunch in peace. I guess I should have gone home, or had it in my office huh?" He scrubs his hands over his face.

"You and I both know none of those guarantee you time alone Logan." I laugh, and he grunts his agreement, but I don't get a chance to talk to him anymore because the others return to the table. Arguing.

"Let Georgie do her job. Leila and Sara for that matter too. They're not here to wait on you hand and foot."

"I know that Makenna, but being the owners should afford us some kind of benefits, right?" he asks, looking around the table for support.

"No." Logan responds. "They're here to run the business, and we don't take precedence over a paying customer."

"Hey! I pay for my food."

"Do you, really?" Kenna asks, while both her and Logan look at their brother, each of them with an eyebrow raised.

This is how our lunch devolves, until Caleb tells Kenna that they have to go back to contractor interviews.

"How many did you set up Caleb?" She asks him.

"As many as I could so that you and Logan couldn't tell me that I hadn't done enough research."

"Sometimes, there's too much research Caleb." Logan grumbles at him.

"Can I have a few minutes with Kenna before you go, please?" I ask, before they go off into another argument of who the hell knows what. I don't think these three know how to communicate if it isn't via some disagreement or other.

"We've got twenty minutes until the next guy will be here, so feel free to go back into the tasting room. I'll stay out here for ten minutes." Caleb tells us.

"And I'm heading back to my office. I'll see you all after." Without waiting for anyone to reply, Logan's gone.

"He's grumpier than usual." Caleb remarks, which can only mean that something's going on with Logan.

"Leave him alone." Kenna says, before taking my hand in hers and leading me towards the back room. When we get back there, and the door closes behind us, she's on me before I can take a breath. Her lips crash onto mine, soft and insistent on mine. Anyone would think we haven't kissed or been in anyway intimate in forever the way she's kissing me. I'm not complaining mind you, but she's usually a lot more controlled when we're at her office or Vines.

I wrap my arms around her waist, pulling her so close to my body that you couldn't get a piece of paper between us. Kenna's hands try to pull my shirt out of my pants, and grip her wrists, tightly to stop her movements.

"We can't Kenna." I say against her lips, but that doesn't stop her, as she pushes hard against my lips again. I pull back from her, as far as I can anyway, because the back of my head hits the door we just walked through. "Kenna." I say her name more firmly.

"I know." She rests her forehead on my chest, while taking a few deep breaths. "I'm sorry."

"What was that?" I ask, holding her tighter when she tried to move away from me.

"I don't know, I just, I miss you. I miss *us*." She says, kind of breaking my heart.

"We're still us baby, we haven't changed." But we both know that's not true. We *are* still us, but we have changed in the last few days, and we're both well aware of it. "It's going to take some time Kenna, but I'm not going anywhere, I'll be right here when you're ready. When we're ready, you have to know that."

"I do." I take my hands from her waist, cupping her cheeks in them and making her look me in the eyes so that she can see that I mean what I say, so that she can't say what she thinks I want to hear. "I do Brady, I swear. I just miss you."

"I'm right here, and I'm not leaving. Well, I do have to go to work, so technically I will leave, but I shall return ma'am. I will *always* return, I promise."

"You shouldn't make that promise." She says quietly, and I know she's thinking about her parents.

"I can, and I fucking will Makenna. I will haunt you until the day you join me in the afterlife, make no mistake about it!"

"Of course you will!" She rolls her eyes, but she can't help the laugh that bubbles out of her, making me smile, because that's what I was aiming for.

"Damn straight baby! I love you, and I will scare off any man that tries to come between us, in life and in death." It's my turn to give her a scorching kiss, just to remind her that she's mine. I pull back, and look into her glazed over, lust filled eyes, and smile. "And on that note, I'm out of here."

"Brady?"

"I need to get to work."

"Hey, get off the damned door, we've got a meeting in a few minutes, and I need to get in there." There's a push against the door, then an even harder push as I move us away from the door, and it flies open. "You could have given me a bit of warning." Caleb grumbles, as he stumbles through the now open door, just managing to stay on his feet.

"You wanted to come in, now you're in." I tell him. "I'm leaving now anyway, I have to get to work. I'll see you later tonight baby. Don't let Caleb push you around too much, OK?" I say with a smirk, causing her to laugh again. It's just what I need to see, her laughing and happy.

"Yeah, cause that's how things happen around here." Caleb mumbles almost quietly enough for neither of us to hear. Almost.

"You better be kind to your sister Caleb, or I'm going to kick your arse." He straightens up to his full height, but he's still not quite as tall as I am, and he looks me dead in the eyes, challenging me. We both know, that if it came down to it between us, I'd win, but it's unspoken knowledge, and not one I'm going to take away from him in front of his sister unless absolutely necessary. Today is not that day.

"I always look after Makenna. You might be her husband, but I'll always be her brother." He slings his arm around her shoulders, and Kenna rolls her eyes so hard, I think she might never look forward again.

"Take it easy baby." I say, kissing her lightly.

"I'm doing all the heavy lifting. Literally, and figuratively speaking."

"OK Caleb." I smile at him, cause it's kind of cute how he thinks he can protect her better than I can, but I can't be here for the rest of the day, so I'm happy to pass the job onto him. For now. "See you tonight Kenna, love you."

"Love you too Brady."

"Love you too Brady." Caleb singsongs at me, and I flip him off.

That is how we spent the rest of the week. Me having lunch with my wife, and one or both of her brothers, and then one of them promising to make sure she's not doing too much, and Makenna getting annoyed because she thinks her brothers believe she lost some brain cells, and can no longer do her job. Margot comes to her rescue more than once, hustling the boys out of her office.

I get a sleepy recount every night when I curl my body around hers when I get into bed after work, and then she drifts back off to sleep.

I wake up every morning when she gets up, and it's my turn to have a sleepy conversation with her about everything that happened the night before at work, before drifting off to sleep again when she leaves for the office.

Then I meet her for lunch. Rinse, wash repeat.

At the end of the week, I wake up knowing that beside me Makenna is awake, but she's pretending to be asleep. How do I know? It's pretty easy actually because her breathing isn't even and her body is pretty tense, and I can tell that just by looking at her, and not touching her.

"Good morning Kenna." I say quietly, not wanting to make her jump, and not succeeding. I pull her back to my front and hug her tightly.

"How did you know I was awake?"

"Years of waking up next to you has taught me a thing or two about you Kenna."

"Hmmm." Is her only response, followed by a few minutes of silence.

"Are you nervous about today?"

"No." It's my turn to stiffen and hold my breath. "I'm not Brady. Well, OK I might be a little nervous, but it's more a nervous excitement to be honest. I can't wait for the doctor to give us the all clear so that we can move forward with our plan. I know she's going to give me a physical clearance, the part I'm nervous about is whether she'll approve of starting the hormonal stimulation so soon after the." She pauses, swallowing deeply before continuing. "So soon after the miscarriage." She spins in my arms so that she's facing me. "But I'm ready Brady. I'm ready to try it. We'd already planned to do this before we went away, so I just want to continue on the timeline we had set before I lost another baby. I think this is our best chance. I truly believe this will work for us. So, yes I'm nervous. I'm nervous that she'll tell me, tell us, that it's too soon, but it's definitely what I want. You do too, right?"

"As long as Doctor Morris says that it's OK to move forward, then yes. I'm all for it Kenna baby. Absolutely." She throws her arms around my neck, and leaves soft kisses all over my face. She's smiling like a loon, and laughing.

I hope that Doctor Morris doesn't break her heart today, but I'm not as certain as Kenna is that she'll be told that we can move forward with our plans so soon. I guess we'll find out in a few short hours.

"Come on then, let's get ourselves organised and ready to go." A second later, Kenna's arms have dropped from around my neck, her body moves away from mine, and she's bouncing out of bed.

I can't help smiling at her enthusiasm, but I can't help feeling her bubble is about to burst, and all I can do is be there for her.

"You joining me?" She asks from the bathroom doorway, throwing his underwear at me, but missing completely because they don't have enough weight behind them to travel far enough.

"On my way." Then I'm out of bed, and stripping off to join her.

Chapter Forty-eight
MAKENNA

I know he's worried, but I can't help the excitement that is bubbling around inside me. I'm pretty sure that Doctor Morris will give me the all clear for physical activity today, I'm just not sure what she's going to say about everything else.

We're both quiet as we move around each other getting ready, both of us in our heads, thinking our own thoughts.

"We can take separate cars if you want? That way you can head to work, and I can head back here." I break the silence that feels a little awkward and strange in the kitchen. Brady takes a sip of his coffee, looking at me over the edge of the mug.

"No." His one word answer startles me.

"What do you mean, no?"

"Exactly that." He says, putting his mug down on the bench. He's leaning his hip against the kitchen bench, one leg crossed over the other at the ankle, arms crossed over his chest, and looking for all the world like he's as relax as he can get. "No means no, Kenna."

"I know what it means Brady, I meant why can't we take two cars? You'll have to drive back into town for work otherwise." Now I'm confused, I thought it was the perfect solution.

"I'm not letting you drive home alone." He gives me a stern look, complete with raised eyebrow. "No matter what kind of news we get today. We go together, and we come back here together. That's just the way it's going to be." I'm expecting him to shrug his shoulders, and stalk towards me like some alphahole, but instead, he picks up his coffee and has another drink, looking over the rim at me again, waiting I suspect for me to argue. Any other day, in any other situation, I would have, but I understand why he wants to go together today.

"Fine." His dark eyebrow arches, a smile twitching at the corner of his mouth. "What?"

"Nothing." The smile pulling at his lips.

"It's not nothing, so what?" I demand.

"It was just easier than I was expecting, that's all."

"I can argue with you if you'd like? Would that make you feel better?" His stance is still relaxed, but that smile of his is getting broader.

"No, that would not make me feel better. I feel pretty great right now, thank you for asking though."

"Are you ready to go then?"

"Whenever you are baby. Although, I wouldn't mind finishing my coffee, if that's OK with you?" He asks, the mug of coffee hiding his smirk.

"Sure." I say sweetly, before I walk up to him like I'm going to kiss him, and then at the last minute, I take the mug out of his hand, and pour the remnants of his coffee down the drain.

"What the hell?"

"You were wasting time."

"We don't have to go just yet Makenna."

"I know, but I don't want to be late."

"Baby, we won't be late, I promise." He says, walking up behind me at the sink, wrapping his arms around my waist, and resting his chin on my shoulder while I wash our few breakfast dishes. "Are you feeling OK?" He asks quietly, his lips lightly touching my neck, sending a vibration of his voice through me, making me shiver a little.

"Yeah, I'm OK I guess." My answer as quiet as his question. He pulls me in for a tighter hug. "I guess I'm kind of nervous though as well."

"Nervous? Why nervous? You're feeling OK, aren't you? Like you're not unwell or in pain, are you?" I pat his hand that's now resting on my stomach.

"Yes, I'm feeling perfectly fine Brady, I promise." I turn my head to kiss him on the cheek. "I'm just nervous about what Doctor Morris will say about starting the hormone stimulation so soon after -." I trip over the word, and I know if I can't say it, and prove that I've dealt with it, then the doctor won't let me move forward, so I take deep breath and continue. "That she'll say it's too soon after the miscarriage."

"Maybe it is, Kenna?" I turn in his arms so that I can face him, and take his face in my hands.

"I know you're worried about my physical and mental health Brady, but we need to be on the same page when we walk in there today, otherwise she's not going to agree to do it. If she senses even the slightest hesitancy from either one of us, she's going to make us wait." I kiss him lightly. "You are with me right? I mean you still want this, don't you?"

"I want nothing more to have a family with you Makenna, you know that. I'm just worried that it's too soon, that's all." It's his turn to kiss me. "*But* if you tell me you're ready, physically, and mentally, then I have to believe you. You're the only one who can know how you're feeling.

"Thank you." I say, giving him a lingering, sweet kiss. "I love you Brady Harris." I mutter against his soft lips.

"I love you too Kenna." He presses a kiss to my lips, tip of my nose, then my forehead. "Are you ready to go see Doctor Morris? We can find out exactly what she thinks, and then we won't have to worry about it anymore."

"I'm ready. No matter what happens today, I'm ready." I say, patting his butt, and giving him a smacking kiss, I pull out of his arms.

"Let's do this." He says, smacking my butt as I walk by him to grab my handbag, and he grabs his keys.

We're quiet as we get in the car, back out of the garage, and slowly drive down the long driveway. As we drive by Vines, Logan and Caleb are standing out on the front deck where they both wave at us and blow me a kiss. I can't help noticing that Jules is missing, but Leila is standing just behind Caleb. Brady rests his hand on my knee, squeezing it gently.

"Whatever happens today Kenna, we'll get through it together." Brady reassures me, and I know that he means it, but it still feels a little empty. Not because I think he won't be by my side through whatever happens, today, tomorrow, and forever, but because at the end of the day, this is mine to deal with. This is about my body either carrying a baby to full term, or not managing to carry a baby to full term. It is my burden to carry, and it will always be my burden to carry.

The drive to the clinic is quiet. The radio is playing quietly, but we haven't spoken since we left Drake Wines. We're both stuck in our own heads, our own thoughts about what can happen today, and what kind of mood we'll both be in when we leave.

Before I even realise it, we've arrived at the clinic and Brady's parking the car. He's not in the same spot as the last visit, but he's not far away from it. It's unavoidable really, it's only a small parking area, but still, it brings back some memories that I'd rather leave behind me. At least this time we'll go in the front entrance.

"Are you OK Kenna?" I jump as Brady's hand lands lightly on my knee, and squeezes, his voice soft.

"Yeah." I sigh deeply, not able to take my eyes of the rear door that we went in a week ago. I shake my head, shaking off the memories of last week, they're not going to help anyone today, and I need to walk into the clinic having put all that mostly behind me. "Yes Brady, I'm OK. It's just being back again this time is a little difficult."

"We can go home. We don't have to do this today baby." He reassured me with another gently squeeze of my knee, and I turn to him and smile. A real, genuine smile, because he makes me so damned happy.

"I know Brady, I honestly know that you would turn around now and take me home if I wasn't ready, but I am ready. I swear to you that I am ready for this visit. I'm ready for whatever Doctor Morris has to say."

"Even if it's not what you want to hear?" He asks, one eyebrow raised in question, but there's no smirk this time, just a serious slight frown.

I take his hand off my knee, twisting our fingers together, and squeeze it lightly. "I'm positive Brady. Even if she tells us that we shouldn't start the hormone treatment yet, I will leave here feeling good. Better than good. I promise." I lift our joined hands to my lips, and kiss the back of his. "I just want an answer, a plan to move forward, today, and I'll be happy."

He sits in the driver's seat, looking at me intensely for a few minutes, his eyes darting between mine to see if I'm telling the truth. He's always been able to read me like a book, so I don't shy away from him scrutiny, I let him see the truth of what I'm feeling.

"OK then, let's do this." He pulls his hand from mine, gets out of the car, and moves around to open my door before I can do more than reach for my handbag and put the strap over my shoulder. He helps me out of the car, takes my hand in his, locks the car, and pockets the keys. "Ready?"

I smile at him, and when he smiles back, I feel a weight lift off my shoulders. If he's smiling with me, then that means he's ready to go in there, and find out what we can do too, and that makes me feel more comfortable with the situation as well.

Brady opens the door for me, waving me inside.

"After you gorgeous." Brady says, and I can't help laughing. The smile that spreads across his face is infectious, and I realise he did this on purpose, he wanted me to forgot about the last time we were here and concentrate on why we're here today. I reach up to cup his cheek, and leave a light kiss on his lips.

"What was that for?" He asks, the smile still on his face.

"Because I love, and appreciate you." I tell him, taking his hand in mine, and walking up to the reception desk. The reception looks up with smile, but it falters when she sees us standing there. "I'm Makenna Harris, we're here to see Doctor Morris."

"I know who you are." She says, and then coughs, and looks at the computer screen in an attempt to cover up her embarrassment. I simply smile at her, and Brady squeezes my hand in his. "Please take a seat in the waiting area, and the doctor will call you back soon."

"Thank you." I smile at her, before Brady guides us to a couple of chairs. As we sit, Brady pulls me into his side, draping an arm around my shoulders, and I rest my head on his shoulder. Smiling I finally take in the other people in the room. It's full of women, some alone, but most with their husbands, or partners. The women *all* have varying degrees of baby bumps, and while I'm happy beyond belief for each and every person in the room, I can't help the twisting that I feel in both my stomach, and my heart. I feel my smile falter for a few seconds, but then the doctor calls us in, and I don't have any more time to think about how lucky the women in the waiting room are, or what I could possibly be missing out on.

"You OK?" Brady asks quietly as we follow Doctor Morris back to a room. I smile, and nod in answer, because I'm not sure I can trust my voice right now. I'm emotional, but it's not entirely because I'm upset, I am truly happy for those women in the waiting room, but they have reminded me of what I'm missing, and what I may never have.

"Take a seat Makenna, Brady." The doctor says as she closes the door behind us. She settles in at her desk, shuffles a few papers around, and then looks up, meeting my eyes when she asks, "How are you feeling?"

"I'm great, honestly." I smile broadly, and I realise that I no doubt look like a crazy person, but I can't help it. The doctor looks over to Brady for confirmation, like I can't tell her exactly how I'm feeling without my damned husband agreeing with me.

Chapter Forty-nine
BRADY

I'm not sure why the doctor needs me to confirm how Makenna's feeling, she has her own mind, and she can tell anyone who asks how she's feeling. I mean I get that she wants to know the truth about how Kenna is truly feeling, but she doesn't need me to speak up for her. I can see the irritation spreading across her beautiful face, so I answer in the only way I know how. Honestly.

"Makenna knows how she's feeling, but if you're asking me if we've spoken about the situation, we have, and if you want to know if we're on the same page? I can tell you that we are one hundred percent on the same page." I smile at Kenna, and squeeze her hand in mine.

"And what page would that be?" The doctor asks curiously. Kenna looks at me, and I nod, telling her without words to go ahead.

"We want to go forward." The doctor doesn't blink, and I can tell Kenna is nervous, which is unusual for her, she rarely gets rattled. "With the hormone treatment that we spoke about before." She swallows, but pushes forward. "Before the miscarriage."

"Are you sure you're ready for that Makenna? You lost a pregnancy a week ago, most women would need some time to process that."

"I know, but I'm not most women Doctor Morris. This isn't my, *our* first rodeo. We've been here before, and had this pregnancy not happened naturally, then we would be moving forward with the treatment. So, if it's all clear medically, and we have the best chance of things working out for us, we would like to continue with the plan, and timeline, please."

The doctor looks away from Makenna, and looks directly at me before asking me the question I've almost been dreading, because I'm worried about whichever way I answer it.

"And you Brady. How are you feeling? Do you agree with this course of action, or do you think it would be best to wait for a few more weeks?" I swallow deeply, and I can feel Makenna's eyes on me, but I don't look away from the doctors eyes. I need her to understand what I'm about to say, and *know* that I'm telling the truth.

"If Makenna says she's ready, then so am I. We both want to start a family, and if my wife tells us that she's ready, then she's ready." I take a deep breath. "So, if everything checks out medically, then I'm all for moving forward with the plans as they were before the miscarriage. I'll be by her side, and support her through all of it."

I hear Kenna let out a breath I didn't even realise she was holding, and the doctor stares me down. After what feels like minutes, but surely must only be a few seconds, she nods, and turns back to her desk, shuffling a few more papers around.

"First, I'm going to have to do a physical, just check everything is all back to normal." She looks at Makenna, who nods her head in understanding. "Once we've done that, then we can sit down to discuss where we can go from here. Is that OK with you?" She asks Makenna, who nods once again. "OK, well, I'll leave the room while you get changed into the gown behind the screen in the corner there, and hop up on the bed." Then she leaves us alone.

"Stop asking me Brady." Kenna says, as she stands up and moves towards the screen in the corner of the room to get changed.

"Say what? I haven't said anything." I didn't get the damned chance.

"Don't ask me if I'm OK. Don't ask if I'm sure about this." She stops speaking for a second. "You need to trust me when I say I'm ready for this Brady."

"I *do* trust you Kenna. I do, I'm just worried, that's all."

"I understand that, but this isn't moving too fast, this is keeping to our plans honey."

"I know, but a week ago." Swallow deeply. "Last week was hard. It was hard to watch you go through it, and it was hard to deal with my own feelings about it. Now, you seem to be forging ahead despite what happened, not because this is something that you want, but because you want to leave last week behind you."

She doesn't answer me until she comes out from behind the screen. "Look at me Brady." I drag my eyes off her legs that I wish were wrapped around my hips, and meet her eyes. "We need to be on the same page honey, because this isn't going to be easy. So, now is your last chance. Do you trust me, and are you ready for this?"

"I trust you unconditionally baby, you know that. I trust you with my life, and the lives of any children we may be blessed to have. No matter how they arrive in our lives."

"But?"

"I'm worried." I say simply with a shrug of my shoulders, but don't break our eye contact.

"That I'm rushing things?"

"Yes." She nods her head slowly as she comes to terms with how I'm feeling.

"But you're on board with it? With the decision to go ahead with the treatment?"

"Yes."

"Just not right now?"

"Well." That's more difficult to answer, but I try to put into words what I'm feeling. "Yes and no. I get that that doesn't really help you, but it's the truth. I know you know your body, and I know you think you're ready."

"You haven't gotten to the 'but', part yet." I can't help laughing a little.

"How about we wait and see what the doctor says about the examination, and go from there? If she thinks that both your body, and your mind are ready, then I'm all for it baby." Her smile is large, and it lights up her beautiful green eyes.

"You've got a deal Brady." She bounces up on her toes to kiss me on the cheek, then moves to the most uncomfortable looking bed, and just as she settles on it, there's a knock on the door, and the doctor comes back into the room.

"Are we ready to go?"

"Absolutely." Kenna says, reaching out for my hand.

"You can pull the chair over and sit right next to the bed Brady."

"I won't be in the way?"

"Not if you stay up that end of the bed, and hold your wife's hand, no." The doctor and Kenna both laugh, and that's when I realise my mistake.

"Right, of course." I say as I drag my chair to the top of the bed, blushing furiously, which doesn't happen too often.

"Ohhh honey." Kenna says taking one hand in hers, the other one stroking my cheek. "You weren't to know, I doubt you've ever had a pelvic exam."

"Not that I can recall, no, and I'm pretty sure I'd remember putting my legs up in those stirrups and someone inspecting my insides." This makes both women laugh.

"Most women try to forget about that happening, especially the next time they need to have one." The doctor laughs.

"No doubt." I mumble in reply.

There's silence for a few minutes, and Kenna holds my hand tightly while staring into my eyes, a small smile on her face.

"OK, we're done." The doctor pats Kenna's leg. "You can't sit up now."

"That's it?" I ask, surprised.

"What were you expecting Brady, a full archaeological exploration?" Kenna asks, laughing.

"Obviously not, but I was expecting it to last a little longer than a few minutes."

"Well, we try to get it over and done with as quickly as possible. Believe it or not, having someone between your legs isn't always a pleasure Brady." The doctor says, struggling hold in her laughter. I don't know what to say to that, so I keep my mouth shut. "Why don't you go and get dressed again Makenna, then we'll talk about where we are, and where we go from here."

"Is everything OK?"

"We'll wait until Makenna is sitting with us to have that conversation." The doctor smiles at me. Does that mean it's good news?

"But she can hear us." I state the fucking obvious.

"I know, but I'd rather have her sitting here." She laughs again. "But yes, everything looks perfect Brady."

"Well, that's good to know." Kenna says, as she slides into the chair beside me. "Does that mean we can start on the hormones stimulation medication?" Kenna asks. I know the doctor and I hear the hope in her voice.

"We can, yes." Doctor Morris confirms. "But I want you to do some blood tests today before you leave so that I can read your hormone levels right now to see if they're in the normal range after last week. If they are then we can move forward. So, yes, I will give you a prescription for the medication today, but I'm not going to give you the go ahead to take it until I get those blood results, OK?"

"Absolutely." Kenna beams.

"How long should it take to work?" I ask, wanting a timeline.

"Honestly? It could happen the first time. We all know that Makenna doesn't have a problem getting pregnant really, it's keeping the pregnancy that her body struggles with." The doctor's honesty is brutal to hear, for me at least, it seems that Kenna isn't bothered at all, because she's nodding in agreement. "I know that's confronting to hear, but it's the truth, and there's no point pulling any punches in this room. We need to do this in an open and honest way. It could take the first time, but it could also take six months or more. The reality is, I can't give you an exact timeline, because it's not an exact science, but Makenna and I have discussed her options at length." She smiles at me with sympathy. I haven't really done any research into the drug that she wants Kenna to take. Honestly, I researched adoption more than any of the treatments that Kenna told me about, but I know that Kenna *has* researched, she's explained the basics to me, and we both know what we're in for.

"Yes, I've told Brady everything that you've told me, and I think this is the way to go for us." Kenna confirms.

"And what about you Brady? Is this the way you want to move forward as well?" I look at Kenna, and I can see the pleading in her eyes, and I know I can't say no, even if I wanted to, not that I do.

"Yes. If this is the way Kenna wants to go, and you're OK with it, then I'm behind her all the way." I pull my eyes from Kenna's to look at the doctor. "As long as you say that she's good to go with it physically, and mentally, then I'm all for it."

"OK, well then let's go through some of the details then, and you can both decide what you want to do." We look at each other, and then back at the doctor and nod. "OK, there are some side effects that you need to be aware of."

"I know, I've read up on it." Kenna says.

"Well, let me just run through them all anyway, and then we can all say we knew what to expect."

As the doctor rattles off the possible side effects, my brain struggles with the information overload. Not to mention all the things that Kenna could possibly have to deal with while taking this stuff. Including bloating, a feeling of being full even though she's not, hot flashes, dizziness, stomach aches, tender breasts, and last but by means least, headaches as well! After all of those I really want to ask Kenna if she's determined to do this, because as much as I want kids, I'm not sure this is worth it. Like doctor Morris can read my mind, and well let's face it with her experience in the field she probably can, she tells us that these are all *possible* side effects. Kenna may get none of them at all. While I know she says that for *my* benefit, I don't find it that reassuring. I feel like I'm asking my wife to go through hell to have to a kid.

"You're not asking me to do this Brady, I want to do it, and we're doing it together, this isn't just about me."

"I said that out loud?"

"Yeah you did honey, but that's OK, I know you're on information overload."

"You can say that again."

'It's OK, you don't have to decide anything today, we still have to get those blood tests done, and the results back before I'll give the go ahead to start. So, I'll get all the paperwork started, and then you can go home and discuss everything. You need to make this decision away from here, and away from me." The doctor smiles kindly at both of us.

"Thank you Doctor Morris. For everything." Kenna says, placing her hand on top of the doctors hand resting on the desk.

"I haven't done anything yet Makenna. Let's hope we can change that."

Chapter Fifty
MAKENNA

Leaving the clinic, I can't hide my excitement. I can feel Brady's hesitation about going forward, he's almost vibrating with his concern that I'm not ready, and I don't know how to reassure him. I don't know if that's what I'm supposed to do either, but I don't have the energy to put into making him feel better.

"So, do you have time to take me to pathology and then the chemist? If not, I can get one of the boys to come and pick me up, I'll understand." We reach the car before he answers my rambling. It feels like I said everything in a one worded sentence, because I'm a mix of nervous, excited, and happy. He walks to my side of the car, rests his hand on the handle before turning to me, and speaking.

"Makenna, baby, I already told you that you won't have to do any of this alone." He closes his eyes, taking a deep breath. "I will be." He kisses the tip of my nose. "Around for every." Another kiss. "Damned step." Kiss. "This." Kiss. "Takes." He presses one last sweet kiss to my lips.

"I know, but I'm telling you if you have to get to work, I can get my own way back to Drake Wines."

"And I'm telling you, I'm taking you home." He takes my hand in his, and guides me towards the pathology lab in the clinic to get my bloods drawn. The conversation between Brady, and the pathologist flows easily as she does what she needs to get blood out of my arm. I hate needles, and Brady is by my side as always, holding my other hand, but I'm dealing with it on my own.

"All done." The pathologist says with a smile. "You did well for someone who says she hates needles. I guess it helps to have your handsome husband holding your hand, hey? You're a lucky woman, that's for sure." She says with a wink, and huge smile as she squeezes Brady's bicep when she walks by him to collect the vials of my blood.

The sudden jolt of jealousy that hits me takes me by surprise. Brady and I have been together for a long time, and not once have I felt that little green monster take me over like this. Brady squeezes my hand, and I look up into his eyes, they're twinkling with amusement, and love. He's not looking at her, he's watching me, and I know he knows what I'm feeling right now.

"I am very lucky, yes."

"So am I. I wouldn't want to live my life with anyone else. I haven't since we were teenagers, and I don't see that changing any time soon." He says without breaking our connection.

"Awww that's so sweet. I wish my boyfriend felt like that about me." She says wistfully, and now I'm feeling sorry for her.

"I'm sure he does." I tell her, neither knowing or really caring if he does. She smiles at me as she puts a bandaid over the spot where the needle entered my arm, and I know she understands.

"I'm sure he does." She smiles sadly back at me. "OK, Mrs Harris, you're free to go. The doctor should have the results in two to three days, but I'd call before coming back in to make sure they're here."

"Thank you." Brady says, helping me out of the chair, and directing me out the door, towards our car. He wraps his arm around my waist, pulling me into his side, and I feel his body shaking as I hear a choked laugh escape him.

"What's so funny?'

"Nothing." He coughs, trying to cover up his laughter, without succeeding. "There is nothing funny about any of this." He tells me as he opens my door, waiting for me to get in the car. I look over my shoulder at him, seeing the smirk he's barely holding back.

"What's so funny Brady?" I demand, putting my hands on my hips, both of us standing in the open door of the car.

"It's not funny Kenna, I was just trying to distract you from getting blood drawn, and it worked." I raise an eyebrow at him. He raises his hands in surrender, taking a step away from me. "OK, you want the truth? It was kind of nice to see you get jealous about someone talking to me like that."

"She wasn't just *talking* to you Brady." I say in disbelief. "She was bla-tantly flirting with you. In front of me. Me, who she knew was your wife, and at a clinic where women are either pregnant or *trying* to get pregnant." I sigh, a big deep one, and try with everything in me not to roll my eyes at him. "She knows what those blood tests are for, she's not stupid, and *still* she came on to you! I have a mind to tell Doctor Morris about her behav-iour, it wasn't very professional." I say in a huff, turning to get into the car. I settle into my seat, and close the door, leaving Brady standing beside the car for a few seconds, before he moves around to the driver's side and gets in.

"Don't say anything to Doctor Morris Kenna, it wasn't Kelly's fault." He says resting his hand on my thigh.

"Kelly?"

"The pathologist."

"Her name was Kelly?"

"Yeah." Brady chuckles. "She could tell you were nervous, I guess she sees plenty of people who don't want to be there. We were talking, and I asked her to distract you. All she was trying to do was to make the experi-ence a little easier for you, she wasn't really flirting with me, not even close. She was trying to get you to relax, and while you didn't relax, you didn't ac-tually notice when she inserted the needle and drew your blood." He shrugs his shoulders. "So, I think we should take that as a win. Usually you go pale, and look like you're going to pass out, but you didn't today."

"You did it to me on *purpose*?" I ask, not knowing whether to be offend-ed or impressed.

"Our intention, *my* intention, wasn't to make you jealous babe, just to distract you while Kelly did her job. I know how much you hate needles, and I was just trying to make it easier for you." He squeezes my knee, then he takes my hand in his, and he moves them up to his mouth, leaving a kiss on the back of my hand.

"OK." I can't stay mad at him for long, that's not quite true, under the right circumstances I can stay mad at him for a days, if not weeks at a time, but not over this one.

"Let's go to the pharmacy, and get this medication so that we can be ready to use it." Without another word Brady starts the car, and heads to the pharmacy. I don't speak because I don't know what to say. When he stops a few minutes later, I move to get out.

"I won't be long, I hope." When he doesn't respond I get out of the car and walk towards the entrance to the store. I feel a strong hand on my lower back, guiding me in the doors and towards the chemist's counter, and I jump.

"I told you, we're doing this thing together Makenna." He says quietly in my ear. "I didn't mean to upset you baby, and I'm sorry that I did, but never doubt my commitment to us, you or having a family. Ever."

"Brady."

"No, I'm sorry if I made you question my love for you for even a second Makenna." He kisses me on the forehead. Before I can respond we're called to the counter, and having a discussion with the assistant, when we're done we walk around the store waiting for the script to be filled.

"I don't doubt that you love me Brady." I say quietly beside him as we look at the toothpaste. "I worry that I'm letting you down."

"Are you sure you want to have this conversation here?"

"No."

"Makenna, you're not letting me down baby, you never could."

"Makenna Harris." My name gets called out before either of can say anything else. We head to the checkout in silence, and pay for the medication, and other things that we picked up. As soon as the doors close when we get in the car Brady speaks.

"I love you Kenna, and nothing you could ever do would let me down. This is an us issue, not a *you* issue baby, and to be fair, for me it's a non-issue. We have a baby, or we don't. Before you say anything, that doesn't mean I don't want a family with you Kenna, nor does it mean I'm not behind you every step of the way with this treatment either. It means, I will have a family whether we adopt, foster, or have our own kids. If we have these treatments, and they work for us then I'll be exceptionally happy, but if they don't, then we'll sort it out. We'll find another way to have a family. Do you understand me? I mean, do you really get me?"

I look him in the eyes, and all I see is a man who loves me unconditionally, and will do whatever it takes to make us both happy. "I do Brady, I truly do."

"OK then." He says with a sharp nod. "That's the last time we have that conversation Kenna. I don't want you to doubt me, or yourself anymore. We're doing this treatment, and we're taking it all one step at a time, but we're doing it *together*. No more second guessing from either one of us, got it?" He asks with a smile.

"Deal." I say with a sharp nod of my own, not trusting my voice to say much more.

"Don't cry baby, we can do this." He says as he wipes away the tears I didn't even know were flowing down my cheeks. "I love you Kenna, we got this." He leans over the centre console of the car, and presses a kiss to my forehead.

"I love you too Brady."

"That's good, because otherwise I'm wasting my time here." He says as he pulls away from me, and starts the car.

"That's just plain rude Brady Harris!" I tell him, as I smack him on the arm.

"Ouch! Don't annoy the driver, you could have caused a crash just now Makenna." He admonishes me. "You can't be doing that when the kids arrive Makenna." He shakes his head like he's disappointed, but the smile on his lips, and the twinkle in his eyes tells me he's joking.

"Well, before they get here you might want to decide who's wasting who's time here Brady." I tell him, not even close to as annoyed as I was. He reaches over and takes my hand in his, weaving his fingers between mine, and resting them between us for the rest of the drive home.

When we enter the gates of Drake Wines, Brady slows down as he drives us to the house.

"You know your brothers are going to be asking you questions as soon as they know you're back. That's if they don't already know, and aren't waiting at the house for us." He says laughing.

"I don't think they'll be waiting at the house." I say, not able to hold back my laughter either, because as the house comes in to view we can see two people sitting on the steps of the porch.

"How the hell did they know we were on our way home?" Brady asks, completely bewildered at their presence. "Did you message them?" He asks as he pulls the car into the driveway.

"No Brady, you were with me the whole time, I didn't even take a call."

"How the hell do they do it then?"

"No idea, but I guess we should be used to it." I laugh, getting out of the car, I meet my brothers at the steps of our home as they get to their feet, engulfing me in a hug.

"How did you guys know we were on our way home?"

"You know, you should just tell him. It's driving him insane that you two know where we are." I say, laughing as I pull out of their overwhelming embrace.

"We have our ways." Logan says simply. He's so damned expressionless, that it makes him hard to read. Unless you've known my older brother for a long time, you think he's a grumpy, unfeeling, and harsh kind of man, but when you know him, you know he loves unconditionally. Having known him almost as long as he's known me, Brady isn't offended by his abrupt, almost harsh reply.

"Of course you do." Brady mumbles. "Why are you waiting out here for us?" Brady asks them as he unlocks the front door and lets us all inside. Logan takes the shopping bag off me, grunting in Brady's direction like he's annoyed that he wasn't carrying the one, very light bag. Logan slings his arm over my shoulders going into protective big brother mode. Which earns him an eyeroll from my husband that rivals Caleb's best efforts, and that boy can roll his eyes until they're in the back of his head.

"Come on, let's make coffee, then you can ask all the questions you want, and if we have the answers, we'll give them to you." I say, leading them all into the kitchen with the hope that Logan will finally tell Brady that he's got tracking apps on all our phones because otherwise I'm going to have to, and he's going to be annoyed that I didn't tell him sooner.

Chapter Fifty-one
BRADY

I follow Makenna, and her brothers into the house. Makenna fills the kettle, and flicks on the coffee maker, while Logan moves around her getting mugs, spoons, tea bags, milk, and coffee.

"Sit." Logan says pulling out a chair for his sister.

"I can make a cup of coffee Logan."

"I know you can, but I'm making them."

"So, are you going to tell me how you know when we're coming home." I ask, looking between my brothers in law expectantly. "No? Can you tell me why you were sitting on our front steps then?"

"Where were you expecting us to be waiting?" Caleb asks me, looking genuinely confused, as Logan ignores both of my questions, and makes everyone coffee or tea.

"Here?"

"We were *here* Brady." His eyebrows furrow in confusion.

"*In the house*, Caleb, it's not like either of you don't have a key."

"But you said not to do that anymore." His eyebrows draw down even further in confusion.

"I never thought either of you, you especially, would take any notice of that."

"So, you mean, we're allowed to just walk into the house again?"

"No!" I yell. "No, that's not what I meant at all. Thank you for respecting our privacy, and my wishes. I appreciate it."

"You're welcome." Caleb says, still looking a little confused, but much happier. I look over at Makenna, and see her smiling behind her coffee mug. So, I look over at Logan expecting my coffee, but all I see is the back view of his shoulders shaking with barely held back laughter. "Thanks for the coffee Logan." Caleb salutes his brother with the mug he picks up off the bench.

"You're welco-." He starts, but he's cut off by Makenna spitting her mouthful across the bench.

"What the fu-!" Caleb gets cut off by Makenna's yells.

"What the fuck is this Logan?" She demands, wiping her mouth on her sleeve.

"It's tea." Logan states easily.

"Tea!" Makenna spits out, slamming the cup down on the bench. "Why the hell did you give me a tea? I wanted a coffee. In fact, I already had my coffee in my mug."

"I know." Logan's pretty calm for someone whose life is hanging in the balance. If there's one thing I learned very early in our relationship, you keep Makenna from her coffee at your own risk.

"I wanted coffee Logan." She makes a move to stand up and make it herself.

"You can't have it Makenna." Logan tells her, placing a hand on her arm to stop her from getting up.

"What. Do. You. Think. You're. Doing?" Makenna spits out each word like it's venom. "I want a coffee Logan, and I'm going to have one, you don't get to tell me what I can and can't eat or drink!"

"You can't have caffeine while pregnant Makenna." Logan says, quietly but with the authority that only the oldest sibling can carry.

"Lucky I'm not pregnant then *Logan*. Thanks for the reminder." I actually see Logan flinch as if she slapped him in the face. Beside me, Caleb sucks in a breath, but I can't look away from what's happening between my wife, and her brother. I don't know which one of them is going to survive this.

"I didn't mean to hurt you Makenna."

"I know that Logan, but I'm not pregnant, and even if I were, you don't get to tell me what I can, and can't eat." Makenna sits heavily in her seat.

"I know, I'm sorry. I'm just trying to look out for you. I want you to have every opportunity to have the family you want."

Makenna's face softens, and she reaches out to take her brother's hand in hers. "I know that Lo, and while I appreciate your concern, Brady and

I have it covered." Logan goes to speak, but she cuts him off with a raised hand, and a shake of her head. "I promise we will ask you for help when and if we need it."

"Promise?"

"I absolutely promise."

"Promise me too." Caleb pipes up, not wanting to miss out on the action.

"We promise to ask one or both of you for help if we need anything. Don't we Brady?" She turns her gaze to mine, and I see the pleading in them, and I can't say no.

"Absolutely. If we need help, we'll ask. Promise." I smile at everyone around the table, but when I get to Logan I can see in his eyes that he doesn't quite believe me. "Promise." I tell him specifically, my smile growing when he grunts in reply. He doesn't believe either one of us.

"Did you know there's more caffeine in tea than there is in coffee?" Everyone turns their attention Caleb's way, and his eyebrows raise in surprise. "What? It's true!"

"Geezus Caleb, there's a time and place for your knowledge of all things that really don't matter in life." Logan grumbles at him, shaking his head.

"It's not useless information Logan, it means that Makenna can have her coffee, she just can't have as much as she usually does." Caleb looks at his sister. "Sorry Sis, but it's true." He tells her with a relaxed shrug of his shoulders. "Decaf would be better, obviously, *but* if you just cut back to one *maybe* two cups a day you should be good."

"You know decaf coffee has been linked to miscarriages, right? We're trying to prevent that here Caleb." Logan says to his brother. "It's better to just cut down your regular coffee to two a day."

"That's not an across the board belief, oh brother of mine. Some studies say that decaf is worse." Caleb asserts.

"How the hell do you two know all this?" I ask, it's not like either one of them have gotten anyone pregnant, well not to my knowledge anyway.

"Research." They say at the same time.

"Why are you researching pregnancy?" I ask, even though I'm pretty sure I know what the answer will be, and not really wanting to hear them say it.

"Because our sister is trying to get pregnant." Logan says, matter of factly.

"Exactly!" Caleb agree with his brother. "And we want to be able to help her out any way we can. You know?"

"I'm pretty sure that's my job, as her husband, you know?" I say throwing his words back at him.

"I'm pretty sure that as a grown woman I can look after myself, but thank you my favourite bunch of alpha boys." She says with a teasing smile.

"Men!" We all shout, then we all laugh together when Kenna says, "I was waiting for it."

When we've all calmed down, there's a few seconds of silence before Logan asks what they're here for.

"So, how did it go today?"

"Well, apart from Brady flirting with the pathologist to distract me, everything went fine. Perfectly I would say."

"What the hell man?" Logan glares at me from across the table.

"Before you get ready to give me a black eye, fat lip or whatever that look on your face is telling me you want to do, let me explain."

"Explain then." Logan demands.

"Kelly did flirt with me, but she wasn't serious about it. When we walked in the room, Kenna was a little out of it. She always goes a little blank when she knows she's going to have a needle, so I told Kelly that we needed to distract her. It's not my fault that's what she chose to do. I get the feeling her boyfriend is an arsehole."

"You got her name?" Caleb asks, surprised.

"It was on her name badge, and it felt a little odd to ask her for a favour, but not call her by her name. Wouldn't you agree?" I glare at Caleb. "You might not care to know a person's name when you're talking to them, but I do."

"I didn't realise you'd gotten her life story while we were there. I wouldn't have thought we were there for long enough, Brady?" Kenna asks me, that look of unhappiness back on her face. I try not to feel too bad talking about it, I mean she's the one who brought it up, but I don't like to see her upset.

"You were zoned out for a while Kenna, but you're right, I didn't get her life story, not even close."

"Then how do you know her boyfriend is an arsehole?" Kenna asks.

"Just by a few things she said, not to mention the look on her face right before we left. She didn't mean anything by it, and the fact is, I came home with *you*. I'll always come home with you, Mrs Harris."

"Did he or did he not flirt with someone that isn't you, Makenna?" Logan asks his sister, always the protector, he just can't let that go.

Kenna looks at me, studying me like it's one of the first times we've met, and I start to get annoyed. She knows me better than this!

"He's good Logan. I know he wasn't flirting with Kelly, even if she was flirting with him, and while I still think it was unprofessional, I'm going to let it go."

"Good, because there's nobody else for me, except you baby." I lean over, take her face gently in my hands, and kiss her.

"Ohh man, don't you have to get to work?" Caleb moans.

"No, I'm working from home today. So, even though I'm enjoying this little party, I should get a few things done." I drop a light kiss to her lips in apology.

"Have some lunch with us first?" Kenna asks hopefully, and I can't say no.

"Of course I will Kenna." I tell her with a smile, work can wait for a few more minutes.

Chapter Fifty-two
MAKENNA

Having lunch with three of my favourite men fills me with joy, and happiness. Watching them laugh and joke around is fun to watch, I love witnessing the bond these three have cultivated from being young men, and while I join in with them now and then, I truly do enjoy listening to their banter.

Caleb being the youngest by a few years, struggles to keep up when Brady and Logan start remembering some of the adventures of their joined misspent youth, I can see that Caleb feels a little left out, but then he joins in by giving grief about being 'old men', because he doesn't remember the events they're talking about.

I sit back, finishing off my cold glass of lemonade, and just enjoy watching the interaction between them. This is what I want for my children, *our* children. The love, friendship, and acceptance at this table is incredible.

"Hey, are you OK baby?" Brady's low voice right beside me startles me out of my daydream.

"Hmmm? Yes, of course, I'm perfect." I reassure him, kissing him lightly.

"You've been very quiet."

"I'm just enjoying the company."

"I don't know about enjoying their company Kenna, but I enjoy *your company.*" Brady says, kissing me with more passion than he should with my brothers in the same room.

"Oh come on you two, give it a rest." Caleb complains, and I smile against Brady's lips, knowing that he did it to get a reaction out of Caleb, and perhaps Logan. Logan rarely reacts in the same way that Caleb does, he seems to be more adult, and perhaps a little envious of our relationship.

"She's my wife *kiddo,* and if I want to kiss my wife, then I damn well will." Brady tells Caleb, leaving him no room to argue. "I'm going to head to the office to get some work done baby, let me know if you need anything, OK?"

"Will do." Brady gives me another, less heated kiss.

"See ya later boys." He says, waving in their general direction, and walking away.

"Men. We're men." Caleb mumbles, and I can't help laughing. It would seem my little brother has an issue with not being considered a man these days, and I can't help wondering who hurt him. I don't get the chance to ask him though, because Logan tells him to stop complaining, and help him clean up.

"I can clean up Logan, you guys need to get back to work." I start to stand up to clean up the few dishes, and Logan stares me down.

"Sit down Makenna, and just let us look after you for a change, please?"

"Yeah Kenna, let Logan clean up the mess." Caleb says with a cheeky smile.

"He won't be doing it alone." I say with a sweet smile back at him. "You're going to help him out too, aren't you Caleb?" He grumbles but I know he's going to do it, both him and Logan will always help me, we'll always help each other. Just when I think he might prove me wrong, he pushes his chair back to stand up.

"Come on then idiot, let's get this cleaned up so I can get back to work." He says to Logan, picking up his own plate and glass, leaving the rest of it for Logan to pick up, who shakes his head, and looks annoyed, but still does it without saying anything to our brother.

I watch them disappear into the kitchen, and when I know they're out of earshot, I laugh. I know they love each other, but damn if the age gap between them doesn't make their relationship difficult, even as adults.

I get up from the table, push mine, and Caleb's chair back in, then join the boys in the kitchen. I can hear them bickering from the doorway, and shake my head. I know they've got each other's backs, but it gets quite tiresome listening to them talk to each other like this. Brady has tried to explain it to me as man slash brother banter, but some days I wonder.

"Can you two give it a rest for just one afternoon. Please?" I ask them suddenly feeling exhausted. They look at each other, and I can see the warning in Logan's eye, always the 'father' figure.

"Of course." Logan grumbles out.

"Sorry Makenna." Caleb says, while walking over to engulf me a bear hug. It feels great. "Love you Kenna."

Next thing, Logan's hugging me from behind, holding Caleb to my front, and we're all laughing.

"You're a fucking arsehole Logan!" Caleb squeals as he tries to move away from us, but Logan's grip tightens, and I'm squashed between the two of them.

"What the *hell* is going on out here?" Brady roars from somewhere behind me, making me jump, and Logan and Caleb jump away from me like they've been caught by our parents doing the wrong! "Some of us are trying to work here, just in case you'd forgotten. I *was* on a call just now, but with all the noise out here I had to tell them I'd call them back." He's looking between the three of us, and I can't help feeling attracted to him, because all I see is the father he's going to be to our kids, and it's sexy as hell.

"Sorry Brady." Caleb mumbles. "Logan started it, I was just giving Makenna a hug and -." He stops mid-sentence because the look on Brady's face says he doesn't give a flying fuck as to the reasons behind the disruption. "Right, sorry man. I'm gonna head out, and get back to work myself." He gives me a quick kiss on the cheek, sends Logan a filthy look, and is gone.

"Look, we meant no harm Brady, we just forgot that you were here, working."

"I expected better from you to be honest Logan. You're always so professional, and all about the work, yet when it comes *my* work, there seems to be a lack of caring."

"That's not true Brady, I just forgot you were working from home. I mean it doesn't happen that often." Logan hesitates for a few seconds, taking a deep breath he continues. "You're right, and I'm sorry Brady, I didn't mean any disrespect, I just meant to piss Caleb off."

"As usual." Brady says. "Well, cut it the fuck out, because soon there will be *actual* children filling this house again and I don't want to have to parent them *and* you two. Do you hear me?"

"Yes." Logan says, short, and sharp. He gives me a kiss on the cheek before heading for the door. "I'm going to go get some work done myself. If you need anything, just call." Then he's gone.

"I can't believe those two. They're supposed to be grown men, holding down professional jobs, and running the damned family business, and yet they *both* still behave like teenage boys sometimes." Brady says in dismay.

I don't say anything, I just walk right up to him, grab his cheeks in my hands and pull his mouth to mine, kissing him deeply, and fiercely. I don't know how long we stand just inside the kitchen kissing like horny teenagers, but I'm not counting either, I'm too distracted to.

"What was that for?" Brady asks, when we finally pull apart, breathing laboured, foreheads resting against each other.

"That was fucking hot, Brady."

"Huh? What was? The kiss? Yes the kiss was hot as fuck, but I don't know what brought it on. Not that I'm complaining mind you." I kiss his lips lightly to stop him from talking.

"Telling my brothers off like that. I mean it gave me a glimpse of what kind of father you're going to be, and it was *hot*."

"Really?" He asks surprised, but before I can answer, he continues. "It was hot was it? Hot like how Kenna?"

"Hot like, I wish you could step away from work for a few minutes, because I'm wet, and needy." My voice low and husky.

"Are you sure you're ready?" He asks me, and the concern is just as sexy as watching him tell off my brothers.

"I am *so* ready right now Brady, that if you don't help me out, I'm going to do it myself." Brady groans at my admission.

"Fuck." He closes his eyes for second. "Let me make sure the doors are locked, then I'm all yours."

"What about your phone call?" I ask curiously.

"It can wait." He says, stepping out of my embrace, and leaving the kitchen. "Meet you in the bedroom once I've locked all these doors."

"They have keys Brady." I yell at his retreating back.

"I know, but they don't have keys to the deadbolts I installed.

"When the hell did you do that?"

"The other day." He yells back. "Now move your cute butt before have to carry you."

His threat gets me moving. I beat him to the bedroom by a minute, maybe two, the man is motivated to get to me.

"Come here and kiss me." He demands, and that's exactly what I do. Before I know what's happened, or how it happened, we're both naked. It's not slow, sweet, or gentle this time. It's the fastest way of getting out of our clothes so that we can get off. Brady runs his hand down my stomach, through what little pubic hair I have, and then his fingers play with my clit for a second, before sliding into my pussy. "Fuck, you're so wet Kenna. Are you ready for me?"

"Fuck, yes Brady." My voice doesn't sound like me, my words are more of a breath than an actual sound.

"Who knew me yelling at your brothers would make you this wet?"

"Don't talk about my brothers when you've got your fingers in my pussy Brady."

"In my pussy you mean?" I nod in agreement because I can't speak. His fingers are pumping in out and of my body, my knees are getting weak, and I would be a puddle on the floor if he wasn't holding me up with his arm that's banded around my waist. "Say it Kenna. Tell me your pussy is mine."

"It's yours Brady."

"What's mine Kenna?"

"My pussy."

"Who's pussy is it?"

"It's yours." I breathe out, willing to tell him anything as long as he doesn't stop what he's doing, but also knowing it's the damned truth. "It's your pussy Brady, always."

"That's fucking right it is." He pulls his fingers out of my pussy, and I cry out at the loss. "It's OK baby, I'm not going anywhere." I don't know how or when, but he's got me pushed up against the wall, and he's lifting me up off the floor. Automatically, my legs wrap around his waist, and before I can take my next breath, he pushes his cock inside me. Taking a second to catch his breath, and letting me catch mine, he stills. Then without warning, he pulls almost all the way out of me, and hesitates. "Look at me Kenna." I didn't even realise my eyes were shut, until they spring open at his command. The heat, and raw need I see in his eyes melts me even further.

"Fuck me Brady." He needs no further permission, as he enters me again in a sharp push, making both of us grunt. I wrap my arms around his neck, and hold on. "Again." I beg. He draws out of me, pausing with just the tip of his cock inside my pussy. "Please Brady." I beg, looking deep in his eyes, I need this. This connection with him. He must see whatever he was looking for in my eyes, because he doesn't hold back another second.

"I won't. Last. Long. Kenna." He pants out to every thrust of his hips.

"Me either." One of his hands that was holding my butt, reaches around past his pumping cock, and strokes my clit until I see stars. I'm sure I black out for a few seconds as I come around his cock, before he roars out his release as well. "Wow!" It's all I can muster right now.

"Mmm hmmmm." Brady murmurs into my neck, and I can't help laughing at his level of response. "Ahhh stop it!"

"What?" I ask, innocently.

"You know what."

"Nope, what did I do?"

"Stop laughing." I press my lips together to stop myself from laughing anymore. "It makes your pussy clench around my cock."

After another minute, he carries me to the bathroom, placing me on the cold benchtop making me squeak from the chill on my rear end, then he cleans me up with a warm, damp cloth, and then carries me back to the bedroom, gently laying me down on the bed. He kisses me gently on the forehead, and then starts getting dressed.

"Stay with me?" I ask.

"I'm sorry Kenna, I would love to, but I really need to go finish that phone call."

"Oh." I know I sound disappointed, because I am.

"Why don't you get some rest, and I'll come back when I'm done?"

"Sure." I say, feeling a little lost, and unsure.

"I'll be back as soon as I can, OK? I promise."

"OK Brady." I can feel my body relaxing into the bed, and as he pulls the covers up over my body, I warm up, which causes me to snuggle into the bed more. "I love you Brady."

"I love you too Kenna." He presses another kiss to my forehead, and that's the last thing I remember before I fall asleep.

Chapter Fifty-three
BRADY

Leaving Makenna to get some rest, I call Damien back, and we discuss everything that we didn't get the chance to before Logan and Caleb behaved like children. I shake my head, because I expect that from Caleb, not Logan, but they don't seem to be able to stop themselves. God knows how they're going to keep working, and running the family business together.

I'm not sure how much later Kenna walks into the office, and drapes her arms over my shoulders, resting her chin on the top of my head.

"Hey handsome, are you almost done?" I save the document I was working on, take her arms off my shoulders, and spin around in my chair, keeping her hands in mine.

"How are you feeling?" I ask.

"I'm fine Brady."

"Did you get much rest?"

"If you're asking if you sent me into a post orgasm coma, then yes, you did, but it was just a nap. I haven't been asleep the entire time." She laughs, and it's the best sound in the world.

"Well, I'm always happy to make the sacrifice and give you more orgasms if they help you to sleep baby." I say, with a straight face, which causes her to laugh even harder. "Is that what you're here for, more satisfaction so that you can relax?" I ask, a smirk on my face.

"No." She says, as I pull down to sit across my lap. "I came in here to see what you want to do for dinner, because I was reading when my stomach grumbled, and I realised what the time was."

My eyebrows draw down in a frown, not because she was reading, but because I have no idea what the time it is. "Are you reading for work, or for pleasure?"

"Pleasure." She tells me with a sexy smile, and deep slow kiss.

"Damn, I love it when you read for pleasure. Those steamy romance books of yours are pure porn, I'm sure of it. Get the right one, and they sure do help a guy out, not that I need any help in that department." I buck my hips to her hips just to drive home my point. Kenna throws her head back, letting out a loud laugh. When her laughter dies down to a beautiful smile, I ask, "So, dinner you say? Don't we still have some meals that Jules cooked?" I hope so, because I don't really feel like cooking, and I'd rather Kenna didn't have to either.

"Yeah, we still have plenty, believe me."

"Will your brothers be joining us tonight?"

"No."

"Are you sure? We've thought that before, and then had to dish up two, sometimes three, extra meals."

"I am absolutely positive." I raise an eyebrow at her in question, because I want to know how she can be so damned sure they won't just show up like they normally do. "I told them not to. I told them I don't want, nor do we need the company tonight. I just want a night where we can do whatever the hell we like, and not have to worry about who may, or may not walk in the door looking for food." She says with a small shrug if her shoulders.

"And they agreed?" I ask, confused.

"They did." She confirms with a nod.

"*Both* of them?" She nods again. "Because you and I both know that Caleb could change his mind. He's like a practice child that one." Kenna laughs, as I shake my head.

"No, he had plans apparently. I didn't ask what or who he had plans with, I'm not sure I want to know." I nod in agreement, I've heard some of his tales, and I know she doesn't want to hear them.

"Why don't you go choose one of Jules' dishes to warm up, and I'll finish what I was doing when you came in." She goes to speak, but I stop her with a gentle kiss. "I promise, it won't take me long, and I will be out to join you in the kitchen. I swear." I plant a light kiss on her lips again, before setting her on her feet, and gently smacking her arse to get her moving out of the office. "The sooner you go, the sooner I can finish up."

"I'm going, but because I'm hungry, not because you told me to!" She declares as she leaves the room, and I laugh as I turn back to my laptop, quickly finishing what I need to.

When I get to the doorway to the kitchen, I pause to watch Kenna as she dances around the space, singing to the music she's got playing on her phone. I love seeing her so happy, and relaxed.

"Holy crap! How long have you been standing there Brady?" She asks with a grin, turning the music down.

"Not long." I smile back at her.

"Sure." She says with a laugh. "You've got great timing, dinner is served."

"Thanks baby." I say, kissing her on the cheek.

"Don't thank me, thank Jules." She laughs. "He did all the hard work."

"Logan helped." I say, taking the plates, and walking them over to the table that Kenna's already set with cutlery, and drinks. Behind me Kenna lets out a loud laugh, and I got exactly what I was hoping for.

"You and I both know Logan wasn't much help."

"Logan can cook." I feel like I should defend the man, because he *can* actually cook, just not the same meals that Jules can.

"You're right, he can, but there's no way in hell that my big brother would have been able to pull this off the way Jules has." She laughs as she sits opposite me at the table. "You and I both know that Jules did the bulk of the cooking, and Logan did the running around, and was Jules' assistant in every way. I'm surprised they didn't kill each other actually. I would have loved to have watched them work together like that." A sad smile lifts the corners of her mouth.

"Hey." I say, reaching over to rest my hand on top of hers. "They'll get it together eventually."

"I know, but I just want it be sooner, rather than later. They both deserve to be happy, you know?"

"Yes, I do baby." There's nothing else I can say, Logan has to live his own life, I can't force him to do anything he doesn't want to.

We eat in silence for a few minutes, before Makenna starts up a conversation. We talk about everything, and nothing, just as easily as we do every day. When we're done, we do the dishes, and clean up together, before deciding to sit down and watch a movie together.

We both know how this is going to end, but we get comfortable anyway, and halfway through the movie Makenna is asleep, her head in my lap. I finish the movie, and carry her to our bed, strip off her clothes, and tuck her in.

"Brady." Her voice is a hoarse whisper as I flick off the light, before walking out the bedroom door.

"It's OK baby, go back to sleep, I'm just going to finish up a few things in the office, then I'll come to bed as well."

"Mmmm kay." She mumbles without opening her eyes, making me smile. I've never known her to be any different when she's half asleep, even when we were teenagers she would mumble answers to my questions. It took me a while to work out that it didn't mean that she didn't want to answer me, but that she was too asleep to actually speak. I found it adorable then, and I still do now.

I'm still smiling as I sit down at my desk to finish up my work. It takes me a couple of hours, and a few phone calls, before I climb under the covers, pull Makenna's warm, supple body into mine, and relax into a restful sleep.

For the next couple of days our routine is almost a carbon copy of the day before. We wake each other up with amazing sex, either while we're still in bed or once we're in the shower. Breakfast and coffee follows. Then Kenna goes to the office and sorts out the days schedule with Margot, I do a few things around the house. Then, she comes back, and we have lunch together. Then we both work in the home office until we break for dinner, and a movie. Where Makenna falls asleep without fail, and I carry her to bed, tucking her in, before finishing off my day's work, and talking to Damien when needed.

Until the third day when Makenna's phone rings, and she stares at the screen.

"Are you going to answer that Kenna, or don't you want to talk to whoever it is?" She doesn't answer me, just continues to stare at the phone.

"Well, at least now I know what you're doing when you don't answer my calls right away. You're staring at the phone deciding whether you want to talk to me or not."

"It's Doctor Morris." She says in a whisper, and I feel like an arse, because now I understand why she's hesitating.

"Answer it Kenna, before she hangs up." I say quietly, resting my hands on her arms in support.

Chapter Fifty-four
MAKENNA

I stare at the screen of my phone, looking at Doctor Morris' name like it's radioactive.

"Answer it Kenna, before she hangs up." Brady says quietly from behind me, and I know he's right. When his hands grip my upper arms, his reassurance gives me the strength to answer the phone.

"Good afternoon Doctor Morris."

"Good afternoon Makenna." She laughs into the phone. "I'll never get used to people knowing it's me on the other end of the phone *before* they answer it."

"I'm sure it's strange."

"Down to business. Is Brady there with you?" I feel like her asking me if Brady's here means that it's all bad news.

"Yes, you're on speaker right now so that we can both hear you."

"Good afternoon Doctor Morris." Brady says, letting her know that he is in fact right beside me.

"Good afternoon Brady, nice to talk to you again."

"You too."

"Right." She sighs, and I don't know if it's good news or bad anymore. "Shall we get down to business?"

"Yes please, Doctor Morris." I say, my voice shaking with nerves.

"Right then, I'll get right to it." She coughs, and I hear her shuffle some papers around on her desk, and all I can think is if this is her getting down to it, then she needs to move faster! "I got your blood test results back earlier today, I read the report and went over the results myself to make sure, but I'm happy to tell you that you're clear to start the hormone stimulant within the next few days if you want to."

I let out the breath I hadn't even realised I was holding in, and look over my shoulder at Brady, who still looks concerned.

"Are you sure Doctor Morris?"

"Absolutely Brady. Unless you have some other concerns about the treatment, and need me to go over things again, or to explain something else to you, Makenna is healthy, and her hormone levels are actually in the perfect range for treatment to start."

"Can I start the tablets today? Or would that be too soon?" I ask, my excitement as the realisation that we've been given the go ahead now reaching fruition.

"Yes, you can." The Doctor laughs. "I didn't want to put too much pressure on you, I guess I should have known better than that. Yes, you can start whenever you're ready. All I ask is that a week after you've taken your first dose, you come in and see me for a check-up. Other than that, if you got the meds after you left here earlier in the week, then yes, you're good to start today."

"Thank you Doctor Morris, that's great news." I say a little breathless.

Her laughter comes through the phone. "I thought you might be waiting for my call, so as soon as I got the results and checked, I called you right away."

"I can't thank you enough."

"You're very welcome Makenna." There's a few seconds of silence, before she asks, "Brady, are you OK with this?"

"What?" He's been standing behind me with his hands lightly resting on my arms, and when I look back at him again, my smile falters slightly, because he looks a little stunned. "Oh, yes I'm fine Doctor Morris. Absolutely fine as long as Kenna is good, I am too."

"This is a lot for both of you Brady, you have to be on the same page as Makenna. She's going to need your support, so if you have any questions, now is the time to ask them."

"No, you answered all our questions the other day."

"No *your* collective questions Brady, if *you* have any concerns, or questions, I want you to know you can ask me. Anything. I'm here for you *both,* and I'm happy to talk to you without Makenna if there's something that you don't want to bring up in front of her. Nothing against you, obviously

Makenna, because I'm happy to do the same for you. You both need to voice your concerns or worries. I've seen way too many couples who think they're ready for this, and then implode because they don't talk about things." She takes a large breath, but before either of us can speak, she continues speaking. "I know you're going to say you're not that couple, and believe me when I say that you're the *most* cohesive couple I've ever met, but this process can put a lot of stress on a relationship. There are some things you don't want to say to your husband or wife, because you don't want to upset them."

"We talk about everything Doctor Morris." I reassure her, smiling at Brady. "Don't we honey?" I ask him, looking for reassurance and agreement. He smiles at me, but it doesn't reach his eyes.

"Of course we do baby. I'm sure we'll be fine Doctor Morris, but we'll keep what you've said in mind. Just in case. Thank you for your very generous offer."

"You're welcome. Now I want to remind you Makenna that I want to see you a week after you start on the medication. It doesn't matter if you start today, tomorrow, or next week, but I want to see you for a check-up the week after you start, OK?"

"Of course." I tell her.

"OK, then I'll leave you to your day."

"Thank you Doctor Morris." Brady says before I can.

"Any time. I have to admit, I've never wanted this process to work more for any other couple I've helped through this. So please, call me if you need anything."

We reassure her that we will, I promise to book that appointment in a week's time, and then we say our goodbyes. When I've disconnected the call neither of us move. I'm staring at the screen of my phone, and Brady is still standing behind me, only now his hands are resting on my hips. I need to ask him one more time, but I don't want to make him mad.

"What is it Kenna?" He asks softly in my ear, his breath tickling the edge of my ear.

"Are you sure about this? You just seem – hesitant still." My voice is barely above a whisper. It's so quiet, I'm not even sure that he heard me.

"I'm not hesitant for the reason you think Kenna." His voice is soft. "I just don't want you to put all your eggs in this one basket, and then get your heart broken if it doesn't work. Before you say anything, no, I'm not saying I don't think it will work out how you want it to, not at all. All I'm saying is that you seem to have tunnel vision. *This* is the only way for you to have a baby."

"Us."

"What?"

"For *us* to have a baby." I say in a louder whisper. "You keep saying we're doing this together."

"You're right." He closes his eyes, and lets out a deep sigh. "We *are* doing this together Kenna, but I wouldn't be doing *my* part if I let both of us walk into this with our eyes shut tight, and all our hopes set on this one process. My job is to make sure that you don't get hurt, and that if you *do* get hurt, it's minimal." He scrubs a hand down his face, and takes another deep breath. "I would feel like I'm letting us both down if I just jumped feet first into this."

"But we're not jumping into this feet first. We've talked about it for months, if not years."

"Starting a family, yes, not taking drugs, taking temperatures, and charting your periods Kenna."

"I know, but this is what we have to do."

"I know, but it doesn't mean that I can't try at least to protect you. You are my everything Kenna, and I don't want to see you in pain again. It broke my damned heart." I turn to face him, and he takes my face gently in his hands. Closing my eyes, I nuzzle my cheek into his hand, and take a deep breath.

"It will be worth it Brady." I tell him quietly.

"Will it baby? Before you say anything, yes I want a family with you more than anything, but this just seems – extreme."

"Yes, it will. You're with me, right?"

"Absolutely baby. I'm with you two hundred percent, but that doesn't mean I'm not going to protect you every step the way, in any way I can. I love you too much not to." He kisses me lightly. "Guess we better start taking your temperature every day, and tracking those periods of yours." I burst out laughing.

"*You* don't have to do all of that Brady." I start before he interrupts me.

"Are you kidding me? There's nothing I'd enjoy more. We're in this thing together Kenna, and is this is what you need to do, then *we* do it." This time I let out a loud belly laugh, and I need Brady to hold me up.

"It's my body honey." I say once I've caught my breath. "Not to mention, I've already been tracking my periods. The only time I forgot was within the couple of weeks before the wedding, simply because I didn't have it. Now, we know that I was pregnant then."

"Well, when are you due for the next time, because you can't start taking the medication until you're a couple of days into it, can you?"

"Nope. So, I should be able to start them in the next day, maybe two." He nods his agreement.

"Let me get you some dinner, then you can relax in the bath for a while, I'll finish up what I need to do for work, and we can watch a movie."

"Another movie?" I tease him. We've settled into such a routine the past few days, that I feel like we're already an old married couple.

"Yes, because you can put your feet up, and we can have time together." He kisses my lips, wrapping me up in his arms, and I don't have the heart to tell him I think my brothers might just crash his plans tonight. It's been a few days since they've been over, and I think a visit is long overdue. Instead, I let him go ahead, and organise another one of Jules' miracle meals that I'm sure are reproducing in our fridge, because they seem to be never ending.

"Do you need any help?"

"No. Go check your social media, and relax for a while. It's not like it takes long to warm up one of Jules' meals." He says with a tender smile as he starts pulling containers out of the fridge. "You could choose the movie we're going to watch tonight."

"Anything I want?" He hesitates with a plate in his hand, and looks at me with a raised eyebrow.

"Yes, anything *you* want to watch."

"Even a Romantic Comedy?" He answers without even looking at me this time.

"Absolutely. Pick a Reese Witherspoon movie, and I promise to enjoy it."

Laughing, I leave him in the kitchen to do whatever, and sit on the couch and start flicking through the streaming service to find a movie. I smile when I settle on exactly the movie I want to watch. Choice of movie done, I sit back, and relax while checking my social media. I probably could, and should have done some more work, but an early dinner never hurt anyone.

Shit, we *have* gotten old! I laugh at my own revelation, and convince myself it's practice for when we have a house full of kids, and have to eat earlier in the day.

Chapter Fifty-five
BRADY

I know I shouldn't have been shocked by the call from Doctor Morris, but I was. It's just so jarring to think of everything that Makenna is going to have to put her body through, to make us a family. I also can't help the smile that spreads across my face, and the warm feeling in my chest at just the thought of becoming a family. Having *children* that share my DNA, and hers.

As I think about the mini versions of Makenna running around the house, and backyard, my smile almost splits my face, and I'm sure if anyone was looking, they'd think I was a fucking lunatic. They might be right, but I can't help the feeling of excitement that's flooding my body now that we've decided that this is the way we're headed.

"What are you smiling about Mr Harris?" Kenna asks when I take her dinner in to the loungeroom, and pass it over.

"Just happy Kenna." I say, and walk back to the kitchen to get my own dinner.

"So, what are we eating tonight?" Kenna asks as I sit down next to her and get comfortable.

"No clue." I crack up laughing when I look up to see the look of horror on her face. "Tonight we have curry prawns with jasmine rice."

"Why didn't you just say that, instead of basically telling me you didn't even look at the container. You and I both know that Jules has everything in that fridge, and cupboard labelled within an inch of its life, so there's no excuse to not know what you're eating!" The look of astonishment mixed with anger on her face is hysterical.

"I do know that, and *you* know better than to believe that I wouldn't look at what I was cooking, or reheating like I did tonight." I say with a raised eyebrow.

"True, but I also know that you trust Jules, and therefore would just pick up any container in there and be more than happy to eat it without knowing exactly what it was."

"Except I didn't." I tell her. Before she can respond, the front door opens and closes, and then both Logan and Caleb are yelling out for us. I can't help rolling my eyes, because they've given us our space for a few days, and even though I knew our luck would to run out soon, I was really hoping it wouldn't be quite so soon. "They're back." I mutter.

"You missed them Brady, you know you did."

"I missed them like normal people miss fungus growing in the bathroom." I mutter under my breath just as they enter the loungeroom.

"Why didn't you guys answer us?" Caleb asks. "I thought you were either not home or we were going to catch you doing things no brother should ever have to see. I think I still need to bleach the fading images from the last time I walked in on you two doing the do." He shivers from head to toe as he plonks himself down on the other side of Kenna.

"Perhaps if you learned to knock and wait until given permission to enter someone else's home, you might not find then in compromising positions." I suggest helpfully.

"Nah, I don't think that would work around here at all." Caleb says, looking for and intents and purposes, very fucking serious. Before I can correct him, Logan speaks.

"Don't let us interrupt your dinner." He says.

"Why are you guys eating so early? Have you turned into an old married couple before your time or what?"

"We're both tired." I tell him, staring him down, but he either doesn't get it or he chooses to ignore me. I think it's the latter option if I know Caleb, and I know him pretty well.

"So, can we raid your fridge for food too, or should we order in a pizza?"

"You could go *home* and do whatever the fuck you like for dinner." I suggest, taking a bite of my dinner.

"Just go and get yourselves something to eat, we were about to start watching a movie." Kenna tells them.

"Ohhh what are we watching?" Caleb asks, even as Logan pulls him up off the couch, and starts dragging him towards the kitchen.

"Get your dinner, and you'll find out." Kenna tells him, and then both of the guys are gone.

"You don't really mind, do you?" She asks me once they're out of ear shot.

"Not really, but it would have been nice to enjoy one more night without them." I know I'm being ridiculous, but I swear, it's only because I want to spend some one on one time with my gorgeous wife.

"I can send them home." She offers, but I shake my head no as I take another bite of food. There's no point in telling them to leave now, they're getting food, and settling in, for a little while anyway.

We eat in silence, the only noise is the low, mumbling voices of her brothers in the other room deciding on what to eat and then arguing over, well everything.

"How are those two ever going to be able to work together in the business Kenna? They can't even discuss what to have for dinner without getting into an argument about it."

"It's all pretty light-hearted Brady, you *know* that. They just enjoy giving each other a hard time. Funnily enough, I've seen them working together, and suppliers don't have a chance against the two of them, and believe it or not, but our clients just love the both of them. I don't know how it works, but it does, and I'm not going to complain about it, not for one second!"

"What aren't you going to complain about?" Caleb asks, as he makes himself comfortable on Kenna's other side again.

"Nothing Caleb." Kenna says with a sweet smile.

"Mind your own business Caleb, if they wanted us to know, we would have been part of the conversation." Logan admonishes as he sits on my other side, making Kenna and I the meat in a Drake brothers sandwich. I nod his way, and he nods back. "So, what movie were you going to watch?" Logan asks, making Kenna smile.

"Watch and find out." She teases, and I hope it's the sappiest bloody romantic comedy she could find. That will teach her brothers for gate crashing our night, again, but a RomCom is not what starts up.

"Ohh cool! Good choice Brady." Caleb says.

"I actually had nothing to do with it, it was all your sister."

"You're pretty cool for a girl you know?"

"Gee, thanks Caleb, I appreciate that!" She says with a laugh, not offended in the slightest.

I take Kenna's bowl, and place it with mine on the coffee table, and pull her into me so that we can snuggle, just as the first explosion lights up the screen. Caleb's not wrong, his sister is the best kind of person there is, she didn't choose a RomCom, no she chose to watch a blow up the world kind of movie for me instead.

The boys both finish their dinner and place their empty plates on the coffee table with ours, and we watch the movie in relative silence. Silence that gets broken by Caleb offering up advice on how not to do things, how to do things the right way or how things wouldn't have worked.

When the movie's finished Logan says, "She fell asleep again huh?"

"Yeah, she's been asleep for about half an hour."

"Why didn't you take her to bed then?"

"Because I enjoy just sitting here, and letting her sleep. I love that she's so comfortable with me that she can fall asleep." I tell him, without thinking.

"You know, she's never been any different. I don't know if she's ever seen the end of a movie in her lifetime." He laughs. "Dad used to carry her to bed most nights, even when she became a teenager."

"Why do you think I make her promise to watch a movie in bed when I'm working?" I laugh.

"Good idea." He chuckles in reply.

"I'm going to take her to bed, I'll be back out in a minute." I take her to our room, strip her down, then tuck her into bed, and she snuggles into the covers.

"I love you Brady." She mumbles in her sleepy voice.

"I love you too Makenna." I say, kissing her forehead, and leaving her to sleep.

When I get back out to the living room, there's no one to be found, and the house is quiet. I walk into the kitchen, because I notice the dishes are all gone, so I figure I'll get them done and then head to bed myself, but I find Logan in there doing the dishes instead.

"Where's Caleb?" I ask.

"He got a phone call and left faster than he gets here when pizzas just arrived." Logan says and we look at each other, and smile.

"Booty call." We say at the same time, and then laugh loudly.

"So, how are you guys doing, really?" Logan asks me.

"We're doing great actually Logan."

"Are you sure? Have you heard from the specialist yet?"

"Yeah, she called today."

"And?"

"And what?" I ask, as I pick up a tea towel and start to dry the dishes he's washing.

"What did she say? Can you guys start the treatment Makenna was talking about the other day?"

"Yeah." I tell him, but don't look up from the dish in my hand that is so dry it might become dust.

"You don't seem so enthusiastic Brady. Has something changed for you? Don't you want a family with Kenna? Does it fit into the too hard basket now?" He asks all the questions at such a rapid pace it's hard for me to keep up.

"What? No!" I almost yell, but remember to keep my voice down. "NO, I love your sister, and I want to give her everything she wants. I want a family Logan, I want kids but I'm just worried."

"About what?"

"I'm worried that it's all too much. That she's putting too much stress on her, mind, and body. I know she's strong Logan, and I know I can and *will* be strong for her, but it's just a lot you know?"

"No, I can't say I do know Brady, I'm sorry, and I doubt that I ever will." He says looking down at the floor searching for his next words, as he dries his hands. "I think you shouldn't take this whole thing for granted, not everyone gets the opportunity that you and Kenna have right now."

"You'll have the chance for a family of your own too Logan." I say patting him on the back, as he turns around to hang up the towel he dried his hands on.

"I don't think that's in the cards for me Brady, but thanks for saying so." He pats me on the shoulder this time. "I think I'm going to head home."

"Thanks for helping me clean up."

"It's the least I could do after making at least some of the mess."

I walk him to the door, say goodnight and lock up behind him, turning off all the lights along the way.

I stand in the doorway to our bedroom just watching Kenna sleep for a minute. Logan's right, we can't take this opportunity for granted, and I'm going to make the most of it. If we don't get pregnant, or we lose another baby, then we'll deal with it, but we could end up with a beautiful baby that looks just like her mum at the end of all this, and that would make me the happiest man alive.

I strip out of my clothes, and place them on the chair on my side of the bed, and climb in beside Makenna. She mumbles something in her sleep, and pushes her body back into mine, and I sigh.

Once again I end the night being the big spoon to my wife's little spoon, and I can't think of a better place I'd rather be.

Chapter Fifty-six
MAKENNA

The days following the call from Doctor Morris I take my temperature, chart my period in my diary, and take the medication. All the while, Brady monitors *me*, while I try to get him to return to work. I appreciate the fact that he's now fallen in line with the treatment, and our new path to starting a family, I don't need him micromanaging me.

Every damned time I turn around, he's asking me another question, or checking to make sure that I've taken what I need to, and written in my diary. It's driving me *crazy*. I shudder to think what he's going to be like when I actually fall pregnant, and I'm carrying his baby.

He really needs to go back to the bar, if for no other reason than to do something that doesn't involve me, and the situation we find ourselves in. The only way I could get the over-protective man to go back though, was to get Margot and Logan to promise to check in on me, and make sure I'm OK, and to call him if anything happens.

Is it nice of him to worry? I guess so, but I've been handling my own life for a long time now, even before we got married, and it's kind of annoying for him to behave like this now.

"You know he's just looking out for you Makenna. He loves you." Logan tells me, defending Brady.

"Well, of course *you* would defend him Logan, he's like another brother to you. Only he's not blood related to you, so he's easier to deal with." I frown at my big brother, whose laugh is more of loud snort, because he knows I'm right.

"You're brother isn't wrong Makenna. Brady loves you, and he knows that you're going to go through a few changes, emotionally and physically, he just wants to make sure you're OK." I go to speak, but Margot holds up

374

her hand to stop me, while shaking her head. "No, hear me out sweetie. He loves you, I think we can all agree on that, it's a fact. He also knows how much this means to you, and yes to him, but he also knows that he can't do this *for* you. He just needs the reassurance that you're OK. It's not that he thinks you can't look after yourself, oh no, he's very much aware that you can, it's that he wants to make sure that you're OK, because that's *all* he can do."

"Margot is right. He can't take the meds for you, or have your period, and it's not his temperature that needs to be tracked. He's doing the only thing he knows how to do, and that's looking after *you*." Logan says, looking at me like he's begging me to argue. "He's a good man Makenna. I'm not saying you shouldn't have sent him back to work, you should have, but his heart is in the right place, and he's not trying to offend you."

"He's not controlling you, or us. In fact, we'd already agreed to check in on you, so he didn't ask us to do anything we weren't planning on doing anyway. It's just this way, his mind is at ease as well." Margot chimes in.

"He knows you can look after yourself. He knows we'll look after you if you need anything but that doesn't mean he's not protective of you and any potential children of yours."

"He's going to make a great dad." I say quietly.

"He will, and you'll make a great mum as well." Logan says while patting my hand, then pulling me into a tight hug. "Now, get back to work, before I send you home to 'rest'." I push against his chest, and laugh at his ridiculousness.

"You can't send me home." I scoff.

"I can and I damn well will if you don't look after yourself." He scowls. "I've got a phone call I have to make, so I'm going to get back to work. On my way back to my office, I'll message your husband and tell him you're doing just fine and that Margot has arranged for lunch to be delivered to your office. That should keep him happy for a while. You're welcome."

"I love you Lo."

"I love you too Kenna." He kisses me on the forehead, Margot on the cheek, and then he's gone.

Caleb comes by an hour later to ask me to join him for another meeting.

"I'll get something to eat at Vines Margot. Did you want me to bring you back anything?"

"No thanks Makenna, I've already got something organised." I nod in acknowledgement, and walk with Caleb over to the tasting room behind Vines. I enjoy our time together, because while he asks me how I am, there isn't an underlying question to it. It's a simple question, that he wants a simple answer to.

We get down to business, have lunch together, and he walks me back to the house afterwards. We have a cup of tea together, then he heads home.

This is how the next few weeks go by. Most of my days, I seem to have someone with me. Whether it's Margot in the office, Logan for one reason or another, Caleb here and there, even Leila the baker at Vines keeps me company sometimes. The only real time I get to myself is after dinner, and before Brady gets home from work later at night.

I start to really look forward to that quiet time by myself in the evenings, because for the rest of the time, someone else is with me, and it's tiresome.

When we go back to Doctor Morris for my check up like she asked, I convince Brady to take separate cars this time, unlike last time, so that he can go to work right after. I told him that I'd organised to have lunch with Beth and Rochelle so that he'd agree. Then, I had to call them both and ask them to join me for lunch, because I knew that he would ask his sister how lunch was, which would create an issue that I didn't want to have to deal with.

Walking back to my car after lunch, and some retail therapy with the girls is when I saw Jules coming out of a café, and I couldn't help stopping to talk to him. He looked so sad, and I wanted to make sure he was ok. That conversation didn't go as well as I hoped, and for the entire drive home, I worried about Logan, because I realised exactly why he was being a bigger grump than usual.

Over the course of the next few weeks, before I can take another round of the medication, life goes back to some kind of normal. Well, what we're calling normal for now anyway. Caleb crashes meals every other day, and I try to coax Logan to join us, but he doesn't.

Then, we start the next round of keeping track of my cycle, temperature, and taking the medication. Brady goes through this weird over-protective change *again* and I have to tell him I can't keep living like this.

"Brady, if you can't reign in this overprotectiveness." I say, waving my hand up and down in front of his gorgeous body. "Then we're not doing this honey."

"It's not *over* protectiveness Kenna, I'm *protecting* you, and our potential child." The frown on his face is so damned adorable, that I struggle to keep the frustrated frown on *my* face. All I can see is our future son with the same deep brown eyes, looking back at me, and I can't help the smile that spreads across my face. "What are you smiling at baby? Is this what they mean when they talk about your hormones making you emotional? Cause you looked like you wanted to kill me a minute ago, and you look like that again." He takes a couple of steps back.

"I *was* imaging a beautiful little boy, with dark brown eyes, and a cute little frown on his face, because I want one that looks just like his Dad. I guess the difference will be that I won't bring him up to blame a woman's hormones for her mood, or desire to *not* be coddled." With my rant over a I take a deep breath.

"OK." He says the word long, and slowly.

"I'm sorry Brady. I'm just frustrated. You don't need to look over my shoulder every second of the day, honey. I'm still *me,* I can still look after myself. I haven't changed."

"I know that, I just can't get my mind to allow that." He moves closer to me, taking my hands in his. "I just can't shake the feeling that something bad is going to happen, and I won't be there for you this time."

"You can't be with me every second of every day Brady. That's not possible, and it's not healthy. You know that honey." I tell him as I drop one of his hands, to place mine on his cheek, and he nuzzles it.

"I know, but that doesn't stop this overwhelming need to be here, to protect you. Both of you, when the time comes." And how can I be mad at him about it?

"You are going to make a wonderful father Brady Harris, and our children are going to love you as much as I do." I say, kissing him with all the passion that I'm feeling for him right now.

"Wow." He says, his breath raspy as he rests his head in the crook of my neck. "I'm not sure what I did to deserve that amazing kiss, but I'd appreciate it if you told me so that I could earn it again." I feel his smile against my skin.

"Just keep being you." I tell him honestly.

"Well, that I think I can manage."

Chapter Fifty-seven
BRADY

After our chat, I try to pull back a little, but it's so damned hard. I just want to protect her from any hurt that comes her way, and I truly don't think *I* can survive watching her suffer if another miscarriage is a part of our future.

She wants a baby, *we want,* a baby so much, but this process is heartbreaking. For both of us.

In the days, and weeks that follow we manage to fall back in to our routine, for the most part anyway. My parents visit, and her brothers still drop in unannounced for meals, but I don't mind as much as I did before. Mainly because my favourite thing to do now is teasing them about needing them to leave so that I can impregnant their sister. That seems to get them moving out of the house pretty damned fast. Well, it works with Caleb, but we haven't seen much of Logan.

Doctor Morris calls us to check in again and asks for Kenna to go in for another check-up after she has another dose of the medication, so we book that in, and I have to say, I'm kind of nervous about it. I don't know why, but I think it's because I don't know what to expect. Makenna seems to be relaxed, and happy, that or the happy constant chatter is a cover for her own nerves, but I don't think so. She seems to be honestly jumping out of her skin with excitement, and it makes me wonder what she could possibly think the doctor is going say to us today, which then sets my anxiety into high alert.

We walk into the office, well Kenna bounces on her toes, and I walk in behind her, check in with the receptionist, who returns Kenna's smile, and enthusiasm, then take a seat in the waiting room. To wait. Among the pregnant women of varying degrees, and for the most part, their partners. Most of them have smiles on their faces as well.

"Makenna, Brady. Doctor Morris is ready to see you now." A nurse smiles at us about fifteen minutes later from the doorway. I'm not sure why, but walking back into the rooms today feels worse than the day I brought Kenna in the last time she miscarried. For some reason, I feel like we're walking into the lion's den, and I can't shake that feeling.

"Just take a seat, and the doctor will be with you in a few minutes." The nurse smiles as she leaves us alone, closing the door quietly behind her.

"Are you OK Brady?" Kenna asks, an adorable frown creasing her forehead as we both sit down.

"Yeah, I'm fine." I smile at her, hoping that I don't look as nervous as I feel.

"Then why is your leg bouncing like that honey?" She says with a small laugh, while placing her hand on my knee to get me to stop moving. "It's going to be OK, Brady, it's just a check-up, nothing more, nothing less. I promise." She kisses me lightly on the lips as we hear the door open, and the doctor coughs quietly.

"Sorry to interrupt." Laughter in her voice, and a smile on her face as she takes a seat in front of us.

"Nothing to interrupt." I say, my voice gruffer than I planned, and Kenna looks at me like I've grown an extra head. I just shrug my shoulders, I have nothing I can say in way of explaining my behaviour.

"How are you feeling Makenna? Have you noticed any of the symptoms we discussed the last time you were here?" Doctor Morris asks, a smile on her face.

"No, I don't think so." Kenna answer with a shake of her head, and a frown on her face. "I've been pretty lucky in that sense I guess. I feel pretty great." With the second half of her answer, she smiles broadly.

I clear my throat with a cough, making both women look my way. "Umm yes you have baby."

"I have?" Kenna asks, looking adorably confused, and I can't help chuckling.

"Yeah, you have baby." I rest my hand on her knee, trying to reassure her that it's OK.

"Which side effect do you think she's had Brady?" Doctor Morris asks with an amused smile.

"Yeah please do tell, cause I'm kind of curious myself now."

Chuckling uncomfortably I start to list off the couple of things that she's started doing in the last few weeks. "You take your cardigan off, then it's back on minutes later, then off again, and on again."

"Well, I keep getting these hot flashes but then they're gone pretty quickly."

"I know, you don't have to defend anything baby. I'm just answering Doctor Morris' question." The doctor smiles at both of us, and I feel myself relax a little. "Your breasts have been a little tender as well."

"Well perhaps if you were a bit more gentle, they wouldn't be quite so tender." Kenna tells me, and then blushes furiously when she realises what she's said.

"I promise I'll work on that baby." I tell her, after kissing her gently on one of her burning hot cheeks. "You had that one dizzy episode too." I remind her.

"I'd forgotten about that."

"Did you fall over, or hurt yourself?" Doctor Morris asks.

"I almost fell over, but Brady was home, and he caught me. Although, I don't think I would have fallen to the ground either way."

"That's why I'm around." I grin at her, proud of myself for keeping all these little things logged in my brain. "I take note of these things, and I'm there to catch you if you fall. Literally *and* figuratively."

"Yeah right, I'm lucky." She says, rolling her eyes, but she's smiling at me like she adores me anyway.

"You're very lucky to have a husband, and partner that takes notice of all the small things Makenna." The doctor smiles at us both. "Well, thanks to Brady, I've noted all that down, but if they get any worse, especially the dizzy spells, don't hesitate to call, or come straight in if you're worried." Her words are directed at me, like she knows that Kenna won't want to come in.

"You got it Doc." I nod at her.

"You shouldn't have told him that Doctor Morris, he's going to take this *way* too seriously now." Kenna rolls her eyes so far back, I'm afraid they won't actually right themselves, all while she lets out a huge sigh. Doctor

Morris throws her head back, and laughs loudly. When she sits back up, she's wiping tears from her eyes.

"You two are positively outrageous." The doctor tells us while catching her breath. "I wish all my patients were like you two. I'm not going to say you're perfect, because no person, or couple is, but damned if I don't think you two won't make the best parents in the world. The love, humour and affection you two have for each other is just so entertaining, and endearing all at the same time."

"Thanks, I think." Kenna says, hesitantly.

"Oh, it's definitely a compliment Makenna. You're the kind of couple I want to help, that I want to see this treatment work for. Don't get me wrong, I want to see it work for every patient that walks through my door, I just want it to work more for some than I do others."

"We're not that special Doctor Morris." Kenna says, blushing.

"You really are, and it's wonderful to see couple like you two every now and then, it helps to reassure me that I'm not in the wrong field."

"Thank you Doc." I say, smiling at her, and taking Kenna's hand in mine. "All I know is, my love for my wife is unconditional, and unreserved. She'll never have to wonder how I feel about her, and I will love our children, when we're blessed with them, with the same unreserved, and unconditional love. I don't care how they arrive, whether they share our DNA, or not, they will be loved." I don't look at Doctor Morris while I speak, I look right in Makenna's eyes, and I see the tears well, before one drops onto her cheek. I swipe at it with my thumb. "Don't cry baby, it's the truth."

"You are the sweetest man on the planet Brady Harris, and I don't know how I got so lucky, but I'm glad that we met." Kenna chokes on the last couple of words, as her emotions take over.

"I know baby, I'm just too good." I smile her favourite lopsided smirk, and I know it's done what I wanted it to do, when she laughs, and calls me an idiot. It's broken the emotional tension, and I think the doctor appreciates the effort too. It was a little uncomfortable in here for a minute!

The doctor coughs, clearing her throat, but her first couple of words are still a little choked up. "So, I need to do a quick physical, now that we've gotten the questions out of the way. When we're done, I'll get you to go to pathology again so that we can test your hormone levels again, and make sure that they're neither too high, or too low."

"Do I need to strip down again?" Kenna asks, and I feel my dick twitch in my pants. Just thinking about Kenna getting naked, no matter the environment, makes me want her.

"No, not today. You can jump onto the bed here, and I'll just feel your stomach to make sure everything is OK." She motions for Kenna to step up onto bed beside us, and lie down. Kenna nods, like this is all normal to her, and I guess it is.

I stay seated, and watch as the doctor goes through all the things she needs to, and Kenna answer the few questions she asks. They're done in a couple of minutes, and then we're saying goodbye. We walk to pathology once again, get her blood drawn, then we're back in the car and heading home.

The nervousness that I was feeling on the way into the appointment has faded, and I'm feeling good about the whole thing. I take Kenna's hand in mine, and bring it to my lips, leaving a light but sloppy kiss on the back of her hand. She looks at me like I hung the stars, and the moons just for her, and I know I would give this woman anything in the world that she wanted. I would fight to give her everything.

Chapter Fifty-eight
MAKENNA

The drive home was quiet, not uncomfortable, but I could tell we were both lost in our own thoughts. As Brady steered the car through the gates of Drake Wines, I suggested lunch at Vines.

"Lunch at Vines hey?" He repeated back to me, before lifting my hand to his lips, and giving it a sweet kiss.

"Yeah. I think lunch at Vines together would be nice." I smile at him.

"You're right, it would be." It's early in the week, so it shouldn't be too busy. "How much do you want to bet that Caleb is already in there?" He asks with a smirk.

I roll my eyes, because I don't think anyone needs to place bets on whether Caleb will be in there. I mean they've given him his own table, and the regulars know not to sit there. Even the group of lovable, but crazy Grandma's with no filters, know better than to sit at 'Caleb's table'. Although, that *could* just be because they want him to be sitting there, so they can check him out.

"I'm not taking that bet, because you and I both know that he uses Vines as his office, even though we gave him a space of his own." I say, rolling my eyes, but truthfully I'm not annoyed. Caleb has always needed to be around people to thrive, and if he needs to sit in Vines to get his work done, then I'm not going to stop him.

Brady laughs as he pulls into a parking spot on the side of the building that houses the bistro. "You're not wrong." He jumps out of the car, and comes around to my side to open my door, holding his hand out to help me out. "Have you ever wondered why he works from here every day?" He's got this cute wrinkle between his eyes, at the top of his nose, which means he's already thought about it, and quite possibly thinks he has the answer.

"I think he just likes being around people, he always has. I think the hustle and bustle of the bistro helps him to settle, and concentrate on his work. Which might sound crazy to you, and me, but he's always needed noise to get his work done." I answer with a shrug, as Brady opens the door to let me enter first.

"So, it's not because he wants to see someone who is also here every day then?" He asks, his eyebrows raised curiously.

"I'm sure part of it is to check in on Leila, they've become pretty close since Caleb came back to work here."

"Hmmmm." Brady replies, but I don't get the chance to question him about it, because the lady in question greets us.

"Good afternoon Makenna, Brady. What can we do for you today? Did you want a table, or are you here on business? Did I miss a meeting we had?" A frown creases her brow, and I can't help laughing. The more I get to know her, the more I understand why Caleb likes hanging out with her.

"No, no missed meeting Leila. We'd like a table if you're not too busy? If you are, we can grab some take out, and eat it at home." I smile at her. I never want to take a table away from a paying customer, that being said, we always pay for our meals.

"We always have room for the Drakes in here." She says with a smile, and starts to walk away, before turning abruptly and saying, "And the Harris's too, obviously." Brady and I both laugh again.

"It's OK Leila, I've been lumped in as a Drake for as long as I can remember, so don't feel too bad about doing it as well." Brady laughs, and I see Leila visibly relax.

"I didn't mean to offend you."

"I know, and I wasn't offended." Brady sends a beautiful smile her way, and she smiles gratefully back.

"Now, did you want a table on your own, or did you want to share with your brother?" We don't ask which brother she means, and she doesn't elaborate. When I look over to Caleb's table, I can see him working hard on something, and I don't want to interrupt him. We're having an early lunch after all.

"How about one on our own? We'll leave him to get some work done, he seems pretty invested in whatever he's working on at the minute."

"Yeah, he is." Leila smiles, and it makes me believe she knows exactly what he's working on right now. She coughs to clear her throat, and moves through the tables. "Follow me." She sits us down at a table that isn't as far as we could possible get from Caleb, but we're certainly not close to him by any stretch of the imagination. "Do you know what you want? There are no new specials this week yet." She takes our order, puts it in with the staff, then walks by Caleb's table, before heading back into the kitchen.

Ten minutes later, Brady and I are deep in conversation about, of all things, making the kitchen baby safe, and putting the knives out of reach, because of course any baby of ours is going to be a mischief making, cupboard climbing terror, when Caleb stops by our table.

"You know you could have sat with me." He says in greeting.

"Why good afternoon little brother, and how are you today? I'm doing fine, thanks for asking." I say, with a sweet smile as I look up at him.

"Ha. Ha. Ha. Very funny Kenna." He proves just how adult he is by sticking his tongue out at me. "Good afternoon Makenna, Brady, how are you doing this fine day?" He asks, giving a slight bow at the end, the smart arse.

"Good thank you, Caleb." Brady answers him without even flinching. "We were just talking about childproofing the kitchen, because obviously any child with Drake DNA is going to be a little hellion, and get into mischief."

"Hey! I can't argue with that, we did give Mum heart attacks every other day. Well, not Logan, cause he's Mr Perfect, but hey, you and me Kenna, we were hell on wheels." Caleb laughs at the memories.

"What the hell do you mean *were*? You both still keep everyone around here on their toes, and you know it!" Brady exclaims, making Caleb and I look at him, and then crack up. We're too loud for the bistro, but I don't care.

There's a quiet cough, then Georgie speaks. "Mr Drake." She says with a smile and a nod at Caleb. "Mr and Mrs Harris, I have your drinks, and your food will be here in a second."

"Georgie, how many times I have told you to call me by my name. I'm Caleb, and they're Makenna, and Brady. We don't stand on formalities here, do we Kenna?" He sounds so annoyed at the barista that I can't help laughing, but I also agree with him whole heartedly.

"He's right Georgie. No pomp and ceremony here. Mr Harris is my Dad, and as much I love and respect the man, I am not him." Brady smiles at her, and I swear I see the poor woman melt a little with both Brady, and Caleb giving her their undivided attention.

"If you're sure, Caleb, Brady." She looks at them both as she says their names, then she seems to collect herself and looks my way. "You too, Makenna."

"Absolutely Georgie. We might be the owners, but we're also just people, and look, Caleb is in here almost as much as you are, so he really shouldn't be called Mr Drake."

"I am not in here that often Kenna!" Caleb declares, and the three of us look at him startled, then laugh.

"Caleb, you have your own table." I tell him between calming breaths.

"No I don't. Do I?" He asks Georgie.

"Umm yes, you do Caleb. Even the crazy Grandma's won't sit at 'your' table." She trying to hold back her laughter.

"I changed my mind, you can't call me Caleb, it's Mr Drake to you." He says with a pout.

"He's being an idiot, of course you can still call him Caleb." I say shaking my head at my brother. "Behave like an adult Caleb." I laugh.

"Caleb is an adult. Georgie you need to get back to the coffee maker please, there are a few orders piling up." Leila says, as she places plates of food in front of Brady and myself.

"Of course." Georgie says, and then she's gone.

"Oh my, that smells so damned good Leila." I tell her, and I think I'm actually drooling.

"Are you good there Kenna?" Brady asks, laughter still in his voice.

"I'm starving, and this smells divine!"

"Well, I'll let you guys eat in peace. Let me or one of the staff know if you need anything else, OK?"

"Thanks Leila." Brady says, but I can't wait any longer to eat.

"Wow Kenna, you could have waited one more minute before you started shovelling food in. I've never seen you behave like that, but I've certainly never seen you eat like that before." Caleb shakes his head, and walks away. I swear I heard him mutter, 'That's disgusting,' as he walks towards the bathroom, but I don't care enough to take too much notice.

"Are you sure you're OK baby?" Brady asks, concern on his face.

"Yeah, I'm just hungry. A girl's allowed to be hungry Brady." I grumble.

We eat in silence for a while, just listening to the chitchat, and noise of the bistro around us.

"You're right, this is delicious." Brady says with a smile. "Leila is a genius! You're lucky you got her."

"No luck was involved. She applied, I saw potential, and I employed her. I'm glad I did, because she is amazing."

"I guess you really were hungry." Brady says, and I look down at my plate, to discover my lunch is all gone, and Brady's plate is almost full still.

"I guess so." I shrug. "I'm not going to apologise for being hungry."

"I didn't say you had to Kenna." He says, holding his hands up in defence. I raise an eyebrow at him as I pick up the coffee that Georgie dropped off earlier.

"Ohhh I think Georgie screwed up my coffee somehow." I screw up my face in disgust.

"That's not like Georgie. Here, let me taste it." Brady says, reaching out his hand for my mug, so I hand it over, honestly I can't get rid of it fast enough. After taking a mouthful, he takes a second one, and nods. "Nope, it tastes perfect, if not a little too sweet for me. Georgie is my favourite barista in Vines, because she always gets everything just right." He passes the drink back to me, but I shake my head no.

"Maybe it's just me then?" I wonder out loud. "Coffee has tasted a little funky for the last few days. Maybe I'm getting sick? A cold perhaps?"

"You should have mentioned something to Doctor Morris while we were there earlier Kenna, she could have checked you out."

"I know she's still obviously a medical doctor, that's not her specialty, and I would feel weird asking her for a consult about me having a simple cold."

"I'm sure she wouldn't mind, and it might affect the medication you're on."

"Yeah, OK, if I'm still not feeling well when she calls about the blood test results, I'll ask her about it." I agree.

"Do you want to get going?"

"Yes, I'm suddenly feeling like I could have a nap now." I say, and Brady grins at me. "Not *that* kind of nap Brady." I laugh, as he holds out his hand for me to take as I stand up.

"No chocolate cake today?" He asks, and I'm shocked to realise it hadn't even occurred to me to get a slice.

"No, not today." I shake my head no to support my words.

"Wow, funky tasting coffee, *and* no chocolate cake. You *must* be feeling unwell! Let's get you home so that you can have that nap baby. You head out to the car, and I'll pay the bill." He hands me the car keys, and head outside to the car, smiling and saying hello to a few customers that I know on the way out. It's not until I settle into the passenger seat that I realise I didn't see Caleb on my way out of Vines.

I hear the car door open, and then I feel Brady's hand on my forehead.

"You don't feel like you've got a temperature. Maybe you just need some rest? The medication you're taking might be making you feel a little under the weather. I'll call Doctor Morris once I get you settled into bed."

"No, don't bother her Brady. I'm sure it's a simple cold or bug, and I'll be over it soon."

It's a quick drive from Vines to the house, and before I know what's going on, Brady's carrying me inside, and heading straight for our room. He gently lies me down on our bed, removes my shoes, then helps me out of my jeans.

"Are you comfy enough for a nap now?" He asks, sweeping a strand of hair off my face.

"Yeah, I am, thank you Brady."

"It is my absolute pleasure Makenna." He says with a smile, and kisses my forehead. "You get some rest, and hopefully you're feeling better when you wake up."

"Promise me you won't call Doctor Morris." I ask him quietly, because I'm already almost asleep.

"I promise baby. Now get some rest." He leaves a light kiss on my temple.

"I love you." I whisper, and the last thing I remember is feeling the covers as he drapes them over me, before I'm sleeping soundly.

Chapter Fifty-nine
BRADY

Over the next few days I notice some small changes in Makenna. She changes from drinking coffee to tea instead, because she can't stand even smelling coffee brewing. Her dizzy spells are happening more frequently, but she seems to be able to pre-empt them, and sit down before she falls down. There are foods that she simply can't stand the smell, or to look at and she sure as shit isn't going to eat them! Plus, she's tired. After work, she eats dinner, and when I come home I find her crashed out on the couch, her empty plate on the coffee table. She doesn't even manage to clear up or even try to get bed. So, I've taken to coming home, carrying her to bed and then cleaning up the dishes, before falling into bed behind her.

Almost a week after our visit to the doctor, Kenna's phone rings while she's in the bathroom.

"Can you answer that Brady?" I don't answer her, I just pick up the phone, and see Doctor Morris' name on the screen.

"Good morning Doctor Morris, how are you?"

"I'm good Brady, how are you? I didn't realise I'd called your number." She sounds confused.

"I'm good thanks. You didn't call my phone, I answered Kenna's phone, because she couldn't get to it."

"Oh, OK. Is she nearby?" I can't tell whether she's happy or not making this call by the tone of her voice, and I start to feel a little wary. "Could you put me on speaker please Brady? I'd actually like to talk to you both, seeing as how you're both there."

"Yeah, of course." I walk to the bathroom, and stand in the doorway. "Kenna, it's Doctor Morris. You're on speaker now."

Kenna smiles at me, but speaks to the phone. "Good morning Doctor Morris, how are you today?"

"I'm very good, thank you for asking. How have you been doing the last few days?"

"Not too bad. Well, OK I've been a little off. The dizzy episodes have happened a few more times, and I've totally turned off coffee, I can't even stand the smell of it."

"She's really tired too." I add in, only to get a dirty look off Makenna. "What? You *are* tired."

Doctor Morris laughs. "Thanks Brady, he was right to tell me Makenna, and it makes a lot of sense that you're feeling tired, and off certain foods. The medication could possibly be causing your fatigue." After a short pause, she asks, "Are you craving particular foods yet?"

"Cravings? No, I don't think so." Kenna looks my way, so I answer as well.

"Not that I've noticed, only foods that you can't stand anymore." I think for a few seconds before continuing. "Nope, no cravings as far as I can recall. Would the medication be causing all of those things? Should we watch out for them? Or is there something else that's causing it?"

"Well, the medication *could* be causing all those symptoms." She answers with a laugh. "But pregnancy could explain them all as well."

"Oh, yes of course it can." Kenna answers. "Do you think I need a lower dosage of the medication then?"

"No, I don't think you're going to need it anymore."

"Oh, you don't think it's working? Am I having too many of the side effects?" The look on Kenna's face breaks my heart, that is until Doctor Morris speaks again, and I finally clue into what she's *trying* to say.

"No, it has nothing to do with those side effects you've listed, well it does, but it doesn't. You won't be needing the medication anymore Makenna."

"Oh, really? What did my blood tests say?" I can now hear in her voice, the disappointment I can see on her face, but I don't get the chance to reassure her.

"You're pregnant Makenna!" Doctor Morris says with a laugh.

"I'm what?" Kenna asks, her quiet voice full of shock. "Are you sure? I wasn't expecting it to work that quickly."

"Well, some people do take a while, and for others, it's quite a quick process. Congratulations, you are one of the lucky couples that it works quickly for."

"Thank you Doctor Morris. For everything." I tell her, because I don't think Kenna can speak right now.

"You're very welcome Brady." I can hear her take a deep breath on the other end of the phone. "But there is something serious that I need to talk to you both about."

"Go ahead." I tell her, taking Kenna's free hand in mine. "We're all ears."

"While we should all be happy about how quickly this worked for you, I think you need to be aware that we know that your difficulty doesn't lie with actually *getting* pregnant, it's with keeping the pregnancy viable. So, I would suggest that even though this is exceptionally brilliant news, you keep it to yourself for a few months. At least until we can get you in here for your first scan, and check up on that growing baby. Obviously, you can choose to tell anyone you want, I can't make that decision for you, but it might save you some heart ache later." Her advice is greeted with silence from us both, and she takes another deep breath, then continues talking. "I also want you to promise to call or come in if you have concerns, or feeling anything weird is going on, or if you have any questions at all. Just because you're pregnant, it doesn't mean my job or concern is over. I really want this to work for you guys, so I want you to call me."

"We will, thank you Doctor Morris." I promise her, while Kenna just stares at the phone in her hand.

"Are you OK Makenna? You're very quiet?" The doctor asks.

"What? Oh yes, I'm fine. I'm just in shock I guess, I truly wasn't expecting it to happen so quickly."

"That's fair enough, but what I want you to remember, both of you actually, is that this is good news. I know you're probably feeling a little nervous about it, but this *is* good news."

"You're right. I know you're right. I just, I don't know I can't explain it." Kenna says, her eyes shut, as she shakes her head.

"You've been here before, and things haven't turned out the way you wanted them to, or expected them to. So, I understand your uncertainty, but we're going to give this pregnancy every chance to go full term that we can. I promise you that. I know I can't guarantee that result for you, but I *do* promise to do everything we can to get you the outcome that you want."

"Thanks again Doctor Morris. For everything." I tell her.

"Yes, yes of course thank you Doctor Morris. We appreciate everything you've done for us." Kenna agrees, with a nod of her head.

"OK, well I'll let you guys go so that the happy news can sink in. Enjoy the rest of your day, and make sure to call and make an appointment within the next couple of weeks so that we can do an examination, and maybe see if we can't work out your due date."

We say goodbye, and I take the phone from Kenna's hand, and end the call.

When Kenna doesn't look like she's going to move on her own, I lead her out of the bathroom, and into the bedroom, helping her to sit on the edge of the bed.

"Are you OK baby?" I ask, quietly as I sit down beside her.

"Hmmm?" She murmurs as she turns her head to look at me. "Pregnant? We're pregnant again Brady!"

"Yes we are baby."

"We're going to have a baby!"

"Ahh yup that was the plan, right?" I reply, slightly confused. "This is what you wanted, what we wanted, isn't it? I mean you can still change your mind I guess, but it won't be very easy to deal with." I mumble mostly to myself.

"No." Kenna reaches up, and cradles my face in her hands, but before I can ask what she's saying no to she kisses me. It's passionate, and hot all at the same time. "We're going to be parents Brady! We're having a baby!" She says it quietly, her voice full of astonishment and awe.

"Yes we are." Both of our grins could almost split our faces.

"People are going to know Brady. Doctor Morris suggested we don't tell anyone, but people will know, we won't be able to keep this quiet." Kenna says, starting to panic, her hands drop to rest on my shoulders.

"Maybe we should keep it quiet until we go for that first check-up that the doctor wants to do? Do you think you can do that Kenna?"

"Yeah, I think I can keep it quiet for a couple of weeks Brady. Can you?" She asks, kissing me lightly, and then resting her lips on mine. I feel her smile widen, then she giggles quietly. "You're going to be a dad. A little human, *our* little human will call you Daddy!"

"I know! It sounds crazy." I kiss her smiling lips. "Our little human will call *you* Mummy." I hold her close in a gentle hug. "You're going to be a mum!" I pull back to look at her face properly, because I hear her breath catch in her throat. "Don't cry baby." I whisper, wiping the tears from her face.

"What if-." A sob breaks free of her lips.

"No. No you don't get to think that way. I have a feeling this time Makenna, this time we're going to get what we want." I swipe more tears off her cheeks. "But even if the worst happens, we'll get through it. I promise you."

"I know we can." Kenna sighs. She takes my hands in hers, and rests them on her stomach, both of us staring at where they're joined. "Our son or daughter is growing in there."

I lean down close to Kenna's stomach.

"We love you already." I say against our hands.

"Yes we do, and I love you Brady Harris." Kenna says, brushing her hands through my hair.

"I love you too, Makenna Harris." I tell her, not taking my hands off her stomach. "And we love you baby Harris."

Epilogue!
BRADY

7 months later

"We need to leave." Kenna says, her words a little breathy. "We need to leave right now, honey."

"Don't we need to tell your brothers we're leaving?." I turn to look at Kenna, and that's when I see her face all scrunched up in pain and she's got both hands resting on her belly.

"NO! I DON'T WANT TO WAIT FOR MY BROTHERS OR ANYONE FUCKING ELSE!! WE NEED TO GO, NOW!!!!!" We don't need to tell anyone what's going on because the boys come running at her raised voice.

She looks at the floor, and my eyes follow her to see what she's looking at. When I see the puddle of liquid between her feet, it hits me. Fuck, she's having the baby!

"I'll get the keys and your handbag. The hospital bag is still in the car, right?" I ask no-one in particular.

"YES! IT HASN'T LEFT THE CAR FOR SIX MONTHS Brady! SINCE YOU FIRST PUT THE DAMNED THING IN THERE!" Kenna yells at me. OK then, guess I'm an idiot.

"What do you need Makenna?" Logan asks, taking charge of the situation, as start looking for my keys.

"Here. They're right here Brady." Caleb says, handing Kenna's handbag and my wallet over to me.

"My keys?" I ask, in a panic.

"Oh you're not driving bro, I am."

"No, I'm driving." I protest. This is my wife and my kid!

"Can you sit with me?" Kenna asks, softly as Logan helps her down front steps. Something I should have done but I'm a bonehead who can't think straight right now.

"Let Caleb drive you both to the hospital Brady. You can sit with Makenna and keep her calm, rather than worrying about driving *and* your wife, OK?" I nod in reply, Logan's right. I need to concentrate on Kenna and our baby.

"Let's go then." I say, nodding towards the door and taking my wife out of her brother's arms and into mine. Then I settle Kenna into the car. "Come on Caleb, move if you want to drive!"

"I'll hang back, and lock up the house. I'll be at the hospital before the baby arrives, I promise." Logan says, kissing Kenna's cheek.

"OK Logan." She says, her breathing getting harder.

"Let's go Caleb. Drive safely, just get us there quickly."

"On it Brady, you just worry about my sister."

As soon as the door is shut, Caleb takes off. Kenna moans and I take her hand in mine, but when she squeezes it tight, I wish I'd let her hold the door handles instead. Who knew she had that kind of strength in her?

"We'll be there in a few minutes Kenna, I promise." Caleb says.

Kenna and I are concentrating on her breathing in the backseat and before we know it, Caleb is pulling into the hospital carpark and opening the door to help us out. A nurse appears beside us with a wheelchair, and we manage to get Kenna comfortable in it, and then we're off at a brisk pace into the hospital.

"The bag!" I yell, scaring a nurse walking by us. "Sorry." I say.

"I've got it." Caleb says, pulling up his shoulder to swing the bag around to his front so that I can see it.

"Thank you!" I cry, giving him a sloppy kiss on the cheek. "What would I do without you? I'm not sure

"Get your hands off your brother in law Romeo and come here." Kenna says, her voice is quiet, and I can hear the pain in it. My heart breaks because I can't take it away for her. Not that she'd let me after everything we've been through to get us here.

We spent the first couple of weeks getting used to the idea of being pregnant. Then after that initial appointment with Doctor Morris, where everything was perfect, and we worked out just how far along Kenna was, we couldn't hide it anymore. We've spent the last six months telling every family member to back off.

I had to get Logan to use some big brother authority on Kenna to get her to slow down at work for a few months. I owe him big time for taking that hit for me.

"No that's going to have to wait Suze, I don't think we're going to have time right now." The nurse wheeling my wife says to the nurse behind the counter with a clipboard, bringing me back to the present.

"Oh we've got a mover and shaker tonight do we?" Suze asks.

"Sure do. I doubt we'll be in there for long tonight. Can you send Doctor Morris in for me as soon as she's free, please?"

"On it Pammy!" Suze says, as we power on to a room.

Nurse Pammy stops in the doorway to a birthing suite, the wheelchair halfway in the room. "I'm sorry folks, only Dad can come any further. You're going to have wait out here in the waiting room just to your left." She tells Caleb.

"Good luck Kenna." Caleb says, kissing his sister on the cheek. "We'll be here waiting for the good news."

"Love you little bro." I take the bag from Caleb, thanking him for the millionth time.

"I love you too Kenna. Now go have your baby." Caleb commands his sister.

As the door begins closing behind me, I curse, and Nurse Pammy gives me a dirty look. "Kenna, baby, I'll be back in a second." I pull my hand from my wife's and lean my head back out the door. "Caleb" I yell out and he comes running.

"What? What's wrong?" He asks.

"Nothing's wrong. Well, I forgot to call my parents." I say sheepishly.

"Oh is that all?" He sighs.

"You've met my parent's, they'll be pissed if I don't let them know it's time."

"Yes I have, and I can take care of that for you Brady. For a second there I thought something was wrong with Kenna and the baby." Caleb sighs again. "Go. Go on. Go help my sister with pushing out your spawn. I'll call Pauline and Jeremy and get them here. Go!"

"Thanks man." I duck back into the room and find Kenna up on the bed, gown on and looking impossibly beautiful. If I tell her how beautiful she looks to me right now though, I know, without a doubt in my mind, I'll lose my god damned balls.

"Brady, honey, please come here." Kenna begs, and I move as fast as I can as I dodge Nurse Pammy and the new nurse that joined her at some point.

"I'm always here baby. What do you need?" I ask, willing to give her anything right now.

"Just you. Here. With. Me." She says between pants.

"Right Mrs Harris, you're progressing really quickly right now, and I'm not sure you're going to wait for the doctor. Are you comfortable doing this with the two of us in the room?" I look to Kenna for her answer, I'm not making that choice for her.

"Yes. I don't think I can wait."

"OK. Now, at this point, we're just going to coach you through the delivery of your baby, OK?" Kenna nods her head. "Mr Harris, can you get in behind your wife, and just hold her up slightly so that she can push when I tell her to?"

I nod my head, not speaking, just doing what I'm asked. "Mrs Harris."

"Makenna. Please, call me Makenna."

Nurse Pammy smiles at Kenna, then says, "OK Makenna, you can call me Pammy. Now, I'm going to ask you to push on the next contraction. Do you understand?"

"Yes." Kenna says, but it's more like a growl.

"OK. Ready. Now. Push!" Kenna growls, lifting the top half of her body off the bed, and I push as much of my body as I can behind her to support her. When she runs out of steam, she drops back to rest on me.

"I love you baby. Always." I say, brushing her damp hair off her forehead, kissing her.

"Are you ready Makenna?" Pammy asks. Kenna nods, and just as another contraction hits Pammy says, "And push!"

Kenna lets out another primal growl, as the top half of her body lifts up off the bed again.

"Oh we're a little further along than I was expecting Nurse Pam." The doctor says, as she enters the room.

"Well, this baby is waiting for no-one Doctor Morris." Pammy responds, and I can feel a little bit of tension between the two of them. She moves to stand up, and move out of the way, but the doctor motions for her to stay where she is.

"No, you're doing a great job, and you're right, it looks like we won't have time to do a swap. That baby is coming."

With one last push, our baby daughter is born, screaming the place down. The other nurse takes her from Pammy, who motions for me to move in, and cut the cord. Then, she takes the baby and does all the weighing and measuring. When that's all done she wraps her up in a warm blanket. She hands me the beautiful bundle, and I lean down to show Kenna. I kiss her like it will be the last time I'll get the chance. "It's a beautiful girl, just like her Mumma." I say through the tears pouring down my cheeks.

"She's beautiful." Kenna says, running her finger down our daughter's cheek, but suddenly she winces in pain again. Like there's another contraction, but the baby is here in my arms.

"What's going on? What's wrong?" I ask in panic.

"You might want to hand your daughter over to the nurse Mr Harris. Your wife is going to need your support again." Doctor Morris says with a smile. Is she a masochist or what? What is she on about? She knows that we read up on everything!

"Shouldn't the placenta be pushed out now? The books all said it was uncomfortable, but nowhere did it say it would be like pushing out another baby."

"There's no placenta just yet Brady, there's another baby coming." Doctor Morris announces like she's announcing another train heading to the station.

"*Another* baby? What the hell are you talking about? What *other* baby?" I ask confused.

"Makenna was pregnant with twins Brady, and we're about to deliver the second baby. I'm as shocked as you are, but we can't stop it from happening now." She says with a smile.

"Twins!" I say, looking at Kenna, and she shakes her head, she had no idea either.

"Well, I'm surprised Makenna not only went full term, but over by a day or two while carrying twins, but that being said, it's not unheard of. Considering that one of those twins was hiding behind the other one for the entire pregnancy, I guess we shouldn't be too surprised with anything about this pregnancy. It's certainly one for the books." She says with a chuckle, like having two babies at once is the most common fucking thing on the planet. The other nurse takes my daughter from my arms as Kenna screams again as another bloody contraction hits her.

"One more push Makenna, and we should be good. One big push OK?" Pammy instructs.

Kenna nods her head, she's so tired, and I can't take the pain or exhaustion away for her. Instead, I get back into position behind her, and kiss her shoulder. "Push baby. One last push." She lets out an incredibly loud roar for someone who looks so damned exhausted, and then there's another baby's cry fills the room.

"Congratulations! You've got a son!" Doctor Morris announces, and I'm about ready to pass out. Fuck me! We're nowhere near set up for two fucking babies. What the hell are we going to do?

The nurse hands me my son after she's done everything she needs to do with him, and I look down at him in my arms, as the shock wears off, all I feel is love. An overwhelming love for my babies, and the love of my life.

Leaning down I show Kenna our son, and the tears flow just as heavily down both of our faces again.

"You did it baby. You gave us two babies. Shit, what are we going to call them?" We had a boy's, and a girl's name picked out, just in case, but now with two babies I can't even think.

Kenna smiles at me, and when she tells me what she wants to name them, I smile. Their names are perfect.

"Why don't you go out and tell your family the wonderful news Brady, while we get Makenna cleaned up, and ready for visitors." Pammy suggests.

I look at Kenna, "I'm good honey. Go tell them, they'll be waiting anxiously, and as much as I'd love to see there shocked faces, I'm not moving right now, and I sure as hell don't want my brothers in here just yet." She lets out a quiet chuckle.

"Good point." I hand my son back to the nurse, and she settles him in his little clear plastic tub next to his sister. His sister! Crap! We've got twins. I feel the smile spread across my face. "I am so proud of you Kenna." I say, kissing her again, then she shoo's me out of the room.

"Let me get cleaned up so that the idiots can come in to see their niece and nephew. Your parent's are grandparents now! You have to go tell them the news. Go Brady!"

I walk out of the room, and find the waiting room full of our family. My parent's see me first, and jump out of their chairs. "Brady!" They shout, getting the attention of Kenna's brothers as well, and within seconds, I'm swarmed.

"Step back and give me some air, then I'll tell you all the news." I say, laughing almost maniacally. I don't think I could be any happier than I am right here in this moment. When they all step back, I take a deep breath. "We have a daughter, Anna June Harris." I say, and the small crowd around me erupts with excitement again. There's a chorus of congratulations, with everyone asking for more details and asking how Makenna is doing. I put my hand up to stop them from all talking. My parents are holding on to each other for dear life, they both have tears rolling down both their faces. "There's more news. Don't panic, Makenna is doing fine. She's perfect in fact, and you can go in to see her in a few minutes after she gets cleaned up, but I have more to tell you." I pause, and take a deep breath. The silence from my family is a little unsettling, but then my smile stretches across my face as I say, "We also have a son. Beau Jack Harris."

"What?!" One word said by four different voices all at once.

"You heard right. We have twins. Two babies. Apparently one has been hiding behind the other for the entire pregnancy, and no-one realised."

"How did they miss two heartbeats?" Mum asks, shocked.

"I have no idea, but again, apparently it can happen. The babies can be so in sync with each other that two heartbeats can be hard to pinpoint." I shrug. "Either way we have a son, *and* a daughter today."

"Ohhh Brady I'm so happy for you both!" My Mum says as she cries uncontrollably.

"Jack." I hear said huskily beside me. "You gave him Dad's name." Caleb says, as he draws me into a hug.

"Yeah, we thought we'd leave April for you." I say back just as quietly.

"Oh geezus man." Caleb sniffles, as he releases me and then wipes a tear from his eye. "Thank you."

"I'm going back in to check in on Makenna, and the babies. I'll let you guys know when you can come in to meet the new family members." There are nods of agreement, and more congratulations all round. I smile at our family. "Babies. We've got *babies*." Then I walk back into Kenna's room. I pull her gently into my arms once she's finished getting dressed, and we take a few minutes just to *look* at our miracles.

Anna and Beau Harris.

TWINS!

I send up a silent thank you to Kenna's parents, because I know they had something to do with our miracles.

Don't miss out!

Visit the website below and you can sign up to receive emails whenever Chelle pimblott publishes a new book. There's no charge and no obligation.

https://books2read.com/r/B-A-FGVL-CXEOB

Also by Chelle pimblott

Built for Love
Built to Last
Built for Trouble

Drake Wines
Vineyard
Sandy Cove - A Drake Wines Novella

Standalone
Barefoot & Dumped!